WARLORD

Doug and Linda Raber

GreenPoint Ventures
Washington, D.C.

Cover design: Melissa H. Miller
www.MelissaInspired.com

Marketing and publicity: Katherine Carr, Silver Marketing Inc.
www.silvermarketing.com

ISBN 978-0-9851905-9-0

Published June 2017
GreenPoint Ventures
Washington, D.C.

WARLORD

Of thy fire thou madest me, and like a true child of fire, I breathe it back to thee.

—Herman Melville[*]

---

[*] "Moby Dick," Herman Melville, Harper and Brothers, New York, 1852.

1

Sudden Death

*It was night, and the rain fell; and falling, it was
rain, but, having fallen, it was blood.*
—*Edgar Allen Poe, Silence — A Fable*[*]

Rockbridge County, Virginia, April 2

The three homes, modest structures clustered together in an
area cleared of trees, were nearly hidden from view. Only
a few lights inside the houses made the scene visible to the
naked eye. A fourth building, which housed the family-operated
automotive repair shop, had been dark the entire evening. It was
Saturday, and the employees had all departed by noon.

The muted sounds from a television ceased, and the silence was
broken only by night noises from the surrounding countryside. Spring
peepers were creating their own symphony with an insistent clamor
that rose from a small stream in the valley.

Winter had released its grip on the foothills of the Appalachians
during the preceding weeks, and the weather was unseasonably warm.
An earlier threat of rain had passed, but there was no moon, and patchy
clouds continued to hide the stars.

Three figures were visible in the grassy clearing. A screen door
opened, and a woman's voice called softly from one of the homes. A
small voice responded with words that were not distinguishable, but
the tone of disappointment was unmistakable. The small figure went
to the woman, the door closed behind him, and moments later the

---

[*] "Silence: A Fable," Edgar Allan Poe, The Works of Edgar Allan Poe, Vol.
2, *Redfield,* New York, 1859, p. 296.

lights were turned off. Shortly after, the last two figures entered the third home. The evening was ending.

When the lights went out in the third house, the small valley was completely dark. The occupants of the homes were isolated from the outside world. The buildings were about a hundred yards from the main road, and the nearest neighbors were almost a mile away on the other side of a small ridge.

The activity in and around the homes had been observed by a man sitting in the woods high on the hill near the crest of one of these ridges. He had been there since just before sundown, sitting on the ground behind a fallen tree. He had not moved in more than two hours, and his legs were stiff.

The man remained motionless for several minutes after the last of the lights had been extinguished, allowing his eyes to adjust to the complete darkness. He could see nothing. Had he not studied the exact location of the houses with respect to his position, he would have been unable to determine where they were. Finally, when he was satisfied that nothing was visible below him in the dark, he slowly reached down to remove something from his backpack.

He lifted the night-vision binoculars to his eyes. He was pleased with this equipment, what the U.S. military unofficially would call "Generation 4" technology. There was no infrared beam that might enable someone to determine his location, even with the latest technology. Instead, the gallium arsenide image intensifiers used the meager light provided by the stars, amplifying it 50,000 times. That was enough to overcome what seemed to the naked eye to be complete darkness.

He could see the three houses clearly, looking at them in sequence, not just once but multiple times. After several minutes, he put down the binoculars to rest his eyes briefly. Then he scanned again.

Nothing.

It was approaching midnight. He had detected no motion for more than twenty minutes.

He did not see the two figures walking away from the homes just as the last lights were being turned off. At that time, his eyes were adjusting to the darkness, and he had not started using the night-vision binoculars. The two figures, one much smaller than the other, moved away from the clearing into the wooded area beyond his line of sight.

The man retrieved another object from his backpack. It looked much like a cellphone, but it could have been some other electronic device. Again, he flipped a switch, this time on the new device. He picked up the binoculars once again.

One last check.

He stowed the binoculars in his backpack, holding the other device in his left hand. Then he grasped it firmly with both hands, his right thumb poised above a button. He pushed it.

* * *

2

Panic Attack

This was a different proposition from crouching in
frozen fear while the unknown lurked just alongside.
Now the unknown had caught tight hold of him.
Silence would do no good.

—*Jack London, White Fang**

Rockbridge County, Virginia, April 3

The call came into the 911 emergency center just after midnight.

"This is Sue Parker. You need to send somebody out here right away. We're just off Bluegrass Trail. There's been some sort of explosion over near the quarry."

The dispatcher was calm. "Yes, Mrs. Parker. Are you saying that they're doing blasting over there at the quarry? This time of night?"

The response was agitated. "No, I told you it was an explosion. We know what it sounds like when they do blasting, and it didn't sound like that at all. It wasn't the same as when they do blasting on the rocks. I don't know what it was, but something's wrong. My husband is outside in the yard in case he can hear anything else. He's pretty good friends with the Sulleys. He told me to call you."

The dispatcher retained her composure, but this time her answer conveyed a sense of urgency.

"We'll get someone out there right away, Mrs. Parker. You just stay in your house, and we'll take care of it. And please tell your husband come back inside so he doesn't get in the way of the deputies.

---

* "White Fang," Jack London, Grosset & Dunlap, New York, 1906, p. 89.

I'm sure there's a simple explanation, and everything will be just fine."

• • • • •

When the emergency center relayed the message to the Sheriff's Office, the deputy on duty decided to call Richard Alkire. It was one thing to go out and pull the bodies out of a wreck on a Saturday night, but this sounded like it was something bigger. Maybe a lot bigger, and his boss would want to be involved from the beginning.

Alkire had been sound asleep but woke quickly when the deputy told him about the emergency call. He gave the deputy clear instructions.

"Get out there and seal the property. Don't even go inside the gate until I get there. In the meantime, I'm calling the feds."

• • • • •

Two years earlier, Alkire had learned that federal agents conducted a raid on the Sulley property. The feds said they were investigating a "tax problem," but he knew immediately that the story was a smoke screen.

Suddenly there were more strange events at the Sulley place. As soon as he put on his shirt and pants, Alkire went to his desk and rummaged through the main drawer. He removed a business card and put it in his shirt pocket. He went downstairs and picked up the keys to his cruiser, gratefully accepting the cup of the coffee his wife handed him.

The business card listed the name of the man he had met at the time of the raid. *Evan Brady.* There was no title or job description, just the name of his employer. *FBI.* A telephone number was printed on the card, but it wasn't the one he called. He used the number Brady had written on the back. Brady had told him to call immediately if anything ever happened, 24/7.

He hit the send key as he turned onto the main road at the end of his driveway.

The phone rang twice before a groggy voice answered. "Brady."

"Uh, yeah. Agent Brady. This is Sheriff Alkire. Richard Alkire, in Rockbridge County, Virginia. We met ..."

"I remember you, Sheriff. No need to explain." The voice no longer sounded groggy. "Why are you calling?"

"An explosion has been reported at the Sulley place."

* * *

Langley, Virginia, April 3

David Hashan had just fallen asleep when his government-issue Blackberry started buzzing. He rolled onto his elbow and looked at the digital clock on the nightstand. It was 2:14. He felt a sudden rush of adrenaline.

"Yeah?" It was more of a grunt.

"Mr. Hashan?"

"Yeah."

"You need to get to your office."

"Now?"

"That's correct."

"Can you tell me what it is?" He knew the answer to the question before he asked it.

"Sorry, sir. Just relaying the message."

"Ten minutes." He hung up.

Hashan lived about a mile from CIA headquarters. His watch said 2:25 as he walked into the suite of administrative offices. He was Assistant Head for Central Asia in CIA's Directorate of Operations. It seemed likely that he was about to confront one of two possibilities. Either an operation under his authority had gone into crisis, or his help was needed with an emergency at a higher level. He knew the answer when he saw his boss waiting for him.

Allan Canterbury, Head of the Central Asia desk, waved Hashan toward a seat. His face was grim. Hashan sat and waited silently while Canterbury read a document on his desk.

"Problems."

Hashan wasn't sure how to respond. He guessed on the basis of current operations that were most likely to be having difficulties. "Tajikistan?"

"No. Virginia. Rockbridge, Virginia. The Sulleys. It's very serious, David."

It took a moment for it to sink in. "I thought we wrapped that up last summer. Everything appeared to be resolved. The entire family was innocent."

"Exactly."

Canterbury continued reading the paper on his desk, and Hashan was getting exasperated. "Jesus Christ, Allan. You didn't bring me over here in the middle of the night to tell me that everything is okay. What the hell is going on?"

"They're gone. All of them."

"Gone? You mean they've …"

"Dead."

Neither man spoke for a few seconds. Hashan broke the silence.

"What happened?"

"We don't have many details yet. But there was an explosion. A big one. The houses were destroyed. There were three of them."

"I remember."

"If it had been an accident, something like a gas leak, it wouldn't have destroyed all three houses. It would have been localized at one of them."

"How did you learn about it?"

"FBI. Evan Brady. He called me at about two this morning. Thought we might want to get something started in response."

"He was suggesting a domestic operation? That we would start up something like that here at the Agency?"

"No, of course not, David. I think he wanted us to be aware of everything so we could consider responding at an international level."

"So he thinks it was a hit. By whoever set up the Sulleys as dupes last year?"

"Probably, but it's too soon to tell. The main thing is that he wanted us to be aware. And ready, so we could start planning our next steps."

"How do we get up to speed on the situation? Is Brady putting boots on the ground?"

Canterbury rubbed his face before answering. "I think so. He should be calling me back any time now. Why don't I get us a couple of coffees? You still have the file in your safe?"

"Yeah. I'll get it."

• • • • •

The telephone rang a few minutes after 3:00 a.m. Canterbury lifted the receiver and stated his name. After several seconds, he spoke again. "I've got David Hashan with me now, Brady. You mind if I switch this to speakerphone?"

Canterbury pushed a button on his console. "Go ahead, Brady. What have you learned?"

The FBI agent launched directly into his report.

"I'll start at the beginning. I got the call came at 12:30 this morning. It was the sheriff down there. Name of Alkire. I met him last year. He told me he was investigating a report of an explosion at the

Sulley place. Said the neighbor who called it in was reliable, and it didn't sound good. He said he'd get back to me as soon as he had more information.

"So Alkire called again an hour later. Said all three of the family houses had been leveled. It looked like there were no survivors, but he didn't let his people to go poking around in the dark. I told him I agreed. That he should stay the hell out and wait for our people to get there."

"Brady, this is Hashan. Do we have any reason to conclude that this was an intentional act? That it wasn't something that went off accidentally? After all, they must use a lot of explosives at the quarry."

"I obviously haven't seen the site myself, but the sheriff seems like a straight arrow. Last year, when we told him that our raid was because of a tax problem, he went along. Didn't believe a word of it, but he didn't make a fuss, either. So, when he says that all three houses were demolished, I believe him. Not one, but all three. I think we can forget about an accident."

"What's the next step?" Canterbury asked.

"I need to hear from my people. We have a team on the way, and they may even be there by now. We sent six agents in a helicopter from Quantico. Part of the Hostage Rescue Team based there. But the people getting off the copter won't all be wearing FBI jackets. Two of their jackets say FBI, two ATF, and two DEA."

"They've all been brought into this operation?" Canterbury's voice conveyed his surprise and a hint of disapproval.

"Nobody's involved in this except the Bureau. We just borrowed a few jackets. I told the sheriff that we'd be sending in ATF and DEA, and he wasn't happy. Told me that the Sulleys were a good family. That they wouldn't have been involved in drugs."

"How did you respond?"

"I said that we had to be sure. That it was standard operating procedure. I reminded him that explosions at meth labs weren't exactly unprecedented. He didn't like it, but he understood."

The noise of a telephone ringing came over the speakerphone. "I've got a call coming in now," Brady said. "My team down has probably reached Rockbridge. I'm putting you on hold."

The was no sound from the speakerphone for almost ten minutes. Then the silence was interrupted by static.

"You still there?" It was Brady's voice.

"Yeah, we're here. Got anything new?"

"I do. And it isn't good. My agents tell me there's no question about it. It wasn't an accident. There were three separate explosive charges. One in each house. But the neighbors heard only a single explosion. That means all three detonated simultaneously. So there's the answer to your previous question, Hashan. Final answer. No accident. This was a hit."

"Survivors?"

"Team leader said there was no way that anyone could have survived the blasts. But we don't have a final body count. They can't do a final search until daylight. The rubble isn't stable enough to go through in the dark. And they need to check for secondary devices."

"Secondary devices?"

"Booby traps. This is a counterterrorism unit. They know what to be worried about. And what to look for. I'll call you back at 8:00. I should have more information by then."

The line went dead.

* * *

3

Bodies of Evidence

A body of evidence has been accumulated, which it would require more ingenuity to explain away than to account for.

—Jeremiah Day, 1810[*]

Rockbridge County, Virginia, April 3

The man stared intently at the Sulley compound beneath his vantage point near the ridgeline. His legs hurt, and his back was stiff from sitting motionless in a cramped position for the last several hours. He would leave soon, but he had to be sure.

He checked his Vostok wristwatch, the luminous hands barely visible in the dark, even when he held it just inches from his face. It was the *Komandirskie* model with the letters *CCCP* printed on the face just below a red star. He had received the watch during his military service, and it had always been reliable.

It was almost 4:00 a.m. First light was more than two hours away.

The helicopter had landed an hour earlier, quickly taking off again after the police agents climbed out. The man was surprised that there were different federal agencies involved. With his night-vision binoculars he had seen the markings on the backs of their jackets. He could understand the FBI and ATF. Both agencies investigated explosives and bombings. The presence of DEA agents did not make sense, unless they suspected that the explosion was somehow related to illegal drugs.

---

[*] "A view of the theories which have been proposed, to explain the origin of meteoric stones," Jeremiah Day, Memoirs of the Connecticut Academy of Arts and Sciences, *Oliver Steele & Co.*, New Haven, 1810, p. 163.

It was time to leave. He had learned what he needed to learn. The police had found no survivors. His devices had worked as intended. That was no surprise. He was a professional.

• • • • •

At 5:30, as the sky began to turn from black to grey, Agent Mike Stover stood at the edge of the clearing on the Sulley property, watching as the first of the black Chevy Suburbans pulled up. His second team was arriving after a hard drive from Quantico. Five agents, men and women, emerged from the vehicle, all of them wearing jackets emblazoned in large block letters that said "DEA."

Suddenly, Stover dropped to one knee and removed his M1911 pistol from his holster, slowly bringing it up to a firing position and aiming at a point just beyond the edge of the clearing. Two of his men saw this, and he used hand signals to direct them closer to that location.

Once his men were in place, Stover rose to a crouch and moved slowly, using the rubble to shield him from the place at the edge of the woods where he had seen something move.

Probably just a raccoon ... maybe a deer.

He moved cautiously along the periphery of the clearing, going from one tree to the next until he thought he was almost at the exact location. Carefully, he raised his pistol and began to pivot toward his target. He wasn't sure what he was facing, but he knew what damage had been done already that night. At least he was confident that his .45 semiautomatic would drop just about any man in his tracks, and two of his agents were on his flank to provide backup.

Stover aimed the pistol at a target he couldn't yet make out, his index finger now inside the trigger guard with very light pressure on the trigger itself. He had chambered a round before his team had reached the investigation scene, and moments earlier, he had cocked the hammer. He froze when he heard the voice.

"Don't shoot. Please don't shoot."

It was a plaintive voice. The voice of a man. A young man. He was shaking, obviously scared. In the dim gray of the emerging dawn, Stover could see that the man was kneeling on the ground at the edge of the woods. And he was holding a younger child, just a boy.

Stover lowered his firearm, carefully decocked the hammer, and holstered the pistol. He signaled to his men to stand down and dropped to one knee as he extended his hands and spoke to the young man.

"It's okay guys," he said softly. "It's okay. Just stay where you are. Out of sight."

Stover motioned for one of his men to move up, and he quietly gave him instructions. Several minutes later, the man returned, followed closely by the Suburban that had just arrived. The vehicle stopped at the edge of the clearing, in a way that made it impossible for anyone else to see Stover and the two people he had just encountered.

The agent handed something to Stover, who turned to the frightened young man. "Here kid, put this on."

It was another DEA jacket. With a baseball cap to match. "Now both of you get in the vehicle, and neither of you says a word. Not to anybody. No matter who. Not until I tell you otherwise."

• • • • •

More than an hour later, the sun at last rose above the trees, and the crews began their gruesome tasks. Several more Chevy Suburbans had arrived, all of them unmarked, all of them black.

High on the hill, not far from the position that had been used by the man with the night-vision binoculars, two pairs of eyes grew wide as they watched events play out below them. Two teenage boys, unable to resist their curiosity, had driven to the entrance of the Sulley property. They had been turned away — no entry, no stopping, no information.

So, they continued past the property line and turned onto the dirt road leading up the hill. The teenagers had not even started high school when the Sulley brothers graduated, but they knew about them. It was a small town, and they wanted to find out what was going on. They were curious. However, they weren't curious enough to notice the fresh tire tracks they obliterated as their pickup truck drove along the dirt track. They were too anxious to view the scene unfolding below them.

From one vehicle, six more agents climbed out, each wearing a dark nylon jacket clearly labeling them as DEA agents. The other two SUVs appeared to be empty except for the drivers. When the hatches were opened, it became clear that those two vehicles had no seats in the rear. The black color was appropriate for their intended use. Today they would serve as hearses.

Two-person teams walked slowly and cautiously into the three burned-out buildings — more accurately, the blown-out skeletons that remained. One by one, the teams returned to the Suburbans carrying stretchers, each loaded with a black body bag. There were six in all. One team — made up of the two men who had provided backup for Stover when he made his discovery at the edge of the woods — delivered the last two body bags.

The teenagers up on the hill considered themselves to be cool and dispassionate. But when Stover lifted the last body bag through the rear hatch of the Suburban, the older boy turned away so his companion could not see his tears. It was a child-size body bag.

* * *

Washington, D.C., April 3

Hashan and Canterbury stared solemnly at the speakerphone as Stover provided the first details from the Sulley site. He had called Brady just after 8 o'clock, and Brady in turn had conferenced in the two men at CIA headquarters.

"We've got six bodies. Positive identification is going to take some time. The fireball from the explosion burned them all beyond recognition. Can't even say for sure whether we're talking male or female for most of them. I haven't seen anything this bad since I did a tour in Iraq."

Hashan frowned. "The count is wrong, Stover. It's too low. You told us before that eight people lived there. You need to keep searching for the other two."

"We don't need to look. We've got them."

"What do you mean?" The question came from Brady.

"Hiding in the woods behind the houses. At least what used to be houses. One is in his early to mid-twenties. Dark hair, about six foot, maybe 170 pounds. Says his name is Martin. Martin Sulley."

Hashan nodded to Canterbury, but it was Brady who spoke. "Sounds right. I interviewed him last year when we picked them up during the earlier investigation."

Hashan repeated a different version of his earlier question. "That's still only seven. What about the eighth?"

"A little boy. Name of Carlo. Maybe seven or eight years old."

"He was the baby in the family," Brady said. "Were they able to provide you with any information?"

"Yes sir, Agent Brady. This is all preliminary, of course, but this kid Martin told us what he could remember. He's pretty badly traumatized by the events, but he gave us the basics. Told us everyone had gone to bed about 10:00 or 11:00. But he — that's Martin, the older one — he slipped out the back of his house around midnight. Said he couldn't sleep. He walked up the path behind the house into the woods. It's only a few yards, so it's unlikely anyone would have seen him, even if they were watching."

"And the child? The little boy?"

"Yeah, Carlo. Martin is his uncle. He's like any little kid, and he could see the back of Martin's house from his bedroom window. When Martin went outside, Carlo climbed out of his bedroom window to join him. It was just going to be a fun adventure, going into the woods at night with his uncle. Didn't work out that way."

Brady interrupted. "Have you moved them to a safe location?"

"Yes sir. We used one of our vehicles to transport the two of them to a safe house up in the mountains. I understand it's near the place you used last year for the other operation."

"Have they talked to anyone but you?"

"No sir. Just me. And except for the two agents who were with me when I saw the kids at the edge of the woods, nobody else ever saw them. We hustled them into the back of one of the vehicles before the sun came up and kept them there. Nobody else knows they're alive, not even most of our investigation team. They were unaware that two of the body bags never had a real body."

"Keep it that way, Stover. We'll be back in touch." Brady terminated the call.

• • • • •

Several minutes later Brady called Canterbury's office again. "It's just the three of us this time. I'm assuming Hashan is still with you."

"I'm here."

"Good. We have some serious planning to do."

Canterbury interrupted. "Maybe we should meet. Face to face."

"Probably so, but it'll have to wait. Right now, I need to be here at headquarters with my people. And my phones. I suspect it's the same for you. Maybe at the end of the day. Let's see how things progress. I live in Virginia, so I could swing by when I leave the District."

Brady hesitated before continuing, "But I think it's going to be a long day. So, for right now, let me tell you how I want to start."

"Go ahead." Canterbury's response was accompanied by a silent nod from Hashan.

"I can give you a preliminary assessment of the incident at the Sulley place. We had been checking up on them on a regular basis. They didn't know we were checking, and neither did any of the other locals. We were careful not to reveal our interest to the Sulleys. Mostly, we were looking out for outsiders. Anybody new to the area. Anyone who just looked out of place. We never saw anything. Maybe our people got a little complacent, but that question is going to have to wait. Right now, we have other things on our plate."

"You think it was the same people who did the other attack. The Fourth of July." Canterbury was asking a question.

"Not attack, Canterbury. Attacks, plural. Don't forget the *E. coli*. But the answer is yes. And I'm assuming that was a rhetorical question. You don't really have any doubt that this was a cleanup effort, do you?"

"No. Maybe I was just hoping you'd tell me I was wrong."

"I don't see an alternative explanation. The people behind those earlier attacks are trying to cover their tracks. Almost certainly, they're trying to sever all connections that could be traced back to them. And we don't even have any damn idea who they are or where they are."

"Actually, I have some thoughts on that, Agent Brady. But it's not for this morning. There's something else we need to address. The two women. The two college students. The girlfriends of the younger Sulleys. If someone is trying to sever all the links, they're targets too."

"We're already on it. I dispatched a team from the Washington field office earlier this morning. We've made arrangements for both women to be briefed later today."

Hashan spoke up. "We need to work together on this. Those two may be key links if we're going to catch the people who killed the Sulleys."

"Don't get uptight. We coordinated our activities before, and it worked out fine. We'll pull it together this time too. But right now, we're working on a domestic crime, and that's not your turf. You need to let us do our job and stay out of the way."

Brady paused and then started again. Calmer. "Sorry, it's been a little tense here. Look, I've got a better idea. Instead of meeting at Langley at the end of the day, can the two of you break free? Or maybe delegate a team of people who can? There's a better place to meet."

"Where's that?" asked Canterbury.

"Hot Springs, Virginia. That place we used two years ago worked out so well that the Bureau has made a permanent arrangement for property nearby. Completely isolated, only one road in, and easy to secure. Elevation is about 3500 feet, with great views. There's about a dozen cabins, and it's run like a bed and breakfast."

"How long will it take for the location to be secured?" Canterbury asked. "It wouldn't work if there were other guests around."

"It's already been taken care of."

"When would you want us to get there?"

"Late afternoon. We've got a full telecommunications setup there. Secure. Even for you guys. If you can arrange a plane, we'll have someone pick you up at Ingalls Field. It can handle jet aircraft, and nobody will bat an eye. Executives fly in all the time for a golf weekend at the Homestead. Only a half-hour drive from there, a lot of it on back roads. You'd probably never find the place on your own."

Canterbury looked questioningly at Hashan, who responded with a nod. "Yeah, we could do that. What about the survivors? We need to talk to them."

"They'll get there before you do. I need to get moving now. I'll see you for dinner." Brady disconnected.

• • • • •

The sun was low in the sky as the Hawker 400 passed over mountain ridge and banked toward the sun. Ingalls field looked like a strip of dirt and asphalt that had been carved directly into the top of the mountain.

Official records would show the two passengers as attorneys from Washington getting away for a few days at the Homestead Resort.

By the time they taxied to the small terminal building, their ride was waiting for them. An unmarked Chevy Suburban.

The driver motioned them into the back seat without saying a word. Only when they had been on the road for several minutes did he finally speak.

"Glad to have you staying with us, gentlemen. I'm Clark Haverford. Perry Ward and I are the co-owners of the property, and we're both retired from the Bureau. Our security clearances are current, and that seems to have satisfied folks from other agencies who've used the place."

* * *

Healing Springs, Virginia, April 4

It wasn't dark yet, but the sun had dropped below the top of the ridge to the west, and they were in full shadow. Haverford dropped them at the main building of the complex. Evan Brady was waiting at the door, and they followed him into a room where a dinner table was set for four people. Agent Stover was already there. Brady made the introductions.

"Okay then, let's get started. It's your show, Evan." Canterbury was the senior person at the table, but for the time being, it was still an FBI operation.

"Okay if we eat first?" Brady asked. "I haven't had anything since breakfast."

"We can talk during dinner," Canterbury suggested.

"I'd prefer to wait, if you don't mind. Some of the topics we have to address aren't particularly appropriate for mealtimes."

Expecting an objection, he preempted it. "Trust me on this."

They ate quietly, their limited conversation focused on neutral topics — weather, sports, implications of potential cutbacks in the federal budgets. Brady explained that the only staff at the lodge that night were Clark Haverford and Perry Ward, who were acting as chef and waiter that evening. And Brady was accurate when he said, "Perry's a pretty decent cook. I've been here before."

When the dishes were cleared, Haverford brought cups and a carafe of hot coffee. No one had opted for decaf.

Brady turned to Stover. "Let's start by getting up to speed on what happened at the Sulley place."

"So here's what we've got. Preliminary forensics verified that there were three separate explosive charges, one underneath each of the houses. They were built without basements, just crawl spaces underneath. Big enough for someone to get in there and place the charge. Like with any bomb, there was some residue, but we don't have confirmation on what it was yet. Best guess right now is plastic explosive. We've got no leads on where it might have come from, but we may learn more from chemical analysis."

"Anything on how it was set off?"

Stover nodded. "The bomb techs are good. They found a few fragments. They're reasonably sure it was detonated by a cellphone. Or maybe just a simple radio transmitter. Whoever triggered it was somewhere out in the dark watching from a hiding place. Probably up on the hill. You've all been there, right?"

He looked at the others to verify that he was right before continuing, "And yes, Mr. Canterbury, we do have teams combing the nearby area. They haven't found anything yet. I don't think they will, either. This guy is a pro."

Canterbury's arms were folded on the table, and he lifted his right hand a few inches. "First off, this 'Mister' stuff is a little stiff. We're going to be working together for a while on this problem, so why don't we just go to first names?" He touched his chest lightly. "Allan. And David," indicating Hashan.

Stover nodded. "Mike. And ..." he turned to Brady. He wasn't on a first-name basis with his superior.

"Evan."

"Good," Canterbury said. He turned back to Stover. "So if this guy is such a pro ... I'm not challenging your logic, Mike, just trying to figure this out. If he's such a pro, how come two people survived? And what kind of condition are they in, anyway?"

"Reasonable questions. The older one, Martin. He's in his early twenties. He said he wasn't sleepy, so he ducked out the back of his house to grab a smoke. Didn't want to tell us at first — it wasn't the legal kind. Turns out there was a direct line of sight from his cousin's bedroom to Martin's back door. The cousin — that's Carlo, who's only eight — he saw Martin leave and climbed out his bedroom window. They walked a few yards along a path and sat down on a fallen tree.

"They weren't injured?"

"Not seriously. Their ears were ringing, but it doesn't look like any permanent hearing loss. Some scratches, but that seems to be from hiding in the woods most of the night. They'll get a full medical checkup tomorrow, but our goal today was to get them the hell out of there."

He paused and looked at his boss, who answered the silent question. "Full disclosure. We're all in this one together."

"So, Agent Brady — Evan, that is — gave us our marching orders right up front. Any survivors were to be protected by any means necessary. Since our initial conclusion was that everyone was killed — one of those errors that you don't mind making — I figured we should keep it that way, at least for anyone who might decide to check up on us. For all I know, the guy was up there on the hill watching us all night. So, when I found Carlo and Martin, I kept them out of sight.

Gave Martin one of the DEA jackets we were using, and a hat too. He would have looked like one more agent if anyone was watching from a distance. The little kid, I just got him inside one of the Suburbans."

"Good thinking," Canterbury said.

Stover continued. "Actually, we went a step further. We put some rocks and blankets into a couple of body bags. Once again, anyone watching wouldn't have known. They were trying to kill eight people, and there were eight body bags. One of them was even the small size. The little kid. Gotta tell you that made me feel like shit, even though it wasn't a real body I was carrying."

Hashan frowned. "What about burial, morticians, autopsies, that sort of thing? Won't the story fall apart?"

This time, Stover deferred to Brady. "No question, that was a little tricky. But I've had some people working on it. First of all, we told the locals that this was a federal crime scene. All autopsies were being done by federal authorities. We took the bodies to Richmond. The medical center there."

"But you're short two bodies."

"Now you'll start to understand why I didn't want to talk about this while we ate, David. I have contacts at a lot of law enforcement offices around the country. Some of them are pretty good friends. People who can be trusted." He paused and looked over his shoulder, as if he were worried that someone might overhear what he was about to say.

"Turns out that there was a nasty car crash several weeks ago in southern California. A guy in a stolen car tried to outrun a traffic stop. Anyway, he drove off the road into a gully. The car caught on fire. The guy died. And he had his little kid with him."

Brady stopped for a moment, looking at each of his colleagues in turn. His expression was grim.

"They were unable to identify them. No DNA matches. Nobody came forward. Two people, burned beyond recognition, one a young adult, one a little kid. The two bodies will be in Richmond by morning. They're being transported in an unmarked plane, and even the people in Richmond won't have any idea how this all came about. Nobody knows any details."

The others nodded, and nobody spoke for a minute.

"What about the two survivors?" Canterbury asked.

"Yeah. We need a plan for them. Especially for the younger one. He's just a kid, so he can't go off on his own. We need something like witness protection."

"Agreed. These kids have no family left. The last of their relatives in Tajikistan were killed a couple of years ago."

"So how do you manage witness protection for a little kid?" The question came from Hashan.

"We'll find something. The child's background is Hispanic. His mom and grandmother came to the U.S. from Mexico. We've got a lead on some relatives from that side of the family who settled in Arizona. They might take him in."

"That would do it. And help us with the older one, too."

"You're still after Martin?"

"Absolutely," Canterbury answered. He glanced at Stover, who had not been involved two years earlier.

"After the Fourth of July plot, we tried to recruit Martin and his older brother to come work for us. But they turned us down. Family ties and all that. They said they needed to help the rest of their family make a go of the quarry and auto-repair businesses in Rockbridge County. To repay their father for sending them to college."

"You think he'll agree now?"

"Wouldn't you, Evan? Revenge is a powerful motivation."

"You'll have your chance when you interview him tomorrow morning, Allan."

* * *

Joint Base Anacostia-Bolling, District of Columbia, April 4

Samantha Summers and Neela Davis were seated at a table in a small room that was sparely furnished with a plain table and a half-dozen straight-backed chairs. The floor was covered in gray linoleum tile, and the walls were painted in what could only be described as institutional green. There were no windows with a view of the outside, although there was a single large pane of glass on the wall behind the two women. It didn't quite look like a mirror, nor could an observer see what was on the other side.

The door opened, and two people strode in. The younger one, a woman, indicated that Summers and Davis should remain seated. The newcomers took seats on the other side of the table. They wore laminated government badges on their jackets, and as they sat down, they placed their credential packs on the table. Each of the open wallets displayed a photo ID and a gold badge.

"I'm Special Agent Roberta Sutherland, and my partner is Special Agent James McElvoy. I'd like to thank you for agreeing to meet with us this evening."

Neither Summers nor Davis said a word.

"The reason we wanted to talk to you was to discuss some recent events. From last night, to be specific. But first, we'd like to ask you some questions, if that's all right."

Summers and Davis remained silent.

Sutherland opened a folder.

"The files we were given on your backgrounds are a little sparse. Am I correct that you've both been in the service for a year and a half?"

"Yes, ma'am," Summers said, answering for both.

"And you both hold the rank of Sergeant?"

"Yes, ma'am."

"It says here that you were questioned by the Bureau two years ago. About your interaction with two brothers — names Richard and Martin Sulley. Something to do with a character referenced here as 'The Warlord.' Is that correct?"

"Yes, ma'am. Where is this going?"

"Please allow us to ask these questions, Sergeant. It will all become clear. Now, have you had any recent contact ... written, oral, any kind of contact with this Warlord since those events two years ago?"

"No, ma'am." They both answered this time.

Sutherland glanced at McElvoy and looked back across the table. "Nothing at all in the past few days? ... weeks?"

Davis and Summers looked at each other, both puzzled and annoyed. They shook their heads.

"No," Davis answered. "Nothing at all."

Sutherland shrugged.

"I suppose that's the answer we were expecting. All right, let's move on. We have to share some information with you. It's classified. Is that understood?"

"Yes, ma'am." They answered in unison.

"There was an event last night. In Rockbridge County, Virginia. At the property owned by the Sulley family."

"What kind of event?" Davis asked.

"An explosion."

"At the quarry?" Davis asked. "They were always so careful with the explosives. What happened? Is everyone okay?"

"No, I'm afraid not. They were killed."

Davis and Summers began speaking at the same time.

"Who was killed? Is Richard okay?"

"What about Martin?" Summers added.

Sutherland looked at them somberly.

"All of them were killed. The entire family. There were no survivors."

"I don't understand," Davis said. "Why were they all in the quarry? Why would they all have been where the explosives are kept?"

"It wasn't at the quarry, Sergeant. They were in their homes. All three homes were leveled by the blast."

"Everyone?" Summers asked.

"How could it have happened?" Davis asked. "They didn't have gas lines to the houses. It doesn't make any sense."

"It wasn't gas. I've got a preliminary account that will be released to the newspapers in a couple of days. It describes the event as some sort of chemical explosion. It says they found residues indicating there was illegal drug activity."

"That's bullshit!" Summers declared. "If you're going to feed us crap like that, there's no point in even playing this game."

She pointed over her shoulder.

"Why don't you tell your friends in the next room to come in and ask their damn questions directly? We've been upfront from the start, and you're just playing games."

In the observers' room, Miguel Garcia, the FBI Special Agent in Charge for the Intelligence Division of the Washington Field Office turned to his colleague.

"Maybe we should take her up on that suggestion, Colonel. I no longer have any doubts that you are correct in your assessment of Sergeant Davis and Sergeant Summers. Anything about their background, their answers, and their reactions supports what you've told me."

Col. Thomas Wolinsky of the Defense Intelligence Agency nodded to the FBI official.

• • • • •

Earlier, Wolinsky had described to Garcia and his team the full background on the two sergeants.

"From the day we learned about their unwitting involvement with the Warlord's terrorist plot, we knew two things. First, that they would be potential targets for retribution, and second, that they could become extremely valuable assets to our intelligence community."

McElvoy asked why it was assumed that the women were not security risks.

"We never assumed that. Not for a minute. That was a major reason we had them enlist in the Army. That and the opportunity to keep a close watch on them. Just the nature of the beast. With them in the active military, we've essentially had them under close surveillance for every bit of the last couple of years."

"How did you convince them to sign up?" Sutherland asked.

"It was relatively straightforward. We knew the Agency was interested in recruiting them, but they can only employ U.S. citizens. The Army was a different story. Moreover, military service offers a path to citizenship, so that was good for both sides in the long term. Their only other choice — at least the only other choice we offered them — was to go back home to Kazakhstan and their Warlord friend. They had no interest in that choice at all. So they got new names and a new career start. Neelam Dâvar became Neela Davis and Zemfira Sumaiyah became Samantha Summers."

"And they did okay in Army training?" Sutherland asked.

"They were good. Really good. And it continued after we brought them into intelligence. Especially Summers. Top of her class all the way. Real kick-ass."

• • • • •

Summers was still fuming when Garcia and Wolinsky entered the interrogation room. Neither she nor Davis had encountered the colonel previously, but they'd heard his name, and his uniform showed his rank. They both jumped to attention.

"At ease, Sergeants. Take a seat."

Everyone sat down warily. With six chairs occupied, the table was crowded. The room was small enough that there seemed to be no opportunity for the tension to dissipate.

Wolinsky spoke first.

"Sergeant Davis. Sergeant Summers. Please accept our apologies for the unpleasantness you've had to endure for the past hour. Those of us in the DIA are well aware of your backgrounds, your capabilities, and your loyalty. It was necessary for our colleagues at the Bureau to observe some of this first hand. I'm going to ask Mr. Garcia to give you and update. He's Special Agent in Charge of the Intelligence Division here in D.C."

Garcia cleared his throat.

"I will echo the colonel's apology, although I think you understand that difficult questions are frequently part of the intelligence business."

Neither Davis nor Summers made an overt acknowledgement of the statement.

"First thing is a correction. What Agents McElvoy and Sutherland told you about the explosion at the Sulley compound was only partially accurate. It is the information that is being released to the public. The most important difference is that Martin Sulley survived. So did his cousin Carlo."

Garcia looked at Summers and saw her swallow hard. Then he turned to Davis and saw the question in her eyes.

"I'm afraid not, Sergeant. Richard Sulley was killed in the blast."

He paused so Davis would have time to compose herself. Her eyes welled up, but she would not allow herself to shed a tear. She nodded to him, a silent indication that he should proceed.

"I want you to understand that the information going to the public is misleading, and we know it is. It has to be. We've got preliminary evidence that it was plastic explosives. Not gas. Not something from the quarry. This was intentional. It was a hit."

"You know who did it." Summers said.

"We have a fairly good idea who did it," Garcia responded. "Do you?"

"I know damn well who did it."

The room was quiet for a few seconds, and Summers spoke again.

"I want in."

"You want in?"

"Damn right, I do. And so does Sergeant Davis, right?"

Davis nodded.

"That's good," Wolinsky said. "That's why we all came here to talk to you."

* * *

4

Disinformation

His main object, however, was to remain in concealment until he could ascertain that his pursuers had left the way open for his journey, by having been deceived into the lower route by the false trail which he had caused to be made with the shoes of the prisoners.

—*The Scout, 1844*[*]

Blacksburg, Virginia, April 4

Shortly after the doors opened on Monday morning, a man walked into to Holtzman Alumni Center on the Virginia Tech campus. After looking around to get his bearings, the man walked up to a receptionist.

"Good morning," she said. "May I help you?"

"Yes, that would be kind of you. I am attempting to locate two recent graduates of the university."

"Certainly," she responded. "You need to check with Alumni Records. Right over there."

The man walked in the direction indicated by the receptionist, and he came to an office door that was labeled "Alumni Records." As soon as he entered, an attractive young woman greeted him with a smile.

"Good morning. I'm Barbara Trimble, Alumni Records Manager. Please sit down. How can I be of assistance?"

---

[*] "The Scout," John Linnaeus Edward Whitridge Shecut, *The Universalist Union,* New York, Vol. IX, November, 1844, p. 668.

"I am wishing to locate two recent graduates of the university. I was advised that you would have such information."

"Of course, Mr. ...?"

"I am Buribaev."

The man's dour expression changed as he attempted to smile, but the curve of his mouth was accompanied by a crease in his brow.

"And the names of the alumni?"

"They are from Kazakhstan. Zemfira Sumaiyah and Neelam Dâvar."

He put a scrap of paper on the desk and pushed it toward her. As he extended his arm, she noticed his wristwatch. It struck her as quite fashionable, probably because it was so clearly designed to be functional rather than elegant. In particular, she noticed the letters, CCCP.

"Are you an alumnus, Mr. Buribaev?"

He looked surprised.

"No, of course I am not. I am not looking for information on myself. I only seek the information of the graduates."

"I understand, Mr. Buribaev. But the university's privacy policy doesn't allow me to give out data on individual graduates except to other alumni."

The man had prepared for potential difficulties, so he tried a new approach.

"I am representing a benefactor in Kazakhstan. It is a man who has become quite wealthy in his international business with America. He is wishing to assist Kazakh students to study in the United States ... at the Virginia Tech."

Ms. Trimble looked intrigued.

"This businessman has made such investment already. The two graduates whose names I show you are only the first such candidates. He paid for them everything. All costs for tuition and for housing and food and even books. He is very generous."

"I'm afraid I don't understand."

"These women graduated from university two years ago. I attempted to visit them yesterday in the evening, but they were not at their address. The people in the next apartment said they moved away when they completed their studies."

"Yes, that isn't uncommon."

"And my benefactor wishes that I give them their final reward. As I said, he is quite generous, and he sent me here quite specifically on this mission."

"But I must nevertheless abide by the university policy, Mr. Buribaev."

He again attempted to smile.

"There is more. As I said, my benefactor wishes to assist many more students. Perhaps as many as six each year. By paying all of the costs of studying here. As the present difficulty suggests, I will recommend to him a new approach. I will suggest that the money be given directly to the university. The procedure will become easier for everyone."

The smile on Ms. Trimble's face returned. She understood the implications of a large donation. It would be good for the university. It would be good for her.

"I'll tell you what, Mr. Buribaev. Let me see if I can find something that would assist you without violating our policies."

"That would be very good of you."

The man's smile seemed almost genuine.

Barbara Trimble began typing on her keyboard. After she entered what the man thought were a few words, or perhaps names, she hit the enter key. A second or two later, she smiled.

"Okay, this looks like it."

And the smile was replaced by a deep frown.

"Oh, dear."

"Something is not right with the computer?"

"It's not that, Mr. Buribaev. Just a moment. I'll print this for you."

The printer began humming, and a sheet of paper emerged. She took a quick look and handed it to him.

"These will not violate our privacy rules. They are newspaper reports that were added to the records of the graduates you inquired about."

CANCUN, Mexico, August 22

The bodies of two women were recovered yesterday from the waters between Yum Balam and Isla Blanca.
Authorities have not released any information on the identities of the women, although two Americans were reported missing from their Cancun hotel last week. Police spokesman Yunel Escobar said more information was expected to be released tomorrow.

CANCUN, Mexico, August 24

Cancun police confirmed today that the two bodies recovered from the waters off Isla Blanca on Thursday

were tourists. They were identified as Neelam Dâvar,
age 24, and Zemfira Sumaiyah, age 22.

In response to questions, authorities clarified that
the women traveled to Cancun From the United States
but were citizens of Kazakhstan according to their
passports. Their home address is listed as Blacksburg,
Virginia, and inquiries to that municipality revealed
that the two were recent graduates in engineering from
Virginia Tech in Blacksburg. No other information was
available.

Foul play is not suspected. Police spokesman Yunel
Escobar said that medical examination indicated
drowning as the cause of death. It is believed that
the two tourists swam too far from the shoreline and
became exhausted in the deeper water.

"I'm terribly sorry, Mr. Buribaev."

He nodded

"It is unfortunate that they have died. But it is not a concern for you. You have been most helpful."

He stood and turned to leave.

"Mr. Buribaev …?"

His eyes met hers.

"Let me give you my card, Mr. Buribaev. If your benefactor has further questions about assisting with scholarships, we'd be delighted to assist him."

She paused, expecting him to provide his own business card, but he turned and left without saying anything further.

She went back to her computer to make some notes.

Just in case. Odd, he never gave his affiliation. Let's see … dark hair … or maybe gray. Glasses? Not sure. That's strange, he didn't seem unusual, but there was nothing about him that sticks out enough to make a note of. And he was just odd in general. He didn't seem to be all that upset when he learned those two young women were dead.

* * *

Washington, D.C., April 7

Allan Canterbury and David Hashan were seated in a small waiting room at FBI Headquarters overlooking Pennsylvania Avenue in downtown Washington.

"I'll be glad when they get around to replacing this building," Canterbury said in a whisper. "It doesn't bother me that they named it after Hoover, but the building is really ugly."

"Brutalist, isn't that what they call it? I'm not sure they'll ever be allowed to tear it down, though. It's considered historic."

The conversation ended abruptly when the door opened.

"Good morning, gentlemen. Sorry I'm a little late. Got caught in another meeting that I couldn't escape." Evan Brady closed the door behind him and dropped some papers on the table.

"There's fresh coffee on the table over there. And some bottled water. If you want anything else, I can ask someone to bring it."

"Coffee's fine," Canterbury said, answering for Hashan as well as himself.

A minute later, they were seated at a conference table.

"I'd like to make sure we're all up to speed on the latest developments. Have you been able to obtain the necessary approvals for your recruiting efforts?"

"Yes. For Martin Sulley and the two college girlfriends," Canterbury answered.

"Are you ready to move forward?"

Canterbury nodded. "Absolutely. As quickly as possible. They're our only link back to the terrorist attacks. And almost certainly the bombing of the Sulley homes. The Warlord."

"You think we could follow the trail right back to Kazakhstan? And send in a team to get him?"

"That's the best-case scenario."

Brady shrugged. "Not much choice, is there? We don't have a name, and we don't know exactly where he is. Kazakhstan is a really big place."

"There's something else, Evan."

Brady looked at Canterbury.

"We'll do our best to work with you on all the legal requirements. Proper forensic efforts, chain of evidence, all that stuff. Obviously, that's the case for everything here in the States. But when it comes down to actually catching this bastard overseas … Let's just say that arresting him may not be an option."

"Understood. We expected that might be the case. The Bureau would have to take a back seat for that kind of operation."

Hashan interrupted.

"We're going off point. Evan, can you go back to reviewing events of the past few days?"

"Sure," Brady answered. "First the autopsies. The lab finished with the six victims. Nothing unexpected based on the initial reports. Pretty damn horrible, though. The bodies were all intact. There was significant trauma from the blast, probably enough to cause severe brain injury, but ultimately, they were all burned to death, so we'll never know for certain."

"And the funerals?" Canterbury asked.

"Just a single funeral. We've been working with the locals. All eight bodies will be transported back to Rockbridge County tomorrow. Burials on Saturday."

"How's it being paid for?" Hashan asked.

"Turns out that the older Sulleys, that's Martin's father and his uncle, had insurance policies that cover all the expenses for the immediate family. Only the grandmother wasn't covered, but we found a way to make a discreet donation to the local church, so it's taken care of. Then the bodies are going to be cremated. It's the only way we can guarantee the necessary security with the last two bodies. There can't be any evidence showing that Martin and Carlo survived."

"Who will be at the funeral? Any of us?"

"Not you, David. And not me, and not Allan. But yes, if you mean 'us' in a broader sense. Mike Stover and a couple of his team members will be there. They'll stay in character, too. Very much law enforcement, acting the full DEA role, looking out for anyone suspicious. They'll talk to some of the local folks to see if they can find out anything more about the drug dealing."

"There's no way around that?" Hashan asked. "I feel like shit, dragging the whole family's reputation through the mud like this."

"Martin and Carlo are the only ones left, and it's for their protection."

"So we're putting out the word that the Sulleys were running a meth lab?" Canterbury asked.

"Just Martin and his brother Richard. Martin was willing to put that label on his brother and himself, but he didn't want anything to suggest the involvement of his father or his uncle. He said it might be fitting punishment for the dumb stuff that he and Richard did a year ago."

"How do we put that word out?"

"Everyone has been extremely cooperative. Take a look at this. It's going to show up in some of the local papers the next few days."

```
ROCKBRIDGE COUNTY, Va., April 9

Funeral services were held today for the family of
eight that died in a fire and explosion last Saturday
night. The Sheriff's Office still has not released an
official statement, but this newspaper has confirmed
that federal authorities took over the investigation
early Sunday morning. Several witnesses confirmed that
multiple investigators combed the scene, all wearing
clothing that identified them as part of the Drug
Enforcement Agency. DEA officials declined to provide
official comment, but a person who would not permit
his name to be used confirmed that the investigation
originated from the Richmond, Va., District Office.

The anonymous source suggested that the blast that led
to the death of all members of the Sulley family was
the result of a chemical explosion at or near the
three residences that were destroyed. He said final
proof was not yet available, but preliminary evidence
was consistent with manufacture of methamphetamine.
"Meth labs are known to be unsafe," he said, "and
large-scale explosions such as the one in Rockbridge
County last Saturday are not unprecedented."

Interment took place at Rockbridge Memorial Gardens.
Former high school classmates of Richard and Martin
Sulley, ages 25 and 24, expressed shock that the
brothers might have been involved in an illegal drug
manufacturing operation. Several of them, all
requesting anonymity, said they knew of
methamphetamine sales in the county but insisted none
of the activity had ever involved the Sulleys. The
Sheriff's Office said only that the investigation
would continue.
```

Hashan shook his head slowly. "That's really sad."

"Best we could do," said Brady. "Anybody does any checking up, the story will hold tight. Martin and Carlo will be safe."

"What about relocation for Carlo?"

"We've found the grandmother's sister out in Arizona. She's willing to take him in. He'll have a completely new identity."

"Isn't there a risk that somebody from that part of the family might come back here and do some digging around?"

"Not likely. There are some people in the extended family who are undocumented. We made them an offer. No details on Carlo's background from us, and they don't go looking. If they hold to that agreement, we'll help out with permanent resident status. That's one of those offers you can't refuse."

"What does Martin say about this?" Canterbury asked.

"We haven't said anything about it to him. We figured that you and David would want to deal with that as part of the recruiting effort."

"Yeah. Probably better that way. David is going back down to Healing Springs this weekend. It will have to be one of the issues on the table."

• • • • •

Later the same morning, the three men were listening to a report from Mike Stover via speakerphone.

"I don't have that much new to report," the FBI agent said. "The bomb technicians have gone over everything pretty thoroughly. The explosive was ANFO, not plastic explosive like they first suspected."

"Ammonium nitrate and fuel oil," Canterbury said. "Can they trace it?"

"Apparently not. The bomb techs said it's the most common explosive used in the U.S., and there was a stash of it in the Sulleys' quarry. It's probably where it came from. But it looks like their record keeping wasn't that great, and the amount needed for this bombing wouldn't register as a discrepancy."

"Unfortunate."

"Yeah. The techs did find traces of the detonators, though. They're trying to reconstruct them to see if there's any kind of match in their databases. If this person has set off similar devices at other places in the U.S., they may be able to get something on him."

Brady spoke next. "Any reason to think this guy has done bombings before?"

"The techs said that the detonators looked fairly sophisticated. One of them is ex-military, and he thought he'd seen something like it back when he was deployed to Kosovo in the late '90s. He thought it was a Soviet-style device. And very sophisticated."

"So we're dealing with a pro," Brady said.

"That's for sure. And there's something else that may interest you. The forensics people have been combing the hillside above the bomb site, and one of them, Jean Burke, thinks she found something. It was just behind a fallen tree, with a clear line of sight down to the three houses. The ground was cleared just a little bit for a couple of square feet. Burke thought it looked like someone had brushed a few stones out of the way to make it more comfortable as an observation post."

"Could it have been wildlife? Just bedding down in a safe place."

"We asked her about that possibility, David. She said no. Said she's been hunting in that part of the country since she was six, and she knows the difference. Plus, she found something else. A small piece of residue from a cigarette or a cigar. Maybe a cigarillo or whatever you call those things that look like a cigarette with a dark wrapper."

Canterbury inhaled sharply.

"Stover, was this a tobacco wrapper or a dark paper?"

"She said it was paper. They were going to do more checking back at the lab. Maybe even find some DNA. She was particularly intrigued because there was a little piece of gold foil stuck to it. She's hoping she can identify it, but she was surprised to even find the scrap. The area was completely clean otherwise."

Canterbury had been holding his breath for most of the time Stover had spoken the previous several sentences. Now he exhaled and began to speak.

"I know what she's going to find out. *Sobranie,* A specific kind of cigarette known as a Black Russian. This cinches it, Stover. You're not going to find out anything more about our guy in any database of American crime scenes."

Brady asked another question.

"Have you obtained any information on how the bomber got in and out of the area? He must have had some means of transportation."

"We're reasonably sure it was a car, sir. Burke followed an animal path just up the hill to an old dirt road. Just wide enough for a car and not many places to turn around. Probably had to be four-wheel drive in any case."

"Tire tracks?"

There was a brief silence before Stover answered.

"Yeah. Two sets. And we've positively identified the second set. A couple of locals drove up there the morning after the bombing to see what we were doing. We stopped them when they came back again on Tuesday. Unfortunately, their vehicle wiped out the earlier tracks almost completely. There were still a few places where you could tell that another vehicle had been there, but there was nothing left that would work for identification purposes. So we've got nothing. Whoever the killer was, nobody saw him coming or going."

Brady rubbed his temples as though he were fighting off a headache. "Stay with it, Mike. Check back with me at the end of the day. Before that if you find anything."

"Yes sir."

Brady disconnected the speakerphone and looked down at the table.

"We're not catching many breaks here."

He turned to Canterbury.

"You think he's Russian?"

"Can't say that for sure, but there's something in his background. There's a Russian connection here. I'd bet a whole lot that this guy's career goes back to the Soviet days."

"If not Russia, then maybe Kazakhstan?" Hashan asked.

"I was in Kazakhstan when the Soviet Union fell apart," Canterbury said. "I even smoked a few of those Black Russian cigarettes myself."

"You both think this might tie directly to the guy you've called the Warlord?"

"I do, Evan. Like David just suggested, I think Kazakhstan is the place. I think the Warlord is trying to sever all the links that might allow us to find him. He's got a well-trained assassin who's taking care of things for him. Almost certainly goes back to *Spetsnaz* or KGB. He's probably my age or even older."

"Is it possible that he's rolling up his operations?" Brady asked. "Maybe we won't have to worry about any more attacks from him."

"We know better than to hope for that possibility. The Warlord is on a mission. We may not know exactly what his goal is, but we can be certain that we'll be on the receiving end of whatever bad things he can cook up. There's only one way that we could ever guarantee he won't attack us again."

"Let's go back to this assassin for a minute," Hashan said. "Remember the business up in Montreal? When several people met mysterious ends? There was even that one guy who just up and died in the middle of a police chase. It all fits."

"It's a reasonable analysis. And it would mean that he's been crossing some borders. In and out of the U.S. In and out of Canada. I doubt that he's based here. That's not how a *Spetsnaz* or KGB agent would operate."

Canterbury looked at Brady.

"The criminal activity is a domestic issue, at least for the moment. So it's officially your turf, Evan. Could you go through channels and get Immigration and Customs Enforcement to look into it? You have the basic dates for Montreal, and now we're looking for a recent trip into the U.S. He might have been in Boston last year for that microbiology conference, too. Let's see if ICE can find any correlations."

"I'll take care of it, but I wouldn't be too optimistic. If this guy really is a pro, I doubt that he's been using the same identity. And he probably doesn't even look the same on successive trips."

"It's a start, nevertheless. I don't expect a positive ID from the exercise, but we might be able to spot something. Some sort of a pattern. Anything at all would be of great help."

* * *

5

Planning Meeting

Two very different things must exist in a man to make him a general: he must know how to arrange a good plan of operations, and how to carry it to a successful termination.

—*The Art of War, 1879**

Kazakhstan, April 8

Kaskyrbai Ghazi sat cross-legged by the campfire with a small band of men. Next to him was Asim Ospanov, his chief aide. Ospanov's official title was chief of security for the KFB, a fitting role for a man whose name meant *protector* or *defender*, even if it was an alias.

Their relationship was filled with contradictions. Ghazi trusted his subordinate with his life, yet he spoke to him in a manner that suggested a lack of respect. His tone was often condescending, and rarely did he give Ospanov compliments or praise.

In contrast, Ospanov viewed his superior with a mixture of admiration and obeisance that bordered on reverence. At the same time, he was ambitious, hoping that someday he would be more than a top aide to the Warlord and would gain the mantle of leadership.

The two men represented the core of the KFB, the Kazakh Freedom Battalion. They were a band of brothers — born of the Soviet domination during the 20th century and united in a nationalist fervor to reclaim their homeland. Typical of the indigenous Kazakh peoples,

---

* "The Art of War," Antoine Henri baron de Jomini, translated by G. H. Mendell and W. P. Craighill, J. B. Lippincott & Co., 1879, p. 327.

nearly all the members of the KFB were Muslim, but their overriding identity was nationalism rather than religion. Their fight was not religious jihad, but a struggle to end what they saw as an occupation of their territory by foreigners. Their goal was a standard of autonomy that would take them back to the 16th century.

Some viewed the KFB as insurgents, while others considered them freedom fighters. Internationally, they were seen as criminals and terrorists. Even among their countrymen, they were increasingly regarded as troublemakers rather than heroes.

Ghazi's family was descended from the nobles of the *Orta Zhuz*, what Westerners called the Middle Horde. They had avoided the Soviet purges, and the men of the family were educated in Russian schools. Born as Georgiy Aishuakov, Ghazi's surname had the Slavic ending that was essential for entering the halls of power.

He studied economics and international law at the Moscow State Institute of International Relations. When not in the classroom, he studied politics by joining student groups that exposed him to a wide range of opinion and philosophy.

The political establishment thought they were training one of the bright young communists who soon would be ready to take the helm of the Soviet Socialist Republic of Kazakhstan. Ghazi was named a junior member of the CPK, the Communist Party of Kazakhstan, because the establishment had misjudged both his loyalties and his aspirations. Ghazi's allegiance was to the *Orta Zhuz*, not the communist party. His ambitions were for himself.

Less than a year after he graduated, he left his post as an apparatchik at the Semipalatinsk Test Site in the northeastern part of his country. He adopted his *nom de guerre* and went underground as a leader of the KFB. As far as the government knew, Georgiy Aishuakov had simply disappeared, likely murdered by drunken workers with counterrevolutionary leanings. For years, no one linked Aishuakov to the KFB leader whose forename, Kaskyrbai, meant *fearless as a wolf* in Kazakh, and whose surname, Ghazi, meant *conqueror* or *warrior*.

Many powerful figures considered Ghazi no more than a vulgar peasant with a rifle. And many men had paid dearly for that view, some politically, others with their lives. Ghazi understood the advantage afforded by his relative anonymity. He was able to travel anywhere in the country without being recognized. He cultivated his swashbuckling reputation and allowed the occasional photograph showing him leading a small band of armed men on horseback, their robes flowing in the wind, bandoliers across their chests, their yurts in the background.

Every available photograph of the Warlord shared a common characteristic. In some, he was partially turned away from the photographer, while in others, a hand, or an arm, or a rifle would obscure a portion of his face. As a result, nobody in any position of authority knew exactly what this man looked like.

On this particular evening, Ghazi and Ospanov were engaged in deep conversation, while others in their band cleaned up after the evening meal. Although the temperature was dropping, it remained pleasant by the fire. The men drank tea as the orange of the sun faded into the neutral colors of the surrounding desert landscape. Ghazi's flowing robe was colorless — not white, but not quite the color of sand, either. As the sunlight faded, so did the remaining color of his features. His face became one with his robes, almost as if he were disappearing along with the day.

· · · · ·

The sun had set, and more sticks had been placed on the fire. Ghazi and Ospanov continued their dialog, the Warlord speaking as a professor to his student.

"To understand what we must do, you must first learn how we came to the place where we are now. It is essential for you to master this history, Asim.

"First it was the Russians. Then they became the Soviets. And now it is the Americans. Our own leaders in Kazakhstan betrayed us. When the Soviet Union finally fell to pieces, when we had the chance to take back our homeland, they failed us. They invited the Americans to come in to our country. They call it diplomacy, and they spoke of economics. But they invited the foreigners nonetheless.

"Half the population of our land is now other than Kazakh in origin. Germans, Ukrainians, Tatars ... but mostly Russians. And now the Americans. They are small in number, but they have dollars, so their voices are loud. Much too loud. And heard too much by our politicians. They must all go, and it will be our task to make it happen, Asim."

The Warlord sipped his tea and continued. "We have had success Asim. Not as much as we would wish, but we have had success. Why do I say this? Our last attack was stopped in the second phase, but it was not stopped completely. We killed many Americans. Think about this, Asim. Why have we succeeded when others have failed? Look at what bin Laden accomplished. And see how our efforts have been still more effective. He had but a single large success, and we have had several.

"It is true that we had misfortunes with our operations. Two times! That fool Orlov thought he was so smart, but he made errors. He allowed his desire for women interfere with the important goals. You will never see that from me. I like what women can do for me, but never will they interfere with our cause. Do you hear me Asim? Do you understand this? The cause must always come first. Women are expendable. Our cause is not."

Hesitantly, Ospanov prodded his commander. "You were saying about bin Laden. Why he failed."

"Yes ... why he failed. It was because he was arrogant. He only wanted big attacks that would be shown on television. His best operations were the early ones when the Americans did not know what to look for. The bombing of the Khobar Towers in 1996 was such a success, although some say it was not bin Laden. And the attack of the warship, the *Cole*, in 2000. That also was good. Those attacks killed American military fighters. Then it changed."

"September 11?"

"It is the most famous. But three years earlier, were the bombings of the American embassies in Tanzania and Kenya. Many of us believed those attacks were tactically wrong. They were aimed at American property, but they killed innocent Muslims, which is against the teachings of Islam. It is the same with suicide bombings. They are perversions."

"And that is why our attacks have been successful? I do not understand, Sardar." He used the term of address that would translate as *commander* or *leader*.

Ghazi smiled condescendingly. "No, Asim. I am trying to explain that bin Laden wanted only to glorify himself. And it was at the expense of other Muslims. At the cost of their lives. What we do is far more heroic. We fight for our homeland. We seek to liberate our fellow countrymen from the domination of the West. From the oppression of the Russians, from the military and financial domination of the Americans. Do you want to know why we will succeed, Asim? Why we will prevail where bin Laden failed?"

"Indeed, Sardar. I wish to know."

"There are two reasons, Asim. One is that our plans will have less complexity. Bin Laden's plan with the airplanes required that nineteen different people would participate at a single time. They had to arrive at three different airports and pass through security checkpoints. Some of them were required to first obtain special training as pilots, and all nineteen had to cross the borders of the United States."

"But they were not stopped ..."

"It was only because the Americans were so stupid that the attackers were not discovered. Even when some of the American agents learned that enemies were in their midst, they failed to act. Bin Laden was not smart, and he was not a hero. The Americans were fools. But they have learned their lessons, and now they watch more carefully. If we are to succeed, our attacks must have less complexity. Do you understand me?"

"I think I begin to understand."

"Good. Sometimes we may use more than two people for an operation, but success will require perfection. Even if we should lose one of our cadre, the mission will succeed. You must understand this Asim. If your plans require that many individual actions all work to perfection, you will fail. It is a question of mathematical probability. The more pieces that must work perfectly for a machine to function, the more likely it becomes that the machine will break down. We will use fewer people. If something should happen to one of our men, the others would complete the mission. We will be victorious."

"You said there were two reasons why bin Laden failed."

"I did, Asim. The first was that he designed attacks that were too elaborate. The second was that his people were not smart. He recruited young men who were religious zealots. Men who were willing to blow themselves apart with explosives because they followed a false interpretation of Islam. Their education was one of memorizing the Koran, not one of learning how to think in a logical and critical way. They lacked training in their mission, and they lacked experience. A few weeks at a training camp is not enough. Our agents are not religious zealots. They are our countrymen. They are patriots fighting for the freedom of their homeland."

"I understand."

"That is good, Asim. And there is yet another reason why we will succeed. Bin Laden and the others who have followed in Al Qaeda and ISIS search out Americans who wanted to fight jihad, and after some small training, they return to the United States where they attempt to recruit others. But as I told you, the Americans have learned their lesson. They watch the young men who have traveled to the training camps, and when these jihadists go asking for people to work with them, they instead find FBI agents. There may be an occasional success, but most will be failures.

"It is only by acting in new ways that success will be achieved. We will do it together, Asim. You are prepared for that?"

"I am prepared Sardar. It is my duty, and it will be my honor. I look to the day when Kazakhstan will be truly free of the Americans."

"Also the Russians, Asim."

"Yes, Sardar. Also the Russians.

* * *

Kazakhstan, April 10

In late afternoon, four men on horseback rode down a path from the hills south of the town of Ereymentau. Before descending to the small farmstead on the outskirts of the town, they had paused atop the largest of the hills. From that vantage point, some 400 feet above their destination, they watched for well over an hour to assure themselves that nobody would be waiting for them other than their friends. Only when certain, did they descend the path to their destination.

Ereymentau itself was a modest town at not much more than 10,000 people, and it was the administrative center of a district with a total population about three times that of the town.

The men had ridden from a part of Kazakhstan that was even more isolated, a place where they and their comrades could pursue their interests without interference, or even awareness, of the central government. They were about to undergo a metamorphosis, transitioning from the ancient nomadic life of the *Orta Zhuz* to the modern society of post-Soviet Kazakhstan.

Two of the horsemen would remain at the farm to await the return of the others. To wait and guard the horses. They would remain out of sight, sleeping in the barn with the horses and their weapons, unperturbed by the tractors and other modern farming equipment.

The other two visitors would undergo much greater transformation. Some twenty minutes later, they emerged from the farmhouse with their host, no longer looking like the peasants who had ridden in from the remote central region of their country. Gone were the *shapans*, the traditional flowing robes of their ancestors, which had been replaced by Western business attire. These were not Kazakh peasants. They were successful entrepreneurs or factory directors.

At the direction of their host, the two businessmen climbed into the back seat of an old M21 Volga, a relic of the Soviets, but one that would draw no attention. They set out on the dirt track from the farm and continued until they were able to turn west on the main road. Two hours later, they reached the outskirts of Astana, the capital city of Kazakhstan. After another mile, the car pulled to the side of the road next to a small café, and the two businessmen climbed out of car. No words were exchanged. The Volga drove away.

The two men entered the café, each of them carrying a small suitcase. They ordered tea and drank it quickly in silence. After they paid their bill, they left the café, found a taxi nearby, and gave the driver their destination. Within fifteen minutes, they were checking in at the front desk of the Radisson Hotel, one of the finest in the city. No particular attention was paid to them. The thriving city was full of Russian businessmen. It would not have occurred to anyone that these two dignified visitors were guerrilla fighters from the KFB.

· · · · ·

The next morning, Ghazi and Ospanov met in the lobby of the Radisson and walked together to a nearby restaurant, where a table had been reserved for them in a secluded portion of the dining area. It was at the back of the room, where they could watch everyone entering or leaving the restaurant. The door to the kitchen was only four or five steps from their table. It provided a means of egress that they did not plan on using, but it was there should it be needed.

"He is here, Sardar."

Ospanov pointed discreetly toward the entrance.

Ghazi said nothing in response.

The man in the doorway walked directly toward their table. Ospanov was mildly surprised that the newcomer seemed to know where they would be seated. Ghazi was not.

When the man reached their table, Ghazi gestured formally.

"Sit down, my friend. We shall take our meal together."

Baluan Aimanov did as the Warlord indicated, exchanging a warm look of friendship with Ghazi. When he was seated, he nodded somewhat formally to Ospanov.

Aimanov had been with Ghazi since the beginning, even before the Kazakhstan Freedom Battalion had been formed. He and the Warlord had been friends at university, and briefly they had worked together at the Semipalatinsk site, near the Russian border some 600 kilometers to the east of where they now sat. They had been young at the time, and in those waning days of the Soviet empire, their talents were welcomed at the site where nuclear weapons were stored and tested. But the political upheaval of the time did more than end the Soviet hegemony, and the two young men left their employment to help establish the KFB.

Even then, Ghazi had been the intellectual leader, so the deference now shown by Aimanov was not new. They were long-time comrades, and the hierarchy had been established long ago.

"Sardar," he said when he was comfortably seated. The single word served as a response to the Warlord's greeting, and it conveyed full acknowledgement of rank and stature.

Aimanov was the Warlord's most important operative. He took orders only from Ghazi and reported only to him, procedures that assured there could be no opportunities for duplicity. Invariably, their meetings took place in public locations, not unlike their breakfast on this particular morning in a small restaurant. Like Ghazi and Ospanov, Aimanov was dressed in Western attire. It looked like a simple meeting of three Russian businessmen. Nobody would notice. Nobody would have reason to give them a second thought.

For several minutes, the men ate their breakfast quietly. A simple meal of tea, bread, and cold sausage. Finally, the Warlord looked at his comrade and spoke.

"Your trip went well, Baluan?"

"I had good success, Kaskyrbai."

Ospanov stiffened when he heard the response. Not because of its content, but because of the name. It was not the first time, but Ospanov was nevertheless surprised by Aimanov's use of the Warlord's given name. It was another reminder of his inferior standing in the unstated hierarchy.

"The last of the connections to our Fourth of July project have been eliminated. There will be no way for them to link any of the activities back to you."

"Explain, please."

"I am referring to the Suleyman family — the ones who went to America from Tajikistan and changed their name to Sulley. We believed two of them were helping us, but I have become convinced they were not. It is now beyond doubt that they caused the failure of our project. But no longer is it a problem. They cannot be a threat to you in the future. They are gone. All of them."

"Gone?"

"Yes, Sardar. There was an explosion. Three explosions, to be precise. The American police have announced that it was accidental. They say that the young brothers in the family were illegally manufacturing a drug called methamphetamine and their chemistry went wrong. It caused the explosion. So they will all be known as criminals. That is good for us."

"But certainly, the police know otherwise. They must be aware that it was an attack."

Aimanov shrugged. "What you say is true. From a hidden place, I watched as the authorities came to investigate. I saw them search the wreckage. Subsequently, I spoke with local residents and learned that the investigators had removed the bodies. All of them. Yet the police cannot know who carried out the attack. They do not know who we are, and the last connections have been destroyed."

"The last? What of the young women?"

"They are gone also. Not by our hand, however. Simply gone. I visited their university soon after the explosions. They graduated from the university two years ago, and the office of records searched for the address where they now live."

"So you found them? Do they not present a danger to us, Baluan?"

"I think not, Sardar. It was a concern also for me at first, but the functionary at the university showed me information from their records. The women have been dead since two years."

"Bodies?"

"No bodies. They went for holiday in Mexico in the summer after graduation from university. They drowned in the ocean waters. It was unfortunate."

"Why did you say it was unfortunate, Baluan?"

"Because they would have worked with us, Sardar. I have checked on this question. They ended their interaction with the two Sulley brothers before their graduation. I believe they would have continued to serve us."

"If you say this, then I accept it to be so." The Warlord's expression did not match his words, and Aimanov understood that the conversation was finished.

* * *

6

New Recruits

A righteous war, and a righteous war alone, justifies
the use of stratagems and spies.

—*Aurelius Augustine*[*]

Fort Benning, Georgia, 18 months earlier

The 14 members of the squad were lined up in two rows. Neela turned her head slightly and looked over at Samantha, who was standing at the other end of the front row. Their eyes met, but they were careful not to smile. Neela's expression conveyed a silent question.

What have we gotten ourselves into?

Her thoughts were interrupted by another question, this one spoken aloud and at high volume.

"What the fuck are you looking at, Summers? When I'm here talking to you, you look at me. This isn't a sightseeing tour here this morning. You're here to learn how to fight."

"Yes, Drill Instructor."

Her response was crisp and loud, and apparently, it was sufficient. The sergeant began explaining the training exercise they were about to start.

"Combatives," he said. "Hand-to-hand combat."

Samantha tried hard to focus.

Welcome to the second week of basic training.

---

[*] "Dictionary of the Apostolic Church," Aurelius Augustine, according to Volume 2, James Hastings, ed., *Charles Scribner's Sons,* New York, 1922, p. 672.

The drill instructor had been explaining the plan for the morning. They were indoors, in what seemed like a high school gymnasium. The mats on the floor made it look like the venue for a wrestling tournament. Each mat was square, about 40 feet on a side, with a circular imprint about three-quarters of that. The drill instructor told them that was where the fighting would take place.

"You will face off at the center of the circle, and your object is to take down your opponent. Put him on the mat. Or her, in some cases."

He looked over at Samantha before continuing, his voice loud and intimidating, as always.

"Remember. This exercise is the takedown. You can push, you can shove. You can grab. But no hitting. That is for another day. Is that understood?"

"Yes, Drill Instructor," the squad answered in unison.

"Then let's start."

He looked around until his gaze settled on the biggest recruit in the squad. Lucas Papelbon was about six-two, and weighed just over two hundred pounds. He was right at the limit for Army standards, and the staff sergeant had been on his case to lose a few pounds.

"Papelbon. Get over here."

"Yes, Drill Sergeant."

Samantha watched as the Papelbon lumbered toward the center of the circle.

I wonder which of these guys gets to fight against him?

She was startled by the answer to her question.

"Summers. You're up."

Samantha started to look around, when she realized he was talking to her. No longer Zemfira Sumaiyah, it took a moment for her to remember the name on her uniform. At five-eight, she was the shortest member of the squad.

"Now listen up, everybody. And start learning. Remember what I told you. Look for a vulnerability. That's how you win in a fight."

Samantha looked at her foe as they stood about ten feet apart. She was in a slight crouch, and he was standing casually.

The sergeant yelled, "Go! Go! Go!"

Before Samantha could think about what was happening, her opponent charged at her. She lunged to her left, and he only clipped her shoulder with his forearm. It threw her off balance, and she fell to one knee. Papelbon's momentum took him outside the circle.

They both knew the rules. They had to start over. Again, they took up positions facing each other near the center of the mat.

"Go!"

This time, Samantha understood her advantage.

He's bigger, but he's slower.

He also learned from his first rush at Samantha. Instead of charging, he began moving sideways. They were circling around each other.

Then she saw it. His vulnerability.

He's crossing one foot in front of the other when he moves sideways.

She waited until he was just beginning his next step, and she moved quickly. He put his arms up to grab her, but it didn't work. She thrust her hands out, and her palms hit his chest. Not hard, but hard enough. With his right ankle behind his left and his weight on his back foot, his balance was gone as soon as she pushed him. He went down hard. Flat on his back. And Samantha was still standing.

I bet I'll get some props for that.

She looked over at the sergeant, who did not meet her eyes. Instead, he looked at the other recruits.

"Hoffman … Warzinski … you're up."

As the two new fighters walked toward the center of the mat, the sergeant did glance at Samantha. There was no expression on his face, but their eyes met for a fraction of a second. And there was the slightest motion of his head. Nobody else would have noticed. Small, but real. A nod of approval.

* * *

Healing Springs, Virginia, April 10

"How are you today, Martin?"

Martin Sulley raised his head from the computer game and looked over his shoulder at the man he knew only as David.

"I didn't hear you come in."

Martin's voice was flat, and there was an emptiness in his eyes that made him look older and harder than his 23 years.

Hashan had seen it before, the first time just before his tenth birthday, when his family had been force to flee their native country of Iran. That was in 1979, just weeks before the fall of the Shah, whom Hashan's father had served as an air force pilot. The senior Hashan's membership in the military elite ensured that any new regime would presuppose his allegiance to the departed ruler. He understood that he was at risk.

As members of the Baha'i faith, the Hashan family found that their religious freedom had departed with the Shah. With the Islamic regime poised to take over, they saw the beginnings of religious persecution against the Baha'i community. They lost some of their closest friends and family members in the chaos of the revolution.

David Hashan's father escaped with his wife and son, but many of his colleagues and family members were unable to do so. David remembered the look on his father's face in 1979 when their aircraft departed Iranian airspace. It was the same look he now saw in Martin Sulley.

Maybe that similarity will work in our favor.

Hashan spoke quietly. "*Sobh bexeyr.*" It meant good morning.

Martin cocked his head and frowned. He seemed puzzled, but as he stared at Hashan, the light returned to his eyes.

"*Soobh-ba-khair.*" He paused for a few seconds, still unsure. "You speak Tajik?"

"Farsi. I don't have much practice with Tajik, but they're very similar. Like you and me, Martin. We have a lot in common. A lot to talk about."

The frown persisted.

"May I sit down?"

"I guess."

"Are you comfortable, Martin? They've given you everything you need? You have what you want?"

The frown was replaced by a flash of anger.

"How can you even ask that? I'm a fucking prisoner here."

"Not a prisoner. Not really. It's just that it isn't safe for you to leave. If you left, they would find you. And they would kill you. Just like the rest of your family. And they would kill your cousin Carlo, too."

Martin's shoulders sagged, and he looked down at his knees.

"Why bother, then?"

"There's still a future for you. And for Carlo. It's just that it's going to be a very different future than what you were planning."

"I want to find the bastards who murdered my family. I want to kill them. And I will. Sooner or later, you're going to let me out of here, and I'm going to find them. It may take the rest of my life, but I'll find them. And I'll kill them."

"Would you like some help?" Hashan asked. "It's time for you to rethink that offer we made a couple of years ago. To come work with us."

"I can't. I have to go back and rebuild the houses. And take care of Carlo."

"You can't do that, Martin. You'd only be targets again."

"Then we'll move someplace else. Where it's safe."

"They would find you."

"So how would it be any different if I worked for you?"

"Not 'for,' Martin, 'with.' There's a big difference. You want to get the killer. We want to get the killer. We do it together. You would be part of the team."

"But what about Carlo?"

"He has to be in a safe place. Probably somewhere far away. We've located your grandmother's sister, Carlo's great aunt, in Arizona. He could live with her. He would have a new name. He would go to school like a regular kid. And he would be safe."

"You're trying to tell me I'll never see Carlo again?"

"It wouldn't be anytime soon. Not if you decide to work with us."

"So, if I tell you to just go fuck yourselves, then Carlo and I could stay together?"

"We couldn't promise that either. The legal system has some strict requirements on child custody, and Carlo is only eight years old."

"He'll be nine next month."

"He's still too young to be without a full-time caregiver. We have to get him into long-term protective custody. The bombing attack killed six members of your family, and the two of you who survived are suffering as a consequence. I can't fix that."

Martin looked at Hashan. His expression was a peculiar mix of sadness and frustration.

"It's like you're trying to blackmail me."

"I wouldn't use that term. But I understand why you said it. Look, Martin. The first thing you have to understand is that your life will never be the same. Your father was killed. Your brother was killed. So were your uncle and aunt, your cousin Della, and her grandmother, Mama Jacinta."

Martin turned his back to Hashan, and his shoulders heaved. Hashan heard the muffled sound of a sob.

"You and Carlo survived by sheer luck, and the only reason you're still alive is because nobody knows. The killer worked for the man in Kazakhstan who set you up two years ago. The Warlord. Nobody expected him to come after you this way, but he did. We can't change that, but we're offering you the chance to work with us and to find him. To bring him to justice."

Martin sat in silence with his back to Hashan. When he turned around, he spoke with resolve.

"If Carlo will be safe, that's the most important thing. But it has to be me that tells him. I have to explain it to him and tell him that I'll come back for him when I can."

Hashan nodded.

"Then I'll do whatever I have to do to get this guy. I don't care if it takes years. I'll help you get him."

"Thank you, Martin. We have the same goal. We're going to hunt the Warlord, and we're going to find him."

"There's something else, Mr. ... "

Hashan spoke in a quiet voice. "David. If we're working together, it will be on a first-name basis."

Martin hesitated, then nodded.

"There's something else I have to ask. What about Zemfira?"

"What about her?" The response was restrained, not quite cold.

"Is she safe? And Neelam? They would have been targets, too."

"They're safe. I can't give you details, but they're both safe."

Martin turned away. The resignation in his voice was apparent.

"We were going to get married. At least we talked about it once. That maybe someday we would. But all that shit happened, and ... And I haven't seen her since."

His voice trailed off. Then he turned back to Hashan. "I won't be able to see her now, will I?"

The answer was accompanied with real sympathy. "I'm afraid not, Martin. Not right away. Maybe after you finish your training."

"Yeah. I understand," he said. But he didn't.

* * *

Columbus, Georgia, 12 months earlier

"I'm gonna stick with beer," Samantha said. "I'll be on my ass if I drink the hard stuff."

"Just one," Espinosa said. "We gotta celebrate. All five of us made it through Darby. And now Mountain Phase."

He was referring to the first two phases of Ranger School at Fort Benning. They had just returned from the Mountain Phase at Camp Merrill. They had the weekend, but then they would all be sent up to.

Samantha was at a bar they called the Hideaway just a few miles from the base. She was with Nate Thurmond, Eric Solis, Jason Harper, and Tony Espinosa. Their completion of the first phase of the grueling training program had earned them passes to blow off some steam. They were all dressed in jeans and t-shirts.

"I'll get this round," Thurmond said, as he stood and began walking toward the bar.

"This one's for you," Harper said as he raised his glass to salute Samantha. "You're one of the first women to ever get through the first two parts of the course."

"We all busted ass, Jason. Not just me. And where are the others, anyway? I thought everyone was meeting us here."

Solis laughed. "They probably stopped somewhere for a drink. They'll show up eventually."

The noise level at the Hideaway was high, but Samantha could occasionally pick out a few words coming from a particularly boisterous table just across the empty dance floor behind her. It was another group of soldiers, but not from their unit.

She heard "... bunch of pussies ..." and "... she looks like a lumberjack to me."

The comment made Samantha turn and look at the other group. Harper noticed too.

Two more phrases made it across the room. Phrases aimed at Samantha.

"... probably a dyke ..." and "... looks like a swamp donkey."

Followed by raucous laughter from the soldiers at the other table. Their next statements coincided with a momentary lull in the noisy room and were completely audible to Samantha and her buddies.

"She's just a bimho ..." and "Yeah, pass-around pussy."

It was more than Samantha was willing to put up with. She stood up and spoke loudly to the other group, her comment directed particularly at the person who had made the last comment.

"Hey asshole! If you think you're such hot shit, come over here and say that to my face."

Harper put a hand on her arm, but she shoved it away. "Stay out of it, Jason. I got this. And I recognize him. Peterson. He's in the 197th."

Peterson never hesitated when Samantha called him out. He nearly jumped out of his chair and almost ran across the room. As he got near, he extended his right arm, maybe to hit Samantha in the shoulder or maybe with the intent of grabbing her by the neck.

Samantha saw the arm go up, and she timed her move for his next step. As Peterson's right leg moved forward, all his weight was on his left. Samantha planted her right foot inches from where his boot would come down.

Peterson's feet were blocked, but there was nothing to slow the motion of his upper body. As his shoulders lurched toward her, Samantha reached up to grab his extended forearm. When she threw her hip into his midsection and pulled hard on his arm, he had no way to compensate. His own weight and momentum propelled his body forward as Samantha exerted downward force on his arm.

Peterson looked like he was doing a gymnastic move. A flip. Except that it was only three-quarters of a flip, and his entire back — heels, hips, and head — hit the floor at the same moment. With a loud *thunk*. It knocked the wind out of him, and he lay there looking up, his mouth moving like a fish trying to blow bubbles.

He started to get up, but Samantha turned and stood between his splayed legs. The room had gone silent, and she spoke quietly as she placed the heel of her right foot against his crotch.

"Don't move, asshole! If you ever want to grow up and have kids, this is a good time to stop."

Samantha noticed that Thurmond, Harper, and Solis were standing, just to her side. She also saw that the other soldiers who had been with Peterson were also standing, and it looked like they were about to join the fray.

A commotion by the door caught everyone's attention.

"What the fuck is going on here?"

Three MPs strode rapidly toward Samantha and Peterson.

Without a pause, Samantha reached down and grabbed Peterson's hand.

"Guy slipped on a wet spot in the floor. Somebody must've spilled some beer. I was just helping him up."

She smiled weakly at the MPs. Her friends backed up and began to sit down again. Peterson's buddies did the same.

The leader of the MPs cast a hard look at Samantha.

"Summers. I've heard about you."

His expression seemed to show disapproval.

"All of you go sit down. And make sure nobody else slips on any spilled beer."

He turned on his heel, and all three MPs went back outside.

• • • • •

A minute or two later, they were finishing their drinks.

Thurmond spoke with his voice lowered. "Nice move, Summers. Too bad those MPs showed up. Looked like we were just starting to have some fun."

"This place has gotten a little dull," Espinosa said. "Maybe we should try someplace else."

"I vote for Soho," Solis said. "I think that's where the other guys were going."

As they filed out, Thurmond walked a little behind the others and turned toward Samantha. He held up his keys.

"Hey Summers. You know my buddy Woltowicz in supply? He lives off base, and he's back in our home town in Nebraska for a week. He asked me to check on his place. Make sure everything's okay."

"Yeah, so what's your point?"

"Well, I thought maybe you'd like to ride along."

"Are you trying out your own moves, Thurmond?"

Samantha couldn't see very well in the dark, but she was sure he was blushing.

"Yeah ... I guess maybe I am."

"Then let's do it."

She followed him to his car, and he yelled to Harper and Solis that he and Summers would catch up to them at Soho.

"Right," Harper answered. "And maybe ..."

Before he could finish the thought, Thurmond cut him off.

"Just shut the fuck up. We don't need to hear any of that."

It had been a good evening, and all five laughed. Samantha got into the car, and Thurmond drove out of the parking lot.

His friend's place wasn't far away, and Thurmond pulled into an empty parking spot in front of a dark apartment. As soon as they went inside, he turned to her. They were standing close.

"Ever since I first met you, I've kinda wanted …"

"You need to be quiet, Thurmond."

"Yeah, maybe. But I'm not sure about this. I mean, we're in the same unit. And now we're going off to Florida for the third phase."

"Actually, no. I'm being transferred."

"No shit. Where?"

"I'm both being assigned to Joint Base Anacostia-Bolling. Washington, D.C."

"Why now? You've almost finished Ranger School."

"You know they don't give us all the reasons. But it's got something to do with intelligence. Remember, I grew up in Kazakhstan, and I've got some language skills."

"That sucks. We're gonna miss you. I am for sure. I …"

"I'm not gone yet, Thurmond."

"No, I guess not."

"Okay, so let's get at it. You asked me here for a reason. Take off your damn t-shirt and then take mine off."

He followed her instructions. Not just her shirt, but her bra, too. They kissed, and he began to touch her. Then he stopped to look.

"God, you're hot," he said. "You're silky. But hard at the same time."

She reached down. "I could say the same about you."

He pulled her toward the couch, and the stripped off the rest of their clothes.

· · · · ·

They held each other afterward.

"Thurmond?"

"Yeah?"

"I'm gonna miss you too."

"Maybe we'll be at the same place again. Like after I finish this training."

"You think they need Rangers up in D.C.?"

"Maybe not."

"Exactly. So be glad we got this time together when we did. It's been nice, tonight. I'm glad you invited me."

She could tell he was embarrassed again.

"Holy crap!"

"What is it?" He asked.

"The time. I was supposed to be back on base by midnight. Look at the time."

They started pulling on their clothes.

"I didn't realize you had to be back tonight. My pass is for the whole weekend. I'll get you on base as quick as I can, but you're gonna catch some shit for this. Sorry."

"Not your fault, Thurmond. I was enjoying this too much."

• • • • •

They pulled up at the entrance to Fort Benning just before 1:00 a.m., and the MP at the gate asked for their IDs, checking their names against a printout on his clipboard. He checked Thurmond's ID first and nodded as he checked his clipboard. Next, he looked at Samantha's and frowned as he scanned his printed information. Then his expression changed as he seemed to remember something.

"Just a second."

He turned and removed a post-it note from the window of the guardhouse. Then he looked again at his clipboard.

"Your pass says 2400 hours, Summers. My advice to you is get your butt back to your quarters in a hurry. You've only got ten minutes."

He stepped back and waved them onto the base.

* * *

Langley, Virginia, April 11

Early the following morning, Brady, Hashan, and Canterbury met at CIA Headquarters. They were joined by Andrea Chang.

Canterbury started the discussion. "Thank you for coming by early, Evan. I didn't want to wait until the end of the day."

"No problem." Brady took out a file folder. "I've got the full report from the interview with Summers and Davis. You want to start there?"

"Perfect. We've brought Andrea up to speed on almost everything else. And she's going to be in charge of the training schedule."

"How much do you know about what the women have been doing for the past couple of years?" Brady directed the question to Chang.

"Only the outline. That they joined the Army. I haven't heard any of the details."

"Then let me start there. That all right?"

The others nodded, and Brady began his recitation.

"It all started with the raid on the Sulley compound two years ago, when we found out about the uranium. We were all there at Healing Springs for the interrogation. All the Sulleys and the two women from Virginia Tech, as well. We figured out very quickly that none of them were directly involved in the terrorist plot, and it was clear they had been duped. By the Warlord. So, the question was what to do next."

"Was the Agency involved with their enlistment?" Chang asked.

Brady glanced at Canterbury, looking for a signal. There was a slight nod.

"Yes. I wasn't involved directly, but I learned about it shortly afterward. It's my understanding that the discussion was between Carter Jennings at the Bureau and Bob Alford here at your place. Maybe others from higher up. Does that square with you Allan?"

"Pretty much."

"So, they recognized immediately that the women posed a risk. Either to us or to themselves. If we were wrong, and they were in fact conspirators who had successfully deceived us, we needed to keep them under constant surveillance. On the other hand, if our conclusion was correct that they were innocent dupes, then it seemed likely that the Warlord might come after them in retaliation for talking to us. Having them join the armed services was a way to cover both bases."

"They were willing to do that?" Chang asked.

"We made them a pretty attractive offer, in my opinion. The deal we cut was a four-year enlistment in the Army, and we would pick their specialty and corresponding training. In return, we guaranteed them — not in writing, of course — that we would grease the skids for U.S. citizenship at the end of that time."

"So that part is still pending?"

"Correct. Officially, they're both still citizens of Kazakhstan."

"Then I'm confused," Chang said. "How can they work with us? The Agency operates under a strict policy of U.S. citizens only. Either as employees or contractors. We're going to get an exception?"

"No exceptions," Canterbury answered. "That's why the Army was the perfect solution. It's a different set of rules, and there isn't anything that prevents a member of the U.S. military from being detailed to work on a task force that would operate here at Langley."

Chang smiled. "Pretty fucking clever. Okay, Evan. Go back to your story."

"Sure. The first step was new names. We wanted them protected, at least for the time they were in the Army. So Zemfira Sumaiyah became Samantha Summers, and Neelam Dâvar became Neela Davis. Legal name changes and everything."

"Wouldn't that let someone track them down?"

"We used the same approach that they use for the Witness Protection program, Andrea. So the answer is, 'no.' The changes are buried."

"What about records at Virginia Tech? Wouldn't that all seem a bit fishy? Two of their students just up and disappear?"

"Good point, but it didn't happen that way. First off, both of them graduated a couple of weeks after the original interrogation. When they agreed to work with us, they had the whole summer to work on conditioning before boot camp. We got them some good personal trainers. Former military guys, who worked them into good shape and kept an eye on them at the same time."

"How did they do in their training?"

"They were great. We already knew they were smart, and their motivation was remarkable."

"Did they go right to Officer Candidate School?"

"No. It was decided right at the beginning that they should be enlisted personnel. We didn't need them to be leaders of other soldiers. We wanted them to be good soldiers on their own. They've both achieved the rank of Sergeant, and they've been stationed at Joint Base

Anacostia-Bolling for much of the past year. Learning the intelligence game."

"So in theory, they're ready to sign up to work with us. The question is, will they? And how do we go from here?"

"They're ready, Andrea. Earlier this week, while I was meeting with David and Allan at Healing Springs, we had two of our top interrogation experts talking to them. As well as the Special Agent in Charge for the Intelligence Division of the Washington Field Office. This was a final check."

"They passed?"

"No question about it. And when they heard about the murders of the Sulley family, we didn't have to do any convincing at all. They're on board one hundred percent."

"Then we need to send them down to Camp Peary for training."

* * *

7

Homeless

*One man, who was both deaf and so ill as to be
utterly incapable of self-support, even if he had been
mentally normal, came to us one evening and
begged to be sent back to New York.*

—*One Thousand Homeless Men, 1911*[*]

Wilmington, Delaware, September 5

Adil Razikov tried to take his mind off the stiffness in his knees by watching the scenery as it passed by his window. His seat on the bus was cramped, but the round-trip ticket had cost only $20, and he'd been told that the return trip would take less than five hours. If that turned out to be true, he would arrive in Washington in only two more hours. Studying the map resting on his knee, he concluded that they had just crossed over the Susquehanna River and were near someplace called Havre De Grace.

Razikov was a large man, about six feet tall and weighing more than 200 pounds. The confined seats on the bus forced him to sit in almost a crouched position, and it made him stiff all over. Not just his knees, but they were the worst.

Eighteen months earlier, he had arrived in the Washington, D.C., area with a renewable L-1 visa designating him as an 'intracompany transferee.' His official title was 'petroleum engineer,' an expertise developed in his studies at the Satpayev Kazakh National Technical University in Almaty. The university had been named in honor of

---

[*] "One Thousand Homeless Men: A Study of Original Records," Alice Solenberger, The Russel Sage Foundation, New York, 1911, p. 108.

Kanysh Satpayev, a renowned 20th century Kazakh geologist, and students such as Razikov felt great pride in studying at a university named for one of their countrymen. They were equally pleased that Lenin's name had been removed at the end of the Soviet era.

Kazakhstan's extensive natural resources include petroleum, natural gas, coal, and uranium, and some economists describe the country as an energy superpower across Asia and Europe. Razikov studied hydrogeology and petroleum engineering, preparing him well for work in the energy field and affording him a choice among several attractive career opportunities.

He received employment offers from several large American companies that had major investments in Kazakhstan's oil industry, but he preferred the smaller company that he believed was free of foreign influence. His family background included a strong thread of nationalism, and working for the interests his countrymen was a goal he had held since childhood. He was recruited by Kazkara, a company that took its name from the Karachaganak Field, a major oil and gas field in northwest Kazakhstan.

Kazkara was not the only organization to recognize his potential. In the late 1990s, Razikov was also recruited by the KFB. Even then, in the early days of its existence, Kaskyrbai Ghazi knew that the Kazakh Freedom Battalion would need the services of technically trained operatives. His sources at the university told him of this patriotic young man who seemed to share his own values.

For a next dozen years, Razikov was an inactive member of the KFB, his ties cemented by a modest stipend and short periods of guerrilla training during times when his superiors at Kazkara thought he was enjoying a restful holiday.

Razikov's situation changed dramatically when Kazkara asked him to take an overseas posting. The company leadership wanted to expand its operations, and they believed the place of greatest opportunity was America. A U.S. office would be established in Alexandria, Virginia, just outside Washington, D.C. Senior management wanted the staff to include someone who had a technical background and also understood the company.

Razikov had been noticed by his superiors from the time he first was hired, and he was soon promoted to the rank of senior engineer. He interacted with visiting Europeans and Americans, and his English language skills, while initially modest, improved tremendously when the company sent him for additional training.

His instructors reported that he had achieved strong proficiency.

We conclude Adil Razikov would work well in the
American environment, and his Kazakh idiom would
disappear completely after a short period of
immersion in the new culture.

Razikov informed the Warlord of his impending transfer to America, and a meeting was arranged. It was a very unusual meeting, because very few members of the KFB ever met directly with its leader. Then again, very few of its members ever paid official visits to the U.S.

· · · · ·

Several months before Razikov's departure, he received a message instructing him to be at the Café Atlantica at 10:45 in the morning on a specific day. The location was a small place in Microdistrict 4 of Oral, the Kazakh city the Soviets had called Uralsk. It was near the intersection of two relatively busy avenues. The railroad tracks were nearby, and several bus lines passed through the intersection. It had been only a fifteen-minute walk from the Kazkara offices.

Five minutes before the appointed time, as Razikov approached the café from the south, another man unexpectedly fell into step next to him. The sound of his footsteps was shortly followed by a voice. "You will please continue walking around the corner."

They turned again after passing several small buildings, and Razikov found himself standing at the edge of a vacant property. Not quite a park, but there was a path with a few trees in the area behind the café. Finally, the man spoke.

"I am Ospanov. May I see your identity card?"

Razikov knew that Asim Ospanov was the head of security for Ghazi. More than a bodyguard, and a frequent companion. He removed his papers from a pocket and handed them to the other man. Ospanov studied them briefly and made an unsuccessful effort at a smile.

"It is in order. Let us go inside, my friend."

As Ospanov spoke, he clapped the other man on the back in what someone might have viewed as a gesture of friendship. But Razikov knew otherwise. Ospanov had just made certain that he was not carrying a weapon.

Ospanov led Razikov to the back of the room where Ghazi waited, his back was to the wall.

"I have ordered tea for you, Adil Razikov. You will please sit down."

Razikov nodded as he sat. "Sardar," he said.

The Warlord gave Razikov his instructions, which were remarkably simple. He should go to America as his company had requested. He should work hard for the ensuing twelve months, demonstrating that he was a competent and reliable employee. Other than that, the Warlord would ask nothing of him in that year.

In that year.

The Warlord also gave Razikov a name and an address on a small piece of paper, about the size of a business card.

"Keep this. He is a friend, and he will be pleased to see you. You should contact him. But only after you have been in America for one year. When that time comes, you must visit him at this address in the city of New York."

"I shall do as you request, Sardar."

"Your work will make you a hero to your countrymen ..."

Ghazi stood abruptly.

"You will excuse me for one moment."

He turned from the table where they had been seated and walked through a small doorway toward the back of the café. Razikov recalled seeing the sign for the toilets when he first walked in with Ospanov. Several minutes later, Ospanov stood, motioning with his hand that Razikov should remain seated. Then, Ospanov went to the front of the restaurant and walked out through the main door.

As Razikov waited for the Warlord to return, he watched Ospanov cross the street and disappear between two buildings. He thought about his future and the challenges he would face in America — both at Kazkara and in the service of the Warlord. Only after another ten minutes passed did he realize that the meeting was finished. The others had left and were not coming back.

* * *

Washington, D.C., September 5

Razikov blinked his eyes and realized he had drifted off to sleep. Looking out the window, he saw that the open countryside had been replaced by dilapidated industrial buildings on the outskirts of Washington, D.C. He was almost there. The bus would let him off in Chinatown, not far from the center of downtown Washington, D.C.

He stared at his hands and noticed how dirty his fingernails were. His hands were filthy as well, and he thought he could smell the stink of his body, but he wasn't sure.

He removed the scrap of paper that had been in his pocket and read the name and address once again. It was the same paper that the Warlord had given him two years earlier. He put it back in his pocket. He might need it again.

This was his second visit to see the man in New York. The first time, back in January, he was told that there would be no more waiting. His year of doing nothing was finished.

In the months that followed, Razikov's performance at Kazkara deteriorated. At first, there were days when he was late arriving at the office. Those occurrences became more frequent, and eventually, there were days when he failed to show up at all. His impeccable appearance declined as well. Two of his coworkers eventually complained to their superior that Razikov's hygiene had declined, and he had begun to smell. His technical reports no longer showed the clarity and insight for which Razikov was known.

In a few short months, everything became unsatisfactory. There were offers of assistance and suggestions that he might consider medical treatment, but these were rejected. His colleagues discussed the growing problem, as did his superiors.

By April, Razikov's promising start in the U.S. had become an utter disaster, and the company could no longer justify keeping him on their books. He would receive no further paychecks. He was on his own.

Razikov looked again at his dirty hands. They matched his pants. And his jacket. He reached up and scratched his chin. What once had been a neatly trimmed beard was now long and scruffy. He had become accustomed to the dirt, and it no longer bothered him.

He stepped off the bus with the two plastic bags that contained his belongings and walked up the block. The driver had announced that their arrival was exactly on schedule at 4:30 p.m. That would give him enough time to reach Farragut Square by the time people began leaving their offices at the end of the day.

•••••

"I don't care who you are, it's unconstitutional! They'll take you to jail! You're going to rot in jail. And I'm going to sue you."

He was speaking in a very loud voice, his strident tone entirely unpleasant.

The responses, though infrequent, were equally harsh.

"You're a disgrace! We don't want you here."

A man headed toward the Metro escalator turned his head in contempt.

"You're just lucky nobody has hit you yet."

"Leave me alone, or I'll call the police," said a woman as she altered her path to walk around him.

Most of the pedestrians did not look at the man, preferring instead to keep their eyes trained on the sidewalk in front of them. One woman sneaked a glance at the large, unkempt man who was shouting, but she quickly lowered her head and continued on her way.

The sidewalks along K Street were crowded at the start of the evening rush hour, and the throng attempted to give a wide berth to the man who was arguing with himself.

His rant in front of the Farragut North Metro station continued for almost twenty minutes, his voice becoming increasingly raspy. Finally, the man grew silent. He went to the corner of the Metro entrance, by the side of the escalators, and retrieved his two plastic bags. Then he began walking slowly across Farragut Square in the direction of Lafayette Square. He paused to scratch his scruffy beard, and passersby took great care to avoid bumping into him.

•••••

Razikov sat down on a park bench. He picked up a half-empty bottle of water and sniffed it. He drank what was left and dropped the empty bottle on the ground where he had found it. Then he leaned back to relax. Over the past six months, he had come to consider a wooden park bench one of the more comfortable places to rest. Certainly, it was better than the hard ground where he would be sleeping that night.

He ate a lot of junk food, and it made him a little fat. He also wasn't as tall has he had been. His actual body hadn't changed, but before he lost his job, he had always worn special shoes. They had made him taller. So now he was shorter and fatter. Even his own mother wouldn't recognize him.

* * * * *

There were a half dozen of them, some with names, others without, but none with a warm bed to sleep in. They were on hard-packed dirt where grass had grown previously — beneath one of the bridges that crisscross East Potomac Park.

This particular location was barely visible from the nearby streets, and most nights nobody bothered them. No fires though. That would attract attention. It didn't matter much, because the weather was still fairly warm. But it had been cold on some of the nights he had spent there the previous spring, and he was worried about what the coming winter might bring.

He listened to parts of the conversation. Not a real conversation. Just words from one person and then responses or perhaps just more words from another. Frequently, nothing made sense.

"This was a good day."

"It was. It was a real shitty day."

"Don't you know it."

"I knew it would be. For certain."

"Tell it, brother. I saw the cat run across the road."

The alcohol always helped. This time, he'd managed to get a small bottle of vodka. Not real vodka, but something that they called vodka in the liquor store. He kept on listening to the conversations but nothing made sense. Eventually, he fell asleep.

* * * * *

"Thus said the Lord! And the righteous shall be punished and the wicked shall go free!"

For nearly half an hour, he kept up a steady string of seemingly biblical quotations. Except that they weren't really quotations, and they certainly weren't from the bible. He'd made up the phrases by listening to others in his new community. He was almost certain that they were paranoid schizophrenics, and he tried to imitate them. In some ways, this wasn't all that different from studying at university. Watch, listen, and apply what you hear and see.

"God will strike down the sinners! He will send the fornicators to eternal hell. They will burn in fire forever."

The horde of workers streaming out of the Metro paid little attention. They only wanted to get away from the shouting and reach the quiet safety of their offices.

He had noticed that the actual words didn't matter. A few things about *God*, about what the words of *Jesus,* or what *the Lord* may have said. The cadence was more important than the actual words. And it had to be loud. If you were quiet, someone might pay more attention, and they might even ask you about it. But if you were loud enough, they just decided you were crazy, and they wanted to stay away from you. If they reached out by talking to you, you might talk back, maybe even touch them. They didn't want that. That was the first thing he had learned. If you were homeless and crazy, nobody wanted anything to do with you.

He had also discovered something else. The more you did it ... the crazier you acted ... the worse you smelled ... the louder you were ... and the more often you were there ... the more you fit those patterns, the less they even noticed you at all. You became completely invisible. You didn't exist. They didn't want to see you, or hear you, or smell you. So they didn't. You were right there, and you could walk right in front of them. But they didn't see you.

· · · · ·

He always followed the same routine. He'd start off at one of the Metro Stations by Farragut Square. He didn't like going anywhere else, because he worried that he couldn't manage a larger expanse. Farragut Square and the couple of blocks down to Lafayette Square. That's what he considered his 'beat.'

He covered the same area almost every day. Tourists might notice him, but not the regulars. They saw him if they came close, but he was just something to sidestep. They didn't really see him. Not as another person. He had ceased to exist.

So once again, after the morning rush hour, he walked the several blocks toward Lafayette Square. He strolled through the park looking for a nice place to sit down. Sit and wait. Nothing was going to happen now. Nor any time soon. Waiting could go on for days. Weeks, possibly. Or months. Maybe even years. Some things just took time.

He saw a couple of places where he might sit. One of them was at the far end of the park, though. The south end. He didn't want to sit there. It was too close to the edge of the park. Too close to the White House. Those people might notice.

* * *

Washington, D.C., September 7

William Desmond stepped off the Metrobus at K Street after a five-mile commute along 16th Street from his modest brick home on the edge of Rock Creek Park.

Desmond knew, or at least he thought he knew, that the White House was the reason his assignment to Washington had happened so early in his career. It started when President Clinton gave a policy speech at the University of Michigan while Desmond was an undergraduate. The poise and proficiency of the President's security detail made a strong impression on Desmond.

He was majoring in Management Information Systems, expecting to launch a career in the business world, but he was soon fascinated by the notion that his education might also be a perfect match for a career in the Secret Service.

Desmond received an official employment offer the week after his graduation. He was sent to the Criminal Investigator Training Program and then to the Secret Service's training academy. Each of these programs was based in Maryland, not far from the District of Columbia. He was partway through these programs when Al Qaeda launched its attacks on the World Trade Center and the Pentagon. Desmond knew for certain that he had chosen the right career path.

His first assignment was to the Dallas field office. A tour for a new Special Agent would ordinarily be for six years, but Desmond's career trajectory didn't follow the standard path. Once again, he attributed it to a Presidential visit. President Bush made frequent visits to his ranch in Crawford, Texas, which was two hours south of Dallas/Fort Worth but only a half hour from the airport in Waco.

The Secret Service had a Resident Office in Waco and maintained staff at the President's ranch, but a speech in Waco meant that extra security was needed. Desmond was assigned to the detail, and he had been standing near Bush for part of the event. As the President was leaving, he paused next to Desmond and smiled.

Desmond thought he hear him say, "Good job."

The President followed the offhand comment with a question. "What's your name, son?"

Desmond never had any concrete evidence, but he felt certain that his early transfer to Washington, D.C., was a result of that simple exchange. He was a rising star.

He never did serve on the Presidential detail. From the start, he augmented his on-the-job training with intensive foreign-language study. He had taken courses in Russian in high school and college, and he next turned his attention to learning Arabic and Farsi.

Toward the end of his first year in Washington, he enrolled in the law school at American University, earning his law degree after four years as a part-time student. By then, his superiors had put him on the fast track for promotion, and his next postings were in Moscow, Bucharest, and Frankfurt. When that phase of his career ended, he found himself back in Washington, firmly established in the Intelligence Division.

• • • • •

On this cloudless October morning, as Desmond walked past the Hay-Adams Hotel, the sun glinted off the bronze statue of Andrew Jackson. Beyond the White House, the Washington Monument rose into the sky. These sights put an extra spring in Desmond's step as he walked at a relaxed pace through Lafayette Square on the way to his office on G Street, a block west of the White House.

He had first noticed her when she stood next to him waiting for the light to change on H Street. When the light changed, she continued walking at a faster clip through the park, and he continued to watch.

She was in her late twenties, maybe five-six or so, and slim. He thought she had a really nice shape. That she was something special. As he walked behind her, Desmond decided that she improved an already beautiful landscape.

He was surprised a few seconds later, when she stopped to engage one of the homeless men in the park. It wasn't anything suspicious, but she had seemed to be in a hurry before that. He saw her give the man several dollars from her purse.

Probably has a heart of gold. And she probably works for almost no money at some non-profit in the neighborhood.

As he approached the edge of the square, he turned back and glanced at them again.

A big overweight, guy with a beard. Not very clean, but not threatening, either.

Desmond filed away his observations of the man for future reference. It was part of his training. He wouldn't have to work to remember the woman.

* * *

8

Martin, Neela, and Samantha

*Where there are compelling reasons in furtherance
of an agency mission, immigrant alien and foreign
national employees who possess a special expertise
may, in the discretion of the agency, be granted
limited access to classified information.*

—*Executive Order 12968*[*]

Langley, Virginia, September 8

The table in the small conference room at CIA headquarters was a jumble of half-empty coffee cups, partially filled water glasses, file folders, and pads of paper with notes scribbled on them. As the morning dragged on, the combination of intense scrutiny and second-guessing of Andrea Chang's proposals was wearing on everyone.

Chang had been tasked with developing a first draft of the operational plan, and this was the third time she had presented a revised version to her superiors. Allan Canterbury, David Hashan, and Robert Alford remained in fundamental agreement with the plan, but they kept picking at it. At the assumptions ... at the details ... and at the potential pitfalls. No matter how good the plan might be, and no

---

[*] "Executive Order 12968 of August 2, 1995, Sec. 2.6, Access by Non-United States Citizens," William J. Clinton, *Federal Register,* Vol. 60, No. 151, 1995, Sec. 2.6.

matter how much they all wanted it to work, they had to keep trying to find even the smallest imperfections.

Only when they could no longer find any flaws could they be satisfied that the plan would succeed. Only then could they ask their superiors to approve the operation. Only then could they subject their agents to the risks that the operation would certainly present.

"Can we talk again about his name?" Alford asked. "If he goes in with his real name, won't that expose him to greater risk? We've gone to all this trouble to show that he was killed, and now you just want to have him stand out there and yell, 'Hey, here I am!'? It doesn't make a lot of sense to me."

"Actually, it does," Hashan said. "Remember, the Warlord and his people believe they killed the entire Sulley family, including Martin. So they're not looking for him. If they hear that he has resurfaced, they might not believe it's true. Either way, it could throw them off balance."

"It's more than that," Canterbury said. "If Ghazi decides to go after Martin, he'll be walking into a trap. We're the ones that have all the facts."

Hashan continued his explanation. "And it's a perfect fit because Martin Sulley actually spent a summer in Tajikistan five years ago. After his sophomore year at Virginia Tech. He lived with his uncle up in the mountains, and he got to know the people in that village. His uncle, the Patriarch, had some dealings with the Warlord, so a link exists. We're going to exploit it."

Alford's doubts had not dissipated. "If I understand the thread here, the uncle subsequently was killed, and we think it was done by the Warlord. But we think the link to the Warlord still exists."

"Almost certainly," Chang said. "Stephan Udrea visited the Patriarch on two occasions, and it was clear that someone in the village was in contact with the Warlord. Someone whose loyalties were not with the Patriarch."

Alford shook his head. "That's exactly my point, Andrea. This person, whoever it is, would alert the Warlord that Martin Sulley is still alive. Martin would become a target."

Canterbury's tone was deliberate when he responded. "You're quite correct, Bob. Martin would look like a sitting duck. But the reality would be just the opposite. Martin would be part of a small force lying in wait. Martin's entire purpose would be to draw the Warlord into the open. It's our only way to find out where he is."

"Does Martin know he'll be the tethered goat?"

"He knows," Hashan answered. "He and I have had some long talks about it. It's what he wants."

"What about the rest of his team?" Alford asked. "He's got to have support."

"It will be first rate," Chang said. "We're working on that now. We think we've lined up two of the very best. Special Operations experience that includes the mountainous region along the border between Afghanistan and Pakistan. And they come with the best and latest equipment. Technology, weaponry, communications. Some of the stuff is barely out of the research lab."

"And don't forget," Hashan added, "Martin won't be alone. Two people who are already part of our team will be with him."

"Tell me again," Alford said. "Why can't we do this in Dushanbe? Or even go directly to Astana, since Kazakhstan is where we think the Warlord is hiding out. Why in such a remote area?"

Hashan answered.

"If we sent him into Kazakhstan to look for the Warlord, others would take notice. And then we'd find Martin dead. We could never protect him in an urban environment. This isn't going to be a frontal assault. It may take more time, but the Warlord will come to us. Martin and his team will monitor trails that are used for opium and weapons smuggling along a key part of the old Silk Road. The Warlord uses those routes to transport drugs between Kazakhstan and the Wakhan Valley in Afghanistan. That's how he originally made contact with the Patriarch."

"You think Martin will be good enough to bring this off?" Alford asked.

"Absolutely," Chang said. "All the reports say he's one of the most talented recruits we've ever worked with. His language skills are excellent, and he learned from native Tajiks, so there's no accent for him to lose. He's been improving his proficiency and comfort level the entire summer, and he's a quick study. The same goes for combat training and tradecraft."

"Okay," Alford said. "I don't see any holes in the operation with respect to Martin. I'll give the green light on that part of the plan."

The others nodded.

"Let's discuss the two women." Canterbury said. "Can you run through that part of the plan, Andrea?"

* * *

York County, Virginia, September 9

The CIA training facility in York County, Virginia, is located on a 14-square mile military reservation on the York River, east of Interstate 64 near Williamsburg. The site is known as Camp Peary, although CIA staff who have trained there frequently call it *The Farm*. Most of the property is unimproved, and it is closed to the public.

Neela had spent the day on a remote section of the base crawling through swampy woodlands while working on her navigation and reconnaissance skills. She was dirty and tired, and she was looking forward to a hot shower, dinner, and a good night's sleep. She was in the back seat of an unmarked sedan driven by one of the instructors. A second instructor was riding in the front passenger seat.

As they followed the perimeter road along the northwest section of the base, the driver suddenly slowed.

"What is it?" the second instructor asked.

"The fence." He had come to a full stop, and he pointed to the high chain-link fence that was topped with multiple strands of barbed wire.

"That looks like it's been cut. I'm going to take a closer look."

The driver unlatched his seat belt and opened the car door. As he started to get out of the vehicle, he looked at Neela and the front-seat passenger in turn.

"Keep your eyes open. I don't like this."

He had barely finished his sentence when the explosion erupted. Neela saw the driver lurch sideways as the car rolled into the ditch at the side of the road, and her head hit the door as the vehicle came to a stop.

Neela yelled to the front passenger, who was slumped in his seat. but he didn't respond. She had no weapon, but staying put wasn't an option. It took two tries to get her door to open, and it yielded when she used her shoulder to push hard. She scanned the ground, looking for the driver. She didn't see him.

As she climbed out of the car, everything went dark. A black cloth had been thrown over her head, and a pair of arms gripped her from behind. Her months of training kicked in, and she twisted so that she would be facing her attacker. She brought a knee up hard, hoping to disable her foe with a blow the abdomen, or even better, the groin.

She heard a grunt, and she felt immediate satisfaction. But she felt the pain in her arm — a sharp sting — before she could deliver a second kick. Another arm grabbed her, and she realized she was dealing with at least two attackers.

Within seconds she experienced a strange taste in her mouth that was followed by a tingling sensation in her midsection. The tingling moved up her body in a wave until she felt dizzy. She tried to kick again, but her leg didn't respond. Then everything went dark.

· · · · ·

She was groggy. She tried to sit up, but it didn't work, and she fell back to her original position, lying on her side. Her arms hurt, and she realized it was because they were tied tightly behind her back. Her feet were tied also.

The hood was gone, but there wasn't much light. Just enough to see that she was on the floor. A hard floor, made of concrete. It was cold, and she was shivering. She attempted to twist her body into a sitting position, but her restraints were fastened to a fixture on the floor. Slowly, the grogginess lessened, and she began to understand why she was so cold. She was naked.

She had no idea where she was or how long she had been there. It might have been an hour. Or maybe a day. She could see just enough to determine that she was in a small room. A cell. There was a drain hole in the center of the floor, so if she had urinated, it would be gone. There would be no liquid to define a time frame.

She tried to remember her training. Certainly, they would interrogate her. But she didn't even know who they were, so how could she plan her path of resistance?

She tried to take stock of her physical situation. Her skin — what she could see of it in the light — seemed to have a uniform color. No signs of any wounds or dried blood. From her cramped position, she tried to move each leg and each arm, one at a time. She understood that these attempts would be unsuccessful, but it allowed her to conclude that none of her limbs were broken. She did the same with her fingers and then her toes, and she detected nothing that indicated significant damage.

The pain did not seem to arise from any specific injury. It was general, it was pervasive, and it was severe. Her mouth was dry, and it made her think she had been there a long time without anything to drink. But when she thought about it, she remembered that some drugs gave rise to a dry mouth. And there was no question that she had been drugged. It had taken a while before she figured that out, but she knew it was true. The whole thing had been planned. They were waiting for her car to drive by.

If she had not been restrained, she would have jumped. The light was intense, coming from sources all around the room. It was so bright, she had to shut her eyes. And sound came at the same instant. Music. It was very loud. Loud enough to hurt her ears. But she couldn't tell what it was. There were instruments, but nothing she recognized. And words, but none that she understood. Eventually she realized that the sound had been distorted intentionally. It didn't matter whether these were songs that she knew, because they had been manipulated electronically to make them unintelligible. Loud, unintelligible, and unpleasant.

After a period during which she had kept her eyes closed tightly, and her mind had tried to do the same with her ears to block the cacophony, she fell asleep.

She woke again to the light and the music, not knowing whether it had ever stopped or if she had achieved any relief through sleep. All she knew was the pain. Her arms and shoulders from the ropes that were tied behind her. Her legs and her hips from the ropes that bound them. Her neck was screaming, because she had no way to rest her head. The ropes prevented her from lying on her back, and when she was on her side, she had to choose between putting her face against the abrasive concrete and holding her had above the floor until her neck muscles were too fatigued and sore to continue.

She thought she fell asleep again, but again, she was unsure.

The cycle continued.

• • • • •

After awaking from one of her periods of sleep, she found herself screaming at her captors. Demanding that they show themselves. Calling them cowards. Shouting obscenities.

Her efforts yielded nothing. She began to feel despair. And she screamed that out as well.

After what seemed like many days or weeks — although she had no way to determine how long it really was, and it might have been only hours — the door to her cell opened.

The person in the doorway wore a mask. The only description she would be able to offer was that he was frightening.

Her first reaction was to cover her nakedness, but her restraints prevented it. She could only lie motionless on the cement floor — cold, tired and completely vulnerable.

He walked toward her and set something down on the floor near her face.

"You should drink."

It was a bowl of water. Reflexively, she again tried to sit up, but her restraints prevented it. Quickly, she realized that she had no choice. She was incredibly thirsty, and the only way she could drink the water was to put her face in the bowl. And drink like a dog.

She greedily consumed the water as quickly as she could without choking, stopping only when a rush of nausea forced her to stop. She looked up at the man, but the only light in her cell came from the doorway, and all she could make out was his silhouette.

He spoke calmly, his voice deep and resonant.

"You will talk to me now. You will tell us everything."

It wasn't until that moment that she realized he was speaking in Kazakh. She was horrified, and she tried to brace herself against a panic that threatened to overwhelm her.

"I don't have to talk to you. I don't have to say anything."

Without thinking, she had answered him in Kazakh.

"You will talk. You will tell us about your work as a spy. You will cooperate with us and be loyal to your homeland."

All this was said calmly and quietly.

She put her face back into the bowl and filled her mouth with water. She turned toward him and spat it at him as hard as she could, but it only reached his knees.

He reacted calmly. His voice remained quiet.

"You really have no choice in this. If you don't cooperate, we will be forced to send you home. There is no doubt you will answer questions without hesitation when the Warlord asks you directly."

The cycle of noise and light resumed.

• • • • •

She did not know how long it had been or if there had been additional attempts at questioning her.

The noise made her look toward the door of the cell as it slowly opened. The same man, stood in the doorway, but this time there were others with him. They stood behind him, waiting for a signal. They were dressed completely in black.

She was too tired to feel any additional fear. Every part of her body ached and she wanted desperately to sleep. If felt like weeks, although she still had no way to determine if it had even been more than a day. She knew only that it had seemed like an eternity.

All three figures walked slowly toward her. The two who had been behind moved out to the sides of the large man. They were smaller. One of them held a black cloth. She saw it and knew they would put the hood over her head once again.

She realized the smaller ones were women, and they seemed less threatening. One of them knelt next to her and held out the cloth. It wasn't a hood. It was a blanket. The woman wrapped it around her, and it felt soft. The other woman began to untie the restraints.

The woman with the blanket spoke.

"It's okay, Neela. It's all over. It's finished. And you did really well. You resisted better than we could possibly have expected.

* * *

Camp Peary, Virginia, September 14

Neela and Samantha walked hesitantly into the small office. Andrea Chang used a small wave of her hand to indicate two empty chairs.

"Come in Neela ... Samantha. Sit down, please."

Chang spoke in a quiet tone, and the young women seemed to relax as they sat in the two empty chairs. Her announcement was short and to the point.

"You're both done with this phase of your training. Your time at the Farm is over."

Neela and Samantha didn't say anything in response. They knew they would learn more in a moment.

"As of today, your assignment has been extended."

Chang handed an official set of orders to each of them.

"The army has detailed both of you to the Agency for a period of two years. It's not likely to take that long, but we didn't want to run the risk of needing to request an extension a year into the operation."

She saw that Samantha wanted to ask something and nodded to her."

"I was kinda wondering ... about our applications for citizenship."

Chang hesitated.

"Yeah. I'd be wondering too, if I were in your shoes. Look, you know the rules. As members of the military, you qualify under the Immigration and Nationality Act for expedited naturalization. But it's not guaranteed."

"Are you backing out of the deal? That's why we signed up for all this bullshit."

"Don't put words in my mouth. What I said was that the policy provides for expedited processing, but it doesn't help any if you fuck up."

"So you're saying we screwed up? After everything we've been through?"

"Just shut up a minute, Samantha! You've done fine. Really well, in fact. You know that, and I know that. So do the others on our team at the Agency. But there are always going to be people who want more proof. People who would bring up everything about the uranium two years ago and say it's enough to turn you down.

"So this isn't the right time. We have a mission to complete, and that has to be our only priority. When it's over ... when we've taken down the Warlord … then we'll put the paperwork through. We'll have the proof of all your contributions. And if anyone tries to give us shit at that point, we'll tell them to shut the fuck up. You have my word on that."

The two young women looked at each other, their expressions impassive.

"Fair enough," Neela said.

Chang nodded.

"Let's move on, then. As of today, you report to me. We've arranged housing in an apartment complex in McLean, only a couple of miles from headquarters. You'll have office space down the hall from me. And you'll go to a lot of meetings. Planning meetings. Strategy meetings. Six, maybe seven days a week. Long days. Whatever it takes for us to bring off the operation to get Ghazi."

"In uniform? As soldiers?"

"God, no. In fact, that's one of the next steps. We've arranged transport for the three of us today. Directly to your new housing, so you'll need to pack all your gear before we leave. Right after lunch."

Neela looked embarrassed when she spoke.

"I'm not so sure … I mean, I don't have gear for working in a civilian office."

This time Chang did smile.

"We anticipated that. The Agency has taken care of it. Appropriate apparel will be waiting for you in your apartment."

"So when do we find out?" Samantha asked. "About the operation. And what our part will be."

"That's why I'm here this morning. Like I just said, we have a lot of planning to do. But the basic outline is in place. So let me tell you about it now. We'll be traveling in an Agency van, and you can ask questions during the trip."

Chang proceed to explain the broad outlines of the operation, noting that many of the specifics had not yet been determined.

"One of the things I want to discuss is your names. Both of you got new names when you joined the Army two years ago. That was partly for your safety and partly for operational secrecy. We didn't want anyone to accidentally figure out the connections."

"So we're getting new names again?" Samantha asked.

"No, your names stay the same. I just want you to understand that the old names are gone. Whether it's just between the two of you or if you're talking with someone else."

"Why the sudden emphasis?"

"There's a fairly good likelihood that you'll be traveling to Central Asia, Samantha. And this may come as a surprise, but Martin Sulley is probably going to be part of the same team."

"Martin …?" was the confused reply.

"Current thinking is to have that team deploy to Tajikistan. To the village where Martin's great uncle lived."

"The Patriarch. But he was killed. Martin told me about it before … before everything went crazy."

"Yes," Chang answered. "The Patriarch was killed, but others in the village are still there. They will remember Martin. They will receive him as a welcome member of the Suleyman family."

"That place is a nest of spies. The last time I saw Martin … it was just after the Patriarch's death. He said it was an attack. Opium traders. But with everything that's happened since, it makes me wonder if there's a link to the Warlord."

"Your training is starting to show," Chang said. "We think it's much more than a possibility. We believe it's a key link. We've concluded that the Warlord was responsible for killing the Patriarch."

Samantha frowned. "If Martin goes there, that information might get back to Ghazi. And someone might make the connection to me. Ghazi might decide to come after us."

"That's correct, Samantha. We've thought about that possibility. We believe it's more than a possibility. It's very likely. That's partly why we arranged for you to have such extensive combat training. Up to and including the Mountain Phase of Ranger School."

Samantha's expression conveyed a mixture of surprise and exhilaration.

"So there's a possibility we might engage him?"

"Exactly. And you would play the same role as Martin. Bait."

* * *

9

Progress Report

*The foreign ministers of the Republic of Kazakhstan,
the Kyrgyz Republic, the Republic of Tajikistan,
Turkmenistan, and the Republic of Uzbekistan and
the Secretary of State of the United States of
America issue this Joint Declaration of Partnership
and Cooperation.*

U.S. Department of State, 2015*

Kordai, Kazakhstan, September 14

The Warlord walked through the doorway of the café into the warm sunlight of the late summer afternoon. He glanced around, although he did so less conspicuously than his aide, Asim Ospanov. Satisfied that there were no threats, the two men crossed a small parking lot.

"Come, Asim. A walk to the park would be most pleasant on this fine day."

They walked without speaking, their pace casual. They turned at the corner just before they reached the war memorials and again as they approached Karagach Park.

Ospanov spoke first. "I observed that you sent messages at the café, Sardar. Were there also messages that you received?"

"Two. Both from America. Our plans move forward. The first must happen soon."

"In Michigan?"

* "Joint Declaration of Partnership and Cooperation by the Five Countries of Central Asia and The United States of America, Samarkand, Uzbekistan," Media Note, U.S. Department of State, November 1, 2015.

"Yes. The message I posted on *Olga's* Facebook page says when the event must take place. Next month."

According to her Facebook account, Olga Dimitrova was a teenage girl whose family lived in a well-to-do part of Almaty, the former capital of Kazakhstan. Her picture showed an attractive girl of uncertain age — more than ten but surely younger than seventeen. She had dark hair, but it wasn't possible to decide from the picture whether she might have a Russian background that matched her name or if she might instead have the Asian characteristics hinting at an ethnicity that was entirely Kazakh. The Warlord had chosen the particular photograph for precisely those reasons.

Olga's latest post was available to her Facebook friends.

> To dearest cousin Rustam-- I am mostly excited to
> learn your new business is doing well. Papa say to me
> how very important our country to have strong
> interaction with America. I study at KIS International
> School in Almaty. It is why I have become good in
> English. Everything at my school goes by schedule and
> we started already in August. Very soon now I will be
> back in my school again for exactly one month. Papa
> says your Uncle Vanya will give to you sporting
> equipment for your hunting and fishing. I hope as soon
> as school is finished you will once again visit across
> the lake. --Your cousin Olga.

"May I ask a question, Sardar? Could you explain to me why these two targets were selected in America? We have attempted two larger attacks, but they were not successful. Does this mean we must now attack in ways that are more limited?"

"Our previous lack of success was not because our plans were inferior but because they were too complex. It was because they took too long to carry out and involved too many people. It is what I have concluded about bin Laden's attacks. The more complex the plan, the more likely it becomes that something will go wrong. Now we will employ smaller, more carefully targeted attacks."

"But there will be less damage ..."

"Less visible damage, perhaps. But the effect will be as great. You must remember our goal, Asim. The Americans must learn that they do not belong in our country."

"Are they truly in our country? More than as guests or diplomats?"

"You have much to learn, Asim. I do not speak of the Americans as individual men or women. When I say they are 'in our country,' I describe their influence. They manipulate our government, they take our oil, they have used our skies to send their bombs to Afghanistan, and they use our highways and railroads to move their troops and military equipment. The Manas Air Base that was used by the American military is less than twenty kilometers west of where we stand, and it means nothing that the border with Kyrgyzstan lies between."

"That American base is now closed, Sardar?"

"Yes. Perhaps it is a sign that the Americans begin to fear us, and therefore we cannot allow our attacks to diminish. We must show them that remaining in our part of the world will cause them great torment. Perhaps the number of people who feel the direct pain of our operations will be small, but our targets have been carefully chosen. The consequences will be more than America's political leaders can hold in their stomachs."

"How many attacks must we make before they learn this, Sardar? We have plans only for two attacks now. Will more be needed?"

"The answer to that question is difficult. We must observe what happens after the next two operations. After that, it will be necessary for me to make new choices. Our people are in place. Five of our recruits are in America now. In several cities, where they appear to be ordinary citizens with ordinary jobs. These are men who were educated at university and also in the harsh conditions of the steppes. They have fought with us, and they have killed with us. They will not be afraid, and they will know how to follow orders."

"But we are always finding it necessary to be in secret. As we are today. Looking behind our shoulders to be certain that nobody listens to us. Even our own government tries to stop us, Sardar."

The Warlord's eyes blazed with anger.

"It is not *our* government! It does not belong to us, Asim. It is a *marionetka*, a government of dolls on strings that are manipulated by the Russians and the Americans. They have tried to stop us — to kill us — but it will never work. We can take to our horses and go to the countryside. We disappear. We are safe."

"But if ... I have fears that something could happen to you, Sardar. What would become of us then? All of us in the KFB? What would happen if the Americans or the Russians should find you?"

A look of sadness tinged the Warlord's face, and just as quickly it faded, replaced by his typical dispassionate expression.

"They do not know me. Nobody but you, Asim — you and several of our comrades are the only men alive who know my face. When I meet with others, they think I am someone else. That gives me great freedom and protection. It means even our own men can never betray me. Only you could betray me."

Ospanov backed up a step.

"Sardar! I would never … It is beyond possibility …"

Ghazi put his hand on his aide's shoulder.

"It is not for you to have concern, Asim. I know you would never intentionally do something to bring me harm."

They walked together in silence for a few steps, and Ghazi broke the silence.

"Is it time for our friend to arrive?"

"Yes, Sardar. At any moment. He knows to meet us here in this park, and my men know they should allow him to come to us."

The Warlord had chosen Kordai for the meeting because it was near the only a few kilometers from the border with Kyrgyzstan. He expected that Baluan Aimanov would avoid the official border crossing and ford the river some distance away. His arrival and subsequent departure from Kazakhstan would not be found in any official records.

• • • • •

At the conclusion of the meeting, Ghazi remained in the park with Ospanov, watching Aimanov walk back toward the street. The Warlord dropped his cigarette and looked down at the brown tube with the gold end. Then he crushed it out with his boot. He didn't like tobacco, but it had been offered by his old friend and comrade.

Aimanov had briefed them on the latest developments with their American operations. Their men were in place in both locations, although the second operation would need more time. Almost five more months. But it was only one month until the first one, and the Warlord told Aimanov that he should return immediately to North America.

"You must deliver the supplies that will allow Rustam Dembay to carry out his assignment and then make his escape."

Unlike some of the other agents who had worked for the Warlord, Dembay was too valuable — too good at his work — to be sacrificed unnecessarily.

* * *

10

Reentry

Had the imperial eagle reposed his head on a scaffold, as in all reason and justice he ought to have done, instead of being permitted to prepare new scenes of carnage amid the mountains of Elba, what torrents of human blood would have been spared!

—*Political Reflections on the Re-entry of Napoleon Buonaparte into France, 1815**

Langley, Virginia, September 16

Andrea Chang and David Hashan sat across from Allan Canterbury in a small conference room at CIA headquarters.

"Could you run through the entire plan again?" Canterbury asked Chang. "I want each of us to be sure it has all the changes we discussed at the beginning of the week."

"Sure. All the tweaks are in, so we should be clear with management. And with legal. You've talked to Alford?"

"Yes. And he's on board. As soon as I get him a final draft, he'll take it up the chain. I'm not sure, but it may have to go all the way to the White House."

"Wouldn't surprise me. Everybody in that damn chain just wants to cover their ass."

"Even if that's the case, it doesn't affect what we are doing now, Andrea. Let's get on with our discussion."

---

* "Political Reflections, Addressed to the Allied Sovereigns, on the Re-entry of Napoleon Buonaparte Into France, and his Usurpation of the Throne of the Bourbons," Edward Hankin, C. Chapple, London, 1815, p. 1.

Chang's frown lasted only a moment.

"All right, I'll start with personnel. Specifically, let's talk about the people we're sending into the field at the start of the operation. That's three altogether: Stephan Udrea, Martin Sulley, and Samantha Summers."

"What cover names will they be using?" Hashan asked.

"All three will use their real names. And that is Samantha's name now. Legally changed from Zemfira Sumaiyah."

"We agreed previously that Martin would use his real name," Hashan said. "But Stephan went by Shayan Ubayda when he was in Tajikistan before. Why not this time?"

"If he can arrange a meeting with Colonel Kholdorov, he'll do that as Ubayda. Otherwise, there's no need for an alias. Not where he's going. It would be an unnecessary complication."

"Remind me of who else you're want to put on the team," Canterbury said.

Chang looked at her list.

"In addition to the three of us and the first three we're sending into the field, I want to use five others. Anja Dalbins, Derek Davenport, Ash Hartwell, and Rachel Pomeranz. And Neela Davis, of course."

"That's good. Everyone but Hartwell has at least some overseas experience, and Ash would be here mainly for his scientific expertise. All of the Agency people have good records. When do the new operatives finish their training?"

"Samantha and Neela finished their program at the Farm this week. We got them set up in a temporary apartment in McLean. Martin completed his Agency training earlier in the summer."

"Do we have written evaluations of their performance during the training?" Canterbury asked. "I'd like to review it before we make our final decisions."

"Not the final report. At least not in writing. But unofficially, their ratings were excellent in all areas. With regard to their assignments for this operation, each of the women is ready to go. And the training officer made a point of telling me that Samantha's work with small arms was outstanding."

"That's good."

"I agree," Hashan said. "Be sure to let me know when they show up here. I'd like to meet with them."

Chang nodded.

"Could you give us an update on Martin?" Canterbury asked. "What's his status?"

"Not much to say, really. He's already teamed up with Stephan, and they're off on their last training exercise."

"Where?" Hashan asked.

"Alaska. They're three quarters of the way through a month at the Army's Northern Warfare Training Center. They're learning how to maneuver, navigate, and fight in hostile environments. Difficult mountains and cold weather."

"They're taking the regular Army courses?"

"They've created a program that is a close match for our needs. I've been in regular contact with the commanding officer at the NWTC for a few weeks, and he had orders to cooperate to the max. He was a little pissed off that we couldn't give him the full background, but he got past it."

"A question, Andrea."

"Yes, Allan?"

"Does the staff out there — and I'm not just talking about the commanding officer — do they recognize the importance of our operation?"

"They understand. I was on the phone three weeks ago on a conference call with a couple of the senior instructors. They know it's a critical mission."

"Have you gotten any pushback from the instructors? They're okay with you running the show?"

"Actually, one of them tried to intimidate me during another phone call. Staff Sergeant Michaels. It was just the two of us, and he started giving me a bunch of shit."

She smiled at Canterbury.

"But then he found out that I could use the word 'fuck' more times in a sentence than he could, and that seemed to resolve our issues. We got on pretty well from then on."

"What about physical conditioning? I imagine these courses could be very difficult."

"Absolutely. Don't forget that both Stephan and Martin were undergoing rigorous physical training at Camp Peary the prior four months. As a result, it appears they're doing well. They've been working at elevations above ten thousand, and they've hiked across a couple of glaciers. They're going to finish up on Mount Denali, which goes up to twenty thousand feet. The Army has this thing under control."

"Stay on top of it," Canterbury said. "Assuming we get our final approvals, we deploy at the beginning of October. Let's be sure we have an operation that's planned well enough for them to carry it out successfully. We can't afford any blunders. Not even the slightest miscue."

* * *

11

Canoe Trip

*After entering Lake Huron, the voyageurs coasted
along its northern shore amid innumerable small
islands and at length reached a fort or post at the
entrance to Lake Superior. To this fort other goods
were occasionally forwarded from Montreal by a
totally different route.*

—*The Saturday Magazine, 1842*[*]

Drummond Island, Michigan, September 18

Rusty Dember drove north from Cheboygan, crossing the
Mackinac Bridge before turning east. He'd been on the
road for an hour and a half when he pulled up at the
loading ramp for the ferry to Drummond Island.

Advertised as a haven for outdoorsmen, the island was a perfect
launching point for his voyage. His canoe was secured in the back of
the old Dodge pickup truck he had purchased earlier in the summer.
One end of the craft was tied to the truck's tailgate, and the other end
was lashed to the top of the cab.

The canoe was the Blackhawk model, manufactured by Savage
River, and it was entirely black, made from carbon fiber and Kevlar.
It weighed less than 40 pounds and was easy for one person to handle.

When he checked into the cabin he had rented, he told the
proprietor that he would be out on the water for a few days.

---

[*] "Fur and the Fur Trade," *The Saturday Magazine,* No. 615, Supplement,
London, January 1842, p. 46.

"The weather forecast is good, so if my provisions hold out, I may not be back again until the end of the week."

"You've paid for the whole week, so it doesn't much matter to me where you're sleeping, Mr. Dember. And I'll keep an eye on your truck until you get back. You just enjoy your vacation."

Late that afternoon, Dember filled his backpack with provisions for five days and secured it to the frame of the canoe. After months of intense training, he was in superb physical condition, but this was to be a trial run for the actual operation. He wanted to be sure he could paddle continuously for ten hours and sustain a maximum effort for at least three. Moreover, he had to be prepared for the possibility of bad weather. When the real test came, there would be no other option.

Dember knew from his map that Drummond Island was the first in a chain of islands, and everything to the east was in Canadian territory. He began paddling along the shore on a course that took him through a maze of smaller islands, most of them less than a half-mile across. The Canadian mainland was about ten miles beyond, on the far side of Lake Huron's shipping channel. The afternoon was cool and crisp, and Dember waited until it was nearly dark before he stopped for his evening meal.

He sat next to the canoe on a sandy strip of ground at the edge of a small cove near the northernmost part of Drummond Island and unwrapped his package of black bread and salami. Quickly, the food relieved his hunger and renewed his strength, and in half an hour he was ready to move again. He lashed his backpack to the supports in the canoe and began paddling, knowing that soon he would be in open water beyond Drummond Island.

Dember was in no rush to cross into Canadian waters, because it meant traversing a major shipping lane. Before undertaking that challenge, he wanted to get a feel for the behemoths that traveled up and down the waterway. The channel was plied by Great Lakes freighters that could travel at speeds above fifteen miles per hour, were as much as a thousand feet in length, and could carry cargos of more than fifty thousand tons.

He had to be certain the he could paddle safely between the moving ships and do so with confidence. On his subsequent trip, he would not have time to stop and think.

Sometime around midnight, he made his third crossing of the shipping channel, but on this occasion, he did not stop paddling when he reached Canadian waters near the eastern edge of St. Joseph Island. His destination for the night was Cedar Island, another ten miles away.

It took him another two hours to reach the site, and he used his GPS to find the exact location.

· · · · ·

Dember slept soundly for six hours. He ate his breakfast quickly, loaded his gear into the canoe, and pushed off. If anyone saw him, he would look like any other paddlers enjoying a late summer vacation.

His trip would be shorter this day, only about six miles. His destination was French Island, an islet about a quarter-mile across that was connected to the Canadian mainland by a small bridge. It was largely uninhabited, and there were no buildings on the western side, so he could make landfall and not be seen.

After verifying that the shoreline was deserted, Dember paddled quickly into a shallow cove and beached the canoe onto the sandy shoreline between some rocks. He looked around once more to be certain there was nobody to observe him, hoisted the backpack across his shoulders, and lifted the canoe above his head.

In a few seconds, he was into the trees. At the edge of a small clearing, he set the canoe down in the brush. He detached his sleeping bag from the backpack and removed a small duffel containing what he would need for the next day. Finally, he placed the backpack and sleeping bag under the canoe, secured them with a nylon rope, and covered everything with pine branches.

Checking that the location's coordinates were properly stored on his GPS, he began walking toward the old roadway that showed on his map. He estimated he would reach the town of Bruce Mines by noon, which would give him more than enough time to catch the bus that traveled the Trans-Canada Highway to Sault Ste. Marie.

* * *

Sault Ste. Marie, Ontario, September 20

When Dember's bus reached Sault Ste. Marie, he walked 600 yards along Bay Street to the Days Inn. There was a reservation in his name, which confirmed that everything was moving according to plan.

The telephone in his room rang early the next morning.

"Mr. Dember? This is the front desk. Your colleague is waiting for you in the lobby."

A man standing by the front door motioned to him, and Dember followed him across the street, where they climbed into a Jeep. They drove a few blocks, and the driver pulled to the curb near the entrance to a small marina.

"Over there. He is waiting."

Dember saw the man sitting on a bench near the water's edge, small boats and great lakes freighters just beyond. Less than a half mile distant, the United States was visible on the other side of the waterway. He walked toward the bench.

"Please sit down by me," Aimanov said. "We have arrangements that must be completed. Everything is in readiness for your assignment?"

"All is in order."

"That is good. We have now three weeks. One day less, in fact. Today, we provide you with the remaining supplies you will need. The Jeep that brought you to me — that will be a satisfactory vehicle for your use?"

The two men continued to stare at the water. "It would be suitable, yes."

"Excellent. The other items are being placed into the Jeep as we are speaking. You and I will next deliver them to your campsite. My associate — the man who brought you to me — will take the Jeep to Blind River. I am correct? That remains your destination?"

"I will go there. Where in Blind River will I find the vehicle?"

"There is a small hotel on the eastern edge of Blind River, near the Trans-Canada Highway. It is called the Auberge Eldo Inn, and the owner advertises it for people on holiday who want to do hiking and fishing. Did you notice that my associate resembles you?"

Dember had discerned that the man was his size and his age. Not a twin, but with similar features.

"I observed that."

"Then you understand. He will check into the hotel in just more than two weeks. He has the reservation already. More accurately, it is you who has the reservation. When he checks in, he will say that he is going on a backpacking trip for five or six days, so the room will be empty during that time. He will hide the room key in the Jeep so you can retrieve it. And now I am giving you a duplicate key for the Jeep."

Aimanov handed the key to Dember and continued his instructions.

"The owner of the hotel will not have seen my colleague for almost a week. When you return to the hotel, he will not realize that you are a different person. If there are any facts that would be necessary for you to know, there will be a note in the Jeep. It will be in an envelope together with your travel documents and the key beneath the driver-side seat."

"I understand."

"After that, it will be for you to continue by yourself. With no further assistance from me."

"Yes."

"Then all is sufficient. Now we go to your campsite."

As they stood, Aimanov withdrew another set of keys from his pocket.

"It is for you to drive. We must be certain the Jeep is satisfactory for you."

Dember forced himself to suppress a smile. He understood that while driving, he could not study the man's face and likely would not even recognize him if they met again at a later time.

• • • • •

They traveled east on the Trans-Canada Highway, and as they approached the town of Bruce Mines, Dember turned onto Bruce Bay Road. He followed it to the end of the mainland and across the small bridge to French Island, where he drove onto the unmarked track along the southern shore. Moments later, Dember pulled into a break between the trees and drove a few yards further, until they could no longer be seen from the dirt road.

Dember climbed out of the vehicle and studied his GPS.

"My canoe is just ahead. We can unload the equipment here."

Aimanov opened the rear hatch of the Jeep to reveal several cardboard boxes, the largest about three feet long. Dember concluded that everything would fit easily in his canoe, once it was unpacked. He planned to bury the packaging before leaving French Island.

When they removed the largest box from the Jeep, Dember estimated its weight at a bit more than one hundred bounds. Three of the other boxes were smaller, but they were heavy for their size. Maybe thirty pounds each.

Aimanov said, "You have three batteries. All appropriate for your purpose. And finally, I have your weapon."

The last package, wrapped in a piece of black nylon fabric, was about three feet in length but weighed much less than the other parcels. Dember laid it carefully on the ground and unwrapped it. Then he nodded.

"You have made the tests? It functions properly?"

"It was demonstrated by the man who provided it to me. These are illegal in Canada, where their laws are much the same as in America. This specimen was imported before the laws became so strict, and there is no record of it."

"And the modifications?"

"Exactly as you specified. Those were demonstrated also. They are impressive."

Dember refolded the nylon and placed the packet on top of the large box. He turned toward Aimanov.

"You said that was everything. What about ammunition?"

"Of course. I was saving it as a special gift for you at the end of our meeting. It is what you requested. What you said we might not be able to obtain. But it is here. You have what you need to complete your mission."

"I shall do so."

"I admire your confidence."

"Our leader expects no less."

Dember walked back to the Jeep's open hatch.

"I can carry the packages to my canoe. There is no need for you to remain any longer."

Aimanov nodded to Dember as he climbed behind the steering wheel. "The vehicle will be waiting for you when you reach Blind River."

Neither man said anything further. Aimanov backed onto the road and drove off.

• • • • •

The sun was still high in the afternoon sky when Dember began the final preparations for his crossing back to the United States that night. He had to pack the canoe, and he wanted to bury, or at least camouflage the materials that he would leave behind with a covering of brush and sand.

He quickly located the canoe and carried it to the water's edge, securing it to a rock on the shore so it could not accidentally drift away. Next, he retrieved the largest of the packages that Aimanov had brought him. He estimated the total weight at about two hundred fifty pounds.

After testing a few loading configurations, he was able to place most of the weight low in the canoe, with the contents of the largest boxes in a large duffel bag that fit snugly in the contours of the canoe's bow. He tied the three batteries to the duffel bag, but he did not secure the entire package to the canoe. If something went wrong and the canoe capsized, he would not be able to right the craft with the full weight of his cargo.

If he met such a catastrophe, he would allow the duffel and batteries to sink to the bottom of Lake Huron. Substitutes for those items would be available at a number of locations near Cheboygan, but only if absolutely necessary. As things stood, there was no link between Dember and the purchase of the materials. There was nothing to suggest what his plans might be, and there would be no way to trace him. No way to follow him.

The canoe rocked gently in shallow water at the edge of the shore as Dember loaded it. Each time he added something, he tested its stability. Each time he was satisfied. The last two items he loaded were his backpack and the black nylon parcel that had been delivered by Aimanov. He lashed those two items securely to the frame of the canoe, and he paid particular attention to the nylon parcel. Under no conditions could he afford to lose the rifle.

By the time he fully loaded the canoe and buried the cardboard packing materials in the sand amid the trees, the afternoon was fading. Dember sat down on a smooth rock and ate.

• • • • •

The craft handled sluggishly with the extra weight, but Dember was able to make steady progress. Using his GPS, he followed a course almost due south from French Island, and after crossing four miles of open water in the North Channel, he approached a large promontory known as Big Point on the eastern side of St. Joseph Island.

The sun fell behind the island, and Dember continued in the twilight for another six miles. He estimated that the ten hours of steady paddling would bring him to his destination, and he stayed on his schedule.

In the early morning hours, he made his break across the shipping lanes, almost holding his breath as he cut behind a large freighter. He was concerned that the ship's wake might wash over the canoe's gunwales, but the craft sliced through the wave without difficulty. He breathed a sigh of relief, realizing that the remainder of the trip would be easy for him.

Shortly before daybreak, he glided into a small cove on the southwestern edge of Drummond Island. For a moment, he thought of the bed in the tourist cabin he had rented, now only a few miles away. But he was not yet ready to go there.

* * *

Drummond Island, Michigan, September 21

The sun was well above the horizon when Dember awoke from his sleep. He walked a few steps to the water's edge and splashed cold water on his face. He ate part of the remaining sausage and black bread and stowed his sleeping bag back in the canoe.

As he pushed off, he felt the soreness in his shoulders, and he knew another long day lay ahead. He would have to spend the entire day on the water.

Night was falling when he approached his destination, but he welcomed the cover of darkness. The absence of lights reassured him that the few nearby dwellings had been shuttered for the winter. He beached the canoe and quickly began to unload its cargo. Once the contents all sat safely on the narrow sandy beach, he carried the packages to a clearing in the nearby trees. He used his *Spetsnaz* Voron-3 knife to cut a half-dozen pine boughs, which he used to cover the shipment. He walked back to the beach to survey the scene. Satisfied that his cache was effectively invisible, he recorded the coordinates on his GPS.

He used a small branch to brush away his footprints and the marks his canoe had made in the sand. Then he paddled several hundred yards along the shoreline until he found a secluded location. After pulling the canoe behind some trees, he unrolled his sleeping bag and settled in for a few hours of rest.

· · · · ·

Shortly after sunrise the next morning, Dember set out for his return to Drummond Island. His cache was well hidden on Bois Blanc Island, only five miles north of his lodgings in Cheboygan, Michigan. Concealed in the brush and covered with pine branches, some two hundred fifty pounds of gear would be waiting for him in just over two weeks' time.

Without the weight of the cargo, it feels like I am gliding on air. In a few hours I will be back to Drummond Island, and it will please me tonight to sleep in the cabin I rented.

* * *

12

Strategic Planning

*Strategy forms the plan of the War, and to this end it
links together the series of acts which are to lead to
the final decision.*

—*Clausewitz, 1832*[*]

Langley, Virginia, September 21

Anja Dalbins waited anxiously in the windowless office.
She occupied one of the two chairs facing a gray
government-issue metal desk. The other chair was empty,
as was the chair behind the desk. A security officer had escorted her
to the room when she first arrived at headquarters earlier in the
morning, and she had been sitting alone and idly since. It had been
more than a half hour, and her nerves were beginning to fray. She
couldn't even check her messages or look at news headlines, because
her iPhone was locked in a small bin outside the secure area.

It was her first trip back to the States in more than a year, and CIA
headquarters seemed more foreign than her office at the embassy in
Dushanbe. Tajikistan had been her home for nearly five years, and she
found immense satisfaction in her work with the USAID Mission.
Most of her efforts had been focused on fighting the continuing
HIV/AIDS epidemic, and she felt that they were making headway.

Hers was an unusual career situation. Officially, she was a Project
Management Specialist for Health, but that title had been assigned as
a cover identity for her actual position as a CIA operative. She always

---

[*] "On War," Carl von Clausewitz, Translated by J. J. Graham, Vol. 3,
Kegan Paul, Trench, Trübner & Co., London, 1908, p. 165.

kept her eyes and ears open for useful information, but most of her efforts had been devoted to helping the Tajik population.

Anja had filed regular reports with Langley, but there was little that seemed to have any significance. The intelligence she collected wasn't winning any wars, nor was it preventing any as far as she could tell. Perhaps in a few instances the information would help her colleagues to keep tabs on members or rebel groups or identify potential terrorists, but it was her daily work that provided her with a sense of accomplishment. In that role, she was helping to save lives.

The exceptions to this narrative were her two trips to the high mountains of Gorno-Badakhshan several years earlier. On both occasions, she was teamed with Stephan Udrea, known in Tajikistan by his cover name of Shayan Ubayda. The excursions were undertaken to meet with a man known as the Patriarch, a man they suspected was somehow linked to a planned attack on the United States.

The plot hinged on a nuclear weapon made from enriched uranium that had disappeared from Kazakhstan more than two decades earlier. Anja had only minimal involvement in the operation aimed at preventing the attack, but she again felt that her contributions had been positive. She never learned the outcome of the operation, and that didn't surprise her. She had no "need to know," so she wasn't told.

A soft knock on the door of the conference room was accompanied by voices engaged in hushed conversation. The door opened, and a familiar-looking woman gave instructions to an apparent assistant before turning to enter the room.

"Good morning, Ms. Dalbins. I'm Andrea Chang. It's nice to meet you. We've heard good things about your work overseas."

They shook hands in a formal manner, and Chang motioned to the chair Anja had been using. They both sat.

Anja managed a smile.

"Actually, we've met before, Ms. Chang. It was seven years ago. You were our 'tour guide,' or whatever the right term is, when we were first here on a recruiting visit."

"We? I'm not sure I follow."

"Oh, sorry. The last few years I've been working with …"

She paused, unsure whether to use his real name or his cover name. "… with Shayan Ubayda. We've both been stationed at the embassy in Dushanbe."

Chang relaxed and returned a smile.

"Of course. Stephan is well known to me … and he's not using the cover name any longer. I had forgotten that the two of you were in the same group of recruits, so please forgive me for not remembering that first encounter. However, I'm certainly aware that the two of you have worked together in Tajikistan. It's the reason you're here now."

"Stephan?" Anja was confused. "Is something going on with him? Some kind of problem?"

"No, not with him. That isn't what I meant. But the operation he's been working on is getting hairy. I want to bring you into it."

Anja knew better than to say anything. It was a time for listening.

"You remember your second visit to the Patriarch?"

"Yes, certainly. But I don't know what became of our efforts. I wasn't read in to the whole operation. Only that Stephan and I concluded that the Patriarch had some knowledge of some missing uranium but I didn't know the details behind our concerns. He showed no reaction when we used the word *sapphire*, but he stopped cooperating with us when we asked specifically about the uranium. Are you thinking we should go visit him once again?"

Chang frowned. Then she took a deep breath.

"I'm afraid that's not a possibility. He was killed shortly after you visited him. There's a lot we need to tell you about to get you up to speed."

During the next hour. Anja learned about Kaskyrbai Ghazi. Not everything, but enough. She learned what he had tried to do, and why he had not succeeded. She asked the obvious question.

"Has he been detained?"

Chang's blank expression hid her underlying frustration.

"No."

"May I ask why? It would seem ..."

"You may ask. And the answer is the reason you're here."

"I don't understand."

"It's actually quite simple. He is an enemy of our country, and we have to find him. We have to prevent further terrorist attacks against us. And we believe you can be helpful. Everything about him is somehow connected with smuggling routes between Kazakhstan and Tajikistan. That's your area of expertise."

"Do you have assets who are tracking him?"

"He's in Kazakhstan, and it's a really big place. We can't trust the Kazakh security forces on this, and we don't have the capabilities for surveillance inside a country that's four times the size of Texas. We need something more sophisticated than brute force, and I've been charged with assembling a team to take on that challenge. I want you as part of the team."

"I don't know what to say."

"Then don't say anything. Not yet. We're meeting later this morning. David Hashan will be giving us our marching orders. You'll have a chance to meet the others and then make your decision."

Anja understood that it might be called a decision, but it wasn't a choice.

* * *

Langley, Virginia, September 22

Anja counted eleven people around the table. She was the twelfth. She was surprised to see two people she knew well.

Stephan and Derek. I thought both were still in Dushanbe.

Other than Chang, the only other person she recognized was David Hashan, whom she had also had met during her recruiting visit to the Agency seven years earlier.

Hashan cleared his throat.

"I'd like to get started please. Before I describe our task, it might be a good idea to make some introductions. Just your name and current assignment. Let me start with myself. I'm David Hashan, and I'm Assistant Head of the Central Asia Desk."

He turned to his right.

"Bob Alford. I'm Assistant Deputy Director for Operations."

"Allan Canterbury, Head of the Central Asia desk."

"Andrea Chang. I'm a Staff Operations Officer, and I'm serving as David's assistant with this task group."

Hashan interrupted. "Just to be clear, Andrea will be running the show. She'll report to me, and I'll report up to Allan and Bob. But the rest of you will be working with Andrea. I'll participate in your meetings when I can, but I won't be running them."

He looked around and then gestured to the next person.

"Ash Hartwell. Directorate of Science and Technology, but I've been officially detailed here as a Specialized Skills Officer."

"Rachel Pomeranz. The Russian Desk here at NCS. I'm an SSO, like Ash."

Anja was followed by Stephan Udrea, and Derek Davenport. All three identified themselves as Core Collectors working in Dushanbe.

Three of the eleven people around the table remained, and Chang spoke before any of them could say a word.

"Let me take over here. The last three members of our group are Martin Suleyman, Samantha Summers, and Neela Davis. Their backgrounds are somewhat different, and their credentials are unique. All three have crossed paths with the Warlord. Neela and Samantha have actually met him, so they are the only two humans we know who are capable of identifying him. Earlier this year, the Warlord arranged the assassination of Martin's entire family. Father, brother, uncle, cousins. All of them."

The room was silent.

· · · · ·

After Chang provided additional background on the newest team members, Hashan gave a bare-bones summary of what they knew about the Warlord's prior efforts to mount attacks in the United States.

Alford, Hashan, and Canterbury had discussed the operation several times during the previous week, and they had decided to use a broad definition of "need to know."

As Alford had put it, "We've assembled a team of people who have been directly involved at some level. If they're going to do the job you want them to do, they've got to be able to talk with each other. So we've got to tell them everything we know."

Canterbury next related how a link had been found between the Warlord in Kazakhstan and the man known as the Patriarch in Tajikistan. That nexus closed a loop among the individuals in the room. He described how Neela and Samantha had been raised as orphans and sent by the Warlord to study in the United States. How, as college students, they met Martin Suleyman and his brother, whose uncle, or more accurately, the brother of their grandfather, was the Patriarch. And how the Warlord had exploited these relationships, asking the young women to encourage the brothers in a seemingly harmless technical venture.

The students had been innocent dupes, victims of the Warlord's schemes. Only a combination of hard work, brilliant insight, and good fortune had prevented the Warlord from carrying out his devastating attack.

Hashan followed by recounting key aspects of the biological attack that had been thwarted earlier that year. Not before there were deaths, but before the attack with genetically engineered bacteria could achieve its full impact.

"We've interpreted these events as indicating that the Warlord has an extensive network inside the U.S., but we don't believe it's what we consider a traditional spy network. It seems to mostly be Kazakh visitors or immigrants who might be asked for a favor. Nothing that an individual would give much thought to. Just typical ways of helping out in an immigrant community."

Hashan looked at his colleagues to be sure he had their full attention.

"Someone might say, 'My cousin back in the old country wrote and asked if I could buy him one of those things.' Or, 'Can you help me find an expert in this area, so I can figure out how to assist my brother-in-law to import his goods to this country.' At that level, these things all seem harmless even if they're not completely kosher."

Hashan turned to Stephan, who had started to ask a question. "Let me finish with a few more things. Then we're going to have time for a lot of questions."

Stephan nodded.

"So, this may not have been what you were going to ask, Stephan, but we have to ask how the Warlord was able to operate this network. Right now, we think that he has a small number of skilled operatives who have taken advantage of the informal immigrant network. Probably not much more than a half-dozen or so. Nothing like the 'terrorist cells' we've always worried about. We think there might have been another five or ten people who were short-term visitors, but we're talking about messengers, not special-operations types."

Hashan realized that once again, he had made a statement that would trigger multiple questions.

"Okay, it's clear there were two or three technically proficient people who were deeply involved in the plot with the uranium. And there were a half-dozen technical people involved in the biological attack. But those six guys were all working as individuals, not as a team. They got their biological samples from a German visitor, and she got them from the Russian scientist who engineered the bacteria. Actually, he was only working in Russia. He was a Kazakh.

"So that brings me to my last point. Part of the reason we think the Warlord doesn't have much of an operational network here is that the people who fit that category wind up dead. The German, the Russian, the biological people. But there's at least one person who's still alive. The man who is probably responsible for killing Martin's family. The only thing we know about him is that he favors a specific brand of Russian cigarettes known as Black Russians."

Hashan flipped the page on his notepad. The next page was blank.

"Andrea, why don't you take over? Or do think we should break for lunch first?"

"Lunch. People can use the time to get to know each other a little."

* * *

Langley, Virginia, September 22

Chang tapped her pen against the desk. "Could we get started again, please?"

The sidebar conversations finished quickly, and the room became quiet.

"As David told you earlier, I've been charged with running this operation. It's going to be a tough one. We're trying to find someone, and we don't know where he is. We don't have a decent photograph of him. And we know it's only a question of time before he launches another attack."

"You're telling us we have to find a needle in a haystack."

She looked at Hartwell and frowned. "No, Ash. We're looking for a grain of sand. A single grain of sand somewhere in the middle of a big fucking desert."

"I've got a number of things to say, but I want a free flow of ideas. So if you have a question, or if you want to add something, or if you just want to disagree … wave your hand, and I'll recognize you. We need some discipline, but I want to be as informal as possible."

Stephan was the first to raise his hand. "Why us? Why this specific group?"

"A fair enough question. Simple answer? Because each of you has been involved in this operation for a long time. Either as an agent or as a participant. A victim would be a better word. Each of you brings important background to the task at hand."

"I don't see the Dushanbe connection," Davenport said. "I'm not objecting, but it seems like you would have been better off with someone stationed in the embassy in Kazakhstan. Closer to the Warlord."

"Exactly the point, Derek. Too close. David, Allan, and I discussed that approach at length. But it would have backfired. There's no way would we could ever bring in the Kazakh security forces. Just not enough trust. If we started reallocating our people in Kazakhstan, it would get noticed. And we don't know how far the Warlord's tentacles extend over there."

Anja was next. "There's an elephant in the room, here. I'm not sure how to address this discreetly, so I'll just ask. And hope nobody is offended. Obviously, this a serious operation. I'm assuming its classification level is high enough that nobody outside this room knows about it."

Alford cleared his throat. "The Director knows. But you were close."

"So, if it's that secret … What I mean is why …?"

Chang interrupted. "You're right, Anja. It is an awkward situation. So let's just face it head on. You're asking why Neela and Samantha are here?"

"Yeah, I guess so. It's just that they're … kind of new. I'm not sure how to say it exactly."

Anja, Neela, and Samantha weren't the only individuals at the table who felt uncomfortable.

"Let me explain," Chang said. "First of all, nobody's worried about how old these two women are. They're the same age you were when you joined the agency. I'm guessing that what may be an underlying concern is whether we can be sure of their loyalty. In part, because they're not U.S. citizens. So you're worried. Can they be trusted? Am I right?"

Embarrassed nods could be seen around the table.

"Well, the answer is pretty simple. Neela and Samantha have no love for the Warlord. They feel no loyalty to him nor to his cause. Two years ago, they tried to assist in what they believed was a business opportunity for a company in their country of origin. Something that any of us would probably do for our fellow countrymen. But it was a setup. They were dupes in a conspiracy that has destroyed the lives and careers they were planning."

"Devil's advocate," Alford interjected. "Maybe that was part of the Warlord's plot. To get us to trust them."

"Of course," Chang answered. "And consequently, it was one of the first thing's we addressed in their interrogations two years ago. Moreover, we have every reason to believe neither of them would be alive today if we had not helped them obtain new identities. Martin's family was wiped out last spring. Neela and Samantha were going to be next."

The two women looked surprised, but they said nothing.

The question came from Martin.

"Why do you say that, Andrea? What makes you think they were the next targets?"

"Because we have some relatively firm evidence. The FBI is still working the investigation of the bombing in Rockbridge County, and they immediately started looking into the possibility that someone might try to find Neela and Samantha. It turns out that someone visited the Virginia Tech campus two days after the attack on your family's compound. He went to the alumni records office to get information on Neelam Dâvar and Zemfira Sumaiyah."

"What does that prove?" Hartwell asked. "People must ask about former students all the time."

"This man was different. The manager of the records office remembered him. Foreign accent. She guessed it was Eastern European or Russian. And he said he was representing a potential donor, who had provided scholarship money for Zemfira and Neela."

"It's intriguing, but it's not definitive," Hartwell responded.

"No, Ash. It's not definitive. But I'll tell you what is. The FBI sent a forensic team in, and they found a cigarette butt near the entrance to the alumni building. Dark wrapper with gold foil. What David previously described as a Black Russian. Residue from the same kind of cigarette was found at the bombing site. This wasn't a coincidence."

"No, I guess not."

"So I'll go back to the point raised by Anja. How trustworthy are these two women? As I told you in the introductions, they're both active members of the United States Army, both with full security clearances. Those clearances don't come easily. And we revisited the issue again this summer during their training at Camp Peary. Polygraphs say they're clean, the shrinks say they're clean, and our counterintelligence specialists say they're clean. They've been scrubbed more extensively than the rest of you."

After a few seconds of silence, Canterbury spoke again.

"I think we can move past this. I know this was an awkward topic, but the discussion needed to be held. Each of you has to be trusted by everyone else at the table, and it was important that you understand why such trust should be extended to Neela and Samantha."

"Thank you, Allan," Chang said. "Let's get back to questions. Does anyone have another topic to ask about?"

Neela raised a hand.

Chang was pleased. Whatever the damage from the preceding discussion, it had not been enough to push the two women out of the conversation.

"Yes, Neela."

"I'm curious about something. I'm referring to when Samantha and I first learned about the attack on Martin and his family, we were stationed at Joint Base Anacostia-Bolling. But it wasn't the Army that interrogated us. It was the FBI. And a few minutes ago, you said that the FBI had found evidence at Virginia Tech."

She paused, uncertain how to ask the question. "I guess what I'm trying to ask is whether the FBI is going to be part of this team … this operation."

Chang nodded. "Fair question. For those of you who might not be up to speed on this, we've been working with the FBI since the murder of Martin's family last April. But now it's gotten a little more complicated. We're setting up an operation outside the U.S., and the FBI isn't going to be a part of it. We want to be agile, and we've assembled our team on that basis. We don't want to find ourselves in a situation where we're held back waiting for multiple approvals."

"Are they aware of the situation?" Alford's voice indicated some concern.

Hashan answered the question. If there was a problem, he didn't want a subordinate to take the hit.

"No. As far as they're concerned, we're cooperating on a domestic investigation. Basically, trying to find out who attacked the Sulley family. We'll keep that going, but there's nothing happening on that front right now. We're not going to tell them about the activities of this group."

"And when they find out?" Hartwell asked. "You know they'll find out at some point."

Chang answered. "They probably will, Ash. And they're going to be really pissed at us. Look, the logistics are difficult. There's a good chance that we'll eventually mount an undercover operation overseas. To take the Warlord into custody."

"Or just take him out."

"Very likely, Ash. That should be no surprise. Not to you, and not to the FBI, either. Doesn't mean that they'll be happy to be excluded, but they'll get over it. Their job is different. Collect evidence, make arrests, and do everything in a way to ensure a successful prosecution. They have to play by the rules."

"And we don't."

Chang's look could have killed. "Of course we play by the rules. But sometimes those rules are going to be a work in progress. If there's anyone in this room who is unwilling to move forward with an operation that may result in termination of the Warlord, you can stand up now, and we'll find you another assignment to work on."

Nobody spoke. Nobody moved.

Chang let the silence continue well beyond the time it had become awkward.

Finally, she spoke. "I think maybe we can move on. Other questions?"

She looked down the table. "Yes, Anja."

"I'm trying to understand something. Not counting the new people ... Neela, Samantha, and Martin. Everyone in the room is from headquarters except the three of us from Dushanbe. You told us why you didn't want to use people currently assigned in Kazakhstan, but I would have thought you'd want people who at least had prior experience there. Sorry, I don't mean to be second-guessing, but it seems like we don't have the right expertise here."

"No offense taken," said Chang. It's a good point, and it was discussed at length before we convened this group. As we said before, using people from the embassy in Kazakhstan could create suspicion through a change in their operational patterns. Same thing for Uzbekistan and Kyrgyzstan. And we do have some expertise at the table that you may not all be aware of. Allan served as a field agent in Kazakhstan a few years back, and his control officer was Bob Alford."

Anja persisted. "I didn't know that. But it seems like reassigning the three of us from the embassy in Dushanbe would be a little questionable. How is it different from using people from the embassies in Uzbekistan or Kyrgyzstan?"

"Derek is the only one of you who worked full-time at the embassy, and he's going back there. He can make trips to other sites as needed. Stephan is also going back to Tajikistan, but not to the embassy, so that makes you the only one of the three who's coming back stateside. You've been overseas for five years, and you're due for a change. Nobody in Dushanbe will make the connection, and if you show up somewhere in Kazakhstan, you won't have any reason to explain."

"You think our language skills will be good enough for this?"

"You're too modest, Anja. You won't have to pass for a native, and all three of you are highly proficient in the several languages of the region."

"There's something you haven't talked about." Stephan's expression showed concern.

"And that is?"

"How do we find this guy?"

Chang smiled darkly. "That's the real issue, isn't it? I need a cup of coffee. Let's take a quick break. Five minutes, and then we can brainstorm Stephan's question."

• • • • •

Even before everyone had taken their seats at the table, Chang started the session.

"Ideas? Anyone?"

Martin lifted a hand. "We have a name for him, right?"

Chang nodded. "Several. According to my notes, the first reports about a charismatic freedom fighter showed up about twenty years ago. He was called Kaskyrbai Ghazi, and we think it's the man we now know as the Warlord. Allan, you reported hearing about him when you were stationed in Kazakhstan back then, right?"

Canterbury nodded. "Yes. And we're fairly sure there's a connection to Georgiy Aishuakov, born 1964. We think that was his birth name."

Samantha spoke softly. "When we saw him in Almaty five years ago, he used the name Kirillov. Arseniy Kirillov. He played the role of a Russian businessman."

"That fits with my understanding of his background," Canterbury said. "Georgiy Aishuakov studied in Moscow before returning to Kazakhstan. We think he then adopted his *nom de guerre* of Kaskyrbai Ghazi."

"And those names have specific meanings, right?" The question came from Hartwell.

"Correct," Chang answered. "Kaskyrbai means *fearless as a wolf,* and Ghazi is *warrior.* And don't forget that he gave names to the two women here with us now. Samantha and Neela. Samantha's name was Zemfira, and Neela used to be Neelam. Both names mean *sapphire,* in Kazakh and Tajik, respectively."

"And also, there's something with the family names," Neela said. "I don't know if it's true, but they always told me my family's name was Dâvar. I never thought about what it might mean until this year. I looked it up, and it seems to originate in Zoroastrianism. There's still some cultural influence of that religion in Tajikistan."

"What's your point?" Chang asked.

"It means *dispenser of justice.* Another name of violence, just like Ghazi. I've wondered if it was a name given to me by the Warlord. If maybe he had something to do with the orphanage right from the beginning."

"It's another piece of information we should file away," Hashan said. "If there's a connection between the Warlord and the orphanage, it could suggest a trafficking operation. It might provide us with another way to get at him."

Samantha spoke out. "If you think Neela's last name might have been assigned by the Warlord, mine makes it even worse. At least for me. They told me my family name was Sumaiyah. There are different ways to spell it, and they change with the alphabets of different languages. But Sumaiyah was the first martyr of Islam."

"He likes to play word games."

Chang looked soberly at Pomeranz. "Not games, Rachel. I think it's a sign of megalomania. He's arrogant and self-important."

Davenport interrupted. "These names may offer some weak spots we can exploit. But they don't answer the real question. How do we find him?"

"Derek is quite correct," Chang said. "Finding him has to be our focus."

She smiled, but her expression conveyed contempt. "He likes to use Facebook. He uses the persona of a teenage girl."

"You're saying he's got some kind of personality disorder?"

"No, Derek. It's an identity he adopts to post messages that are likely to fly under our radar. We've seen a few of them now, and they may give us the best chance of finding out when he plans to visit a specific location."

"So we're all going to become his Facebook friends, Andrea?"

"Don't be a smartass, Derek. It's one of the reasons why you're here. You're the computer geek. We've got to find a way to turn his attempts at secrecy into a vulnerability."

"Do we know anything about what he looks like?" This question from Hashan.

Alford surprised everyone by saying, "I have a couple of photographs. They're new. From a friend who works for the Kazakh National Security Committee." He passed the sheets of paper around the table.

Everyone was quiet for a few moments. Then Hartwell spoke.

"You can't see his face in any of these. Either he's turned away from the camera, or his hand is in front of his face."

Alford nodded. "That's exactly the complaint of the Kazakh security forces. They've been trying to get a photograph for a dozen years. His Kazakh Freedom Battalion has been a thorn in the government's side for a long time, and nobody knows what he looks like."

"I know. So does Samantha. The FBI made drawings."

"Yes. Thank you, Neela." Chang opened a folder and took out photocopies that she passed around.

"This is the best we've got. I'm told the FBI has some very good artists for this sort of thing."

Samantha shook her head doubtfully. "It looks like him a little bit. Maybe even a lot. But it was from a memory of five years ago. And there's something about the drawings that isn't quite right. It would tell you that a lot of people are not him. But I don't know if these drawings would let you pick him out in a crowd."

Chang shrugged. "Maybe not, but it's all we have."

Stephan posed a question. "What do we do if we find out where he's going to travel? Neela and Samantha are the only ones who could make a positive identification. But he knows them, so it would probably be too risky."

"Correct," said Chang. "However, there's something else we've learned about him that we haven't discussed yet. It could afford entrée into his sphere of activity. Provide a way for us to get close to him and make an unequivocal identification. Now, I've told you why we're not using our agents in Kazakhstan as members of this group, but they've helped us with background work. Locating places he's been in the past. His business meetings take place in cities, especially those with modern hotels."

"How does that help?" Stephan asked. "It seems like he's too careful to go back to the same place repeatedly."

"Probably so. And that's where it's going to be essential for us to intercept plans such as his Facebook posts. He plans his visits in advance."

Stephan was impatient. "So what exactly did our people in Kazakhstan tell you?"

"That Ghazi likes women. Young women. It seems that he's very fond of getting massages during his visits to these cities. Preferably by a masseuse who is young and attractive ... and maybe a little bit ... how should I say ... a little bit more than a masseuse."

"So that would be the contact?" Stephan asked.

"Yes. A masseuse would be able to meet him directly, and he wouldn't be suspicious. It would be a way make a contact and confirm his identity. But we would need someone to ..."

"So where do we find someone like that?" Hartwell asked. "Seems like you're talking about two kinds of expertise without much overlap. You've got your nice garden-variety spies like us, but now you're talking about someone who sounds more like a hooker. Are you planning to audition for that role, Andrea?"

Hashan interrupted. "That's out of line, Ash!"

The exchange was followed by an awkward silence.
"I could do that."
All eyes turned to Anja.

* * *

Langley, Virginia, September 24

Andrea Chang looked up. Her expression remained neutral, but her eyes betrayed a hint of surprise.

"Have you got a minute?"

Chang nodded and pointed to the empty chair by her desk.

"You caught me off guard, Anja. You look … a bit unconventional today."

"The hair, huh?" Anja's bleached hair color contrasted sharply with her complexion and dark eyebrows.

"It's different. Your appearance is a little …"

"Slutty?"

No trace of a smile. "I suppose that's accurate."

"Good. That's part of my new persona, isn't it?"

Chang's smile reflected Anja's, but it disappeared quickly.

"This is serious business."

Anja's smile faded as well.

"I know it is. That's why I'm working on the image. I'm willing to suffer a little now to reduce the risk of pain later. I even added this. And it hurt a bunch."

Anja stood, turned her back to Chang, and lifted her shirt to reveal a tattoo.

"My tramp stamp." She turned back to face Chang and extended her hand to show another tattoo — this of a snake wound around her ring finger.

"It's a Central Asian pit viper. I thought it would be just about right for this mission. I wanted to do this before we started the next step, Andrea. I think it will make things easier for me."

Chang nodded.

"I called the woman whose number you gave me," Anja said quietly.

"And?"

"I'm meeting her today. This afternoon."

"Come see me tomorrow morning. Tell me how it went. Your reactions."

"I will. And thanks for letting me discuss it privately. It's still a little embarrassing. The idea of talking about it in front of the whole group."

"I understand. You can change your mind, Anja. This isn't a requirement for you."

"Maybe not, but it's necessary. We already went through that. Someone has got to do it, and you'd never be able to train somebody from outside the Agency in the time frame we have to work with. The next terrorist attack won't wait for you to find the right woman and put her through all the training needed to go undercover. All I need to do is learn how to give a better massage than what I've done before with boyfriends."

Chang's expression no longer revealed any trace of a smile. Her eyes indicated concern. Or maybe sadness.

"Come see me in the morning."

• • • • •

After her conversation with Chang, Anja drove past Tyson's Corner to a small strip mall on Route 7. She checked a handwritten note to be sure she was at the correct address and parked her car.

A single street number encompassed multiple businesses in a two-story building, and she walked past several storefronts before finding the location of suite 6D. The shabby exterior suggested that considerable time had elapsed since the building had been able to attract high-end clients, and a sun-bleached sign indicated that suite 6D was on the second level. The glass door opened only after a hard pull that was accompanied by a scraping noise, and Anja climbed a set of creaky stairs to a landing on the second floor. A windowless door with no identification other than the designation 6D was on her left. She pressed a plastic doorbell button that was old and discolored.

A soft chime rang on the other side of the door, and a few seconds later there were sounds of someone approaching. Then silence. Anja realized that whoever was inside must be looking at her through the peephole. She tried to look relaxed and nonthreatening.

The loud click of a heavy deadbolt startled her, and then the door opened a few inches until it was stopped by a chain. Part of a face appeared in the opening.

"Yes?"

"Uh … I'm Anja. I'm supposed to be meeting Destiny."

"Just a second."

The door closed again, and there were sounds that Anja couldn't make out. Then she heard the metal bolt slide in its track, and the door opened again.

"Come in."

Anja walked into what had once been the waiting area of a small group of offices. She could see a faded place in the carpet where a receptionist's desk might have been, where now there was only a decrepit sofa and two nonmatching chairs. Beyond were three doorways, each of the doors partly open. The rooms beyond were the right size for small offices, perhaps ten feet on a side. They looked empty, or at least largely so from her angle. The third room was larger, almost certainly intended as the manager's office a decade earlier. Anja could see furniture in that room, and a hand motioned her in that direction.

"C'mon in. These are my digs when I don't have a client. I'm Destiny."

The voice was hesitant, the smile tentative.

They shook hands awkwardly. This wasn't a normal business interaction for either of them.

"Sorry to be so cautious about letting you in. I know we talked before and Andrea said it was okay, but you have to be careful in this business. You never know when the cops are going to set up some kind of sting. And there's also a lot of crazies out there. I got beat up once."

Anja shuddered visibly. "Yeah, I understand."

Destiny pointed to a pair of comfortable-looking imitation leather chairs.

"Take a load off. You want a Coke or something?"

"Diet?"

"Sure. Probably all I got anyway."

She turned to a small refrigerator. "Is a can okay? I hate to wash dishes."

"That's fine." Anja took one of the drinks. "Thank you."

They were silent for a few moments. Both were ill at ease.

"So what exactly is it you want from me? I told Andrea I'd do what I could, but she didn't say much."

"How do you know her?"

Anja realized she was probably on thin ice even asking the question, and it took a few seconds before Destiny answered.

"We used to live in the same apartment complex. She helped me out of a jam once. Introduced me to a guy with some influence. So I owe her."

"You give massages, right?"

"Yeah." Then a pause. "I mean it's not like I'm a licensed therapist or anything. But I can rub someone's arms and legs and back and stuff."

Another pause. "And the men who come here ... they're usually pretty satisfied when they leave."

"So it's a little more than a massage?"

Anja's question was greeted by a hard stare. For five seconds, there was no answer. Finally, Destiny spoke slowly.

"Andrea said you were okay, so I guess I can talk. So yeah, sometimes it's more. Most of the time it's more like ... I'd just say they go away satisfied. And it's no big deal to me. It's not like I'm ... I mean, I'm not sleeping with all these guys."

"But sometimes?"

"Christ! You're a real piece of work. I guess I should have expected it if you work with Andrea. I've never understood what the fuck she really does, but I know she's one tough cookie. She does the same thing. If she wants to know something, she just comes right out and asks. No apology or anything. She just asks."

"So ... sometimes?"

"Yeah. Sometimes. But it's only if I know a guy. If I've seen him before and I'm pretty sure I can trust him. And it's not like I bring him back here into my private area to hang out. It's just the massage room. Nothing else. He gets his jollies and he leaves. That's it. Over. Done. Finito. And I go back to my life. Or to other clients. It's all just a job."

For the first time, she smiled.

"Couple different kind of jobs, right? What the hell, it brings in the money. Overall, I do pretty good. I got some regulars, and they recommend me to their friends. As long as I stay young and look sexy, I'll be fine."

The look on her face made it clear that she understood the limited lifetime of her chosen career. She was an attractive woman, but not a girl by any means. Anja looked at her and saw someone her own age, or perhaps several years older, but either way she had a lot of mileage. It gave her a hard look.

Anja glanced at the satin robe Destiny wore.

The robe covered Destiny's body, but it fell on her curves in a way that showed them off. Her calves, visible below the robe, suggested that she was fit and trim.

"So, I'll go back to my first question. What is it you want from me?"

"I want you to teach me how to do massages."

"I already told you I'm not a real masseuse."

"I know. That's the whole point."

"You want to learn how to do my kind of massages? Special massages — what we call *sensual* massages."

"Yeah."

"Why the fuck would you want to do that? Andrea said she works with you, so I assume you got a decent job already. In spite of what I just said, this isn't the best way to make a living. And if all you want to do is get laid, you're better off meeting some nice guy in a bar."

"It's complicated."

"Meaning you can't tell me, right? Same shit I get from Andrea. I know she works for the government, but she says it's all confidential so she can't talk about it."

"Yeah, kinda like that."

"Whatever. I guess it doesn't matter all that much. If you want to learn to new tricks for getting guys off, I can probably help you. When do you want to do this?"

"Whenever. My schedule is fairly open."

"I have a client coming in this afternoon at … I guess it's in about a half hour."

"That would be okay for me."

As soon as she said it, Anja felt a strange sensation in the pit of her stomach, almost like nausea. She realized she was about to move beyond the talking stage.

"All right, then. Let's do it."

For the first time during their encounter, Destiny was engaged.

She stood up and walked to a cabinet at the back of the room. She rummaged through items of clothing on hangers and turned back to Anja. "Strip."

"What?"

"I said strip. Take off your fucking clothes. You don't think you can do this dressed like you work in a goddamn office, do you? Just put your clothes on that chair for now. We'll hang them up in a minute."

Anja unbuttoned her shirt with her back to Destiny but turned to face her as she pulled it off and laid it on the chair.

Destiny's eyes went up and down Anja's frame, focusing momentarily on her breasts. Then she looked lower and motioned for Anja to continue.

Anja kicked off her shoes and unzipped her jeans. Leaning on the arm of the chair for balance, she slipped them off one leg at a time and placed them next to her shirt.

Destiny moved her hand in a circular motion, and Anja pivoted as instructed. Then she faced Destiny with a quizzical look.

"Not bad. Your body is okay. Flat stomach, nice ass, good legs. Your tits are a little small, but there's not much we can do about that right now. There's still enough for a guy to grab onto if he likes chicks. Okay, let's do the rest."

Anja hesitated until Destiny waved her hands in a motion that clearly meant, *Get on with it.*

She took off her bra, and then slid her panties down to the floor. Both items went on the chair with her other clothing. Destiny again motioned for her to turn around.

"Pretty good. Waxing is important. And your tits have a nice shape, even if they are small. If you really do decide to go into this business, you should think about implants. Most guys like big ones a whole lot better."

Destiny removed a garment from the cabinet and tossed it to Anja. It was a bright red chemise that felt like silk but was almost certainly synthetic.

"Go ahead, put it on."

Anja pulled it over her head, and as Destiny indicated, she walked to the mirror to inspect herself. She tugged on the sides after noticing that it didn't come down very low over her hips.

"It's kind of short."

"Yeah. It belongs to a girl who's nowhere near as tall as you. I have a couple of friends that sometimes come over and help out. Like if a guy I know calls and says he's bringing a friend. Or if he says he wants two of us at the same time."

"She won't mind? If I wear it."

"Nah. And besides, it'll get washed. You have to wash these things pretty often around here. Always getting … stuff on them."

Anja shuddered and hoped it wasn't visible. She looked over her shoulder into the mirror.

"Jeez. It doesn't even cover all of my butt."

She turned to face the mirror.

"And the front doesn't come down all the way either. You can see …"

Destiny smiled. "It'll be okay. You look sexy in it."

She removed something else from the cabinet.

"Here, try this."

Anja slipped into the black satin robe and tied it demurely.

"Lookin' good, girl. Now, you look completely innocent."

"You think so?" Anja asked uncertainly.

"Yeah. It's just a question of where you start and how far you want to go. Everything you do is going to be something you play by ear. Although 'ear' isn't quite the right part of the body. Point is, if you want to get the guy a little excited, you can loosen the belt a little, so the front comes partly open. Then he can see the chemise, and your tits show right through it. You'll be able to look down at the guy and see right away just how much he likes it."

"Do you wear the same thing?"

"Depends. Sometimes I'll skip the robe and just wear a teddy. Other times I'll wear a bra and panties. It's all a question of whether the guy is new and what I'm interested in doing. Or not."

"Speaking of which," Anja began tentatively, "I feel a little naked here without panties."

"That's because you are, dummy. That's how I want you to get started today. So you can get used to the feeling. We're going to do this guy together. Mostly you're going to be able to watch me. Watch and learn."

"Just watch?"

"You want more? Okay. Tell you what. You take the top half, I'll take the bottom. I'll work his legs and stuff, and you can massage his head and shoulders. He'll love it. And when he's lying on his back, he'll look up and see you. Let that robe come open, and he's going to love the view."

"Is this going to be anything more than a massage?"

"Nah, not today. And for sure, not for you. Maybe while I'm down there I'll give him a little kiss, but nothing special. He wants more, he's gonna have to come back and see me again another time. And I'm pretty sure that'll happen. Having you there should be good for my business."

"So, what do I do?"

"Follow my lead. You want to take off some of your clothes, that's cool. If you feel like you need to keep them on, that's good too. You want to lean over and let him kiss you somewhere, that's your option. Or let him touch you if you want. The real point is that if we do it right, it's gonna be easy. No big deal."

* * *

Langley, Virginia, October 8

Andrea Chang and David Hashan were seated in his office. The atmosphere was tense.

"Do you really think we're ready, Andrea?"

"There's no choice. We have to get people in place before the winter snow. There's every reason to believe that Ghazi is getting ready to mount another attack."

"Then let's move. How soon can we start putting people in place?"

"About a week if we have the resources."

"We have them, Andrea. We have approval to act at our discretion. I confirmed with Alford yesterday."

* * *

13

Solar Storms

Because they serve as vital nodes and carry bulk volumes of electricity, High Voltage transformers are critical elements of the nation's electric power grid. HV transformers are also the most vulnerable to intentional damage from malicious acts.

—*Congressional Research Service, 2014*[*]

Cheboygan, Michigan, October 10

Rusty Dember pulled up the collar on his dark sweater. The sky was gray, and it seemed much darker than usual at 3:15 in the afternoon. He thought it was ideal.

He saw the yellow vehicle moving slowly on the side road. Then he watched as it turned onto the highway, although it was difficult to see clearly at a distance of nearly eight hundred yards. The vehicle was exactly on schedule.

He reached for his phone and called the same number he had keyed in a few minutes earlier. His call was answered on the first ring.

"Hallo Jimmy." He said the name with an odd pronunciation. It sounded more like *Chimmy*.

"I'm calling so you know that your friends are on their way home. The time is for you to get started."

Dember had never learned Jimmy's last name, and Jimmy had never learned his. Not that it would have mattered, since Rusty Dumber wasn't a real name.

---

[*] "Physical Security of the U.S. Power Grid: High-Voltage Transformer Substations," Paul W. Parfomak, Congressional Research Service, June 17, 2014, Summary.

They had made their final check by phone a half hour earlier, and everything was set to go. Dember disconnected the latest call and at the same instant pushed a button on a second phone. The second phone was no longer configured for conversation, however. When he pushed its "talk" button, a third device located a hundred fifty yards away received a signal and closed an electrical circuit. Dember saw the flash, not because it was particularly bright, but because he knew exactly where to look. Anyone who wasn't looking right at the pole would have guessed that the flash resulted from the failure of the high-pressure sodium lamp in the overhead streetlight. It would have been the obvious conclusion, because the streetlight immediately went dark. In the dim light of the overcast afternoon, everything was perfect. The drivers would have to slow down as they approached the intersection.

Dember thought about the wires he had attached to the terminals of the transformer mounted on the pole. And he thought about the device he had fastened to the back of the transformer with electrical tape. He smiled. It had worked as planned.

Climbing up the previous night under cover of darkness had been the only part of the operation that made him nervous. The night had been completely dark, and he had waited until the moon went down. The streetlight had seemed like another sun. He knew he was in the shadows, but it was nerve wracking nevertheless.

The original plan had been to target a traffic signal, but there were almost none in the relevant area. There were a few downtown, but it was essential that the planned events take place on the outskirts of the small city.

Dember had been pleased the week before, when he saw his letter to the editor in the online version of the *Cheboygan Daily Tribune*. He was fairly certain it had also made it into the print edition:

```
Space weather threatens our power system.

The 2003 Halloween Solar Storms caused a major
blackout, and we still have not solved the problem.
That was during Solar Cycle 23, and now we have Solar
Cycle 24. It won't be over until 2020, and nobody has
fixed the problem. Large transformers in the
electrical grid are especially vulnerable and one of
them is in our area, right near Boyne City. We all
should tell to our elected officials that they have to
enhance industry response and mitigate the threat from
a solar storm.
```

He had signed it Rusty Dember. He had copied most of the words for his letter from a scientific report he found on the web. He figured it would compensate for his writing skills, which he knew were weak. If local authorities had noticed the letter, it would slow their understanding of what was actually happening.

He looked down at the polished wooden stock of his rifle. He wiped off several raindrops in what was almost a tender caress.

* * *

14

Sub Rosa

Paris — After a legal battle of two months, during which a revision court confirmed the decision of a court martial. Mata Hari, Dutch dancer, seeker of adventure, must face the greatest adventure of all. Today the Supreme Court confirmed the previous findings, and the dancer was again sentenced to be shot as a spy.

—Issues and Events, 1917[*]

Langley, Virginia, October 10

"Good morning, Anja. May I come in?"

Chang stood at the doorway to Anja's office.

"Of course. Is there a problem?"

"No problem. I just wanted to talk privately. Things are starting to move, and I want to make certain that I've got my ducks in a row."

"There's something you want me to do?"

"More like some questions," Chang said, pausing for a moment. "It's a delicate topic."

"Yeah, I get it." Anja looked directly at Chang.

"You need to know about my evenings working with Destiny."

"Yes."

"So, it's been every night for the last two weeks. I think I've got it down."

"A little more detail, please. Just what does 'it' mean?"

---

[*] "A French Cavel Case: Mata Hari, Beautiful Parisian Dancer Sentenced to Death as a Spy," *Issues and Events,* New York, Vol. 7, No. 16, October 20, 1917, p. 249.

"The massages. And the extras."

"Don't make me pull teeth, Anja. I don't give a fuck about the morality, but I need to know exactly what you've experienced. We're sending you out into a snake pit, and I don't want you to get bitten."

"Sorry. I'm not trying to be coy. I'm not exactly used to talking about this kind of stuff with my boss."

"Doesn't matter. You need to start doing it right now."

Anja was surprised at Chang's intensity.

"Okay. For the first week, I always worked with Destiny. Both of us together. The customers — clients she always calls them — never seemed to mind if I was there. Especially when I joined in. Each time …"

"How many times, Anja? I've got to have a sense of your experience."

"I guess it was three or four per night. Maybe a couple more sometimes. Starting around five … going until midnight, with a few minutes between the one-hour sessions. Okay?" There was a hint of anger in her voice.

"Proceed."

"So, each time, Destiny had me participate a little more. First couple of times, I just sort of rubbed the guy's shoulders, but then she had me do more. Like I let my robe fall open a little, so he could catch a glimpse of my … my breasts. You could tell it turned him on. It was always fairly obvious."

"I'm sure."

"And then, maybe on day five or so, she had me switch locations. I worked on the client's feet and legs … and the rest."

"You mean all over? Everything?"

"Yeah."

"And the client was satisfied?"

Anja rolled her eyes. "Let's just say there would have been plenty of opportunity to collect DNA evidence."

Chang smiled, but it was a serious smile. "Okay, I get your point. The second week was different?"

"Yes. Destiny has two massage rooms, and once or twice a night she booked two clients at the same time. Then I was on my own."

"And how did that go?"

"Pretty good, I think. I was nervous the first time, but there were no problems once I got started. I just followed the same routine that I did with Destiny. The first few turned out to be nothing more than regular massages. Maybe a little extra touching but no big deal."

"And subsequently?"

"After the first day or two, I started to feel more comfortable. I let things get a little more … intimate. The men got to see a little more of me. Maybe do a little touching. And I got so I was finishing up with some very … satisfying conclusions."

"But we're only working on your perception. It's just a self-evaluation."

"Actually, no."

Anja reddened and looked down for a moment. Then she continued.

"Destiny set up a small video camera in the corner. And she recorded everything."

Chang started to raise an objection, but Anja continued. "She erased the videos afterward, so there's no record of what happened. But Destiny looked at them and commented on things that I could have done better. Or maybe just in a little different way. The point is that overall, she said I was doing a good job."

"Understood. Anything more?"

"Yeah. The last day. Yesterday. My last client, in fact. He was someone who had been there earlier in the week, so the opportunity was there. I tried something that Destiny had showed me."

"Which was?"

"After the regular start, after I worked on his back, I had him turn over like usual."

"Yes."

"He was pretty excited. It showed. And he told me he had more cash in his wallet. I'd already taken off my robe, and I wasn't wearing anything under it. So I got onto the table, and … well, let's say there wasn't anything else he could have asked for."

"The whole deal? You actually fucked him?"

"Yep."

Chang nodded. "I guess that's good. You understand you may need to do the same thing with Ghazi?"

"For Christ's sake, Andrea, I'm not a complete moron. That's why I did it."

"I didn't say it to offend you."

"It's all right. Sorry … I overreacted."

* * *

15

School Days

Of the large number of foreign students who come to this country to study, there is a risk that a small minority may exploit their student status to support terrorist activity.

—*National Commission on Terrorism, 2000*[*]

Cheboygan, Michigan, October 10

When Dember had used his reconfigured cellphone to remotely short out the transformer on the nearby electric pole, it wasn't just the streetlight that went out. As he surveyed the landscape for the next several minutes, he could see that a much wider area had lost power.

Maybe even all of Cheboygan.

But that was only a guess. The important thing was that he had created a diversion. It would keep authorities from anticipating the events taking place along Highway 23 where Dember was watching.

He was perched on the roof of a small outbuilding on the edge of a commercial property, his position shielded from the road by a long building with a red roof. Behind him was East Avenue Park, and then a relatively open field. Finally, beyond that, was Lake Huron.

Dember had chosen the site carefully, finding a location where trees would obscure his position from several houses that were about two hundred yards away. At the same time, he still had a clear line of

---

[*] "Countering the Changing Threat of International Terrorism," Report of the National Commission on Terrorism, Pursuant to Public Law 277, 105th Congress, L. Paul Bremer III, Chairman, transmitted to the President and the Congress on June 7, 2000, p. 29.

sight to the highway for at least five hundred yards in both directions. His eyes shifted back and forth from left to right, and he forced himself to breathe slowly as he saw the two vehicles coming in his direction.

From his left, the truck was coming into clearer focus. It was an eighteen-wheeler, and the flatbed trailer was loaded with steel reinforcing rods destined for highway and bridge reconstruction on the interstate north of the city. The load looked modest, a bundle of steel rods about three feet high, four feet wide, and only ten feet long. But with its load, the big rig weighed almost eighty thousand pounds — forty tons — and was traveling at a high rate of speed.

I hope Jimmy can do this. He only gets one chance.

The second vehicle, in the distance on Dember's right, had also become clearly visible. It was large, although not as big as the truck. It rode high off the ground and was more than thirty feet long, but its weight was less than a quarter of the fully loaded tractor-trailer. It was also travelling much more slowly. That was to be expected for a school bus.

Dember watched closely as the vehicles approached from opposite directions, their speeds such that they would pass each other at the intersection of a side road with the highway, a location that would give him the best possible view. The big rig would be out of his line of vision for several seconds as it drove past the building between Dember and the highway, but after that both vehicles would remain fully visible.

Do it right, Jimmy.

It all seemed to take place in slow motion. Just as the vehicles were about to pass each other, the truck swerved slightly to the left. The truck driver never applied his brakes, but it didn't matter. From a distance of less than two hundred yards, the sounds reached Dember at almost the same instant that he saw the initial impact. It wasn't a head-on crash. Instead, the left side of the semi ripped into the side of the school bus, the truck's grille making initial contact with the bus just in front of the driver's seat.

Amid a shrieking cacophony of breaking glass and twisting metal, the truck continued along the side of the bus, almost without slowing, shearing off the entire side of the bus.

The side did not come off cleanly, because the front end of the truck had not merely grazed the bus. It had penetrated the passenger compartment, tearing into the children, crushing them, and spilling seat benches and small bodies onto the pavement.

When both vehicles finally came to a complete stop, the big rig was only a few yards past the bus. Dember had a clear field of vision into the side of the bus, and he could see the horrifying results of the collision. In addition to the bodies on the ground, there were others inside the bus. The screeching and scraping of metal had ended. That raucous din had been replaced by the horrified screams of the children who survived the initial impact.

Dember looked intently at the cab of the truck, surprised that Jimmy had not jumped out. The plan was that he would run away from the truck and make his escape in the old Dodge Neon that was waiting for him only a few yards beyond the place where the truck had come to a stop. But Jimmy was unable to go anywhere. When the truck had first made impact, the rear-view mirror on the bus broke free. The mirror's iron frame was directly in front of Jimmy, and its main support rod penetrated the truck's windshield and continued its trajectory into Jimmy's forehead.

None of this mattered to Dember. Eventually, the authorities would have found Jimmy, and this way it would be sooner instead of later. Jimmy had a history of associating with right-wing militia groups, and Dember had made sure that incriminating documents would be found. The authorities would eventually discover that Jimmy was only a dupe, but the ruse would slow their investigation. And it was all just an act, anyway. The first act of a drama that was still developing.

• • • • •

The collision took place at 3:18 p.m., and the first ambulance reached the scene by 3:27. The EMTs were completely overwhelmed, and they pleaded desperately over their radios for more assistance. A single deputy responded promptly to the initial call to the sheriff's office, but the rest of the county's dozen patrol units were spread across an area of almost a thousand square miles. It was another fifteen minutes before a second cruiser arrived at the location, and the deputies focused on traffic control and logistics. As tragic as the events were, they had to treat it all as nothing more than a terrible traffic accident.

One call that did go out from the sheriff's office was directed to the Michigan State Police. Traffic enforcement was the responsibility county officials, but the state police had a special unit that handled investigations involving commercial motor vehicles. This horrific crash of a semi-tractor trailer certainly fit that description. The

Cheboygan Post of the State Police had been closed down several years earlier for financial reasons, but a detachment of several officers was still based in the city. One of those officers was able to reach the site by 3:55.

When Trooper Lucien Chevereaux pulled up, he quickly realized what his next step had to be. He walked over to the county sheriff, who had arrived moments earlier. His face was grim as he nodded to his colleague.

"I've got to contact headquarters on this one. They'll want to alert the Governor."

"You've got to be kidding. If you do that, we'll be facing a media storm. We've got enough to do here without adding that to the mix."

"It's worse than that, Sheriff. The Governor is hosting a conference at the official summer residence. This isn't the kind of disaster a governor can ignore."

"Shit! I guess there isn't any choice. Go ahead Trooper, but tell them to hurry up. We want to get the wreckage cleared before dark."

"They'll be here a lot quicker than that. A helicopter can make the trip from Mackinac Island to the county airport in fifteen minutes. Then it's only five miles by car. We might be looking at less than an hour. And if the Gaylord Post can't find any additional troopers, we'll need your help with an escort from the airport to get the Governor here."

"Yeah, if you need it. But see if you can get some of your guys. My people are already overwhelmed."

The sheriff turned and walked away. He didn't like the notion that he'd be taking orders from the state police, especially a mere trooper. But he understood.

That's all we need now. The damn Governor.

• • • • •

Dember had been watching the exchange through a pair of binoculars. He couldn't hear their words, but he had a good idea what they were saying. He pushed on the earbud in his left ear and flicked his radio receiver to the channel used by the state police. Within two minutes, his suspicions were confirmed. The Gaylord Post was contacting the Executive Division of the state police — the group responsible for the Governor's security detail.

Five minutes later, the response was confirmed. The helicopter was revving up, and the Governor would land at the Cheboygan County Airport in twenty minutes. They had inquired about landing directly at the accident site, but given the low cloud ceiling and the absence of a nearby area that was clear of trees, the cost of a few extra minutes was outweighed by the Governor's safety.

Dember checked his watch. The radio communications suggested that the Governor would arrive by 4:30, but he estimated it would be at least ten minutes later. Either way, he would be ready. He dropped back behind the peak of the small building's roof to do a final check of his equipment.

Not that much to check. I just listened to the radio, and everything else is secure in the pockets of my fatigues.

He patted the pockets of his camo pants to be certain. On this overcast afternoon, the pattern of varying shades of gray provided the perfect camouflage. With the additional concealment provided by the balaclava covering his face, he would be invisible to anyone more than a few yards away.

The first communication of real interest to Dember came through at 4:33.

"The helicopter is on final approach. Should land in thirty seconds or less."

Then another.

"The bird has landed. We're escorting three people to the accident site. The Governor and two members of the security detail are in the Chevy Tahoe. Scott is driving. Lindberg and Sorenson are providing escort in their vehicles. Our ETA is 4:44."

Five minutes later, Dember could hear the sirens in the distance. Reacting to that signal, he removed his earbud and put it in one of his pockets along with the radio and secured the pocket. Everything was packed up — everything except the black nylon package that lay on the surface in front of him. Carefully, he unfastened the clasps on the nylon container and looked fondly at his Valmet 78 rifle. It was a military firearm made in Finland three decades earlier, and it was based on the Kalashnikov he had used during his military service.

But it wasn't a standard Valmet 78. The man Dember had met in Sault Ste. Marie had been able to obtain a model 78/83S, designed for use as a sniper rifle. In contrast to the heavy, large-caliber weapons used by many military snipers, this was a relatively lightweight and maneuverable modification of a basic assault rifle. It weighed about five kilograms and was a favorite of the Special Operations forces Dember had trained with.

This particular weapon was outfitted with a scope and a bipod to improve stability and accuracy. It was chambered for the 10-gram

7.62x51 mm NATO cartridge, and his bullets were armor piercing, just in case his target might be wearing a Kevlar vest.

The rifle had been modified in several important ways, exactly as Dember had requested. In addition to single shots, it was capable of firing a three-shot burst. Dember didn't want anyone in the target area to know where his shots originated, and with a total elapsed time of only three-tenths of a second for the burst, there was little more than the sound made by a single shot. Even more important, the rifle was equipped with a flash and noise suppressor.

Dember hoped that a single burst would take out his target, and it would all be over before anyone understood what had happened. He was about to learn if that was an accurate prediction.

The sirens grew louder, and the vehicles moved into Dember's field of view.

Three of them. Bright blue with a single light on the roof. State Police ... the Governor's security detail.

The convoy slowed as it approached the accident scene, passing several cars that had been halted on the highway. When the police vehicles came even with the wreckage, they pulled to the side of the road in a tight group. Dember was unable to identify the occupants as they emerged from the vehicles, but he wasn't concerned.

They will walk over to the bus. It is why they came.

His expectation was correct. A group of several people, two of them in uniform, walked tentatively toward the school bus. At this point, Dember was watching through the scope, getting ready for a body shot. If the recoil from the first round caused movement of his rifle barrel, the next two rounds of the burst would strike higher on the body toward the shoulders. He forced himself to breathe slowly, knowing that it would happen in the next few seconds.

There! The shortest of the three. Long blonde hair. No question. It is her.

He stopped his breathing for a moment and carefully squeezed the trigger. At a firing rate of 600 rounds per minute and a muzzle velocity of nearly three times the speed of sound, the first bullet made impact before the third round left his rifle. All three projectiles struck the target before the sound of gunfire traveled the same distance. As Dember saw the Governor crumple to the ground, he pulled the rifle back toward his hip and ducked below the peak of the roof. Quickly, he scrambled to the edge and jumped down, first a five-foot drop to the makeshift landing mat he had fashioned from some old cardboard boxes, then another five feet to the ground, rolling to dissipate the impact. Two seconds later, he was up and running.

• • • • •

"What the fuck ...?"

Another ambulance was pulling up to the accident site, and State Police Sergeant Sorenson had not heard the shots above the blare of the siren. Even as a seasoned trooper who had pulled bodies from more crashes than he cared to remember, he had been horrified by the carnage that was evident as they approached the school bus. For a moment, he thought the Governor had fainted. Then he saw the blood.

"She's been shot!" he screamed. "The Governor has been shot! I need a medic here!"

He knelt down next to his boss preparing to administer first aid, but as soon as he turned her over, he knew it was too late. She was dead.

Dumbfounded, Sorenson stood and scanned the area. His police training and military background kicked in. Those were exit wounds in her chest, so the shots came from behind. He wheeled around and pointed toward the commercial building across the road.

"Over there! The shots must have come from over there."

If the gunman were still there, Sorenson knew they all would be sitting ducks. His fellow law-enforcement officers understood this as well. He yelled for everyone to take cover.

"Scan the area! Scott, you circle around to the left. Lindberg ... take the right. I'll cover you."

As he shouted these instructions, Sorenson ran for his cruiser and opened the trunk to retrieve an assault rifle.

Chevereaux, who had been the first representative of the State Police to arrive on the scene, came sprinting up to Sorenson and crouched next to him behind the cruiser.

"We're going to need help here, Sergeant. There's not enough of us to carry out a search."

"No shit. Call the Gaylord Post and tell them we need all the help they can give us. I don't even know how to call this in. 'Shots fired'? Sure, but it's a hell of a lot more than that. If it was sheriff one of us, we'd say 'officer down,' but that doesn't begin to describe the situation. This is the fucking Governor, and she's dead! This is a bad day, Chevereaux."

Sorenson saw the sheriff crouching beside a nearby vehicle and sprinted over to him. "Can you call in any extra support, sheriff? We need everything we can get from jurisdictions all across this half of the state."

"We've already put out the alert to the rest of my deputies. Also the Tuscarora Township Police Department and the Mackinaw City Police. Can you reach your people at the Gaylord Post?"

"Trooper Chevereaux is calling it in. Maybe we'll get some help chasing the shooter, but first we have to find out where he is. Or at least where he was."

• • • • •

Dember sprinted hard for about thirty seconds, then dropped into a crouch and began walking. He held his rifle across his body in the position, ready to fire if any threat arose. He was near the center of the park, and beyond its edge he still had another half mile to go. The important thing was to be out of their field of vision. He knew well, both as a hunter and as a special forces operative, that motion was what made it possible for people to see you. If you were motionless, you were safe. But he couldn't just remain where he was. He had to hope that the low brush and trees would provide adequate cover.

The deteriorating weather made it nearly certain that no aircraft would be searching for him. That gave Dember some reassurance as he continued moving away from the site of the shooting. After five minutes, he picked up his pace to a steady trot, and in another five minutes he could see the road ahead of him just beyond a few trees. When he reached the line of trees, he dropped into a prone position, both to rest and to survey his surroundings.

Across the road was an area of fairly dense brush, and beyond, he could see the water. This was the path to his immediate objective, the same path he had used early that morning under cover of darkness to reach the shooting site.

When he caught his breath, he checked to be sure that the road was clear in both directions and crossed into the brush. Twenty seconds later, he reached the canoe. In another fifteen seconds, he was on the lake, paddling north across Duncan Bay. Farther to the north, about six miles away, lay his next destination. Bois Blanc Island.

• • • • •

It was dusk when he put the canoe ashore on Bois Blanc Island. He knew he needed to maintain his strength, so he took a few minutes to rest, drink some water, and eat a piece of dried sausage. Using the GPS coordinates recorded on his prior visit, he quickly located his cache. Then he returned to the canoe, pulled it into the brush several yards from the water's edge, and covered it with pine boughs.

He was working on a small sandy area by the water, and one of the batteries from his cache was providing power to a small air pump. Dember watched with satisfaction as the inflatable boat began to take shape. There were several chambers, and he filled them in sequence. Then he mounted the small electric motor on the transom, tossed in his other gear and the rifle, and pushed off. Several minutes later, he was lying on his side steering the boat on a slow but steady course.

Due east. About forty miles.

It would be a long night, and he thought he would reach his destination around dawn, maybe earlier if he could maintain the craft's top speed of more than five miles per hour.

At least this time, I don't have to paddle. And it's calm. There's no wind.

Around three o'clock the next morning, Dember's GPS told him that he was approaching the shipping channel. The overcast continued to block any moonlight, and he was nearly invisible. His profile above the waterline was only about twenty inches when he was lying on the floor of the eight-foot Zodiac. It meant no passing vessel would even see him, much less take action to avoid him.

He would need to steer between freighters as they passed through the channel. At the start of his voyage, he had been on full alert from the time he started paddling north from Duncan Bay, watching for freighter traffic between Lake Huron and Lake Michigan by way of the Straits of Mackinac. Here it was the traffic between Lake Huron and Lake Superior.

In contrast to his previous crossing in the heavily laden canoe, the Zodiac seemed much less vulnerable to the wakes of passing ships. Nevertheless, these hulking vessels were giants in comparison with his tiny rubber boat.

And despite their enormous size, they were extremely difficult to see in the darkness. Fighting his nerves, Dember slowed the Zodiac to a near standstill and waited. He felt it before he heard it, and he heard it before he saw it. His first thought was that it was coming right for him, but after a moment of panic, he realized it would pass by safely. Nevertheless, he was unable to see the freighter's wake before it was on him, and suddenly his boat rose in the air by what he estimated to be three feet or more.

When he cleared the wake, he knew it was time. He checked his compass heading and steered a course to the northeast that was perpendicular to the shipping channel. For the next five minutes, he hardly dared to breathe, knowing that he was at his most vulnerable position. And then he heard the sound again. He felt it.

Another ship. A big one.

But he quickly realized it was well behind him. He was beyond the shipping channel. He was on the Canadian side. He was safe.

With daybreak nearing, Dember decided to put in for the day on one of the small islands along his route. He followed what had become his standard procedure, and before sunrise he and the boat were well hidden among the trees and brush near the shoreline. He unrolled his sleeping bag and stretched. He would have no difficulty sleeping through the entire day.

* * *

Lake Huron, October 11

When Dember awoke, the sun was low in the western sky. He felt ravenous, and he ate nearly all of his remaining rations. Two of his three batteries were now dead, but that left him with more than enough for the remainder of the trip. One of the original three had been intended primarily for inflating the boat rather than for propulsion, but he had used it until it died part way through his crossing the night before. By his calculations, the second one was at least 90 percent depleted as well, so he dug a shallow hole with his knife and buried both of the expended batteries beneath a covering of sand and brush. That was a decrease of 80 pounds in his cargo, so his craft would now travel both faster and more efficiently.

He waited for dusk and pushed off on the final leg of his voyage, a distance of about fifteen miles. He would arrive in the middle of the night, but that did not discourage him. He would finally be sleeping in a bed.

About a mile from his destination, he undertook his final cleanup. There was nothing suspicious about his GPS and binoculars, not even his knife — not in a location where hunting and fishing were a way of life. But the police receiver was too specialized, and there was no question that the rifle was inappropriate. They went over the side, unlikely to ever be found.

Before discarding the rifle, he removed the clip and discarded most of its 20 cartridges. The clip was still heavy, and it would serve his purpose. He wedged Rusty Dember's driver's license and college ID card into the clip, reinserted several cartridges to hold them in place, and dropped the clip into the water.

He thought about the ID from the community college and how well it had served him. His identity as a student insulated him from questions about why he had come to Cheboygan, and it had provided opportunity to recruit a partner.

Jimmy had been perfect. He had joined the army as a troubled teen, but he washed out before completing his basic training. He fell in with a right-wing militia group that blamed all society's problems on the federal government. Dember met Jimmy in a local bar, and his dislike of government authority was apparent after only a couple of beers. Recruiting him had been easy.

The plan was nearing its conclusion as Dember piloted the Zodiac into shore. He would quickly deflate the craft and cover it with sand among the trees at the edge of the lake. Nobody would find it for a long time, because there was no reason to look on the Canadian shore near Blind River, Ontario.

The last traces of Rusty Dember were at the bottom of Lake Huron, and Rustam Dembay was ready to get some sleep. The following day he would drive the Jeep to catch his return flight to Kazakhstan. His passport and his plane ticket were waiting in the Jeep.

The Warlord will be pleased.

* * *

16

Launch

*We could move almost instantly when the president
gave the order to launch strikes.*

—*U.S. Navy Secretary, 2014*[*]

Langley, Virginia, October 11

The meeting of the operational team had been called for 1:30 p.m. on Tuesday. At 1:40, Andrea Chang still had not arrived, and the team members were getting restless.

At 1:46 Chang finally showed. Her face was taut and colorless, and when Hashan, Canterbury, and Alford followed on her heels, the others new something was up.

"Sorry to be late. Have any of you been following the news?"

Chang's eyes swept the table, and she could see that the answer was yes.

"You mean the Governor of Michigan?" Stephan asked. "It's been all over the newsfeeds since last night. Everyone is reporting that it was a radical militia group from that part of Michigan. What does that have to do with us?"

"I'll tell you what it has to do with us, Stephan. We have reason to believe it was Ghazi."

Hashan, Canterbury, and Alford all nodded, almost imperceptibly. Everyone else looked dumbfounded.

Chang motioned to Canterbury, who clearly would be taking the lead in the subsequent discussion.

---

[*] "Mabus: Airstrikes Illustrate Unique Navy Capabilities," Jim Garamone, *DoD News,* U.S. Department of Defense, September 30, 2014.

"I don't think there's much doubt. The evidence is circumstantial, but everything fits. And we were expecting another attack, so maybe it shouldn't be a big surprise."

"What evidence?" Hartwell demanded. "We've started wars before on the basis of unfounded suspicions."

"Nothing unfounded, Ash. There's a couple of things. First of all, they recovered the brass. The FBI has been working through the night, and they sent these photos over this morning. They may not be part of our operation, but they know we're working on it."

Canterbury took a stack of papers from a manila folder and passed them down the table. He paused for several seconds so everyone could look at them.

"The shell casings are shown clearly in the second picture. It's a standard NATO cartridge, and the recovered bullet fragments were from 7.62x51 mm rounds."

"NATO?" Hartwell asked. "How does indicate anything more than a disgruntled local who hated the governor?"

"The cartridge isn't limited to American and NATO use. It was also used by the Soviets. The third photo will convince you. The markings are in Russian."

"So what? I could buy Russian ammunition online without a problem."

"Be patient, Ash. From almost two hundred yards, the shooter fired three rounds in a tight group. We're talking about someone who is an expert marksman with an accurate weapon. The eyewitnesses were cops, and there's no doubt that it was a fully automatic three-round burst. This wasn't a garden-variety hunting rifle."

"Still could have been one of ours. Either the rifle or the shooter. Or both."

"There's more. The Soviet special forces — the *Spetsnaz* — had a favorite weapon that was derived from the AK-47. Much lighter than the sniper rifles used on our side, but it was still a heavy-barreled assault rifle. Highly accurate at distances of several hundred yards, which was the shooting distance in Michigan. I'm talking about the Valmet M78, a sniper rifle made in Finland that was produced for using the NATO rounds. A very nasty weapon. It's illustrated in the fourth photograph."

"They recovered the weapon?" Stephan asked.

"Unfortunately, no. Or at least not yet. But that adds to the evidence. It had to be a weapon that is easily carried. The shooter definitely wouldn't have been able to get away from the scene if he'd been using one of the big .50-caliber sniper rifles used by our forces. They run about four times the weight of the Valmet. This guy was mobile."

"Which means they haven't found him."

Canterbury frowned. "No. At least not yet. But there are some links. Like the identity of the shooter."

"We know who the shooter was?" Anja asked.

"We think so. This part of Michigan is sparsely populated, so strangers can't hide too well. The FBI identified a man by the name of Rusty Dember who attended the local community college. And he's disappeared. His teachers and fellow students haven't seen him for a couple of days."

Hartwell interrupted. "What's his background, Allan? A local?"

"We don't have anything solid, but one of the other students at the college said Dember told him he was an immigrant. That he originally came from Russia."

Before Hartwell could ask the second part of his question, Canterbury held up a hand.

"I know. Ghazi is in Kazakhstan. But it's consistent with his M.O. Always a little subterfuge. Almost like a game. And the Russian connection has been strong. Ghazi studied in Russia. The microbiologist who did the genetic engineering of the *E. coli* last year was working in Moscow. The Kazakhs also have a continuing military alliance with Russia, so nothing is out of line."

"Do the authorities in Michigan have any idea where this guy Dember went?" Hartwell asked.

"Not yet. The FBI found the exact location where the shots were fired. They think they've got footprints leading to the edge of Duncan Bay, so their current thinking is that Dember escaped using some kind of small boat. That he probably moved down the coast a mile or so and then used a vehicle to get away from all the police activity."

"In other words, they don't have the slightest idea."

Canterbury shrugged. "No, Ash. Probably not. But we've started working the international connections. Our people are asking for help from both Russia and Kazakhstan. We're looking at travel records for the name 'Rusty Dember' and anything that might be a simple variant. Maybe we'll get lucky."

Rachel Pomeranz spoke hesitantly. "When we worked the *E. coli* thing last year, Ghazi was using a Facebook page to communicate. Under the bogus name for a teenage girl. Svetlana."

Derek Davenport responded to the question. "That's been part of my assignment for the past few weeks. Svetlana's page has been shut down. No posts for almost a year now."

"It was worth asking, I guess."

"More than you know, Rachel." Canterbury took some papers from a folder and began passing them around the table.

"FBI headquarters sent us this information about an hour ago. From the Facebook page of a Russian girl named Olga. That's all I know right now."

There was a short silence while everyone read the message:

```
To dearest cousin Rustam-- I am mostly excited to
learn your new business is doing well. Papa say to me
how very important our country to have strong
interaction with America. I study at KIS International
School in Almaty. It is why I have become good in
English. Everything at my school goes by schedule and
we started already in August. Very soon now I will be
back in my school again for exactly one month. Papa
says your Uncle Vanya will give to you sporting
equipment for your hunting and fishing. I hope as soon
as school is finished you will once again visit across
the lake. --Your cousin Olga.
```

"Rustam could be Rusty," Martin said. "It fits the way the Warlord plays with names."

"That's what the FBI concluded," Canterbury said. "They dated the message to mid-September. They don't know what all the details mean, but they're reasonably sure about two things. First, the 'sporting equipment' was probably the rifle used in the shooting. And second, they think that 'across the lake' gave him instructions for his escape. To return to Kazakhstan. Not just across a lake, but across the ocean. Unfortunately, there's a good chance he's already done that."

"I have a question, Allan. Why the Governor of Michigan?"

"You've probably been out of the country for too long, Stephan. She took some very strong political stands over the past year. Some people thought she was preparing for a presidential run next time around. One of her themes was a strong international presence, and she argued that the U.S. should establish permanent military bases across Asia. Specifically, in Kazakhstan, Kyrgyzstan, and Tajikistan. All places that have borders with Russia or China."

"And our presence is what the Warlord is fighting against?"

"Exactly. You win the prize, Stephan."

Chang cleared her throat.

"I think we ought to move on. You certainly noticed that the presence of Allan Canterbury and Bob Alford at our meeting this afternoon is unusual. Obviously, David and I met with them prior to this session. The timing was precipitated by the assassination, but that wasn't our sole topic of discussion. We've all been pushing hard, and we now have the necessary approvals. As of this afternoon, our hunt for the Warlord is operational. The bastard is almost impossible to find. He's like a ghost, so we're calling it *Operation Gray Ghost*."

She nodded toward Hashan. "David will meet with you individually for your final briefing, but you already know what the basic plan is. Travel orders have been cut, and most of you are scheduled for overseas posting. Starting the day after tomorrow. So after you meet with David, pick up your plane tickets from his staff assistant. And pack your suitcases. It's time to go."

* * *

Tyson's Corner, Virginia, October 11

"Thanks for coming to dinner with me, Stephan."

"No problem. It's a good way to have a sendoff. We're all heading out in the next couple of days."

Anja looked around the small restaurant, making certain that there was nobody within earshot, yet knowing at the same time they couldn't discuss much about the upcoming operation in a public setting.

"Actually, it's more than just a launch party. I kinda wanted to clear the air between us … after the way things went three years ago. Just in case …"

"You're talking like we won't ever see each other again. We may not be a couple, but we still work together."

"We both know it isn't that simple, Stephan. We have no idea how this operation is going to turn out. One of us … both of us … it might not end up the way we want it to."

"We've always known the risks are there. I don't know what to say."

"Then don't say anything. I just wanted you to know that I still care about you. I really liked you when we were together. From the first time we met. That first night. It was just across the street from here, remember?"

"You think I could forget?"

"No, maybe not. Anyway, I thought our time together when we were both in Dushanbe was special, too. We had some real adventures. Outdoors and indoors."

He reached across the table and took her hand.

"It wasn't just you, Anja. Those were special times for both of us. It was just that I …"

"Let's not go back to it, Stephan. I know why it didn't work out, and I'm not asking to start it over again. I guess I'm a little freaked out about what's coming next, and I'm looking for a little … I don't know … validation of the whole thing between us."

"It was good, Anja. It's just that things sometimes don't turn out the way we hope."

"We were both a lot younger then. Not just in years."

"Yeah, I know. I think sometimes you grow up a whole lot in a really short time. Like that first trip up into the mountains."

Anja laughed. "That was a trip all right. In lots of ways. And an education."

Her expression turned serious.

"Stephan?"

"Yeah?"

"Would you come back to my place tonight? I think a need some reassurance. I'm not sure that's the right word, but I'd like to be with you. I'm not trying to go back to what it was before. At least, not unless it could be like that very first time. Only tonight. No commitments. Just two people who know each and share some important history."

"And who care about each other." Stephan squeezed her hand.

"Let's pay our check and get out of here."

• • • • •

Stephan surveyed the apartment as they walked in.

"Not too bad. The Agency is paying for it?"

"Yeah. It's only for a month. It's more like a hotel room than an apartment, except it has a real kitchen. It's kinda small, but it's worked out okay."

"I'm still in a hotel room. They've been moving me around so much for training, they said it wasn't worth arranging an apartment."

He looked at the sofa. "Okay if I sit down?"

"Of course it's okay. You know you can always be comfortable around me. You want a drink?"

"Love it. How about ..."

"A scotch?"

They both laughed.

"Just like that first time. What was it ... seven years ago? Don't tell me you've got an ice bucket ready and waiting."

"Sure do." Anja turned to the kitchen and picked up the container of ice and a bottle of scotch. She set them on the coffee table next to Stephan.

"The only difference is that this time it's a real bottle. Not those little things they put in a minibar. Why don't you pour us a couple? There's some glasses on the shelf."

Stephan poured the scotch, and they made small talk while they drank. The first one and then a second.

"This is just like when we met, Stephan. And it's making me a little ..."

"Horny?"

"You too?"

"Bet your ass."

"I'll bet more than that. Why don't you help me get comfortable? Just like that other time, and undo my zipper."

"Except this time, you're wearing jeans."

"So what? It gives me a chance to watch you while you're doing it. That time, I was wearing a dress, and I had to turn my back so you could unzip it."

"I'm just as nervous as I was then, Anja. Come here."

He pulled her to him, and they kissed deeply. Then she stepped back a few inches.

"My jeans."

"Yeah, okay."

He did it slowly. First the button, then the zipper. She let him move the jeans down her legs, leaning on his shoulder so she could kick them off her feet. Then she stepped back another few inches so he could look at her.

"Lace panties. They can't be the same ones."

"Of course not. But they're as close as I could find. I went shopping before dinner. I guess I was thinking about this as a possibility."

"Last time, you were turned around. It was your butt I saw first."

"I'm going to give you that view again. Ready?"

"Do it."

She turned, and spoke in a husky voice. "What do you think of the ink?"

"Unbelievable. I'm not sure it makes you look like a tramp, but you're incredibly sexy."

"You really think so? Still?"

"You kidding me? Of course."

He reached out for her again. His hands were all over her, under her shirt, beneath her bra, and into her panties. Then she stopped him.

"I want to show you something else."

"What?"

"I'm not completely blond."

"No?"

"Take a look." She again turned her back to him, pushed her panties down, and wriggled out of them. Then she turned to face him.

"I see. Not much, but it isn't blonde."

"Just a patch."

"It's sexy."

"Let's go into the bedroom, Stephan. Let's do this right."

Anja pulled Stephan's clothes off him as quickly as she could, touching him as she did so.

"Feels like maybe you do still think I'm sexy."

"No shit, Sherlock."

She pulled him toward the bed. "I want you in me."

They made love, and they held each other for a while in silence. Then they made love again. And then it was morning. Time to embark on the next phase of their lives. Separately.

* * *

17

Commencement

Dushanbe, Tajikistan, October 17

"So what do you think, Martin? Settling in?"

They were sitting in Stephan's room at the Hotel Avesto, where he had checked in early the previous day after a 25-hour flight via New York and Istanbul. The room was registered in Stephan's old cover name, Shayan Ubayda.

"I feel better today, but I'm not there yet. Basically, I still feel kinda shitty. The time change really wiped me out. Ten hours is big difference. At least I could get to sleep with the pills, so I should be okay by tomorrow."

"Sounds right. I don't feel that great either, but I've done it enough times to know it doesn't last."

"Have you sent him a message, Stephan?"

"Yeah, but I haven't heard back yet. He'll get back to me soon, if I know him at all."

"You're using your old contact information?"

"Yeah. The embassy knows I'm here, but they probably wouldn't contact me for a low-priority message. I'll walk over there in a few

---

minutes and see if he's responded. Trust me. It won't be long before we hear back."

"I don't doubt you. It's just that I'm getting a little antsy. Just sitting here in the hotel."

"Get used to it, Martin. We're going to be doing a lot of waiting in the next few weeks. Maybe for a lot longer. At least you won't have to stay all locked up, once we leave Dushanbe."

"Yeah, I get it. And I understand that I don't exist during this part of the mission. But it doesn't make it any easier. What did you say in your message to Kholdorov?"

"I asked if we could meet this afternoon for a coffee. Knowing him, it will be a vodka. I suggested two places, and I think he'll pick one of them. It would be the polite thing for him to do that."

"He won't be mistrustful? Because you've selected a specific place?"

Stephan smiled. "No question about it. He'll be very suspicious. And that's why I picked two locations. One is right across the street from here, and the other is across the street from your hotel. They're a kilometer apart, so it's not like I picked a couple of places right next to each other where somebody could watch both places. Not just one person, at least."

Martin walked closer to the window. "And both locations are on Prospekt Rudaki?"

"Exactly." Stephan pointed, and like Martin, he remained far enough back from the window that he would not be visible to pedestrians below.

"That's one of them down there. There's a clear line of sight. And your room also looks onto the street. Just as we planned."

"I think the hotel clerk thought I was a little weird. He offered me a room facing the park, but I told him I would only be here a few days and wanted to see the sights of the city. I said I wanted to see all the shops across the avenue."

"Perfect. And don't worry about the desk clerk. I'm sure he's had a lot of requests that were a whole lot stranger. If you go back to your room, I'll get you a message confirming the time and place. If he picks your location, it's easy. If he picks the one across the street from here, you have my spare room key. Either way, all you have to do is watch. Just be careful to stay inconspicuous when you're outside."

"Photos?"

Stephan frowned. "If you're absolutely fucking certain that the flash on your iPhone is off. I suggested five thirty to him, and it'll be getting dark around then."

"You don't need to treat me like a kid."

"Yeah, I guess not." Stephan shrugged. "Sorry. Guess I'm still a little tired myself."

"I'll take off now. You want to check the hallway for me? I'll use the stairs for a couple of flights before I get on the elevator. At least nobody has asked me if I was a tourist. Maybe all that language training has paid off."

"We had good teachers, Martin. And don't forget, you lived here a couple of summers ago. So if anything, your accent would make you sound like you come from up in the mountains. You're cool."

"Then I'll see you tomorrow, assuming everything goes smoothly tonight. If there's a hitch, I know the fallback procedures for contact through the embassy."

* * *

Langley, Virginia, October 18

"Come in, please." Canterbury walked from behind his desk and pointed to the sitting area in his office. Hashan and Chang joined him at the small conference table.

"What's up, David?"

"We just heard from Derek Davenport. He found a new Facebook post. Take a look."

Hashan put a printout on the table. He and Chang already had copies.

```
Good news for my family. My uncle Cyril will be
visiting friends in the capital in three weeks. He
will obtain information on his latest business
ventures, and he said he is certain it will be good
news. He told me that reports from the new store he
opened yesterday was a smashing success, and he is
looking forward to the next one in the winter. I hope
he will tell me stories of the empire. --Yelena
```

"It's not Olga this time," Canterbury said with a frown.

"No. it looks like he's shifted to a new persona."

"What does it mean?"

"Andrea and I have been kicking that around. We think Ghazi is telling everything. A lot more than he'd want us to know. He's going to the capital. That's Astana. And the last line? About the empire? He's got to be staying at the Imperia G, the Empire Hotel."

"When was it posted?"

"Derek said it went up on the eleventh."

Canterbury shook his head. "Then 'yesterday' means the tenth. The 'store opening' was the assassination in Michigan."

"Probably."

Chang spoke for the first time. "Not just probably. It's pretty fucking certain."

"Does this mean he'll attempt another assassination this winter?" Canterbury asked Hashan.

"Sure looks like it. But we have no idea where. Or who. Or when. Winter lasts three months."

"We've got something here we can act on," Chang said. "We know he'll be in Astana the first week of November. We've got to get Anja there, Allan. Do we have any contacts at the Empire?"

"I'm not certain. I used to know some people in the hotels when I was in Kazakhstan, but it's been a long time. Maybe somebody in our embassy could help."

Chang handed him a sheet of paper. "You'd be better. I managed to get a list of employees at the hotel. There's always a chance that one of the names might ring a bell."

Canterbury looked at the paper, his finger tracing the names. Halfway down the list, he paused, then tapped a name twice.

"This one is a possibility. Maybe more than that. There was a young woman when I was in Almaty. Either it's her or someone with the same name. Tatiana Gruzhnova. She's listed here as an assistant manager now. Sounds about right for the elapsed time. If I've identified her correctly, she'll help us. In fact, she owes us big time. We helped protect her and her kid back then just after the Soviets left. She'd be about fifty now. Maybe forty-five."

Chang pulled another sheet of paper from her folder. "How about age forty-eight? Her son is about to turn thirty. She worked at the Hotel Kazakhstan in the nineties."

"Sometimes you amaze me, Andrea. No question. That's her. I'll prepare a message that will ensure her assistance."

"You're going to threaten her?"

"No. Not by threatening. She'll be glad to help us, once she knows it's me asking. And she knows how to be discreet. We can trust her."

"The hotel offers massage service," Chang said. "But it doesn't look like they have a regular spa."

"That's a problem?"

"Just the opposite. It means we can arrange for Anja to go to his room. She won't have to suddenly fit in as a regular masseuse in a fitness center where it might raise a few questions."

Canterbury looked at Chang, then at Hashan, and then back at Chang. "This is forcing our hand on the operation. And we haven't discussed the last step in any detail. Does Anja try to take him out?"

"I don't see how we can do that," Hashan answered. "Not until we get a positive identification. And killing him in the hotel would just be asking for trouble. Remember the Israeli operation in Dubai? They entered on British passports, all fake identities. But everything was caught on surveillance video. A complete public relations disaster. It's not an option for us."

"So how do we make the ID?" Canterbury asked.

"We've got Anja set up with the latest high-tech stuff. She'll have a shoulder bag for her massage oils that's fitted with a digital camera the size of a pea. The lens is virtually indistinguishable from one of the rivets that anchors the handle. Another one of the so-called rivets is a homing device we can interrogate from nearby locations. And she'll be wearing a sort of a housecoat, like a lab coat or something. At least when she arrives …"

Hashan paused, slightly embarrassed. Then he continued. "So there will be full redundancy. And Anja is first rate. She knows what she's doing." Again, he looked uncomfortable.

"What about you, Andrea? You're running point for this operation. You're satisfied with everything? And what about operational safety? We're putting Anja in an extremely dangerous position."

"I think we've got it covered. Neela will be in the hotel, so she can look at whatever photos Anja gets and confirm the identification. If we're really lucky, she'll spot him in person, either entering or leaving the hotel. We've disguised her appearance well enough that she won't be recognized by anyone who isn't interacting with her directly. And we won't let that happen."

Canterbury nodded, but he remained apprehensive.

"If there's a positive identification, what next?"

Chang grimaced.

"Depends a little bit on the Warlord. Once we confirm the ID and what room he's in, the plan is to arrest him. We'll have a team ready to roll. There will be an SUV in front of the hotel, and a helicopter waiting at the embassy. As soon as we grab him, the bird will leave the embassy and land in the parking lot of a supermarket across the street."

"How is it going to land in the middle of a busy parking lot?"

"We've got some contractors through the embassy who are construction workers. We'll get them to block off part of the parking lot, so the bird will have plenty of room to land. Keep in mind that Anja is going to be working by appointment, so that gives us plenty of opportunity to prepare. By the time anybody in authority might realize that something strange is going on, we'll have transferred our boy to a plane at the airport, and he'll be on his way stateside."

"Sounds like a lot of variables. Chances for things to go wrong."

Hashan shrugged. "We don't have a choice, Allan."

"Which brings up one more thing," Canterbury said. "What about arrest authority in Astana?"

Chang shot him a look of annoyance. "It's iffy. You know damn well it is. But we have the legal attaché office at the embassy. The FBI should be willing to cooperate."

"Have we asked?"

"Not yet. Not since we shut them out of the operation."

"But you think they'd help?"

"I sure as hell hope so. But it doesn't matter, Allan. We're going to do what we have to do."

* * *

18

Preliminaries

*Wolf hunting, or rather shooting, always takes place
at night, the sportsmen preparing themselves with
short hunting knives and ready loaded rifles.*

—*Russia Illustrated, 1844* *

Dushanbe, Tajikistan, October 17

Martin stood in his hotel room, several feet back from the
open window, his binoculars trained on the café across
the street.

*Amazing. Stephan had him pegged perfectly. I can do the
surveillance from my own room without the risk of anyone seeing me
outside.*

He had been monitoring the street since five o'clock, and it was
nearly half past. Kholdorov arrived early as Stephan had predicted and
entered the café about fifteen minutes after Martin began watching.

Identification of Kholdorov had been straightforward. His military
demeanor, even from two hundred yards, had permitted a preliminary
identification, and when the colonel came closer, Martin saw that the
man was an exact match for the photograph Stephan had provided. His
arrival a half hour before sunset made the task easier.

Several minutes prior to the colonel's arrival, two men had strolled
past the café, seemingly uninterested in the people around them. One
man had entered the café, while the other continued walking. Several
minutes later, the man on the street reversed direction, and the two

---

* "Russia Illustrated: An Historical & Descriptive Account of that Immense
Empire," Linney Gilbert, London, 1844, p. 131.

apparent friends met again on the sidewalk. They continued a short distance and then stopped at second establishment on Prospekt Rudaki. Martin watched them scan the area and check the sightlines back to the café, nodding discreetly rather than pointing.

They seem satisfied that their location will be adequate for their surveillance of the café. And they won't be able to see me with the lights off in this room.

Martin and Stephan did not view the colonel as a direct physical threat, although they fully expected him to be accompanied by his own watchers. Nevertheless, they were apprehensive. Even if they were not in immediate danger, they were certain the colonel was playing a double game.

Stephan arrived at the café at 5:30, precisely on time. Upon entering, he glanced around and saw Kholdorov in the back. It was exactly as Stephan had predicted. Walking briskly to the table, Stephan extended his hand in greeting. The colonel stood and offered a formal handshake that was accompanied by a steely gaze and no hint of a smile.

Stephan was equally cool in his greeting. "Colonel Kholdorov. It has been a long time."

Kholdorov nodded. "Mr. Ubayda. Indeed, it has been more than one year."

"More than two, Colonel."

The smile on Kholdorov's face broadened, but it was no friendlier.

"You will please to have a chair. Mr. Ubayda. I have taken the liberty of ordering vodka. This is acceptable for you?"

It was as Stephan had anticipated. He smiled dispassionately, confident that his reserve would not go undetected.

"I would be delighted, Colonel."

They were silent as the proprietor brought their vodka. Russian style, in small glasses. Two rounds were delivered, but Stephan said nothing. The vodka was accompanied by pickles and black bread.

"To your health, Mr. Ubayda."

"And to our friendship, Colonel."

They drank the first vodka.

"You asked to meet with me quite urgently. A reasonable man would conclude that you wish to ask me some questions."

"Yes, Colonel. Of a somewhat delicate matter, I am afraid."

Whatever tension might have faded from the conversation returned with even greater intensity.

"You will proceed."

"Thank you, Colonel. The last time we met privately, I asked you some questions about a mutual friend. The man known as the Patriarch. And also about his brother who had been assassinated during the civil war."

"I recall the conversation."

"And I also asked if you knew anything of the possible involvement of those men with nuclear materials. You said you would telephone me if you could find any information. You never called."

"Did it make any difference?"

"Perhaps not, Colonel. The specific problem was resolved."

"It would seem there was a good outcome. We shall drink to it. May all of your problems become solved."

They drank their second round of vodka.

"Tell me, Mr. Ubayda. If your problem was solved, what is it that you wish to ask me now? I am hopeful there is not some new difficulty."

"There is a difficulty, although I cannot be certain it is new, Colonel. It may be related to the old problem. At our last meeting, I told you that the Patriarch may have provided more information than he had intended."

Kholdorov's gaze hardened. "I might recall that."

"After that conversation, Colonel … only a few days later. The Patriarch was killed."

The hardened gaze turned to barely disguised outrage. The Colonel rose partway from his seat.

"You would suggest that I was responsible for his murder?"

"I suggest no such thing, Colonel. You have always been a good friend to me and my colleagues. You have helped us when we needed help, and you have guided us when we needed guidance. It is what we ask of you now."

Kholdorov returned to his sitting position. "You would please be more specific."

"We hope that you could help us identify … identify and find the man who killed the Patriarch. We believe this person also killed others — the entire family of the Patriarch's brother. And those killings took place in the United States. This person is an enemy of our country."

The colonel's face was devoid of expression, and his voice carried no warmth. "This is something I must think about. It is something I must think about in solitude. It would be best if you left me now."

Kholdorov did not rise when Stephan stood, and he extended no hand in parting. But he spoke quietly as Stephan turned to leave.

"Mr. Ubayda. I will contact you after I have thought about this matter."

Stephan nodded.

"I will leave a message at your hotel. You are staying at the Hotel Avesto, I believe."

Stephan couldn't prevent the small expression of surprise on his face, although he stopped himself before voicing it. All he said was, "That is correct."

"Then please, Mr. Ubayda. You should be on your way. I wish you a pleasant evening."

* * *

Dushanbe, Tajikistan, October 19

"Hop in, dude. We're going for the ride of a lifetime."

Martin tossed his canvas duffel bag into the back seat and climbed into the passenger seat next to Stephan.

"Nice ride. How in hell did you score a Land Cruiser? And it looks like a new one."

"Last year's model. I'm not sure why we got it, and the guy at the embassy motor pool was pissed off. I think he figured I probably wasn't going to bring it back again. I guess they don't get many vehicles that are this nice."

"You think Andrea pulled some strings?"

"Probably Canterbury. Maybe even Alford. But considering where we're headed, it's not that hard to justify having the best vehicle available. This thing is supposed to be really good off road, and we'll need it. They also told me the sides and undercarriage have armor plate. I can tell you it handles like a tank."

Stephan pulled out from the front entrance of the Hotel Tajikistan and turned south toward A384, the highway that would take them out of the city."

"What's the plan, Stephan? Did they give us a specific route to follow?"

"Yeah. I got it this morning when I picked up the vehicle. We go south from here, and it's pretty much a straight shot to the Afghan border. Should take us about three hours, maybe a little less, and crossing shouldn't be a problem. We're not carrying any cargo, and they know we're coming. Once we're in Afghanistan, it's another thirty or forty miles to Kunduz."

"What happens after we reach Kunduz?"

"We head east to Fayzabad. Another four hours according to what they gave me. We stay there tonight."

"A hotel?"

"Don't know," Stephan answered. "I've got an address, but that's all. Whatever it is, it'll be the best we get for a while."

"What about Samantha?"

"The rendezvous is set for tomorrow. Pretty much as soon as we enter the Wakhan Corridor. A Special Ops team is going to fly her in from Pakistan. They're also going to send another vehicle for the next part of the trip. Probably from Kabul. The guy who briefed me said they'd look like Afghanis, but they'll be our guys. It wasn't clear whether they'd be CIA or military."

"They'll be armed?"

"Bet your ass. Andrea sent a message saying that they're going to bring us a whole buttload of weapons. Assault rifles, RPGs, mortars, light machine guns, the whole deal. And the Special Ops guys are staying with us."

"Like overnight? Or longer?"

"Sounds like it's for as long as it takes. That's good. Even with the training they gave us, I was a little nervous about doing this mission on our own."

"Are we going up through Khorugh?"

"Nope. We're taking the back way. Too many problems with bandits and rebels near Khorugh. Andrea's note said they contacted the guy who drove Anja and me when we first went to see the Patriarch four years ago, and he's informed the villagers that you're coming back. They're expecting you. And your wife."

"That still seems weird to me."

"But it's how it has to be, Martin. We can't risk upsetting anyone's moral sensibilities. Besides, you like each other, right?"

"Yeah, but this isn't the way it was supposed to play out."

"None of it is like it was supposed to be. Maybe it'll be different after we finish the operation. If things work out, maybe you two will want to get married for real."

"Maybe so. It's hard to even think about that kind of stuff right now."

"Something else, Martin. We need to watch out for a possible ambush on this trip."

"Taliban?"

"Probably not. The embassy gave us an all clear on that. If something happens, it'll mean they're after us specifically."

"Because the driver told the villagers I was coming back?"

"Not exactly. The villagers aren't going to be threatened by you. You're one of them. Family. If it happens, it'll be a consequence of my conversation with the colonel."

"You don't trust him very much, do you?"

"Actually, I do. At least in an ass-backwards kind of way. He may be duplicitous, but his words can't be ignored. Take a look at this note he sent me last night."

Martin read it aloud.

When you go hunting, you must always be afraid of the
wolves.

"I've already sent it on to Andrea in a secure e-mail."

"I don't get it. What does it mean?"

"His name, Martin. Think about his name."

"The colonel? I don't see … Oh shit. You mean the Warlord.
Kaskyrbai Ghazi. *Kaskyrbai* means *fearless as a wolf!* I forgot about
that."

"Right. That message from Kholdorov confirms it was the
Warlord who took out the Patriarch — and also your family. I don't
know what role the colonel might have played in passing information
to Ghazi. But I have a gut feeling that he was involved."

"You think Kholdorov was part of the plot? My family?"

"I don't see him as an active player, no. He's not a militant, but he
seems to deal in information. And we caught him doing it. Maybe
that's why he got so angry when we met."

"You think he might still be playing a double game?"

"Count on it. That's why I'm worried about an ambush. And if the
colonel didn't provide the information that led to the attack on your
family, there's an informer in the village who did. So there's going to
be some sort of attack. For sure. On our way to the village or sometime
after we get there. It's only a question of when."

* * *

19

Abdurrahim

A Russian party under Colonel Yonoff, making its annual promenade of the Pamirs, came up to them, fired on them, and killed every single man.

—*The Heart of a Continent, 1904* [*]

Wakhan Valley, Afghanistan, October 20

Stephan and Martin had been on the road since early morning, and the smooth asphalt road had long since given way to a dirt and gravel track of distinctly lesser quality. Martin laughed as Stephan swerved around a large pothole.

"At least we know what we're in for later. We'll probably look back and think of this as a parkway."

Stephan grunted his agreement. "What have you got on the GPS? Seems like we should be getting close to Eshkashem. That's we cross the frontier back into Tajikistan, right?"

"Almost there. Up ahead, where the road turns to the right? That should be on the outskirts. Then another four miles or so to the crossing. And maybe some better roads on the Tajik side."

The border crossing was uneventful.

"I really expected they'd give us some shit," Stephan said. "I wonder if someone was here ahead of us to grease the skids a little."

"Wouldn't surprise me. So far, everything's going like clockwork, but I'll feel better when we meet up with the Special Ops team. You

---

[*] "The Heart of a Continent: A Narrative of Travels in Manchuria, Across the Gobi Desert, Through the Himalayas, The Pamirs, and Hunza, 1884-1894," Francis Edward Younghusband, John Murray, London, 1904, p. 264.

said the embassy told you it would be safer on the Tajik side, but either way, it sure isn't Kansas."

"Agreed. My instructions from Andrea said that the Tajik militants haven't been active along this next stretch of road, but she's seven thousand miles away. God knows who's providing the information to her."

They drove, mostly in silence, for several hours, awed by the majesty of the Wakhan corridor ahead of them. They were at an elevation of 8,600 feet, and the mountains rose on each side of the river with peaks ranging from 15,000 to 20,000 feet.

"Pull over a second," Martin said.

"What is it?" Even before the vehicle came to a complete stop, Stephan was reaching for the M4 carbine mounted on his side of the center console."

"Nothing's wrong. Sorry. I just wanted you to be able to see this."

High on the hill above them were the ruins of a fortress.

"My uncle — the Patriarch — told me about these forts when I stayed with him that summer. It shows why the Wakhan has been so important historically. It's a straight shot from here to China, and the mountains on both sides are huge. Before modern weapons, nobody could ever march an army through the mountains. And if they were crazy enough to try, a fortress like that would stop them."

"Impressive. Any idea how old it is?"

"Doesn't say anything on the map. My Uncle showed me a couple of old forts, and he said some of them were built a thousand years ago. Maybe two thousand. Pretty amazing, isn't it?"

They were across the river from the Afghan town of Khandud. They drove past several miles of farmland, a narrow island of arable land in what otherwise seemed like a vast sea of barren rock.

Suddenly, a pickup truck pulled out from a cluster of houses on the road ahead and accelerated rapidly toward them. Without a word, Martin grabbed his M14 and slid out the passenger door of the SUV. Stephan dove across the front seat behind him, pausing only to remove his own M14 from its mounting. Crouched in a small ditch to the side of their vehicle, they silently considered their options. Stephan used hand signals, directing Martin to crawl toward several trees near the roadside, while he positioned himself at the rear of the truck.

Moments later, Martin shouted. "All clear! It's them. The front license plate is number twenty-three."

Stephan nodded but didn't move.

"Stay put until they get closer and identify themselves."

The truck slid to a stop a few yards short of the SUV, and for several seconds nobody moved. Then, the driver-side door slowly opened, and a man climbed out. He was dressed in peasant clothing, a turban on his head. A large man, but even the loose clothing couldn't hide a high level of fitness. He kept his hands in full view, raised to head level.

He spoke only two words. "Jordan rules."

Stephan smiled. "Shaq was better at the end."

The password and response had been exchanged. Stephan and Martin stood up, and the driver of the pickup truck relaxed. A second man emerged from the passenger side. He was taller and more intimidating than the driver.

"The end doesn't matter. Right now, they're both old and I could beat either one of them. But Jordan was the best."

The four men converged halfway between their vehicles. Stephan and Martin identified themselves, and the pickup driver spoke.

"Mike." No affiliation, no rank.

"And I'm Travis." Only first names had been offered.

Handshakes were exchanged.

"Just the two of you?" Martin asked.

"You mean the woman?" Travis answered. "She's back at our camp. About fifty klicks from here. Let's move out. Follow us, and we'll be there before dark."

• • • • •

They drove fast, at least for the conditions of the road. For several minutes, Stephan and Martin were quiet. Then Martin spoke.

"They're big guys. They look like linebackers."

"I hope they're as tough as they look. We need really top support for this operation."

"I'm thinking we'll be okay. They don't act like this is their first rodeo."

• • • • •

For most of the drive, they followed the Pamir River in a northerly direction, gaining nearly 3,000 feet in elevation. When the road made a sharp turn to the east, the pickup truck turned onto an old washed-out track, and the campsite came into view a half-mile later.

The four men climbed out of the vehicles, and Samantha emerged from a tent, an assault rifle at the ready.

"You can stand down, ma'am," Mike called to her. "We're all friendlies."

Samantha put down her weapon and walked over to the men. She shook Stephan's hand in a warm greeting and then reached out to give Martin an awkward hug.

"If we're supposed to be married, we have to start acting like it," she said. "At least in public."

"Maybe we …"

Samantha's elbow hit Martin in the ribs, just hard enough to keep him from finishing the sentence.

Stephan decided to change the topic.

"Where do we go from here?"

Mike gestured toward Travis. "He's our navigator."

"This is the Matz River." Travis pointed to the nearby stream that was running at barely a trickle. A dirt track ran along the river bank.

"We take it up toward the Matz Pass. The village we're going to is off to the north side a couple of klicks before the pass. Unfortunately, this nice dirt road only goes about a quarter of the way. The river is pretty dry right now, so when the road ends we drive right up the river bed."

"Damn good thing," Mike added. "Otherwise we'd have had to walk over these mountains. Maybe we could have used horses, but we'd never have had a prayer of getting the vehicles where we're going."

"Can your truck make it?" Stephan asked. "It doesn't look all that solid."

Mike laughed. "It's a four-by-four. May not look like much, but you should see the engine. This baby is hot. And the tarp in the back is covering a .50-caliber machine gun. One of the new versions of the M2. Really sweet. Anybody tries to give us any trouble on this trip, we've got enough gear here to blow them right off the fuckin' mountain."

He glanced nervously toward Samantha. "Sorry, ma'am."

"No problem," she said. "I told you what my training was, and I've heard a lot worse than anything you've got to say."

"Yes, ma'am," Mike replied.

Samantha rolled her eyes.

"You think we should expect trouble? An attack?" Martin asked.

"Truth? Not too fuckin' likely. Travis and me, we covered everything between here and where we met up today. Nobody around. No militants. No insurgents. No Taliban. Just a few farmers, and they were scared shitless. They know what a technical is when they see it. That's what they call this kind of truck. The Taliban use them."

"The road was clear from when we crossed the border at Eshkashem up until we met up with you. Stephan and I didn't see anything unusual, either."

"That's not a complete coincidence," Travis said. "There was another team that cleared that part of the road before you came through, so you wouldn't have seen anything. It's been a pretty damn big operation getting you in here. The other team left at dawn, and they got to Eshkashem before you crossed. They were watching you from up on the hill, and they let us know you were on the way. We got some good radios here. Secure communications, the whole damn thing."

"So what about the rest of the trip up to the village, Mike?" Stephan returned to the prior topic.

"It's gonna be a real adventure. I'm confident we can make it the whole way with these vehicles. Our people flew some kind of recon flight a couple of days ago. Probably a UAV. And the experts back home analyzed the video feed and told us it was clear the whole way to this village. Both the dirt track and the stream bed. No matter what, we gotta drive over some big f... some big damn rocks. But they said we could do it."

"I've got a question." Stephan looked at Mike, then Travis, and then back again. "What are your plans? I mean, after you get us up to the village."

"We thought we'd hang with you for a while," Mike answered. "Our truck is carrying a whole lot more than just that machine gun. Our orders ... our instructions are to help you set up an airtight defensive perimeter around that village. We understand that you might be expecting some visitors in the near future. The unfriendly kind."

"I'm not sure how soon. But yeah, we expect it."

"Probably within a month," Travis suggested. "After that, there should be enough snow in the mountains to keep anyone from moving around with anything bigger than a Kalashnikov. So we'll make sure you and the people in the village are ready for whatever they throw at you."

"It's probably best if we keep a low profile with some of this stuff, Mike. The villagers know Martin, and they've met me. But they're going to see you guys and Samantha as outsiders. At least to begin with."

"You think that's going to be a problem?"

"I think we just want the villagers to see us as being here to help them. You agree, Martin?"

"Depends on how you look at it. I don't think it's a bad thing for everyone to know we're well armed. They haven't forgotten about the attack that killed the Patriarch. But headquarters said that someone in the village is on the other side of this fight. So we don't want to advertise everything we've got planned. And we sure as hell don't want to give away our defensive strategy."

"Fair enough," Mike said. "The original idea was for Travis and me to stay for a few weeks and then get out before the snows come, but it wasn't a fixed arrangement. There's no point in us checking out, if it's going to screw things up. Our instructions say that in the final scheme of things, you're in charge."

"Maybe so," Stephan said. "But only for setting goals. For tactics and implementation, we're amateurs. You and Travis give us the advice, and we'll follow it."

"Fair enough. You've all had some kind of Special Ops training?"

"Martin and I both spent a few weeks at the Northern Warfare Training Center in Alaska. No claim to be experts, but we hung in there with the training program."

"Excellent. What about you, ma'am." His expression suggested he wasn't expecting much.

"Infantry. Fort Benning. 198th."

Mike's eyes showed a hint of surprise, but his answer was neutral. "That's good."

"You didn't let me finish," Samantha said. "Then I went to Ranger School."

"You completed the program?" his tone betrayed some skepticism.

Samantha's eyes flared, but she controlled her reaction. "I finished Darby and Mountain Phase. Then they pulled me out and assigned me to intelligence. So here I am."

He whistled. "That's fucking impressive."

"Looks like we got a good team," Travis added.

Mike appeared to relax, and he sat on a crate by the pickup truck. "Yeah, I think we do."

He returned to the previous topic. "So, I guess we'll play a lot of this by ear. Working together, like Stephan suggested. My advice at this point is we should give the three of you a quick refresher on tactics, with emphasis on the specifics of the local terrain."

"Mostly defensive?" Martin asked.

"For right now, yeah. And we'll check you out on all the weapons. It's probably a good idea if we all start using the same weapons. Let's put the M4 carbine and M16 rifles in reserve and switch to HK416s. They're all based on the AR-15 design, and they all use the 5.56×45mm NATO cartridge. So the learning curve is going to be minimal. The HK is a superb weapon, and you're going to like it."

"Still sounds like it'll slow us down so we can get familiar with it," Stephan said.

"Not a problem. We can take an extra day getting to the village, and you should be pretty well set when we get there. Plus, you'll get used to the altitude. We can evaluate features in the terrain as we go. That way, we can discuss defensive strategies as well as attack and counterattack scenarios. After we get to the village, we can go out on a couple of day hikes to scout the area. Pick out the best recon and ambush sites and shit … and stuff like that. Sorry ma'am."

Samantha shook her head and smiled.

* * *

Pamir Mountains, October 23

After a two-day trip up the trail toward Matz Pass, the five visitors arrived at the village in midafternoon. They had been observed for the last several miles of their expedition. All of them experienced heightened levels of anxiety.

Stephan was surprised to discover that his apprehensions were offset by a sense of pleasant anticipation as he neared the village he had visited twice previously. Similarly, any foreboding Martin might have felt was outweighed by a feeling of joy as he returned to the place he now considered his ancestral home. Samantha's feelings were a combination of suspicion and doubt as she contemplated the challenges she would soon confront. The other two travelers, Mike and Travis, felt the intense thrill of embarking on another dangerous assignment.

They halted the two vehicles several hundred yards from the first visible structure and walked slowly toward the building that had been the Patriarch's home. They carried no visible weapons, although the others were certain that Mike and Travis were not completely unarmed. They could see no one as they approached, nor did they hear any sounds.

Suddenly a shout pierced the silence. "Mumin!"

A man emerged from behind the Patriarch's house, and Martin recognized him as Shahram, his uncle's most trusted subordinate. He was of indeterminate age, somewhere between forty and sixty, with leathery skin that suggested long exposure to sun and harsh climate. Martin was immediately certain that this man had become the village leader.

"Mumin! It is splendid that I am again looking at you. I knew it was you as quickly as I saw you walk up the path."

The initial greeting was in English, but subsequent conversation took place in Tajik.

"It is good also to see you again, Shahram. I am called Martin now. That is important. *Martin*, not *Mumin*."

The puzzled look lasted for only a second. "Yes, of course. I am delighted to see you once more, Martin. It means you have been kept safe. From the enemies of your family."

"You are a wise man, Shahram." Martin smiled fondly.

You have changed. When I saw you last, you were but a boy. Now you are a man."

Martin was momentarily embarrassed, but he knew it was a tribute.

"It has been five years, Shahram. Much has changed."

The man's expression darkened. "Your uncle ... You have the knowledge that ...?"

"I know he was killed, Shahram. In part, that is why I am here."

The village leader didn't fully comprehend Martin's statements, but he understood their significance.

"The Patriarch was a great man, Martin. When you came to us, he explained that you were his family. That you and the others in America were all that remained of his family. That we must accept you and your brother as part of our family here."

"It is only me now, Shahram. There is no longer anyone else."

Martin's expression betrayed the emotions that he managed to force beneath the surface of his voice.

Once again, the villager didn't know the specifics of what had happened. But he understood.

"Then I welcome you back as my brother."

He turned to the others. "Forgive me. I am ill-mannered. You are friends of Martin, and I welcome you to our village. The village is called Abdurrahim now. It is in esteem of Abdurrahim Suleyman, who was the uncle of Martin's father."

Abruptly, his expression changed when his eyes locked with Stephan's. Not an unfriendly look, but one of surprised recognition. "I know you, as well. You are ..."

"I am Stephan Udrea. I come as a friend to Martin, and I thank you for your kind welcome. We all thank you."

Shahram smiled happily. "We receive few visitors here, so you bring us great joy. You have not told me the names of the others in your group, Martin."

"Forgive me. I have been too excited at seeing you again. These men helped us to reach the village from the Wakhan. Their names are Mike and Travis."

The village leader looked at the two men. Two immense figures, they were dressed as Pashtun warriors, but to someone who had witnessed the unrest of the previous decades, everything about them screamed 'American soldiers.' Shahram nodded politely, and yet again, he understood.

He then turned toward Samantha. "You have not told me of this lovely woman who travels with you. She is to be a secret?"

His calculated smile was rewarded by a broad grin from Martin.

"There is no secret, Shahram. This is my wife. Her name is Samantha."

Shahram spoke happily. "This is wonderful. A welcome to you also, Samantha. Welcome to our village of Abdurrahim. You also are now part of our family. You are my sister!"

Then, he turned to the others. "You must all forgive me. I am so busy to speak with my family that I have shown no manners. Your visit is cause for a celebration, and we are honored to have you as our guests."

A shout, without specific words that could be identified, provided the necessary signal. Nearly every member of the two dozen families of the village seemed to materialize from nowhere.

The words came next. Shouted, so all could hear.

"Martin has returned! You remember him. The nephew of the Patriarch. He is here with his friend Stephan. And his other friends. And most important, with his wife. Her name is Samantha. You must welcome them. Today is an illustrious day, and we must prepare a feast for our guests."

• • • • •

While others in the village worked to prepare the celebration, Shahram escorted the newcomers on a walking tour of the village and its environs. Samantha, Stephan, Mike and Travis were included, but there was no doubt that Martin was the focus of attention. He and Shahram conversed in Tajik.

"Everything remains much as it was when you last were here, Martin. Your uncle was Abdurrahim Suleyman, the Patriarch. For him, the village needed no name. He merely called it 'his home.' Now we call it Abdurrahim. It is in tribute to him. He protected us and helped us to prosper. It has been for us very difficult without him for these two years. He was a very wise man."

Martin answered formally.

"I am honored by your respect for my family. If you will have me, I will make my home with you in the village."

He paused and looked around, in part for dramatic effect.

"But I must warn you of the possibility that the people who killed my uncle may also want to kill me. It could bring danger to the village. They have already killed my brother and the rest of our family."

Shahram's happiness over the reunion with Martin disappeared immediately in a pall of gloom.

"I am most saddened to learn of this news. It has the appearance of a vendetta against the Suleyman family. Wherever you go this evil may follow you."

Martin was concerned that the request for safe haven might be refused, and he was prepared to use that moment to divulge the existence of the supplies and weapons his team had brought to the village. He knew they would constitute a powerful bargaining chip. But the disclosure wasn't necessary.

"It would be a great privilege to have you live among us, Martin. We too have feared that your uncle's enemies would attack our village once more. We named the village as a continuing reminder of his leadership. And we will always be prepared to protect his legacy, with our lives, if necessary. You are part of that legacy, Martin. You are welcome here, and we offer you our protection."

"Thank you, Shahram. I owe you a great debt, and I will work hard to repay it."

They stood briefly in silence before the walking tour continued.

"You can observe, Martin, the improvements we have made. While he lived, the Patriarch extended electricity from the diesel generator to nearly half of the homes in the village, and those same homes have flowing water in them. It was a great accomplishment."

"I don't remember this large building, Shahram." Martin pointed to a structure in the center of the small village.

"Yes, that is our gathering place. It is large enough that everyone may come together for holiday celebrations and meals. As we shall do this evening."

Martin next pointed to one of several partially built structures.

"What are the structures that are unfinished?"

The answer was accompanied by a look of chagrin. "It is an unfortunate thing. We were constructing new homes for others in the village. With water and electricity. They were to be quite grand."

"What happened?"

"When your uncle was killed, the construction stopped. Abdurrahim was a very wise man, and he had many books. So he knew how to do those things. But the rest of us did not. We thought there might be assistance from the government or from the Americans. Your uncle told us of a project of cooperation that would begin."

He turned to Stephan. "We hoped that your ... that the woman named Anja who accompanied you on your visits to our village ... that she would begin the program. We hoped that other Americans might help us build our village and make it modern. But that did not happen either. Those of us who were left could not do it. We are strong, but we do not understand how to do these things."

Martin looked at Stephan, then at Mike and Travis. They had understood the conversations in Tajik, but they were not yet comfortable speaking the language. Martin asked them in English.

"Does the gear you brought include stuff so that would let us help them finish these buildings?"

Mike nodded, and Martin turned back to Shahram.

"We would be pleased to assist you in completing the project. My friends have equipment we could use to complete the homes."

The offer was clearly unexpected.

"We would be grateful, Martin. To you and to your friends." He looked at the others, smiling broadly.

The next structure they approached was the former home of the Patriarch, a place where both Martin and Stephan had been guests.

"This will now be your home, Martin."

"I don't understand, Shahram. It looks occupied. Who lives there now?"

He was embarrassed. "I do, Martin. I was second in charge after the Patriarch, and when he was killed, the others wanted me to live in his home. But I will now move back into my previous dwelling. Your uncle's house will become yours. A home for you and your wife. It is proper, as you are the only relative of your uncle."

The offer was unexpected. They were still walking, and Martin continued for several more steps before responding. He turned and put a hand on Shahram's shoulder.

"I am honored that you would do this for me, but I cannot accept your generosity. Do not forget that I have lived among you, so I know something of your ways. The leadership of the village cannot be designated as a birthright. It must be earned, and I have not done so. Only one man in the village has earned the full respect of the others, and that is you."

Martin gestured toward the others and continued his explanation.

"We are newcomers, and we must be treated as such. Anything more would show disrespect to you, to the others in the village, and to the memory of the Patriarch. Is there not some other building that we could occupy? If you deem it wise, we could also sleep in one of the unfinished buildings until it is completed."

Martin knew he had said the right things, and Shahram seemed to grow in stature as he answered.

"There is certainly a building that would accommodate you and your wife. It is my old home. My son has been living there with his wife and son, but that has only been for the time needed to make small changes to the large house. Those changes are now completed, so I shall ask them to live with me. They will occupy the rooms that once were used by you and your brother. It will be good for my family all to be together again under one roof."

"Your generosity overwhelms me, Shahram."

* * *

Abdurrahim, Tajikistan, October 28

After less than a week of work, the progress was remarkable. Samantha's voice conveyed her astonishment.

"Look at these homes, Martin. Even yesterday, they looked like they were months away from being finished, and now they're almost done."

"No question. I thought my background was fairly good, but it seems like Mike and Travis can do just about anything. And they didn't just do it themselves. They've got the villagers believing in themselves again."

"It's not just Mike and Travis. The people also look up to you, Martin. I've seen it get stronger ever since you started. The first day, they looked at Shahram for guidance, then to Mike and Travis. Then it was to Mike and Travis first, and to you and Shahram almost equally. Now they're looking to you first."

"I felt a change, but I don't understand it. I haven't done anything."

"That's where you're wrong. First off, you're a Suleyman. That's huge. Even more important, you've been running things. A lot of it has been the way that Mike and Travis have looked to you as the leader in working with the villagers. Same thing for Stephan. All three of them know they're senior to you. And more experienced. But they're playing their roles. If this exercise is going to work, it's going to depend on the people accepting you in a leadership role. And so far, you're doing great."

He smiled at her. "Thanks. You're doing pretty damn well, too. The other women don't know what to make of you. Most of what you've been doing ... they probably think of it as men's work."

"I'll make some compromises, Martin, but I won't become a fourteenth-century woman. I'm trying to keep it low key, and I think they'll all come around. Mostly, I think they're surprised, but nobody seems to be offended. There's a lot of respect for hard work, and it's not like the women haven't been working hard forever here."

Shahram walked up to them hesitantly.

"May I speak with you, Martin?"

"Of course. There is no need to ask."

He paused when he realized the meaning of the question. "And we can speak before Samantha. She and I have no secrets."

With obvious distress, Shahram began to speak. "I am worried. It is Tohir."

"Has something happened to him? He is injured?"

Tohir Shohtemur was one of the younger men in the village, and Martin had met him during his previous visit. He was a hard worker, but he kept to himself, often preferring a solitary hunting expedition to a joint project with the other men. Martin had never considered this behavior suspicious, only a bit peculiar.

"He has disappeared."

"Perhaps he has gone hunting, Shahram. Why should that worry you."

"I don't think he is hunting. He has acted strangely since you arrived a week ago. Now he has gone, and he took enough provisions for a week. He did not speak with me first, and he left in secrecy."

"Perhaps he is jealous of the attention you have given to me."

"I think not, Martin. This happened once before. Two years ago. He had an explanation then, and I believed him. It was the same as what you have suggested. That he was on a hunting trip. He even returned with meat from an antelope he told us he killed."

"Then why do you suspect something else now?"

"Because of what happened after he returned the previous time. I did not think of it before today, but I am certain. Exactly one week after he returned. That is when we were attacked. It is when they killed Abdurrahim Suleyman."

• • • • •

Later that afternoon, the Americans held a meeting in the structure that had become home for Martin and Samantha. They were seated on cushions surrounding a low table. Everyone knew that something serious was to be discussed, but first they drank their tea. It was a question of appearances.

Stephan broke the silence. "What is it Martin?"

"Tohir. I think we have our first break."

Martin related the story Shahram had told him.

"If the same timeline holds, we probably have a week to prepare," Mike said.

Travis was less certain. "We can't count on it. You're assuming that Tohir has to make contact with people who would need a week to get here. But Stephan told me there was intel on a possible drug route in this area from the Wakhan corridor north toward Kazakhstan."

"You think there might have been a scheduled rendezvous?" Martin asked.

"Yeah, it's a possibility we have to consider. Because that would reduce the time for them to organize and send a team to only three or four days. What do you think, Mike?"

"We've got to start getting our positions ready. Tomorrow afternoon, we break early from working on the houses, and I'll show you how we're going to respond when the bad guys show up. The biggest question is whether Tohir is the only one we have to worry about. Stephan, you've been here since Martin left. Any thoughts?"

"I met Tohir when I came to see the Patriarch. He seemed a little aloof, but it didn't set off any alarms. I think we should take the advice of Shahram on this topic. Martin, would you talk to him when we're done here?"

"Yeah, I can do that. And he's going to ask how to deal with Tohir. If he shows up again, do we call him out?"

Mike answered. "Let him think he's in the clear. If he does anything unusual ... repeat, anything ... then we grease him."

Mike looked at the other four members of the group, and all of them nodded. He stared at Samantha for an extra moment, and her eyes flashed.

"These bastards wanted me dead, too. I've got no problem with fighting back."

"Okay, let's get back to what we were doing. Travis and I will check out some things tonight. Martin, let's make sure that Shahram joins us tomorrow afternoon. We're going to set up a perimeter that includes all approaches to the village for five hundred yards in every direction. That entire area will be a kill zone."

* * *

20

Contact

*Special warfare is the execution of activities that
involve a combination of lethal and nonlethal
actions taken by a specially trained and educated
force that has a deep understanding of cultures and
foreign language, proficiency in small-unit tactics,
and the ability to build and fight alongside
indigenous combat formations in a permissive,
uncertain, or hostile environment.*
—*Special Operations, U.S. Army, 2012*[*]

Abdurrahim, Tajikistan, November 2

The small group clustered together atop the ridge five
hundred yards north of the village. Under other
circumstances, someone would have commented on the
incredible scenery. However, their purpose on this day was not
sightseeing but planning for surveillance of a more serious kind. As
they laid out the plans, the two Special Ops men were garnering
further respect from their three CIA counterparts and the village
leader.

Everyone crouched around a map spread out on the ground,
studying the different locations as Mike described them.

"This is the key position for the entire sector," he said, sweeping
his arm across the landscape. "From here, you can see the entire
village plus the near approach from any direction. To the south and

---

[*] "Special Operations," Army Doctrine Reference Publication No. 3-05,
United States Army, August 31, 2012, p. 1-5.

east, your view is unobstructed for a couple miles. Factor in the sensors we just set out, and nobody is going to make a surprise arrival, no matter how careful they are."

"I think you've nailed it, Mike. But what about our vulnerability from north and west, where our clear sightline is probably only a half mile?" Stephan's question raised a concern shared by the others.

"Fair question, but look here at the map again. There's only three reasonable ways to reach the village. These guys don't have aircraft, and we'd know about any vehicles way in advance if they tried that. So we can be fairly certain they'll come on foot. One alternative is the same way we came in, from the southeast, but it's highly unlikely, because it's from the wrong direction. Whoever comes after us will almost certainly be approaching from the north. From Kazakhstan.

"Couldn't they skirt the village and use the southern approach?" Samantha asked.

"Anything's possible. I'm just telling you what's most plausible. It doesn't mean we're leaving ourselves exposed. We're going to cover every alternative, so it's a question of how we prioritize. An attack from the north is the most logical. The map shows that the village is between these two river valleys, right above their confluence. Not rivers, really. Just streams most of the year, if that. So we put our main focus on those two approaches and the southeast as a secondary. They'll be walking into an ambush no matter what."

"You're assuming they'll try a frontal assault," Martin said. "Couldn't they try something from the ridges? Even starting with artillery or a mortar attack?"

Mike smiled. "You're pretty good. I like that. And yeah, they could. It's unlikely, because they're not a regular military force. Their capabilities are going to be limited, and they'll have to carry their weaponry on their backs. Worst case, it would be mortars. Now, look again at the map. From the southeast, they'd come under visual surveillance, and from the west, they'd have to scale this thousand-foot rock face. The danger comes from the north. From the next ridge over there. It's out of our line of sight, even here. That means it wouldn't be hard to lob a few shells right over where we're sitting and into the village. It would really fuck things up down there."

Martin persisted. "So how do we react if they try that?"

"It's simple, Martin. It's just like the Boy Scouts: 'Be prepared.' Travis set up sensors that will alert us if our visitors approach the top of that ridge from the valley."

"And then?"

Mike took a device resembling a cellphone from his pocket. "Travis also buried some explosive charges up there. If the sensors identify an attacking force near the top of that ridge, I just turn this thing on and push the button. Then, 'boom,' they're toast."

"What if they're spread out? The blast could miss fighters at the rear."

"On top of the shit Travis buried on the ridge, I'll have my 'Punisher' up here at this position."

Mike wore a cocky grin.

"That's an XM25. It's what they call a 'Counter Defilade Target Engagement System.' It's new, and officially it's still in the testing stage. Totally unbelievable. Basically, it's a 25-millimeter grenade launcher. But it's programmable for distance, and you fire it like a regular assault rifle. It's got a laser rangefinder, so you can tweak the distance setting for just beyond whatever barrier the bad guys are hiding behind. You get an air burst as the shell passes over the target."

The others nodded, as they began to appreciate the remarkable superiority they would have in a firefight. Samantha spoke for the first time. "What's the actual response plan? What do we do when these guys show up if we're all down in the village? Maybe even asleep?"

Mike pulled a piece of paper from his pocket and unfolded it. At the top, he had written "Battle Position."

"The site we're at now will be my station. Travis will be across the way at the top of the eastern ridge. He'll be farther away, but he'll have a clear line of sight for any approaching force, no matter which of the three routes they use."

Travis pointed to his assigned position on the map and showed how he had sightlines for the various approaches to the village.

Mike continued his explanation. "Travis will have the M249. The M2 stays mounted on the truck, so that gives us two belt-fed machine guns. Samantha, you'll man the Browning in the truck. When we're done here this afternoon, we'll move the truck closer to the southeastern edge of the village, so you'll also have a clear line of fire for any of the three most likely approaches."

"And the rest of us?" Stephan asked.

"You're the core of the village. Your first job is to make sure the villagers take cover, and then you prepare ready to engage anyone who gets through the outer perimeter. You'll each have an HK416. That includes you, Shahram. The north side of the village is shielded by this hillside we're on, so Martin will cover the west side, Shahram the south, and Stephan the east."

Shahram was surprised, and his expression showed that he was pleased to be included as a full member of the team. "Thank you, Mike. I will protect my village with my life."

"It shouldn't get that far. But to be on the safe side, I want everyone to get in a full round of weapons training tomorrow. One at a time. Travis and I will accompany each of you to your stations. The rest of you will make sure that nobody wanders into the field of fire while we're training."

. . . . .

Stephan and Martin stood a few yards from each other in the village, making certain that nobody wandered into the danger zone. For previous training exercises with the weapons, Mike had taken the Americans over the next ridge, so the sounds reaching the village had been muted. On those occasions, Shahram had convened his compatriots in the village gathering place, instructing them on their roles during what amounted to a simulated attack.

The first round of fire came from above the village. The staccato sound of Mike's HK416 was followed by the intimidating explosions of several rounds from the M25. Travis had set up a small pile of scrap material behind several large rocks on the south side of the village, and even without a close examination, it was clear that the grenades had destroyed the target. Stephan used his radio to relay that information to Mike.

Each of the five members of the American unit carried a handheld Falcon III multiband radio, enabling them to communicate quickly with fully encrypted signals. Mike acknowledged Stephan's call and directed Travis to take his turn shooting. Again, those down at the village level heard an HK416. Several individual rounds followed by two three-round bursts.

Stephan had a pair of binoculars trained on the hillside on the southwest side of the village, where they had set up a target made from a 30-inch square of leftover cardboard. About half of the shots hit the target, and the others kicked up dust from the nearby rocks. Stephan was impressed by the accuracy of the shooting from 500 yards, and he reported the results by radio.

When Travis changed to the M249, the results were strikingly different. The daunting sound of automatic weapons fire was reinforced when the cardboard target disintegrated during the first burst.

"Okay, Samantha. Your turn. Everyone get ready for this one."

The sound of the M2 Browning machine gun was fearsome, even to this group who had undergone extensive weapons training. Again, a target had been placed against one of the hillsides, and within seconds, Samantha had obliterated it.

"Good shooting, Samantha. You're up Martin."

Martin and Stephan took their turns, firing a half dozen single rounds followed by several three-round bursts. Their targets had been placed next to each other, so the competition was clear. Martin scored several more hits than Stephan, and when it was over, he flashed a grin at his senior companion.

Mike was back on the radio. "Good job, guys. I can see it clearly from here with my scope. Let's give Shahram a turn. Martin, you get him to join you and then wait while Travis and I scramble back to join you. About five minutes and then he can wrap it all up."

It was nearly ten minutes by the time Travis got back.

"Sorry, it took me a couple extra minutes to get the right camo over the SAW." He was using the acronym for a *squad automatic weapon* to describe the M249.

"Where's Shahram?" Mike directed his question to Stephan.

"He's coming now with Martin. Something's not right."

A wave of concern passed through the group.

Mike tried to keep the mood upbeat. "How about it, Shahram. Why don't you take a turn? Your target is over there. Just about two hundred yards. Two hundred meters, I guess."

"I no longer require any practice. Not now."

"I don't get it."

"I have had my practice."

"I still don't understand." Mike looked at the others, but none seemed to have any knowledge of what was happening.

"It is Tohir," Shahram said. "As you instructed, I have watched him closely since he returned to the village yesterday. He seemed normal, and all his explanations were reasonable. He brought us meat from his hunting, and he helped with the work this morning. But when the shooting began, he became very agitated. I told him to remain in the gathering place, but he ran outside. He was at the edge of the hill, so most likely you could not see him. When Samantha fired the larger machine gun, he fled rapidly. It was clear. It was everything we feared."

Martin's expression was a combination of surprise and anxiety.

"Then we must go after him, Shahram. He's going to alert the attackers to our plans."

Shahram shook his head. "No, Martin. It is why I do not need to practice with my rifle. You could not hear, because Samantha was also shooting. I learned that this rifle can shoot well, and I can aim it well. It is something Tohir also learned."

• • • • •

That evening, Samantha and Martin sat on cushions in front of the hearth in the living area of their dwelling. They had just finished their dinner and were sipping cups of tea.

"Martin …?" Her voice was hesitant.

"Yeah?"

"I'm afraid. Of what's going to happen."

"You mean, when they come? I guess I am, too. I think we'd be idiots if we weren't afraid."

"Yeah. But that isn't what I meant. I was thinking about the longer term. Afterwards. After we get the Warlord."

"I don't think we'll be the ones who get him. He probably won't be part of the force that comes after us. It will only be some of his men."

"I always hoped he'd be there, too. You have no idea how many times I've seen his face when I pulled the trigger on my rifle. I think it's why my shooting is so good."

"I understand. In some of the hardest times, those same thoughts were all that kept me going. These are the people that wiped out my family. My father, my brother, my grandmother, my aunt, my uncle, my cousin. All of them."

"You mean cousins, right? The girl and the little boy."

His face went completely blank. "Yeah. Cousins. Plural. That's why I know I could kill these bastards now."

"There's something I don't understand."

"What's that?"

"What you said a minute ago … that the Warlord wouldn't be part the attacking force. If we never expected the Warlord to come after us in this village, why are we here? I always thought it we were trying to lure him here so we could kill him."

"I think it's more complicated. In my training, they told me that his organization, the KFB, has been getting smaller. That he hoped it would grow if his terrorist attacks were successful. But they weren't successful, so now we have a chance to fight back and make him even less of a threat. It's just like a regular war."

"So we kill them, and we don't let them kill us."

"That's a big part of it. But there's more. In part, our posting here to the village is a diversion. If he thinks we're the main threat — or even the only threat — it will help Andrea with the operation she's setting up."

"I guess that makes sense."

She paused.

"Martin …?"

"Yeah?"

"What about later? Will it ever be the same?"

"In what way?"

"With us. I've never felt the same way about anyone else. Before all this happened, we had plans. Or at least we were starting to make plans."

"I know. It's part of what the Warlord took from us."

"But we could get some of it back? We're both still alive. And we're together. We tell people we're married, even though it's not true."

"I'd like it to work out, Samantha. I really would. But we don't even know if we'll be alive next week. It's all so …"

She turned to him. "I want to be close to you."

He reached for her and pulled her to him. His hand slid beneath her clothing, and her sudden gasp surprised them both.

"Come to me tonight, Samantha. In my bed. At least for tonight. Be my wife, and let me be your husband."

* * *

Astana, Kazakhstan, November 4

Anja sat in a chair watching CNN in Andrea Chang's room at the Ramada Plaza Astana. They had adjoining rooms on the 12th floor, so they were able to stay in close contact while maintaining a reasonable level of privacy.

Anja stood and walked to the other side of the room, where she parted the curtains and looked out at the cloudy sky. Then she returned to her chair and changed the channel.

"Try to relax, Anja. I know it's tough, but it doesn't help to pace around."

"I know. It's just that we've been cooped up here for almost a week. I'm going stir crazy."

"We all are. But it's part of the job." Chang was referring to other members of the team who were staying nearby at the Empire Hotel in anticipation of Ghazi's arrival."

"At least I've been getting some practice. It's good that Canterbury's old friend put me on their list of contract employees. I've had one a day for the last three days. I'm getting a lot more comfortable with it, especially with different languages and stuff. Nobody said anything to make me think I was incompetent or that I seemed out of place. And I think I give a pretty decent massage now. One of the clients even told me he was very pleased with it. And that's with no funny stuff at all."

"That's good. Being relaxed and confident is going to help when the time comes."

"I know that, Andrea. I just wish it would get here."

"Any time now. It could have been yesterday, but it wasn't. Likely today, but almost certainly by tomorrow. Derek and Neela are both in place. Derek is assessing his gear, and our two local assets are helping him with the tests. He sent me a text before that indicates it's all working fine."

"And Neela? I still worry that the Warlord could recognize her."

"You haven't seen her. One of our people stationed at the embassy helped her with her appearance. She's an attractive young woman, but you'd never know it. She's registered as a representative for an entrepreneur from Turkey, and she speaks Kazakh with a Turkish accent. She has a real gift for languages, so that's step one. Then her clothing and her hair just add to the picture. Absolutely frumpy. She looks like those pictures we used to see of women during the Soviet era. Worst haircut I've ever seen, and glasses like Coke bottles. Plus, she walks around all stoop-shouldered. No man would ever give her a second look. No woman either. She's just too blah. Makes her almost invisible."

"As long as she doesn't have to confront him ... and talk to him."

"I'll grant you that, Anja. But in the remote chance that he somehow gets near her, one of our other people will break in quickly. Her only assignment is to identify him when he arrives. Any time someone shows up at the Empire who's remotely close to his description, she's going to be on her way through the lobby. Either going in or out, but she'll pass through. The hotel staff has already become familiar with this strange young woman who has a lot of business meetings."

• • • • •

Half an hour later, Anja reached for the TV remote again, as CNN began repeating a news cycle she had already seen twice. Before she could change the channel, Chang's encrypted phone rang. Quickly, Anja she hit the mute button, and the CNN anchor continued his news report in silence.

Anja couldn't make out the details of the conversation from what Chang said, but as soon as the call was finished, Chang turned to her and spoke.

"He's here. And Neela is absolutely positive that it's him. Registered under the name of Semyon Ignatiev."

"I know that name."

"Right. Ghazi is continuing with his same stupid tricks. Using other people's names. Ignatiev was a long-time Soviet politician. He was head of the secret police for a while under Stalin. He's probably been dead for thirty or forty years."

"Do we know where he is at the Empire?"

"He came as one of a party of four. They've got four rooms total. On the fifth, eighth, and ninth floors. The two on the ninth are adjoining, and one of them is a suite. The one on the eighth floor is also a suite."

"Any hope of just busting in and grabbing him?"

"Not a chance, Anja. We're going to need you. You're sure you can do it?"

"Yeah. He won't be any worse than some of the other clients I've had in the past few weeks. Especially if I'm really nice to him."

"Let's hope so. But don't get overconfident. That's not a good thing in our business."

"I'll be careful. We just have to hope he's in the mood for a massage."

They didn't have to wait long. Fifteen minutes later, they heard the telephone ring in Anja's room. Anja jumped up and bolted through the connecting door to answer. During a brief conversation, she gave Chang a thumbs-up.

"Four o'clock this afternoon. Shit! It's happening, Andrea. It's for real. That's only an hour from now. I need to shower and get ready."

"Did they give you a room number?"

"No. He's being cagey, just like we expected. I'm supposed to call Mr. Ignatiev through the hotel switchboard when I'm ready."

"Okay, let's move. I'll have your 'sister-in-law' come by to pick you up in thirty minutes. It's only a block away, but I want everyone to get used to the traffic patterns. You'll be at the Empire with plenty of time to put your coat in the employee's locker room, or whatever they call it."

"What about the stuff from Derek?"

"He's sending over the device now. It's sewn into the handle of the carrying case that has your massage oil and stuff. Shouldn't be any problem at all."

· · · · ·

Almost an hour had passed after Anja left her room in the Ramada Plaza, and Chang was in Davenport's room at the Empire, ostensibly for a business meeting. He had taken a suite in preparation for such meetings, and this meeting included Neela and the two agents who were based at the embassy in Astana.

Chang ended her call and put her phone on the table.

"The embassy says the helicopter crew is ready. They only need one or two minutes after we call them."

She pointed out the window.

"And you can see down there, that our people have cleared the space we need in that parking lot. Where is she now, Derek?"

"She's on the move." Davenport was tracing his finger along one of his computer screens. "All they told her on the phone was to go to the fifth floor. That someone would meet her when she got off the elevator."

"We know which room they have on the fifth floor," one of the local agents said. "Are we absolutely certain that we can't just go up there and grab him now?"

"It's not an option," Andrea answered. "We have no idea if he's actually in that room or if they'll take her to one of their rooms on a different floor. For all we know, there could even be another room we don't even know about."

"Yeah, I guess so. This really sucks."

Davenport started to get excited. "She's stopped. She's on the fifth floor. Look."

He paused. "Hold it, she's moving again … sixth floor … wait a second. The elevator has stopped again … somewhere between the fifth and sixth floors."

After thirty seconds, the tension in the room had nearly reached the breaking point. "It's moving again," Davenport said. "But something's fishy. She got off on the seventh floor. They don't have a room on the seventh."

"And that's our floor," Neela said.

The two local agents looked at each other. One of them said, "I think it's time for me to go down to the lobby and buy a newspaper. If they do have a room on this floor, I can't just go snooping around. They'd spot me in a minute."

He took a room key from Davenport and walked through the main door of the suite. Everyone waited in nervous silence for nearly five minutes, until they heard the door click open once more.

"What did you find?" Chang demanded.

"Her bag. It was placed neatly underneath the little side table across from the elevator."

"Did you check it?"

"I didn't go near it. If someone was watching, they would have seen me. And Anja would be dead."

"So, where is she?" Neela asked. "Eighth floor? Ninth floor?"

Chang knew the answer to that question.

"We have no fucking idea."

· · · · ·

Just after 5:30 that afternoon, the telephone in Davenport's room rang. The room was filled with the stink of nervous sweat, and nobody had spoken in more than twenty minutes. There was nothing to say.

Davenport pushed the button for speakerphone and answered with a simple "Yes."

A woman's voice responded. "Oh, I'm sorry. I must have dialed the wrong number. I was trying to call my sister-in-law."

The line went dead.

Chang said aloud what everyone was thinking. "She's okay."

Davenport picked up his secure phone and pushed a button for one of his saved numbers. After a moment, he spoke a single phrase.

"She's ready for pickup."

"You need to get back and talk to her, Andrea."

Chang's voice was icy. "I know what I have to do, Neela. But we have to maintain security. There can't be any connection between her leaving and my departure. I'll go in five minutes."

· · · · ·

At six o'clock, Chang heard the click of the door to Anja's room. The connecting door between their rooms was open, and Anja appeared a moment later. Chang resisted an overwhelming urge to embrace her. Instead she offered nothing more than a neutral request.

"Come on in and tell me about it."

Anja swallowed hard and nodded. "Got anything decent in your minibar?"

Chang withdrew a half-liter bottle of Snow Queen vodka. "Might as well do this Russian style. Whatever is going on, we aren't on the clock anymore today."

She poured two small glasses, and handed one to Anja.

"Cheers," she said, and each drained her glass in a single swallow. There was silence for another ten seconds.

"That was really fucked up," Anja said. "Scared the shit out of me."

"Did they hurt you?"

"No, nothing physical. Mostly just scared me. I got off the elevator like they told me, on the fifth floor. Two men were in the hallway waiting for me."

"What happened then?"

"They pushed me back onto the elevator. They pushed the button that keeps the elevator stopped. One of them took my carrying case. The other was very polite, almost apologetic. He said he had to search me."

Chang shuddered, and the distaste showed on her face.

"It wasn't that bad, Andrea. Not much different than a pat-down at the airport. Except it was a guy, and I was just wearing lingerie under the robe. You know he was getting his jollies."

"But he was satisfied? And he didn't check the case?"

"There was nothing to find on me, and they didn't seem to care about the case. They just stopped at another floor and stuck it in the elevator lobby there. They told me I could pick it up again after. I asked about my massage oils and they said not to worry about it. Later, they told me it was the seventh floor."

"And what room did you go to, Anja?"

"I couldn't tell. It was above the seventh, but I couldn't see which. They put some kind of a hat on me that came down over my eyes. So I don't know which room. I don't even know which floor."

"Shit! That's unfortunate. What happened next?"

"Almost exactly what we planned on. And he was even more polite than I expected. Toward the end of the massage, he made it clear that he'd like a little more, but I told him that I didn't do that with my clients the first time I met them."

"He bought it?"

"Yeah. It kind of surprised me. Even better, he said there should be a second time. I can't be sure I remember his exact words, but I'll try."

Anja spoke in Kazakh, attempting to reproduce Ghazi's demeanor, if not the specific words.

I will be here two more days. Not tomorrow, but the next day. At the same time. We shall use the same procedures.

"I think we can get this motherfucker, Andrea."

"Then we need a better way to track you. We had no idea where you were for more than an hour, today."

"The transmitter has to be something I can wear. Either on my body or my clothing."

"We'll meet with Derek and the others tomorrow morning. We'll figure out something."

* * *

Abdurrahim, Tajikistan, November 5

Travis climbed down from the makeshift ladder and looked over at Mike. "We're almost done with these houses. I wish we had a couple of cold ones to celebrate."

"It'd be nice, but we would have had to bring them with us. And the truck was full, so we'd have had to leave something else behind. With the visitors we're expecting, I'd rather have the guns and ammo."

"I suppose. But I'd still like a beer."

Mike laughed. "Couple more weeks and we should be with friendlies. Then you can drink as much as you want. For now, we got to stay cool."

"Yeah, I guess. Let's get back to work."

Less than two hours later, Mike was talking with Martin and Stephan, when Mike's laptop emitted a series of beeps. Stephan looked at him quizzically.

"That's my TIGR system. I told you about it. *Tactical Intelligence Ground Reporting.* One of the sensors has a hit."

The three men crowded around the laptop as Mike brought up a 3-D map of the region. To the northeast of the village, a red dot was flashing.

"What is it?" Martin asked.

"Can't be sure yet. Something is moving on that trail. Could just be an animal, but there's a camera a little farther down the path."

He clicked an icon at the top of the screen, and a second window opened in the top right corner. All that was visible was a group of rocks.

"It'll be about a minute," Mike assured them.

They saw the motion at the same time. Just a blur at first, but then a human figure was visible. Then another. Then three more. As quickly as they had appeared, they moved beyond the narrow range of the camera."

"I count five," Martin said.

Mike nodded. "I think so. Could have been only four, though. We're pushing the limits of our video resolution with the placement of that unit. But we know they're coming."

"But we know they're on foot. And no big weapons."

"None that we can see. No way to be sure they don't have more people at a distance bringing up the rear. But we don't have the luxury of sitting around to watch. I'll get Travis. Stephan, let Shahram know it's happening. Martin, you tell Samantha to get to the truck. Everyone needs to be in place in three minutes, and be sure all your radios are turned on. If things start happening before Travis and I reach our positions, make sure you provide covering fire. Now, let's move!"

• • • • •

Nothing happened for the next fifteen minutes. Then the silence was broken. A whooshing sound was immediately followed by an explosion. Only fifty feet beyond Shahram's location, a wooden cart had been obliterated.

Mike's voice came over their receivers. "That was an RPG. We start shooting in twenty seconds, or they'll get to a place where they could score a hit on the village. I'll give the signal. Ten … nine …"

When Mike called "zero," the entire village and its surroundings erupted in a tumult of gunfire and the larger explosions of grenades. In accord with their plans, Mike had waited until the group of attackers reached a point that would be directly in the sights of Samantha's Browning machine gun. Travis and Mike could see what they hoped were the trailing members of the attacking group. As soon as Samantha opened fire, Travis unleashed a fusillade from the M249, and Mike fired several 25-millimeter grenades programmed to burst just behind the attackers bringing up the rear.

In accord with their orders, the defenders ceased firing after twenty seconds. Samantha and Travis had each fired four bursts of several seconds each, pausing long enough between bursts to sight in on anything that was still moving. The machine guns fired between nine and fifteen rounds per second, and they couldn't risk overheating the barrels.

Everything was silent again until Mike's voice barked over the handhelds. "All okay up here. Travis?"

"I'm okay."

"Samantha?" Mike called the names of each member of the team in succession, and each responded positively.

"Looks like we waxed those bastards. But we wait ten minutes. Keep your eyes peeled."

Within five minutes, nerves were fraying. Shahram stood and spoke into his radio.

"I am going to check on the others in the community building. I must be sure they are all right."

Two things followed more or less simultaneously. Just as Mike yelled at him to get down and stay in place, Shahram twisted and fell forward against the wall he had been crouching behind.

Stephan was the first to react. He turned and brought up his HK416 carbine, yelling into his radio that lay on the ground next to him.

"We're taking fire from the west! Shahram is hit."

"Fuck!" Mike yelled. "They had a second unit and we missed it."

Then he called out his orders. "Stephan. You lay down fire. Make sure they don't get any closer. Travis, you and Samantha get ready to fire in that direction. Martin, you check on Shahram, but stay out of the line of fire. I can't see the western approach from here, but I'm maintaining my position. We have to keep watching the northern approach until we're sure we got everyone that came that way."

Stephan fired several three-round bursts in the general direction from which the shots must have come. Meanwhile, Martin crept closer to Shahram.

"Shahram, are you okay? Can you hear me?"

He heard Shahram groan weakly and saw the spreading red stain on the village leader's upper body. He set his carbine down and sprinted the last fifteen feet, dropping to the ground when he reached him. Remaining in a crouch, he began dragging Shahram to safety. He was pulling sideways, trying to get behind a building that would shield them. Three more rounds hit the wall just behind them. The attacker had not fled.

Samantha and Travis fired bursts from their automatic weapons, but a rock outcropping prevented them from scoring a hit. Martin told Shahram to lie still and crawled to where he had set down his carbine. He picked it up and spoke into his radio.

"I saw where the shots came from. I'm going to move to the south to get a clear shot. Give me some cover!"

Mike responded. "Move fast and stay low. Travis, Samantha, and Stephan: the second you see Martin move, fire short bursts. Keep this guy pinned down."

Martin dove behind a low mud-brick wall at the south end of the village. He knew that there were some low rocks that would obscure the attacker's view, and he crawled a dozen feet farther. He checked his rifle to be sure the barrel was clear, inserted a new clip, and set it for a three-round. Slowly, he raised his head until he could just see above the wall. Moving as little as possible. Any motion would make him a target.

There he is! He's scanning the village with his rifle, and he doesn't see me.

He rested the carbine on the wall to steady his aim and slowly brought the attacker into his sights. Just as he centered on his target, Martin saw the attacker move his own rifle. They were aiming at each other.

Martin had begun his careful squeeze of the trigger. He heard the sound of a mosquito flying past his head, but he knew it wasn't a mosquito. It was a bullet, and if it was close enough to be audible, he was in trouble. As these thoughts were going through his head, a second bullet hit the mud-brick wall, kicking sand and dirt into the side of his face. Only then did he realize that he had already fired his burst. He saw his target lurch to the side and fall a dozen feet down the hill.

Martin pulled the handheld from his pocket. "He's hit. He's down."

"Is he the only one?" came Mike's response.

"Don't know! But I can't see anyone else.

"Everybody stay put. We're starting the ten-minute clock over again."

"I'll stay low, but I've got to check on Shahram," Stephan yelled.

"All right. Check in as soon as you get to him."

Stephan crouched low and moved behind one of the small buildings, approaching Shahram's location from a safe direction. The man lay motionless on his side, and he was unresponsive when Stephan turned him onto his back.

"I've reached him. I can't tell how bad it is, but he's unconscious. I've got to cut off some of his clothing to check the wound."

Several minutes later, Stephan spoke into the radio again. "It doesn't look that bad. His shoulder's messed up, but it looks like the bullet passed completely through. Definitely didn't hit any internal organs, and it seems like it missed the big bones. There's not that much damage. I've pretty much stopped the bleeding, and I'm giving the basic first aid for shock."

"Okay, Stephan. It's all quiet, so I'm thinking we're in the clear. Five more minutes and we all come in. I'll keep an eye on the TIGR alerts. Travis, you meet me on the trail to the north, so we can check for wounded and make sure there isn't someone up there hiding. Martin, you do the same thing for the guy you took out. At the very least, secure his weapons. We'll all get together and talk about it in about a half hour."

• • • • •

The six members of the team had gathered in Shahram's home, where they were joined by Shahram's son. It was crowded, but Shahram could not be moved. Although morphine made his pain bearable, he needed rest.

Mike and Travis had surprised the others with their skill as medics, cleaning Shahram's wound and treating him with antibiotics. They declared that his injuries weren't life-threatening, even in harsh conditions of their remote location.

Mike reported on the attackers from the northern approach.

"We got their weapons. There were five of them. All dead. Not surprising, when you consider what we were firing at them. What about you, Martin?"

"Same thing. Just the one. He was dead. I was lucky to get him in my sights before he shot me."

"It was good shooting," Mike replied. "I'd have you on my team anytime."

"You saved my life."

Although Shahram's voice was subdued, it conveyed strength. He looked at the others.

"All of you have saved our village. We owe you great thanks."

He nodded to his daughter-in-law, who had brought tea for his guests. She picked up an ornate cup and poured tea into it. Martin remembered it from the time he had visited the village five years earlier. It was his uncle's cup.

His favorite.

Shahram motioned for her to give it to his son, who in turn carried it to where Martin sat.

In a remarkable act of humility, Shahram's son knelt before Martin and handed him the cup. Martin demurred.

"This cup should go to your father. He is the leader of the village."

The son replied with emotion. "He has spoken with me, and he asked me to do this. He asked me to give you this cup. It is for you, Patriarch."

* * *

Astana, Kazakhstan, November 6

Anja knocked on the door that connected her room and Andrea Chang's. It was 2:00 p.m., the time they had agreed on.

Chang opened the door and spoke in a reassuring voice. "Come in, Anja. Have you been able to rest?"

"Yeah. A little."

"What about food. Have you had anything since breakfast?"

"No."

"You need to eat. You know that."

"Yeah."

"Okay, let's sit down. We need to talk about this."

Anja sat on the sofa, and Chang took a chair on the opposite side of the coffee table.

"Scared?"

"I guess."

"It's not surprising. You really put yourself out there on Wednesday. There were some surprises, but you handled them like a pro. Now it's almost over. Once more this afternoon and it's finished."

"You're assuming that Derek will come up with something for a tracking device."

"You've known him almost as long as I have. He's the best. He'll have something when he gets here."

Chang's comments were interrupted by a soft knock on the door.

"That should be him now." She checked the peephole on the door to the hallway, nodded, and unlocked the door. Davenport walked in, his mood subdued. He smiled hesitantly at Anja.

"Hey. I got some stuff for you, and I think you'll like it."

He opened a nylon bag and extracted the robe Anja had worn two days earlier. He tossed it across the couch, and she caught it with one hand.

"Try this on."

She looked at him with a look that was almost impish. "If you think I'm going to strip down so you can see me in the robe, you've got another think coming."

"Of course not," Davenport replied. "I mean, not with Andrea sitting right here."

Chang was glad that Davenport's simple playfulness had snapped Anja out of her funk. Caution was needed, but her team had to be in top form in only a few hours.

"That's enough!" she said. "We've got serious work to do here. Derek, show us what's up."

Anja had been examining the robe.

"It looks just like it did yesterday."

Davenport smiled. "Bingo. But take a close look at the button on the sash. We'll know exactly where you are today."

He stopped when he heard a knock on the door.

"That's the rest of the team," Chang said. "Right on time."

She went to the door, once again checking to see who had knocked. She opened the door and ushered them in.

"Derek, show them what we're working with."

Davenport started at the beginning with his description of the sash.

"The best part is that it's passive. They could scan this baby a million times and never find it. It only emits a signal when it's interrogated with the right frequency and the right coded interrogation signal."

"How close do you have to be to track the button?" Chang asked.

"Obviously, the closer the better, but we've got that problem solved. I've installed an interrogator chip in each of the elevators as a first step. And we've tested it. I can sit in my room at the Empire and watch the elevators go up and down on my screen. I can find the sash no matter which elevator it's in."

"And when she leaves the elevator?" Chang continued her probing.

"We know our guys have rooms on floors five, eight, and nine. And we know which rooms. I've been able to install the same type of interrogator near the doorways of rooms that are either one floor up or one below each of the possible locations. Since I was on a different floor, it means none of our targets had any chance to see me doing it. And it wasn't a big installation. I just fastened it in a molding where it was hidden by a curtain or the edge of a carpet. Now that we've deployed several of these chips, we get full three-dimensional tracking."

"How do you know it's going to work? Anja hasn't been there yet."

"Good question, Andrea. We tested it by putting a button on one of the housekeeping carts to verify that we could see it moving around the eighth floor. Same thing for the ninth floor. We didn't want to go there ourselves in case our friends are watching. But we could see the housekeepers making their way up and down the hallway. Works like a dream."

Chang nodded seriously.

"Okay, so we've solved the problem of tracking Anja. What about grabbing the Warlord?"

One of the other agents answered the question.

"As soon as Anja leaves his room and gets on the elevator, we move in. We'll be on the seventh floor, and we'll use the stairwell. We can get there quickly, no matter which floor they take Anja to. We go in with force. Anybody gives us any shit, they're dead. That includes Ghazi. But the plan is to incapacitate him and get him out of the hotel."

"The original plan, right?" Chang asked.

"Exactly. As soon as we clear the room with Ghazi — or without him if that's how it turns out — we send the message for the SUV to meet us at the hotel entrance. We'll be out of there in two minutes and boarding the plane less than ten minutes after that. Smooth as silk."

• • • • •

"Ninth floor. She's in the room. It's working perfectly. You can see her moving around. I can almost see her doing the massage."

Davenport stopped speaking, recognizing that he was too close to saying something inappropriate.

Twenty minutes later, a puzzled expression crossed Davenport's face.

"What is it?" Chang asked.

"She stopped moving around. It's almost like she took off the robe and dropped it on the floor."

Chang rolled her eyes. The others remained silent.

Davenport said, "Oh."

Fifteen minutes passed. Very slowly.

"I'm starting to get nervous," Chang said.

"It's only five minutes longer than Wednesday. Maybe this time it's just a little more ... involved?"

"I hope you're right, Derek."

The telephone on the desk rang, and Davenport picked it up nervously. He said nothing, listening silently to the caller. His face took on a vacant look, his eyes glazed over. Then he hung up without a word.

"They're gone."

"What the fuck are you talking about, Derek? What do you mean they're gone?"

"That was Canterbury's contact at the hotel, Andrea. The assistant manager. She said that she thought I'd want to know. That the people we were interested left the hotel. About ten minutes ago."

"All four men?"

"Yeah. And she said there was a woman with them."

* * *

Astana, Kazakhstan, November 10

The small room at the U.S. Embassy in Astana was quiet. Only an occasional muffled sound penetrated the closed door. The office had been assigned to Andrea Chang for the active phase of Operation Gray Ghost. Chang looked at Davenport, then at Neela, then back at her hands folded on the desk. Nobody made a sound until finally, Chang spoke.

"It was a very unpleasant conversation. They're extremely angry."

"Not everybody," Davenport said in a tone that suggested he didn't quite believe his own words. "They can't all be. Hashan and Canterbury ... and Alford. They've got to understand. Sometimes shit happens. That doesn't make it your fault, Andrea."

Her look could have frozen Davenport's coffee. "Nice of you to say that Derek, but this isn't horseshoes. Close doesn't count. And the point is, Alford may understand, but he still had to report it up the chain. I got the sense that the news has gone all the way up."

"To the Director?" Neela asked.

"No, across the Potomac. To the House and Senate leaders, and probably to the President."

"But why? Their biggest concern was that we would do something to cause an international incident. And that didn't happen. The Kazakh government, city officials, even our own people here in the embassy — none of them have any idea what we were doing. We've kept a lid on the whole operation."

"That's not the point, Derek. They're mad as hell because we've got a CIA agent who's gone fucking missing. They've booked us on tomorrow's flight back. If we don't get new information by tonight, we're being sent home."

"That sucks."

"Yeah, it does."

• • • • •

The office was silent. Chang had nothing more to say, and the others knew better than to say anything. All they could do was wait, although nobody knew what they were waiting for. They tried to kill time by writing drafts of the after-action reports they would each have to submit.

Thirty minutes passed. The telephone on Chang's desk rang, and she answered. She spoke quietly. Just an occasional "yes," a periodic "no," and several monosyllabic grunts that had no obvious meaning.

Part way through the conversation, Davenport saw her cringe, as if from a physical blow. Her shoulders sagged, and all expression disappeared from her face. She was silent until she uttered a final "yes," and hung up the phone.

Andrea looked up. "They got a package. It was addressed to me. Here at the embassy."

A long pause. "There was a note. Just one sentence. It said 'The wolf is most dangerous in winter.' No signature."

"It's not winter yet," Neela said. "Is it a warning?"

Davenport interrupted. "What was …?"

He hesitated. All three of them knew what he was going to ask. What he had to ask.

"What was in the package?"

"A finger."

Silence again. It lasted ten seconds.

"Do they have an identification?"

"They told me they would have a fingerprint analysis this afternoon. That they could get a DNA comparison by tomorrow."

They stared at each other. Three silent figures in a silent room.

"There's something else," Chang said in a voice that was barely audible.

"The finger. It had a tattoo of a snake."

* * *

21

Postmortem

It frequently happens that a Postmortem Examination is conducted under circumstances which render it extremely difficult to put on record a faithful history of all that is really desirable or even necessary to be known.

W. P. Cocks, 1832[*]

Langley, Virginia, November 12

Alford and Canterbury walked side by side along a path on the outskirts of CIA headquarters.

"This is truly fucked up, Allan. I know it isn't your fault, but we're taking flak from all directions. The director is pissed, and he said the President is mad as hell. It's my understanding that the heads of the House and Senate intelligence committees are getting ready to go public."

"God Almighty, Bob! They can't do that. Everything about this is classified."

"Sure it is, but it won't stop them from trying to cover their asses. It isn't every day we lose one of our agents, and they need to hang someone out to dry. And they want to make sure it isn't one of them."

"But they've got to consider the ramifications. Aside from disclosing classified information, they'd also be jumping the gun. So far, we don't know what's really happened to her."

---

[*] "Forms for Facilitating the Records of Post Mortem Appearances," W. P. Cocks, Longman, Rees, and Co., London, 1832.

Canterbury saw the look of cold resignation on Alford's face, and he paused momentarily.

"Look, I know it's a long shot. Everything we've learned about Ghazi suggests that he's killed her. But Christ, they've got to at least let us confirm it before they start leaking to the media."

Alford's face remained grim, and Canterbury realized there was something more.

"What is it?"

"This is why I wanted you to go for a walk with me. I didn't want anyone watching us, or even to be within earshot."

Canterbury cringed.

"We just got a message from State. The embassy in Astana has a police report."

"They found her body." It was a question.

"They found two bodies, Allan. One is Anja's. We don't have DNA yet, but a finger was missing. And someone on embassy staff did a personal identification. There's no doubt anymore."

"And the second body?"

"Another visual identification. It was the woman from the Empire hotel. Your contact. Tatiana Gruzhnova, the assistant manager."

Canterbury slumped and muttered something that Alford couldn't make out. It didn't matter. They walked in silence for several minutes.

"The Kazakh police found a note pinned to Anja's body."

Alford pulled a piece of paper from his pocket and read aloud.

```
You must now understand that Americans should not be
in Kazakhstan. Also not in Tajikistan. Nowhere in this
part of Asia. It belongs to us. We have sent warnings
to you before. In Washington and again in Boston. And
most recently in Michigan. You are fortunate that they
were not more than warnings, but you know what to
expect. Now you also know what will happen if you send
another of your incompetent spies into our midst.
```

"Was it signed?"

"Did it need to be? Nobody else knows those things, Allan. It was Ghazi. There isn't any question."

"How did he find out?"

Canterbury answered his own question, or at least he offered one of the possible explanations.

"Anja wasn't that experienced. She may have let something slip that made him suspicious. And once he took her, it was only a question of time. Christ, that means that our entire operation is blown."

"She was the only one he saw, Allan. She may have given him names, but he doesn't know what anyone else looks like. The big question is, what do we do now? If we're going to keep the big shots from going public and blowing the rest of the operation, we need to have our next steps laid out."

"You're asking me for a response plan? For God's sake, Bob! I just found out. I don't have the slightest idea what we're going to do next."

"Then that's the good news."

"What in hell are you talking about?"

"It means that Anja didn't know either. She couldn't give it up no matter how much they tortured her."

* * *

Sterling, Virginia, November 16

For the second time in a week, Allan Canterbury was walking along the edge of a wooded area in suburban Northern Virginia. This time, he was just north of the Dulles Airport Marriot Hotel. He was accompanied by Stephan Udrea.

"How was the trip?"

"A grind. Just like it always is. It seems strange to be in the States again. Especially after what happened in the mountains. It wasn't even two weeks ago. I take it that's why you called me back? For a full briefing?"

"Actually, no. It's the other part of the operation that I wanted to talk about. It isn't going that well."

"The other part."

"Yes. Our effort to zero in on the Warlord."

"With Anja, you mean."

"Yes, that's right." Canterbury's voice caught.

"What? Is she okay?"

"No. That's the problem." He paused to maintain his composure. "She's not okay. They killed her, Stephan."

Stephan looked at Canterbury with incomprehension. Then he turned on his heel and walked away.

"Stephan …"

Behind his back, Stephan waved off the question with a push of his hand. He continued walking, knowing that Canterbury would be watching. It wasn't a question of being rude. It was simply the need to be by himself for a time. He resisted the urge to scream, or to smash his fist into the side of a tree, or even to just kick at a rock. None of it would help. It was a cold day, and he could feel the warm tears running down his cheeks.

He didn't understand his emotions. It wasn't just sadness, and it was more than anger. He only knew that it was visceral. He turned back toward Canterbury.

"I want to get that bastard, Allan."

"So do I."

The walked in silence for a few minutes.

"Tell me what happened."

"We don't know, Stephan. It seemed to be going okay. Not too different from what was planned. She made contact with him for a massage. That seemed to work all right, and he made a second appointment for two days later. That was Sunday. Almost two weeks ago. We had all the tracking in place, and everything seemed to be in order. We expected her to be out of contact for a little over an hour, and we didn't start to get concerned until after her tracking device stopped moving. That's when we got the phone call."

"The phone call." It was a question.

"Yes. Our contact at the hotel. The assistant manager. Someone I knew from years ago. She called Davenport's room, where the monitoring team was. She told him that they had left the hotel. And they took Anja with them. They left her robe and her carrying case behind, and that's where the tracking devices were. So we had no hint."

Stephan had a thousand questions, but none that he was willing to ask.

"I'm sorry," Canterbury said.

"It's what we signed up for."

They walked a few more steps.

"Jesus, Allan. A week ago, two weeks ago, I'm not sure. I was working with Martin and the other two guys, and we were in a firefight. We killed all six of them. It was probably the same day he was killing Anja."

"The day before, to be accurate."

"Doesn't matter. But I want to get him, Allan. I really want to kill that motherfucker."

"We will, Stephan. It's not going to be easy, but we are going to get him."

"How?"

"I don't know yet. Andrea is due back from Astana tonight. We'll talk to her tomorrow and start putting together a plan."

* * *

Langley, Virginia, November 17

"How did he know?" The question came from Andrea.

Canterbury turned to Stephan with an inquisitive look.

"Maybe it was our trip to the Patriarch's village. Somehow the Warlord found out. Made the link."

"That's bullshit!" Chang was agitated. "If anything, your presence in the village was a diversion. He sent a team up to kill you and Martin and everyone else of importance. It had nothing to do with Anja."

"I didn't mean the trip last month, Andrea. I'm talking about when Anja and I went there two years ago. Remember, I met with Colonel Kholdorov a month later, and I told the colonel I thought the Patriarch knew something about the missing uranium. Then a few weeks later, the Patriarch was killed."

"What's your point?" Chang asked.

"I think my conversation with Kholdorov was conveyed to the Warlord. And he assassinated the Patriarch because he knew too much. We were getting too close."

Chang shook her head.

"Maybe Ghazi killed the Patriarch, but he knew the Patriarch. Even if you hadn't talked to Kholdorov, the Patriarch might have been taken out. We sure as hell know the Warlord killed other people when they presented some sort of a threat. He killed the whole fucking Sulley family."

"That's exactly my point, Andrea."

Chang's frustration showed.

"Anja was different. She wasn't one of the Warlord's collaborators, unwittingly or otherwise. You're grasping at straws, Stephan. It's too much of a stretch."

"Too much of a stretch? Anja's dead! You think that's a fucking stretch?"

Canterbury interrupted. He spoke quietly.

"Let's take it down a notch. We're not here to blame anyone, and we don't need to get angry with each other. We have to work together to figure out our next steps."

He looked at Stephan. "Tell us a little more about how you think your visit to the Patriarch ultimately might have made Ghazi suspicious of Anja."

"There were several people who had seen me with Anja in the past. The colonel, for one. And people in the Patriarch's village. And don't forget, I made two visits total. The one we're talking about was two years ago this spring. The other was two years earlier. When I was first posted to Dushanbe. Anja came with me both times."

"You think the Patriarch somehow told the Warlord about her?"

"I don't think he would have done that, Andrea. He liked her. But there was a spy in the village."

"Why would her presence have been significant?" Canterbury asked.

"Not her presence during those past visits. Her absence from the group this last month. The traitor in the village, his name was Tohir, it's all in my written report. He knew we were setting up a defensive perimeter, and he disappeared for a couple of days. It was pretty clear he got a message to the Warlord. Tohir remembered me from before. He also knew Martin from when he visited the Patriarch with his brother."

"You think he alerted the Warlord to Martin's presence in the village? And yours?"

"I do. I think it was the main reason for the attack on the village. The Warlord already tried to kill Martin with the rest of his family."

"Have you interrogated the spy?"

"No. He's dead. He tried to run away, and the village leader shot him."

"But before that. Before the attack, he would have had the opportunity to send a message telling the Warlord about Martin's presence?"

"We're reasonably sure of it, Andrea. Shahram, the village leader, told me the man had disappeared once before in the same way. It was just before the Patriarch was killed. It was no coincidence that it happened again. Tohir would have passed the information that there were five Americans. He recognized Martin, and he recognized me. And the last time he saw me, I was with Anja. He would have passed on that information. He would have given the Warlord her physical description."

"We should have thought of that," Canterbury said. "We were so anxious to reach the Warlord, we never considered that possibility."

"If anyone should have thought of it, it was me. I'm the one that went to the village with her. But we trusted Anja to bring it off."

"Don't try to pin the blame on her. It wasn't her fucking fault," Chang said.

"That's not what I meant …"

Davenport interrupted. "We all know it wasn't her fault, Andrea. I should have done better with the monitoring."

He'd only gotten a few hours' sleep since boarding his plane in Astana. Stephan had told him he looked like shit, and he felt worse. His eyes were bleary, and nobody thought it was only from lack of sleep.

"If I'd set up my equipment better, I would have known that her carryall had been set down. That it hadn't been moved for a long time. If I'd been on top of it, Anja ..."

Hashan interrupted him. "Don't try put it on yourself, Derek. We don't need to place any blame. It was beyond our control. Maybe if we'd had a year to plan the operation, we could have thought of all the possibilities. Keep in mind why it was necessary for us to act quickly."

"David is correct," Canterbury said. "Things don't always work according to plan. But at the same time, it's always our job — my job — to make sure the bad shit happens to someone else. Not to one of our own agents. I don't fault any of you, and I'm confident that everyone on the team did their best. Turns out it just wasn't enough."

Canterbury knew full well that blame would be assessed by others, and if it came down from above, he was the one who would bear the brunt of any condemnation. He also knew he would make sure it stopped there.

"So what do we do now, David?" Chang asked. "You tasked me with leading this team, and we can't quit now. We have to find a way to get the Warlord."

"Basically, we have to start over," Canterbury said. "We don't know where he is."

Hashan spoke again. "We go back to watching and waiting. Derek, you make damn sure we see everything that might be one of his Facebook posts. We've got two agents in Astana that know about the operation now, so we'll tell them to stay alert as well."

"What do we do when we find out where he is? Or where he'll be?" Neela asked. "Don't forget that I know him. I could make the next contact."

"You wouldn't last ten minutes, Neela." Hashan's voice was harsh. "That's not a criticism of you. It's just a fact. Like you said, he knows you."

"What are you thinking of, David?" Chang asked.

"I honestly don't know at this point. It has to be something short of a military operation, although we can probably get special forces help if we can justify a surgical strike. The main thing is to come up with a plan that has an acceptable risk-benefit ratio."

Canterbury looked around the table, his gaze lingering briefly on each member of the team.

"Start thinking about it. Talk to each other. When you come up with something, we'll meet again."

* * *

22

Nousafarin

Be subtle! be subtle! and use your spies for every kind of business.

—Sun Tsu, The Art of War, 6th Century B.C.[*]

Langley, Virginia, November 25

"Let's get started, people." Chang was impatient as she took her place at the head of the table.

"I've got some important updates for you, and I don't want this meeting to last long. A couple of you have flights to catch."

Nearly the entire team had assembled in the conference room. In addition to Chang, those present were Davenport, Davis, Hashan, Hartwell, and Pomeranz. When Stephan and Canterbury walked in, only Martin and Samantha were missing. They were still in Tajikistan.

"We have a new plan. It's been approved." Chang glanced at Canterbury.

"Preliminary approval," he said.

"What is it?" Hartwell asked.

"We've identified someone we think can get to Ghazi. And we've got a plan to make him think it was his idea."

"It doesn't sound any different from the last time, and look where that got us."

"There are differences, Ash. Try listening to the proposal before you crap on it."

---

[*] "The Art of War," Sun Tsu (Sun Zi), 6th Century B.C., translated by Lionel Giles, 1910.

Chang took a deep breath and continued. "Three main differences. First, we've got better tracking technology to deploy. Not that Derek didn't have good stuff before, but this is really state of the art. Stuff they weren't willing to give us previously. Second, it will go down as a personal encounter. The Warlord is going to ask a mutual friend to introduce him to this woman. That will reduce the risk tremendously. There isn't going to be any way to make a connection to us. And third, we're talking about someone with … *experience.* This woman isn't an amateur. She knows how to seduce a man."

Hartwell was stunned.

"Are you telling us that you want to send in someone without any experience in the intel field? Someone whose only useful qualification is that she's a slut?"

Stephan turned toward Hartwell, his eyes blazing, his voice caustic. "Shut the fuck up, Ash. You don't know what you're talking about."

"Then why the hell don't you explain it to me, smartass?"

Others in the room reacted to the exchange with a mixture of annoyance and surprise. The meeting had spun out of control before Chang even realized anything was wrong.

Canterbury banged his hand hard on the table, and the noise shocked everyone into momentary silence.

He spoke softly and deliberately. "This is a matter of extraordinary sensitivity. I suggest you all remain quiet and allow Andrea to continue her explanation."

Stephan sat back in his chair, and Hartwell looked down at his hands, now folded on the table in front of him. Chang looked around, trying to make sure that no one else seemed ready to interrupt.

"The woman we're talking about is an amazing person. Her name is Nousafarin Rahmon, and she's been in this country for more than fifteen years. She's a U.S. citizen and an honest taxpayer. She also has a highly unusual background.

"She started as a victim. When she was thirteen, she was abducted from her home in Tajikistan by an international trafficking operation. They took her to Russia and forced her to work in a brothel. She was just a kid, and they kept her in that brothel for five years."

Chang knew the story well enough that reciting it had made her angry.

"In 1998, she saved Allan Canterbury's life. He was seriously injured and caught without papers on the wrong side of the Russian border. Nousafarin contacted a Russian she had met, and he provided emergency assistance. We learned subsequently that he previously had been KGB, and he arranged safe passage to the West for both Allan and Nousafarin. Neither of them had papers.

"Allan helped Nousafarin make a new home in the D.C. area, and she went to school here. College degree in art, and now she runs a gallery in Tyson's Corner. She's an amazing woman. Smart. Competent. Talented. And absolutely beautiful. Nobody in our society likes to talk about these things, but she's also a very sexual being. She has continued to see different men, and she has accepted money. In the movies, they used to call it money for the 'powder room,' and that made it okay. But it's the same thing. Nousafarin prefers the term 'courtesan.'

"I first met her about ten years ago, and she's helped us out a few times. There's no question about it. Men are like putty in her hands. Allan has kept an eye on her over the years, making sure she stays safe. Stephan has met her also. I think you can see pretty damn clearly that those of us who know Nousafarin think very highly of her."

She turned her gaze toward Hartwell and stared for several seconds. He met her eyes. Then he looked at Stephan and Canterbury in turn.

"I'm sorry. I didn't know."

They both nodded. Then Canterbury spoke.

"The decision to use her for this mission was not an easy one. We all know what happened to Anja, and now we're turning to another woman with whom some of us have close ties. True, she's not an Agency employee, but those ties are very strong. We trust her, and she trusts us. We just have to plan this operation in a way that justifies that trust. Let's work together on that."

* * *

23

Ivan

*We did not consider ourselves to be separate from
those who stayed in the FSB. We shared everything
with them and we saw our work as just another form
of serving the interests of the state.*

—*Former KGB special-forces officer, 2007*[*]

Langley, Virginia, November 30

Canterbury sat across the desk from Alford. The atmosphere
was strained.

"That's it, Allan," Alford said. "The approval is still
only tentative. I can't get you final go-ahead until you provide a
specific action plan. You've got to lay it out every step of the way."

"Is this just you, Bob? Or is it from above?"

"Doesn't really matter, does it? The simple fact is, after what
happened with Anja, we need some serious cover. If the next effort
misfires, we've got to be able to show that everything was carefully
planned, fully thought out, and thoroughly vetted. It may be bullshit,
but if something goes wrong, the Agency doesn't want to take the hit."

"But we would. Both of us. The blame would come right down to
those of us who are genuinely trying to do something."

"It's always the way, Allan. You know that."

"I do. But it's difficult enough without having to play these
authorization games."

---

[*] Igor Goloshchapov, former Major in the KGB Directorate B, in "The
Making of a Neo-KGB State," *The Economist,* August 23, 2007.

"This discussion isn't helping. Let's move on. Tell me how you plan to set it up. How are you going to arrange for her to make contact with Ghazi?"

"Do you remember the guy who helped Nousafarin and me get out of Sochi in 1998?"

"Vaguely. You weren't reporting directly to me at that time. He was Russian, right?"

"Yes. Ivan. A businessman. He acted like he was part of the new Russian mafia, but I always thought he was KGB. Obviously, not in ninety-eight, but before the Soviet collapse. There was something about the way he operated. His training showed. I think he maintained his contacts when the KGB became the FSB, even if he wasn't an active agent."

Alford nodded. "You think he can help? Could you even find him at this point? That was more than fifteen years ago."

"I've had contact with him since then. A couple of times. On one occasion, I was in Moscow, and all of a sudden he was walking next to me on the street. He came out of nowhere. 'Fancy meeting you here, Adrian,' he said. That's what I mean about how he operated. And his contacts."

"Yes. Not much doubt, is there? So what would you ask him to do for us?"

"I want him to facilitate an introduction between Ghazi and Nousafarin," Canterbury said.

"You have reason to think he might be willing to assist us?"

"I do. It all goes back to our original meeting in 1998. He saved my life. Nousafarin's too. But he was no Santa Claus. He made it clear that he was making a deal. I got back to the safety of the U.S. along with Nousafarin, and he got money. I'm not sure exactly how much, but it was a lot. The transaction was unusual, because we had never met before, and he held all the cards. But he took my word when I promised to make sure the payment was made."

Alford offered a wry smile.

"I suppose I do remember signing off on that expenditure. But it was a long time ago. Why do you think you could trust him to help now?"

"Two reasons. Remember, I told you I met him a couple of times subsequently. Once, it was that supposedly accidental encounter in Moscow. But the other time, it was a straight-up trade of information for money. He had his fingers in a lot of things, and he was able to provide some details on insurgent activity that might have affected our troops in Afghanistan. He knew about the various groups in Kazakhstan and Kyrgyzstan. The information he gave us was useful, but he made out well in the exchange. At this point, he's the one who owes the next favor."

"That's still only one reason. You said there were two."

"The second one is Nousafarin. There's a special bond between her and Ivan. He visited her regularly in the brothel in Sochi, and it seems he genuinely liked her. That speaks not so much to why he would help us as it does to why I would trust him."

"You'd better develop something a lot firmer than that," Alford said. "We can't justify this operation on the basis of your gut feelings."

"I understand. And I know what I have to do. I have to go to Moscow. I've got to meet with Ivan face to face."

Alford put his elbows on the desk and rested his chin on his hands. He said nothing as he processed the information. Finally, he spoke.

"You've been out of the field for too long. I don't want you going by yourself."

"Who?" Canterbury asked.

"Rachel Pomeranz. Her language skills are outstanding. She acquitted herself very well last year with that Orlov stuff."

"But she isn't a field agent. It wouldn't answer your objection to my going alone."

"You have a better suggestion?"

Canterbury wasn't sure if Alford was leading him or simply letting him offer an alternative. He decided it didn't matter, and the answer came quickly.

"Stephan Udrea."

"Why Udrea?"

"He has good language skills, and you couldn't ask for more recent field experience."

"And ...?"

Canterbury was certain he was following rather than leading. But he could do nothing other than provide the answer.

"And he also cares about Nousafarin."

"No doubt, Allan. And he also wants to get the Warlord just as much as any of us. Maybe more. Just make certain that his emotions don't color his vision in a way that might cause him to make a bad decision."

"We'll have a talk about it. He'll be okay."

"Then go to Moscow and find your friend Ivan. And while you're doing that, be sure to flesh out the rest of your strategy. I want a detailed blueprint for this operation. And you'll have to convince me it's unassailable before I'm willing to send up a request for final approval."

* * *

Moscow, Russia, December 7

The two men walked at a fast pace, small clouds of condensation forming every time they exhaled.

"I'm freezing," Stephan said.

"We're almost there," Canterbury said.

"It that it?" Stephan pointed to a massive stone building at the northern end of the square.

"Yes. It doesn't look all that heinous from here, does it? But just because the KGB is gone, don't think it doesn't still intimidate people. The prison is still there, and the FSB still uses it for one of its directorates."

"Then why are we …?"

Canterbury smiled as he gestured toward the Lubyanka.

"Because we're just like any other visiting Americans. We have a few extra minutes, and we take time to see the sites. Certainly, we wouldn't want to miss the famous headquarters of the Soviet secret police."

"You think someone might be watching?"

"That was always the assumption in Moscow. It still is. If you act like you're trying to avoid surveillance, they assume you're up to something. If you look like a tourist, they may conclude you're a tourist."

"I suppose that makes sense. And that's why we're using the Lubyanka metro station? According to the map I got at the front desk, there is another station closer to the hotel."

"You're catching on. It's the closest metro station on Line Seven, and it takes us to the Barrikadnaya station. About a half-mile from the embassy. It's the route recommended in the travel guide."

"That's why you were asking the concierge about getting some documents notarized."

"Exactly. And he told me that the best place to get that done was at the embassy. Apparently, they do it all the time for American visitors."

Stephan smiled. "And you didn't know that?"

"No, did you?" He suppressed a smile.

"Okay, I'm beginning to understand how you scored rooms at the Ritz-Carlton. I thought it was just that you had pull, but it's all part of the cover."

"We look the part. American businessmen. Definitely not dressed for Moscow in the winter months, and I'm starting to agree with you about the chill. At least the metro entrance is right over there. Make some mental notes of the station, Stephan. It could be important later."

"You can access two different lines, right?"

"That's one consideration. If we need to lose a tail — or if one of us does — it could be a big help. More places to disappear. You know the recent history of the station?"

"Not really." Stephan answered.

"Five years ago, there was a bombing. Probably Chechen separatists, and about forty people were killed. The bomb was on a train, but it went off when the train was in the station. The other line, not the one we're using today."

"So there's a lot of surveillance?" Stephan asked.

"Almost certainly. And again, that's to our advantage. We're not doing anything out of the ordinary."

"So how are we going to find …?"

Canterbury interrupted.

"Not here. That sort of question can wait."

• • • • •

An hour later, Stephan sat with Canterbury in a borrowed office at the embassy.

"That was tedious, but now we have some notarized papers," Canterbury said. "When we go out to dinner tonight, I'll leave them in my room. If they're any good at all, they'll find a way to check our rooms, and the documents will strengthen our cover."

"How did you come up with consumer electronics, Allan?"

"It was a suggestion from one of our economic analysts back home. I thought it was a very good piece of advice. We're not supposed to be the inventors, so we won't look like idiots if someone asks a technical question we can't handle. At the same time, we both use enough electronic devices that our basic familiarity with the market is good."

"And Ivan?"

"He has dabbled in this area in the past, so it makes sense to say that we're looking at him as a potential business partner."

"How do we contact him?"

"I sent a text message this morning. To a phone number he gave me five years ago."

"So we just sit on our thumbs and wait?"

"I don't think we'll have to wait that long. It's been four hours since I sent the message, and that's enough time for him to verify that it's really me. I'm not sure what his relationship is with the FSB these days, but I have no doubt that his contacts remain in place."

Canterbury gave a sudden start and thrust his hand into the pocket of his suit coat.

"I bet that's Ivan calling now."

It was a text message, designating a time and location. They would meet late the next afternoon at the bar in a hotel in the heart of the city.

"Hotel Baltschug Kempinski," Canterbury said. "A top hotel, just on the other side of the Moscow River from Red Square."

* * *

Moscow, Hotel Baltschug Kempinski, December 8

Just before 5:30, Canterbury walked into the lobby of the Hotel Baltschug Kempinski. Stephan followed several steps behind. Canterbury scanned the lobby for a face he was certain he would know.

They walked toward the bar at the side of the lobby. When Canterbury stopped, it was clear that he had recognized his old acquaintance.

Ivan rose from his chair and walked toward them. He stopped several feet from Canterbury, and his severe expression suddenly changed into a broad smile. He spoke English with a heavy accent.

"Adrian Carter. My good friend. It makes me real happy to see you."

Each man took another step forward, but before Canterbury could finish extending his arm for a handshake, Ivan put both arms up and embraced him in a bear hug. Ivan was shorter than Canterbury, but he was considerably heavier. Broad shouldered and barrel chested, he looked like a wrestler in a well-tailored suit.

Ivan released Canterbury from his embrace and looked past him at Stephan. "So, Adrian. I see you have brought with you some protection."

He immediately laughed at his remark. Stephan may have been slightly taller than Canterbury, but he definitely lacked the hulking physique expected for a bodyguard.

Canterbury smiled. "It is good to see you again, Ivan. Please allow me to introduce my colleague, Stephan Udrea. I'm afraid he is new to this game, so it is I who must provide protection to him."

They both laughed, and Ivan nodded to Stephan. "It makes me pleased to meet you, Mr. Udrea. I am Ivan Fyodorov."

They shook hands, and Ivan continued. "But I do not believe anything of what my friend tries to tell me. He and I are becoming old men, and you are young. I have no question to my mind that he should be following orders from you."

All three laughed politely.

Ivan turned and motioned for the two Americans to follow. "Please. You will come with me this way. I have made special reservation here at the hotel. We will go to the private room. The hotel makes it available just for us. It is a specialty occasion."

A uniformed waiter showed them into a room with a table large enough for a dozen people but set for three.

As soon as they were seated, Ivan waved to the waiter.

"I have asked the restaurant to give us a feast. You are my guests. Shrimps and lobsters and smoked fishes. The very best in the city. And to start …"

The waiter placed an ice-cold bottle of vodka in front of them.

"Only the best," Ivan continued. "Tonight will be a celebration that I can again see my old friend Adrian."

Ivan offered a toast, and they drank their first round. Then Canterbury followed, thanking Ivan for his hospitality and praising the beauty of the city. Stephan knew he would be next, and he planned ahead for a few words that would be both congenial and flattering.

• • • • •

Later, after they had consumed considerable amounts of food and multiple rounds of vodka, Ivan thumped a hand on the table.

"So, my good friend Adrian. You have told me of your ideas for exporting electronics products to Russia, but we both know that is not why you have come to see me. It is something else, and I am thinking now is time you tell me."

"As always, you are perceptive, Ivan. There indeed is something I wish to discuss." He paused for a drink of water before he went on.

"Fifteen years ago … closer to twenty, now … you saved my life. In return, I've done favors for you over the years. And I think it's fair to say I've more than repaid you."

Ivan nodded but said nothing.

"Now I need another favor from you."

"Of course, Adrian. It is good business, what we have done for each other. We have become capitalists here, no? And you have been great help to me and my economics. But it is also more than buying and selling. I remember. You helped me to avoid certain situations that were of difficulty. So I owe you. Of course. Tell me what is it you need from me."

"There is a man. You may know of him. He was educated here in Moscow, but he is a Kazakh. He is with the KFB. He is their leader."

"You mean Ghazi. I know him. I know him since before he was Ghazi. When he was Aishuakov."

"Yes, it was at that time. It was when we first met."

"You wish to kill him."

"What I wish is of no concern," Canterbury replied.

"But you wish me to help you find him."

"Not exactly. I wish you to help him find us."

Ivan frowned. "You speak in riddles. And this is a very dangerous game."

"It will not be dangerous for you, if you play the role I ask of you. Nor will it be dangerous for me. Not physically. But there is someone else involved. She could be in great danger."

They looked at each other, and Canterbury's eyes conveyed an equal mixture of threat and fear. They also revealed his personal concern, and Ivan knew what it meant.

"She is okay?"

"She is fine. As of now. If you do as I ask, she will continue to be fine."

Do you doubt my honor? You think I cannot be trusted.

Ivan, you are a businessman. We have done business together, and it has been successful. However, I do not know who else you might conduct business with. What we are discussing must be more than business. If you betray her, she will die. And if she dies, you will also. And so will your family. Your wife — the mother of your children — and also your children. And also your mistress in Sochi. And your business partners here in Moscow. Most unpleasant deaths, Ivan.

His face darkened, and his eyes narrowed. "You threaten me? After everything I have done for you?"

He started to get up.

"Please, Ivan. It is not a threat. It is merely a statement of how strong my feelings are. Just in case there is some other businessman who might wish to compete with us. You must give me your assurance that Nousafarin will not be betrayed. We will make this business arrangement profitable for you. Better than anything that a competitor might offer. But Nousafarin is taking a grave risk, and she must survive. It is essential. So you have my trust, if you can assure me that I have yours."

He was still angry.

"You say I have your trust, but you act like not. I gave you your life a decade ago, when you surely would be dead if I didn't help you. Now you offer me a threat but say it is otherwise. Without our business over these last years, I would leave now. Probably I would have you killed. But that is not how things should be."

"There is something else. Information you should know."

An arched eyebrow. "Tell me."

"I think Ghazi was involved when she was first brought to Sochi. Five years before you and I first met. When she was only thirteen. He kidnapped a child and sold her into slavery.

His eyes darkened.

"I only learned of this possibility quite recently. In the early days of the KFB, it was how he raised money for his movement. Buying and selling young girls."

"When I met her she wasn't a girl. She was already a woman."

"I recognize that, Ivan. I know you helped her. She bears no hatred for you. Nor do I."

"But Ghazi …?"

"Yes. Hatred for him."

Ivan nodded.

"That is not the reason I am searching for Ghazi. It is much more than that. It is of no concern to you, and it is of no concern for our business arrangement."

"But it is of concern to me. I cared for Nousa. Certainly, you understood that. From the very beginning. My reason to help you at that time was not for business reasons, although it has worked well for both of us. You were incidental. It was Nousa I tried to help."

"I understand, Ivan. I never thought anything else. It is why I have come to you now. There is something she must do, and she needs your help."

Ivan looked intensely at Canterbury, and their eyes locked.

"I will help you, Adrian."

"Thank you, my friend. Let me tell you what we need."

* * *

24

Feint

*Make a sound in the east, then strike in the west. In
any battle the element of surprise can provide an
overwhelming advantage. Even when face to face
with an enemy, surprise can still be employed by
attacking where he least expects it.*

—*The Thirty-Six Stratagems, China, ca. 1600*[*]

Langley, Virginia, December 15

Stephan was the last to arrive. Chang, Davenport, Hashan,
Hartwell, Neela, Pomeranz, and Canterbury were already
seated at the small conference table. Everyone looked
uncomfortable. Canterbury had just finished telling the others about
the trip to Moscow and Ivan's agreement to provide assistance.

"What exactly is he going to do?" Hashan asked.

"He's going to facilitate the introduction."

"You mean he's actually going to introduce Nousafarin to the
Warlord?"

"No, that would be too obvious. He won't make the actual
introduction. That's why I chose the word 'facilitate.' He'll help it to
happen, but he won't do it himself."

"For those of us who haven't met your friend, could you please
tell us just what the fuck he's agreed to do?"

Canterbury turned to Chang with an expression that was a cross
between annoyance and affection.

---

[*] "The Thirty-Six Stratagems, A Modern Interpretation of a Strategy
Classic," Peter Taylor, Infinite Ideas, Ltd., Oxford, U.K., 2013, p. 31.

"Of course, Andrea. I was just getting to it. Ivan doesn't know all the reasons we want Ghazi, but he accepted my assertion that Ghazi had been responsible for terrorist attacks in the U.S."

"Does he know the details of those attacks?" Hartwell asked?

"Not from us. But his FSB ties will likely permit him to learn a lot. And I think, Ivan understands that Ghazi's group poses a serious threat to Russia in the long term."

"That was enough to secure his assistance?" Pomeranz asked. "It's a fairly nebulous premise for someone as savvy as you say Ivan is."

"It's only part of it. Most of all, it was Nousafarin's involvement that closed the deal. He still cares about her, and he understood that helping us would help her. He can keep her from getting killed."

Canterbury continued his briefing. "Ivan has played ball with the Warlord on several occasions. I didn't ask for much detail, but I think it's safe to assume that he has supplied the Warlord with arms. As I've told you, Ivan seems to walk a fine line between his background with the KGB and his current life as an entrepreneur. Ivan has met the Warlord met face to face, but for the most part, he's used others as intermediaries."

"So we're going into business as arms dealers?"

"Don't jump to conclusions, Derek. All we're going to do is have Ivan arrange a business meeting. Nothing unusual, except that Ivan will set it up so the intermediary who makes contact with Ghazi will first encounter Nousafarin. That will set the stage."

"Sounds a little iffy," Hashan observed. "How do we get Ghazi to take the bait?"

Canterbury resumed. "The plan is to use a man named Ostrakov. His full name is Gennady Ostrakov, and he's a reasonably wealthy merchant who has acted as a link between Ivan and the Warlord in the past. His business includes arms, but he also provides things like communications gear and vehicles that the KFB doesn't want to buy on the open market. Ostrakov will arrange a meeting in Kazakhstan. Probably in Astana or Almaty."

"You think the Warlord would agree to meet him in one of those cities? After our operation with Anja, won't he be worried about another trap?"

"It's a real concern, David. But we know Ghazi likes his creature comforts. Both of those cities have nice hotels and good restaurants. Ostrakov will offer to host him for an expensive dinner. An expression of thanks after their last lucrative deal, and a sales pitch for the next one. And that's our opportunity."

"What's the connection with Nousafarin?"

"Ivan will arrange an unrelated business opportunity for Ostrakov. Something that will cause him to arrive several days early. And by sheer coincidence, Nousafarin will be staying in that same hotel — while she's on tour looking for new artists to show in her gallery."

Chang interrupted again. "I agree with David. It all seems iffy. I suppose you can get Nousa in the same city as the Warlord at the same time. But we need them to be a little closer than that. A lot closer."

"Yes, Andrea. As soon as the business dinner between Ostrakov and Ghazi is confirmed, we'll set the other parts in motion. The unconnected business deal for Ostrakov will be with one of our people, who will find a way to introduce Ostrakov to Nousafarin. We can't be completely sure how he'll react, but I have faith in Nousa."

"What happens between the two of them probably doesn't matter that much, but on the night of Ostrakov's business dinner with the Warlord, Nousafarin will make dining reservations at the same restaurant. The Warlord will notice her. And when he learns that Ostrakov has met her, he will ask to be introduced."

"You want to base the entire operation on that assumption?"

It was a direct challenge, and Canterbury was momentarily nonplussed. "I can't guarantee it, Andrea. We can't guarantee anything. But we don't have any other options. And we've got every reason to trust Nousafarin's abilities."

"Sorry, Allan. I wasn't trying to disparage Nousafarin. I agree we can have faith in her. It's Ghazi I don't trust. I've never met him. None of us have. So we don't know how he's going to react."

"That's not entirely accurate."

The room went silent, and everyone turned to stare at Neela.

"You're forgetting that I've met him. I have the personal experience of knowing exactly how lecherous he is. I haven't met Nousafarin, but if she is even half the woman you've described, the Warlord will be like a moth to the flame. And all the time, he will think it was his own idea."

"It won't be easy," Hashan warned. "If Ghazi suspects anything, Nousafarin will be at great risk. And he should suspect. We tried once. He's got to know we'll try again. He's not stupid."

"We need a diversion." The comment came from Davenport.

"Do you have a suggestion, Derek?"

"Nothing specific. Just that it would be good if the Warlord expected our next attack to come from a different direction. He'd be less likely to view Nousafarin as a threat."

"Derek is correct. I've been thinking about something that fits his suggestion. I'd like Stephan to go back to Dushanbe."

"How would that help?" Chang asked.

"It would allow him to meet with Colonel Kholdorov again."

"How in hell would that be useful?" Stephan asked. "we can't trust him for anything. The last two times I met with that bastard, someone wound up dead. First the Patriarch and then Anja. You want Nousa to be next?"

"Hear me out, Stephan. We can't trust him to support our interests. But we can be confident of his response regarding information he considers valuable. We can be certain that he will pass it on, and it will find its way to the Warlord."

"How would that create a diversion?"

"We have to tell Kholdorov something that will make the Warlord look in the wrong direction. Ghazi expects us to make a move, and if he believes himself to be in imminent jeopardy, it will divert his attention from Nousafarin as a potential adversary. It's essential that he view her as an object of desire and a source of pleasure, not as a threat."

* * *

Dushanbe, Tajikistan, December 21

Kholdorov was already seated in the café when Stephan arrived.

"Good afternoon, Colonel. I am grateful that you agreed to meet with me."

The colonel stood and extended his arm to shake hands. "Should that surprise you, Mr. Ubayda? Have I not always been of assistance to my friends?"

Stephan had put considerable effort into planning the meeting, and he was determined that Kholdorov not catch him off guard. His smile was cold as he shook the older man's hand.

"Of course, Colonel. I meant only that it seemed as though my request at our last meeting might have offended you."

"In our business, we cannot afford to be offended. It was only as I told you. It was necessary for me to think carefully about your request. It was necessary for me to be alone. You must not make unwarranted conclusions to the contrary."

"I shall make no such conclusions, Colonel."

The waiter came to their table and set down a bottle of vodka and two small glass cups.

"I asked them to bring this when I entered the café." Stephan said as he poured them each a vodka. "Will you drink with me? I wish to thank you for the information you provided two months ago. It was most helpful."

"As I said, Mr. Ubayda. I attempt to be of assistance to my friends."

"And as you also said, Colonel, a man must be afraid of the wolves when he goes hunting."

Kholdorov nodded sagely, but he was surprised by the next statement.

"And now I go hunting."

"Your plan is to hunt for wild boar or small game?"

"We have spoken of an excursion to hunt wild boar and ibex. But our real objective would be a wolf."

"Here in Tajikistan?"

"That is where we would begin, Colonel. In several days, I shall meet my comrades in in the village that was home to the Patriarch. I expect we will travel in a northerly direction, and it is likely we will reach Kazakhstan."

"It is a most ambitious endeavor. Have you decided where you will hunt?"

"It has not yet been decided. It was my hope that you might have a recommendation."

Stephan poured another shot of vodka into their glasses, and at the same time he pushed an envelope across the table. The flap was not sealed, and a thick wad of banknotes was partly visible. This was the moment of truth. If the colonel was prepared to engage in this maneuver, he would suggest a location where the Warlord might be encountered.

Kholdorov frowned and then spoke quietly.

"It is said that the wolf is most difficult to hunt. It is a dangerous predator and very clever. If I were conducting such a hunt, I would travel to the north and to the east, through Kyrgyzstan and into Kazakhstan. Beyond Almaty. I would circle around the east end of the Kapchagay Reservoir. There I would enter the Altyn Emel National Park, and I would remain in the foothills of the mountains. It is where I would expect to encounter my wolf."

Stephan nodded soberly, and Kholdorov continued.

"Or perhaps the wolf would find you."

"I will heed your advice, Colonel. Will you drink with me once more?"

As they raised their glasses, Kholdorov made the toast. He spoke in Russian.

"За нашу дружбу!" *Za nashu druzhbu!*

Stephan echoed the words in English.

"To our friendship."

Once more, the colonel poured from the bottle of vodka. Then he raised his cup.

"I drink to your hunt."

They drained their glasses. Stephan noticed that the colonel had not proposed that they drink to the success of the hunt.

• • • • •

Several minutes later, as Stephan walked toward his hotel, he reviewed the meeting with mixed emotions.

He was angry.

The Colonel had never asked about Anja, and that led to an inescapable conclusion. He already knew what had happened to her. And Stephan understood that it meant even more than that. It meant that the Colonel knew he was responsible for her death. Maybe not directly, but he had conveyed information to Ghazi. Information that caused the Warlord to kill her.

Stephan was also elated.

The Warlord had provided the information Stephan had requested. He divulged where the Warlord could be found. It was somewhere in a very large area, but Stephan knew that his team would be able to go after him.

And still, he was wary.

He knew Ghazi would be waiting for them. They would be trying to lay a trap, but they might also be walking into one.

In sum, he was pleased.

He knew he and his comrades would be well armed. They would be able to ward off the enemy even if they walked into an ambush. They would be on guard, and ultimately, it would not matter whether they actually found Ghazi. The entire point would be to divert his attention from the possibility that the threat could come from Nousafarin.

It was all like a game of chess, with Kholdorov helping each of the players to make another move. Stephan believed his plan was well formulated, and he was convinced that the diversion would succeed.

* * *

25

Diversion

Direct action entails short-duration strikes and other small-scale offensive actions conducted with specialized military capabilities to seize, destroy, capture, exploit, recover, or damage designated targets in hostile, denied, or diplomatically and/or politically sensitive environments.

—*Department of Defense, 2014*[*]

Abdurrahim, Tajikistan, January 12

S tephan took a drink of his tea and looked at his host with a warm smile. "The village is looking good, Martin. It's hard to believe that I was only gone for two months."

They were sitting in the main room of the home where Martin and Samantha were living. It reminded Stephan of when he and Anja visited the Patriarch two years earlier. It struck him that he was once again in the Patriarch's home. Except it was a different structure, and Martin was now the Patriarch.

Samantha sat next to Martin, their physical closeness hinting at an emotional intimacy that had grown since Stephan had last seen them. She looked earnestly at their guest.

"Are you only here to check up on us, Stephan? If so, you're going to have a very good report to take back. Everyone is doing great, we've got our provisions all set for the worst months, and everybody here has been pitching in like a real community."

---

[*] "Joint Publication 3-05, Special Operations," Joint Chiefs of Staff, Department of Defense, July 16, 2014, p. x.

She noticed that Stephan did not share in her excitement, and she turned to Martin. Her quizzical look changed first to one of anxiety.

"Oh, shit! It's not a report at all, is it? Is there going to be another attack? I thought we were past that."

Martin remained silent, but he nodded to Stephan.

"That isn't it, Samantha," he said. "There's nothing to be concerned about for the village. As far as we know, everyone is safe here. It's somewhere else. We need to go off on a hunting expedition."

"All of us? Who will take care of the village? We can't leave everyone unprotected."

"The villagers will be okay. Our orders are for the operation are that I'm going with Martin, Mike, and Travis. You'll be staying here."

Her emotions shifted in an instant from dismay to anger.

"You think I can't do it? You haven't even been here for two months. I can handle anything you might encounter. Maybe I don't have as much experience as Mike and Travis, but you know what my training is."

"That's the whole point, Samantha. You proved your abilities in the attack last fall. Headquarters has assigned you to take charge while we're gone. It should only be a couple of weeks, and it's highly unlikely that anything will happen during that time. You've shown you can handle things if there's an attack on the village. The other villagers know how to handle their weapons now, and Shahram will listen to you."

"Where are you going?"

"Kazakhstan. That's partly why you can't come. If we get in a jam, we're U.S. citizens. You would still show up as a Kazakh national. You'd be completely screwed."

She didn't like it, but she knew he was right.

"It sounds like the trip is going to be dangerous. What's it for?"

Stephan looked her in the eye. "There will be some risk. But we'll be prepared."

Then he broke eye contact and looked down at the floor.

Samantha realized that her last question would not be answered. And she understood why. It didn't make it any easier.

• • • • •

Stephan and Martin sat on the floor of the house that Mike and Travis had used since the firefight. The dwelling previously had been occupied by Tohir. The four men stared intently at Mike's iPad, which displayed a map of southern Kazakhstan.

Mike pointed to a location on the map. "This is our target area, over here at the bottom right. It's about eight hundred klicks from here. That's as the crow flies. By road it's about twice that. It would be a real bitch of a trip in the winter."

Stephan frowned. "Sixteen hundred kilometers. About a thousand miles. How the hell do we cover that kind of ground in the middle of winter?"

"Travis and I have been in touch with our operations center, and it looks like they're going to help us out. We don't have all the details yet, but we only have to get to the main road north of here — that's the M41 highway. It's less than twenty miles, and they'll bring in a helicopter to pick us up. Take us all the way to Manas, over here about three hundred klicks west of Almaty."

"I thought Manas was closed."

"Yeah, we vacated the Transit Center in 2014, but the airport hasn't gone anywhere, and there's still some back-channel cooperation. The Kyrgyz government isn't big on militants any more than we are."

"Even if we can get there, it looks like it's still a couple of hundred miles to the target area."

"It would be, but we'll get a second ride over to a staging area just northeast of the Issyk Kul. It's really remote, so nobody is going to notice us. Our friends will use transport helicopters to drop us and our vehicles right near the Kyrgyzstan-Kazakhstan border, and we'll only have a hundred miles by ground."

"They can't drop us off any closer?"

"Shit, Stephan. I didn't think you were such a pussy."

Mike flashed a big grin before continuing. "A hundred miles is a lot better than a thousand. Point is, we can't do the staging inside Kazakhstan. They said there would be too many political problems."

"Looks like we don't have much choice. When do we move out?"

"Day after tomorrow. Travis and I will keep working on the logistics, but there's not much to do here. Everything we need is going to be waiting for us when we get to the rendezvous in Kyrgyzstan. All you guys need to bring is a small pack. Toothbrush and clean socks and underwear."

* * *

Kyrgyzstan, January 15

Following a half-hour flight from Manas, the helicopter set down on a deserted stretch of road several miles south of the Kazakh frontier. The four passengers jumped down and crouched below the whirling rotor blades. A hundred yards away they could see two vehicles with several men standing by them. The pilot kept the engines running.

Mike and Travis led the group as they jogged toward the waiting men. Mike greeted one of them by name. No introductions were made for Stephan and Martin. Travis reviewed a list with the leader of the other group. Then he turned back to Mike.

"It's all here."

"Good. We're ready to roll."

"Thanks guys," Mike said. "Appreciate the help. We'll be talking to you."

Stephan and Martin watched as the three men with no names walked to the aircraft and climbed aboard. They shielded their faces against the sting of dust and snow from the rotor wash as the helicopter took off and flew directly overhead before banking hard and accelerating into the distance. In seconds, it had disappeared.

"So, whaddya think?" Mike asked Martin.

"It's awesome. I was expecting another beat-up truck or maybe a Toyota four-by-four. What are these? Humvees?"

"Next generation," Mike answered with a big grin. "Joint Light Tactical Vehicle. These JLTVs can drive through damn near anything. Rain, snow, mud. Hot weather or cold. Whatever you throw at it. And nothing's going to stop it. It's completely armored from top to bottom, and it can go damn near straight up the side of a goddam mountain. Best of all, it even has fucking cup holders."

"You and Travis are driving?"

"Bingo. Stephan and I will take the lead. You and Travis will follow in the vehicle with the trailer. We've got everything we need. Plenty of food, lots of extra fuel to keep our heaters going, and weapons up the wazoo. HK416s for each of us, an M249 light machine gun like the one we had back in the village, and two M107s."

He paused to look at Stephan and Martin.

"The M107s are real nasty fuckers. Some guys call them the Barret Light Fifty. Semi-automatic .50-caliber sniper rifles that can throw down accurate fire on targets as much as two klicks away. So, if those assholes we're looking for make an attempt to pick us off, we can turn them into road kill. The best weapons they could get hold of would only have about two-thirds of that range."

"What about an ambush?" Martin asked.

"Like I said, the vehicles are armored. I mean, it's not like we'd want to just sit there and let them shoot at us, but we'd have time to get into a safe position. Then we could return fire. In addition to everything else I just said, we also have a couple of XM25s, so we can throw up some air-burst grenades if we need to. No way in hell these fuckers are going to have anything to match up with our firepower."

Stephan had his own question. "What about communications gear, Mike?"

"We got that covered, too. Two satellite phones in each of the vehicles, so we each get one. Iridium Extreme 9575. Best thing out there. And I can use a data link to my iPad for up-to-date maps. We're even going to get twice-a-day satellite images. Operations said they couldn't give us real-time coverage, but they're directing one of the satellites so that the cameras will give detailed coverage of our zone when they fly over."

"Drones?" Martin asked.

"A drone would have been better, but they said they couldn't put anything into Kazakh airspace for this operation. Too sensitive."

"What if we get in a real jam. If we need help getting out?"

"We're kind of on our own here, Stephan. No cavalry to call in. But we'll be okay. You and Martin are pretty good. I've seen you in action. Travis and I are better. No offense, man. Worst case, we'll need to run like hell to get back across the border into Kyrgyzstan. Then we can get a helicopter to pick us up again. My worry isn't that we might lose a fight. It's that we won't find these dickwads in the first place. If we find them, their ass is grass."

"I hope you're right."

"I know I'm right."

• • • • •

Later that morning, the four Americans were traveling north on the A-362 highway. Stephan looked up from the iPad map.

"We're making good time, Mike. Looks like we'll get there well before dark."

"That's the plan. We'll need some light to set up camp. The images Travis downloaded were a huge help in planning, but it's always a little different when your feet hit the ground. Right after we reach the village of Koktal, we'll head west on A-353."

"I've got a couple of questions, Mike. Wouldn't it have been faster to stay on the A-351 highway all the way to the outskirts of the Altyn Emel National Park? That's right at the eastern end of the Kapchagay Reservoir. Right where Colonel Kholdorov said we should look for Ghazi."

"Think about it. Didn't you tell me that you don't trust this guy?"

"That's right. At least, not completely. I think he plays both sides of the field. So, I suppose he's probably let Ghazi know that we're going to be up here looking for him."

"Exactly," Mike said. "Kholdorov told you to start your search at the east end of the reservoir. There's probably a lot of value in his advice. But we should plan on Ghazi expecting us. Kholdorov was very specific about the east end of the reservoir. Zoom out on your map and look at where we crossed the border. All logic says we should go through Almaty and then turn east along the reservoir. We'd enter the park right about where you just suggested. It's where they'll be looking for us."

"Now I see. Coming from the east, there's a good chance we'll approach their position from behind."

"Exactly. They'll be looking west, and we'll be coming from the east."

"You think we'll be able to mount an attack without them seeing us first?"

"Not a chance, Stephan. They're probably pretty good. We learned that in November. But they're not as good as us, and they sure as shit don't have the weapons and technology we have. I just want to be sure that we aren't walking into a trap. I trust this Colonel Kholdorov a whole lot less than you do."

"Fair enough."

"You said you had two questions?"

"Yeah. We've passed a couple of small towns. Shouldn't we be worried that the villagers might alert Ghazi to our arrival?"

"Not likely. Everything we know about this guy is that he's not exactly welcome most places in Kazakhstan. Their government, just like ours, considers him a terrorist. Maybe they aren't looking as hard for him as we are, but he still doesn't control a lot of territory. He's a lot like bin Laden was before we first went after him in Afghanistan. As long as he stayed up in the mountains, nobody gave a shit. So, I figure Ghazi is about the same. He doesn't come down to these villages, and the locals don't worry about who might be after him."

"But we're still gonna look a little strange."

"A little different, maybe. But they've seen it before."

* * *

Kazakhstan, January 15

Travis drove the second JLTV, and Martin navigated.

"That's the A-353 highway they just turned onto, Travis. As soon as we make the turn, we'll be heading west. According to the map, we're only about two hours from where we leave the highway to go off-road."

"That's good. We're still on schedule. Shouldn't be more than another hour after that. I marked the route along the contour at a thousand meters. It's a pretty straight shot for about ten klicks, and then a little bit of an incline. If we can start setting up our camp by four thirty, we'll have about an hour before sunset. It's starting to cloud over, so it'll get really dark after that."

"I have a question, Travis."

"Fire away."

"Why did we get through the border crossing so easily this morning?"

"We all played our parts perfectly. You and Stephan are a couple of rich guys, and we're your guides for a hunting excursion in the Altyn Emel National Park. All our papers were in order, and it's just the kind of high-end tourism the Kazakh government encourages. We paid some big mother fees to get all the permits and everything. And just in case you didn't notice, a little cash changed hands this morning, too. That's why they didn't search our stuff."

"You think we'll find the Warlord?" Martin asked.

"Don't get your hopes up. Chances are fairly slim that we'll have any direct contact. I think we'll have to be satisfied with a few members of his supporting cast. That's how he works."

"I thought we were coming here because it's where Ghazi would be."

"Yes and no. Mike and I talked a lot about this. And we got a lot more information from our operations center as well. Take a look at your map, and zoom out a little to show the mountains at the north end of the national park."

"Got it."

"Now look at the elevations. Those peaks get up above twenty-five hundred meters. That's damn near ten thousand feet. There might be some nice mountain goats up there but it's a terrible place for military operations. So nobody is going to have that as their home base. That's why we're staying a little west of there. That and the fact that we don't want to be exactly where Kholdorov told you to go."

"You don't think we'll find Ghazi's base?"

"Not likely. You see the ridgeline along the mountains? Near the middle of the national park? There's a pass that goes through to the north side of the mountains. Maximum elevation is less than fifteen hundred meters. About five thousand feet. Same elevation as Denver, so you don't need to be an alpine climber to get across. There's no road, so we're not looking for vehicles, but we're pretty sure that's where Ghazi's men will come from."

"You think his base is on the other side? North of the park?"

"Look at the terrain. It's isolated, and it's relatively flat. Plus, it's a straight shot to Almaty. He'd be isolated and protected but not too far from the city. Mike and I are convinced he's somewhere in that region."

"How do we pinpoint it?"

"Switch to the satellite view. Just flick the screen to the next image. Got it?"

"Yeah. I see what you mean. It's from last summer, and you can see farms all around. A perfect place to hide. He could be anywhere in the area. The locals wouldn't give a shit, and we'd never see him."

"Exactly.

"Then what's the whole point of our coming up here, Travis? If Ghazi isn't going to come meet us, why did we bother?"

"It's the world we live in, Martin. At least the world we work in. 'Need to know.' I can't be positive, but my guess is our mission is actually a smoke screen. Something to take Ghazi's mind off another operation somewhere else. As long as we make enough noise and wave something shiny in front of him, he'll start focusing his attention on us. And someone else will make him pay for that."

• • • • •

"Another eighty yards, Travis. They've got it too. They're stopping."

"Perfect. I'll pull up to their right. Get ready to hop out."

The four men climbed out of the JLTVs and walked around the vehicles to assess the location.

"Looks good to me," Mike said. "You and the guys at command headquarters picked a good place. And we've got the perfect amount of snow. Looks to be between four and six inches. Enough to help us disappear but not enough to hinder our mobility. The JLTVs performed every bit as good as they told us they would."

"Let's throw up a frame over the vehicles, Mike. We've got a lot to do." Travis didn't wait for an answer and began taking a set of struts from the trailer. "Here, Martin. You and Stephan snap these together to set up a lean-to over the JLTVs. Then throw this fabric over it and sprinkle some snow on top."

Travis and Mike began unpacking the remaining gear in the trailer, carrying it about 200 feet toward the hillside. They set it down on a flat area that was sheltered on three sides by the hillside and rock formations. Then they returned to the lean-to that Stephan and Martin had nearly finished.

Travis nodded approvingly. "Good job. Let's move the vehicles over by the other gear."

Stephan reacted with surprise. "I thought we just built this frame to hide them."

"That's exactly what we want it to look like. Just in case anyone was watching us, they saw us put the vehicles under this shelter before dark. If they have any kind of thermal detection, it won't be very sophisticated. We know from the November attack that they fight hard, but their equipment isn't hi-tech."

"You're saying they won't know if we move the vehicles tonight?"

"Exactly, Stephan. It's much darker now. But we'll put both JLTVs behind the rocks, and they'll be protected from direct fire. Then we cover them with thermal blankets. White blankets, a little snow, and no infrared radiation. Nobody will be able to see these things, even if they get within spitting distance."

"Then why the lean-to?"

"Just a little distraction." He pointed to a small gasoline generator and a five-gallon can of fuel. "The lean-to is just regular fabric, and we'll run the generator on low. We won't need much electricity tonight. It puts out a little bit of heat, so if somebody's looking for a thermal signature, they'll figure it's the vehicles. That way, if they try to go after us with an RPG, they'll just wind up taking out a generator. And it wouldn't matter that much, because the JLTVs can supply external power."

Martin was curious as well. "What about our thermal signatures?"

"We brought plenty of thermal insulation. We'll set up two small tents with full visual and thermal camouflage. You and me in one,

Mike and Stephan in the other. We'll be warm enough, and nobody's going to see us."

"And we better get moving," Mike said. The sun is behind the mountains, and it'll be pitch black in a couple of minutes. We need to be inside our tents. Except for one of us. We'll take turns standing watch. Does the place you flagged on the satellite images still look good, Travis?"

"Yeah." He pointed to a location about 150 feet away and slightly above them on the hill.

"That gives a good line of sight in every direction except up the mountain, and nobody's coming at us from there. Night-vision goggles will let us spot anything that's moving out there. Even wildlife, so be sure you know what you're looking at if you see something. No shooting at anything unless you get the word from me or Mike."

· · · · ·

Two hours later, Stephan and Mike finished their evening meal. Martin returned from his turn on watch, and Mike began his shift. The temperature was only a few degrees below freezing, and they remained comfortable in their parkas, sheltered by a thermal camouflage cloth that extended from the roof of one of the vehicles.

"So, what did you think of your MRE?" Travis asked Stephan.

"I've had worse. It's better than being the guest of honor at a tribal meeting and having to eat the eyeball."

"No shit. I never had to do that. Guess I've never been anybody's guest of honor. But these things aren't so bad. And it's only for a couple of days."

"I don't understand why all the jargon, Travis. 'Meal, Ready-to-Eat'? It's just a package of food, so why call it an MRE? And the FRH? For a 'flameless ration heater'? It's works fine, but it's just a chemical packet that gets hot."

"That's the Army, dude. They invented it. They need a set of letters for everything."

"You guys want to talk about tomorrow?" Martin asked.

"Why not?" Travis answered, his words distorted by a mouthful of food.

"I was looking at the images from the last couple of satellite passes. Both visible light and infrared. The software is fucking amazing."

"How's that?" Stephan asked.

"Well, you know how you see things easier when they change? Like when something is moving?"

"You mean how it's hard to spot something if it's motionless?"

"Exactly. Well, this software lets me compare successive satellite passes. Look."

Martin held out the iPad and clicked through several images. "See anything?"

"Nothing sticks out."

"Mostly, yeah. But check out this one place. It could be a heat signature, or maybe it's just a blurry spot on the ground. Now look at what happens if I digitally superimpose the images. And do it with a time lapse."

The three men stared intently at the screen.

"There's something there," Stephan said.

"Bet your ass. About one klick away, on the far side of the ridge to the southeast. It's exactly where you said they'd be, Travis. No question that somebody's there, and there's movement. It's some sort of a base camp."

"Any idea how many people?"

"Can't tell."

Travis's voice turned serious. "I'll let Mike know so he can keep an eye out, but they're almost certainly hunkered down for the night. I imagine we'll have more information in the morning when we get a new set of satellite downloads."

* * *

Altyn Emel National Park, Kazakhstan, January 16

Just before daybreak, Stephan left the campsite to take his turn on watch. Mike returned to join the others several minutes later, stamping his feet as he ducked under the camouflage awning by the JLTV.

"Nice and warm in here," he said as he crawled into the tent. "Got some breakfast ready for me?"

"Everything you could ask for," Travis replied, handing him a packet. "Best oatmeal this side of Almaty. And it should be just about ready. I got it started when Stephan left."

"Thanks."

"You see anything during your shift?"

"Nada. Nothing moving out there. You got any thoughts, Travis?"

"Just that we should stick with the original plan. Make it look like we're sitting here like idiots. Get them to come to us."

"They didn't do anything last night."

"I think we surprised them by coming from the east. Or maybe, they haven't even spotted us yet. You think we should start up the generator?"

"Good idea," Mike replied. "Hardly uses any gas, and we can get all our battery-operated stuff fully charged. Martin, why don't you go crank it up. It'll make a little noise and throw off some heat. If we're lucky, they'll make that their primary target. But stay low. Just in case we miscalculated somewhere."

As soon as Martin left the tent, Mike turned to Travis. "How long do you figure?"

"No way to be sure, but I'd guess a couple of hours. The generator should get their attention. I'll head out as soon as Martin gets back. By the time they start to move, I'll be watching."

"What are you taking?"

"Just the spotter scope and a light fifty."

"Take an HK, Travis. If there's a real firefight, I don't want you climbing back down here to get it."

"More weight, but I guess you're right. I'll have my radio and iPad with me."

"How much ammunition are you planning to take?"

"Three magazines for the 107. That's thirty rounds. Whaddya think? Maybe a half dozen thirty-round clips for the HK?"

"Sounds right. Better to have it with you."

"You're taking the other 107, Mike?"

"No. I watched Martin shoot the other day, and he's deadly. I want him up on the other side of the ravine. He'll have a good sightline for everything to the south and across the entire opening of the ravine. He'll have the same weapons as you. Sniper rifle and the HK416."

"And you?"

"I'll take a position on this side of the ravine, just uphill from Stephan. I'm going to bring him the one of the XM25s. I'll take the other, and I'll also have the M249 light machine gun. We'll both have our HKs as backup. We'll get most of the ammo up to those positions, too. I just hope our friends don't make us wait all day."

• • • • •

By midmorning, increasing cloud cover made it a gray day, although ground visibility remained clear.

A period of extended silence was broken by a transmission over the handheld radios. It was Travis.

"I see movement. To our west. Two or three men. Maybe four. They're moving downhill at a cautious pace. Doesn't look like they have a real trail to follow, so it's going to take a while for them to reach the base of the hill. Stephan, you should be able to see them in about thirty minutes. Same for Mike. Martin, probably a little longer before they're visible from your location. Just hang tight. I'll keep you informed."

It only took 25 minutes. Stephan spoke in an even voice.

"I see them. You were right, Travis. Four of them. Doesn't look like they have a lot of firepower. Just AK-47s. I can't tell for sure yet, but it looks like two of them may have under-barrel grenade launchers mounted on their rifles."

"This is Travis. They've moved, so I have an unobstructed line of sight. You got it right, Stephan. We don't want to let them get too close with those things. They're not real accurate, but they're deadly. Maximum range is around four hundred meters. Can you read their position, Mike?"

"I've got them at about five hundred meters. They seem to be moving exactly how we expected. We can see them here, but they're following a line that will keep them out of sight from the lean-to until they within two hundred meters. A little farther away from our positions up the hillside. That's when we can expect them to start firing. Another fifteen minutes."

"Martin here. I may have something interesting. I've been scanning my whole field of view since I got here. From Stephan's position, almost directly west, all across the flat area to the south, and over to the other ridge on the east. A couple of times I thought I might have seen motion, but I wasn't sure. Now I am."

Mike was the commander for the operation, and the others waited for him to respond.

"Are you talking about something on four legs, Martin?"

"Only two legs. Just moved into a place where I have a clear view. Correction … make that four legs. There's two of them. Both carrying weapons."

"How far away?"

"Rangefinder on my scope says just under four hundred meters."

"Are you sure they're part of the assault team? We don't want to take out a couple of friendly locals trying to put food on their table."

"I know what a Kalashnikov looks like. And at least one of them has a grenade launcher mounted. I can't get a clear look at the other yet."

"Okay, guys." Mike's voice was serious. "We didn't expect this. They're smarter than we gave them credit for. The two Martin just spotted must have circled way to the south to try a two-pronged attack. Not sure why we didn't pick up their trace last night. Maybe they came down behind the next ridge over. Either way, we gotta to deal with it now."

"This is Stephan. I don't see anything to the south."

"Me either," said Mike.

"You won't," Martin answered. "They'll be hidden from your line of sight until they close to about two hundred meters. According to my map, they won't have a clear shot at your positions even then. They look like they're doing the same thing as the first team. Focusing on the lean-to as their primary target."

Mike spoke again.

"All right. Just stay put. We don't want an extended firefight, so we let them get close. Two hundred meters is about right, since they can't place their grenades accurately at that distance. They could still get lucky, though, so everyone make sure you got your body armor on."

Several minutes later, Martin's voice came over the radio.

"Got some progress here. First off, it's definite that only one of them has a grenade launcher. The other looks like it's just a standard-issue Kalashnikov. Even better, they've split up. When you give the signal, Mike, I'll go for the guy with the launcher. If I can take him out, we'll all be a lot safer."

"Good thinking, Martin. Be careful you don't expose yourself to the second guy. For now, just sit tight. Wait for my order before anybody fires. We're going to wait for them to shoot first. That way we know for sure who we're dealing with, and headquarters said it gives us legal cover."

Ten minutes later, Martin spoke again, his voice hushed.

"My guys look like they're getting into firing position. They're about fifty meters apart, both about a hundred-fifty meters from me. And I've got a clear line of sight on each of them."

Mike responded. "Good work. It looks like the other four are getting ready, too. But I'm losing my targets. They're going behind that small hill."

"Same here," Stephan reported.

Travis spoke next. "I've only got one of them left. He's taken a position behind a boulder, but that's with respect to the lean-to. From my position, I have a clear shot. And he doesn't have a grenade launcher."

"Okay." It was Mike's voice. "We probably only have a few seconds left. As soon as they initiate hostilities, I'll give the signal to return fire. Travis, you take out the guy you're watching. Martin, take out the one with the grenade launcher. That leaves two other grenade launchers out of sight behind the hill on our side of the ravine. Stephan and I will throw out airburst grenades. Stephan, you set yours for an elevation of ten meters above the hill and ten meters beyond the crest. I'm assuming they'll be near the top, so I'm going for two meters above the crest and only one meter past it."

Less than twenty seconds later, they heard the first explosion. A second followed immediately, and then there were two more. The lean-to suffered two direct hits, and pieces of the simple structure were thrown high in the air in all directions. A fireball erupted from the five-gallon gasoline can.

Mike gave his signal between the first and second pairs of explosions. Martin had kept his target in the crosshairs of his scope, and he fired three .50-caliber rounds. Two of them were direct hits. He then turned his sniper rifle toward the position where he had last seen the other attacker on their southern flank.

Travis squeezed the trigger of his sniper rifle a single time. He could see the results clearly through his scope. It was a head shot, and all he saw was a motionless body crumpled on the ground. He next turned his attention to the small hill that shielded three more of the attackers. As he moved his head, he saw the first two explosions. Then there were two more. One of Mike's rounds had impacted a rock on the near side of the hill, but the other three exploded as planned. Unless they had moved to a different location, all three attackers certainly had been hit. Likely eliminated.

Mike and Travis kept their attention on the hill, while Stephan turned to follow the action near Martin's position. He couldn't see either Martin or the other attacker, but he heard a burst of automatic weapons fire. Small arms, almost certainly a Kalashnikov. Then he heard a second burst in response, and he saw a flash up on the far hillside. He was certain that Martin was firing back with his HK416. A third burst was followed by silence.

A few seconds later, Stephan was startled by the sound of sustained automatic weapons fire behind him — from the position that Mike had taken. He turned back to the hill where the attackers had taken cover and could see a figure running away from them. As he looked, it fell downhill, twisting grotesquely, like a rag doll thrown by an angry child.

Mike's voice came over the radio.

"I think we got all of them. Check in. Travis?"

"All okay here. I took out my one target."

"Good work. I got one for sure with the M249. We probably got the other two with the XM25s. Stephan?"

"I don't see how they could have survived those airbursts. But one of them did. We have to check."

"Right. But we wait a couple of minutes. Travis, you keep watching with your spotter scope. Martin, how's everything on your side?"

There was no response. Mike's voice became urgent.

"Martin! What's your status? Answer me, motherfucker."

There was only silence on the radio. After five seconds, Mike spoke again.

"Travis, you keep watching from your position. If one of them is still alive, we don't want him sneaking off on us. I'm going to cross over to Martin's position. Stephan, you cover me. Anything moves out there, shoot the fuck out of it."

"Yeah."

Mike clambered down the slope on the west side of the ravine. When he reached Stephan, he gave him the light machine gun and a 200-round belt of ammunition. Then he began moving toward the position Martin had taken on the east side of the ravine. He moved quickly down the hill, and then ran at a crouch as he crossed the open area between the two hillsides. Just as he reached the cover of a boulder on the far side, he saw several small rocks near him shatter into bits and he again heard the burst of automatic weapons fire. It had been directed at him.

He screamed into his radio. "Stephan. He's still out there. I can't see where, but he's out there."

"I see him, Mike."

A long burst of automatic fire came from behind him, and Mike realized that Stephan was using the SAW. Even if Stephan didn't score a hit, the attacker would be frozen in place by the machine gun.

Mike scrambled up the hill toward Martin's position. There was no further sound of automatic weapons. In fact, it had become eerily quiet. When he reached Martin's elevation, he was still about 75 feet away. He could see Martin clearly, lying motionless next to his weapons. The boulder he presumably leaned on to steady his aim was covered with blood.

Mike picked up his radio.

"Martin's down! Stephan, get over and check on the guy who was shooting at him. Make sure you got him with the SAW. Then circle around and verify that we got the last three you and I were shooting at. I'll go see if there's anything I can do for Martin."

• • • • •

The two JLTVs traveled in tandem toward the outskirts of the national park. Mike had decided that they should leave quickly to avoid the possibility of a second wave of attackers. Even more important, he knew it would be an utter disaster if the Kazakh authorities somehow showed up while they were still at the scene of the firefight.

Mike drove the lead vehicle, accompanied by Stephan in the passenger seat. Travis drove the trailing vehicle. The seat next to him was empty.

"Do you think this damn operation did any good, Stephan? We killed at least five of them, and maybe a sixth. The guy who shot Martin was hit. You said there was a trail of blood in the snow."

"Did I screw up not tracking him down? From the amount of blood, I don't think he could have gone far at all."

"It would have cost us too much time. And it would have been too risky. They might have had another member of their team sitting back and waiting. Regardless, we took out five or six experienced fighters, and that has to seriously damage the Warlord's capabilities."

"Hard to say, Mike. But we'll know soon enough. I wasn't read in on all the details, but I know other operations are underway. If only as a diversion, our mission was a definite success. And they can't have that many foot soldiers, so even if we didn't cripple their capabilities, we put a big dent in them. Ghazi is going to spend a lot of time looking over his shoulder now, and that's going to make him a lot more vulnerable."

"I hope you're right. This mission was tougher than I expected. I know there's always risks, but those guys were better than I expected. Who's going to tell Samantha what happened?"

• • • • •

In the second vehicle, Travis was singing one of his favorite Country Western tunes, his voice loud and off key.

"Could you please shut the fuck up? If you're not going to let me sit up front, at least let me get some rest back here."

"Don't be such a pussy, Martin. Two lousy stiches — that was all Mike needed to fix you up."

"Maybe so, but my head sure is pounding. The helmet saved my life. So did the radio."

"That's the weirdest thing I've ever seen in combat. You're supposed to use your radio to communicate. Not to stop bullets."

"Maybe not, but it worked, didn't it? Just enough that most of the fragments hit my body armor."

"You were damn lucky. I'm glad. You did a good job out there, Martin. I'm proud to have you on my team."

"Thanks."

He paused. "Travis?"

"Yeah?"

"Who's going to tell Samantha what happened?"

* * *

26

Progress Report

*While terrorist group members occasionally are
arrested in Kazakhstan, the level of terrorism in the
country has been low in part because regional
groups regard Kazakhstan as a safe haven.*

—*Congressional Research Service, 2011**

Kazakhstan, January 17

The Warlord sat in a chair in the central room of the structure that was his residence and base of operations. The dwelling was the largest of four mud-brick buildings inside a walled compound situated on an old farmstead. The wall was almost six feet high and several feet thick, making it an effective barrier against potential enemies, whether they might come on foot or by automobile. A heavy metal gate made from discarded farm equipment offered the only means of entering or leaving the compound. The gate could be opened to allow a visitor through, but only if someone first moved the pickup truck parked in front of it.

There were other farms in the vicinity, but it was a remote area some 150 kilometers north and east of Almaty. To the west, the ground was relatively flat, and the small farms produced a meager income for the peasants who lived there. To the southeast rose the mountain ridge that formed the northern border of the Altyn Emel National Park. As the crow flies, his home was 35 kilometers from the place where his

---

* "Kazakhstan: Recent Developments and U.S. Interests, Jim Nichol,
Congressional Research Service, June 1, 2011, p. 14.

friend Colonel Kholdorov had told him the American force would come seeking him.

The Warlord's home was comfortable if not ornate, although it was considerably more refined than a passer-by would have expected. The mud-brick façade completely obscured the internal wood frame. The interior was simple, yet warm, and each of the several sleeping rooms had its own fireplace.

None of the compound's other three buildings had such amenities. Those structures, where Ghazi's guards were quartered, were much more Spartan. Nevertheless, his men accepted their inferior living conditions without complaint. They were soldiers in the KFB, and Ghazi was their leader. If anything, the willingness of their unquestioned leader to reside in such an ordinary-looking home was a source of inspiration.

One room in the Warlord's house was more luxurious than the others. At its center was a large bed, which was covered with fine fabrics and soft pillows. On one wall, a doorway led to a Western-style bathroom with a shower and sufficient hot water to please Ghazi and anyone he might entertain. Female visitors had been observed entering the home on several occasions.

None of his soldiers had ever seen the bedroom — not even Asim Ospanov, who had served as his chief aide for more than five years. Only the two housekeepers, daughters of the farm's original owner, were permitted to enter the room, and then only when specifically instructed by Ghazi himself.

The housekeepers, who looked after the Warlord's home and private quarters, understood they must never speak of him to anyone. Not to anyone in the small village down the road. Not to their cousins whom they visited every year. Not even to his most ardent followers. The two women understood that their livelihood — and probably even their lives — depended on a loyalty that was to be maintained at all costs.

Ghazi heard the automobile in the distance, the sound of its engine growing louder as it approached. He was on alert, but the details would be looked after by his guards. Consequently, he sat in his chair and waited. When the automobile came to a stop just outside the compound, he knew there was no threat. Not because he could see it or see who was in it. And not because he recognized the sound of the car's engine or the voice of its driver or passenger. It was quite the opposite. He recognized the absence of certain sounds. Had this automobile been bringing a threat to his door, he would have heard gunfire.

A knock on the door was accompanied by a muffled voice. "It is I, Sardar. It is Asim."

"Enter," he responded.

When Ospanov stepped into the house, Ghazi made no indication that his aide should take a seat.

"You are late. I expected you two hours earlier."

"Forgive me, Sardar. I was learning about the foray of our warriors into Altyn Emel. The message sent by Colonel Kholdorov was accurate. The Americans came. Four of them. But our men were waiting for them, exactly as you planned."

"And the outcome?"

"Also as you planned. They will not be a threat to us any longer."

"Details, Asim."

"They came just before dark, two days ago, and they attempted to hide their vehicle under a cloth covered with snow. But a heat-sensing device permitted our warriors to see exactly where it was. The team divided into three parts. Two men left the camp high on the hillside that evening. They remained out of sight and circled around the Americans to approach from the south. Four more men came down the hillside in the morning, positioning themselves to the west of the Americans' camp. The seventh man remained at the base camp as an observer."

"Our men were not seen making their approach?"

"Certainly not the two who circled to the south. I cannot be certain about the four who came from the west, but it is of no consequence. They were able to take cover behind a hill within striking distance. And the attack proceeded exactly as planned. The observer witnessed it all. Our men fired RPGs at the hiding place of the Americans' vehicle, and it was destroyed with a glorious explosion."

"What of the four Americans?"

"All dead. Our men are outstanding warriors."

"And our men? They are here? If so, I must congratulate them."

"One of them was wounded, but it was not serious. The others have taken him to a physician near Almaty. They said it was possible that someone outside our organization might have heard the gunfire and the grenades. They said it would be unwise to have them leave tracks that came here. It would be unsafe. Consequently, they are in hiding. It is to protect you, Sardar."

Ospanov's voice had revealed a growing nervousness as he related his story, and the Warlord looked at him icily. He asked no further questions about the engagement.

"We must make preparations for the coming week, Asim. I have scheduled meetings in Almaty. Money must be made available quickly for the final phase of our operation in America. Everything depends on this, so there must be no mistakes. Book me into the Royal Tulip. I have not been there for some time. Be certain it is a suite, the very best. Register me under the name of Nikita Volkov. You and two others shall accompany me. Much effort will be needed to ensure our security, and you will have little time for relaxation in your hotel room. Consequently, you will not require deluxe accommodations. A standard room will suffice. You three will share it."

* * *

Almaty, Kazakhstan, January 21

The Warlord, registered as Nikita Volkov, sat in the living room of his suite at the Royal Tulip Hotel in Almaty. He picked up the telephone and called his security detail in the adjacent room.

"Asim, please come and speak with me about this evening's arrangements." Without waiting for a reply, he placed the handset back into the receiver.

The knock on his door came seconds later.

"Enter."

Asim used one of the room keys to enter the suite. The Warlord did not rise to greet his aide but waved him toward another chair.

"The plans for our meeting have been made?"

"They have, Sardar. Baluan Aimanov will be at the Central State Museum tomorrow when it opens at ten in the morning. At thirteen minutes after the hour, he will be in the Fourth Exhibition Hall inspecting the photograph by Bagaev. The famous picture showing State grain procurements in 1929. The museum will be quiet at that time of the day, and your discussion will not be disturbed."

"It is a good location. We will discuss the remaining details of our next strike. Next month's operation will be the time of our greatest victory. The time of the greatest defeat for the Americans. They will understand they have lost, when their President is dead."

"Yes, Sardar."

"And what of Gennady Ostrakov?"

"I have spoken with his assistant in Moscow. He is *en route* and will arrive in Almaty tomorrow evening. He will join you for dinner the following day as you requested. The reservation has been made for nine p.m. at the Royal Café downstairs."

"You have investigated this place? It is adequate for us?"

"Very much so. I was told the food is quite good, and the location is excellent. I have arranged a specific table so that one of our men can keep you in view from the hotel lobby. It is a private table, away from the windows, to guarantee your safety. I also will eat my evening meal there. I will be seated where I can observe your table and also the entrance. I must protect you with my life."

"I think it will not come to that. Aimanov and Ostrakov are the only two people who know we have come to Almaty. And Ostrakov knows only of the restaurant. He is unaware that I also stay in this hotel. You appear nervous, Asim."

The aide looked up, startled. "I have no nervousness, Sardar. I only wish to be cautious."

"Then proceed with the preparations. You have advised our contact at Eximbank Kazakhstan that significant funds will be transferred?"

"It has been done. They will carry out the transfer as soon as they receive the request from Alfa-Bank."

"Excellent. And have you made an appointment for me at the Alfa-Bank?"

"At nine tomorrow morning. It is ten minutes to drive from the museum, so there is adequate time. The car will wait nearby."

"That will be satisfactory. I shall take pleasure in moving these funds to the Alfa-Bank. Their origin already is obscure, and the transfer from Eximbank Kazakhstan into what is seen as a Russian bank will raise no questions. At that moment, the funds become clean, and they can be aimed directly at the heart of our enemies."

"But one additional transfer will be necessary?"

The Warlord smiled. "The Americans, in their greed for money, now have opened all the doors so we can provide the dollars our compatriots need to complete their task. The funds will move from Alfa-Bank into an account in Barclay's Bank, where our friends can access it. Just imagine ... the money for our attack will flow through the heart of New York City, and the Americans will congratulate themselves on the success of their capitalism."

"Yes, Sardar. It will be good."

Ghazi leaned back in his armchair and stretched.

"The schedule for my business dealings here is set. It would appear that tomorrow afternoon, after I have met with Aimanov, I can turn to relaxation for the remainder of the day."

"That is correct."

"Then I will do so. You will arrange for a mid-day meal to be brought to my room. Later that afternoon, I will take a massage. I have seen the women who work in the hotel spa. One, in particular, is quite young and quite attractive. I do not wish to use the facilities in the hotel spa, so the woman will come to my room. You will make certain she understands. That she will minister to all my needs."

"What if ...?"

Ospanov stopped when he saw the Warlord's expression.

"It will be done, Sardar."

* * *

27

Insertion

Indirect tactics, efficiently applied, are inexhaustible as Heaven and Earth, unending as the flow of rivers and streams; like the sun and moon, they end but to begin anew; like the four seasons, they pass away to return once more.

—*Sun Tzu, The Art of War, 6th Century B.C.*[*]

Almaty, Kazakhstan, January 22

"**D**amn, I'm cold," Neela said.

Davenport extended his arm and squeezed her shoulder, as might be expected of the husband of this attractive young woman.

"Get used to it," he whispered. "I think it's mostly the wind, though. The weather report said it was supposed to get up to thirty degrees tomorrow and stay above twenty for the next few days, even at night. Not much different from back home."

She scowled at him as they walked into the Holiday Inn.

"Although I guess it depends on what you call home," he continued. "Don't forget I'm from North Carolina."

Neither of them mentioned that they were in a part of the world that had been her childhood home.

"Let's check in and get up to our room," Neela said.

Ten minutes later, they were inspecting their accommodations. Neela started to ask a question, but Davenport held up a hand.

---

[*] "The Art of War," Sun Tsu (Sun Zi), 6th Century B.C., translated by Lionel Giles, 1910.

"Give me a minute."

He removed a device that looked like a TV remote from his briefcase and began moving it around the room, especially in proximity to electrical outlets and connected devices. After several minutes, he smiled and nodded to Neela.

"You were going to ask something?"

"Yeah. How did we manage to get a suite? Even if they waive the rules, we're still supposed to be here on business."

"A couple of reasons. First off, Andrea's probably going to use part of the suite as our operations room. And second, even though our cover is that we're married, they're not going to tell us to share a bed. So one of us gets the bedroom, and the other sleeps on the sofa bed."

"Who gets which, Derek?"

"I have seniority."

"Why don't we fight for it? I'm willing to arm wrestle."

Davenport, who had been a desk jockey for the preceding five years, winced and then shrugged his shoulders. "Okay, you win. I'll take the sofa bed."

Neela's fleeting smirk was replaced with a serious look.

"Who else is going to be here? Besides Andrea?"

"No one else we know. Probably some local people. Andrea will give us the details when she gets in."

He pulled out his phone and looked at the screen.

"Looks like she's arrived. She'll be here in forty-five minutes."

•••••

Davenport opened his laptop and began typing.

"Got some prep work to do."

He was still engrossed in his screen when Chang knocked. Neela verified it was her and then opened the door.

"Good flight?" Chang asked by way of a greeting.

"Pretty good," Neela said, and Davenport mumbled something unintelligible while nodding his head.

"You doing a crossword puzzle, or is there something useful on your screen?"

"Huh? Oh, sorry, Andrea. Actually, I've found something that could be important. Take a look at this."

Chang walked behind Davenport and leaned on the back of his chair to get a better view of his laptop. "Facebook?"

"Yeah. Remember how the Warlord was using Olga as his Facebook persona?"

"Of course. But this is a page for someone named Natalia."

"Exactly. First it was Svetlana, then Olga, and then Yelena. All names from the 1988 Soviet gymnastics team that won the gold medal. There was only one first name he hadn't used before."

"Natalia?"

"Bingo. Natalia Laschenova. I've been keeping an eye out for all of them, but given his past behavior, I don't have any doubt. Check out this paragraph here."

Chang read the text aloud.

To my dear friends.

I had a wonderful Christmas vacation. There were some vermin near our home last week, but we arranged for friends to exterminate the pests. My cousin Cyril is now sending everyone nice presents from the old capital, including money to the family members who have traveled over the ocean. Such a large gift, and it will allow them to complete their vacation in great style and return home in less than one month. I wish a happy new year to all.

Sincerely, your friend, Natalia.

"It sounds like him. When was it posted?"

"Earlier today."

"Then there's no question. Everything fits. It says he's in the old capital right now. Cyril was the name he used in the last post, and we know he's supposed to be here tomorrow to meet with Ostrakov. And he's talking again about the family members. He flat out said that they're in the U.S. What else could he mean by saying they traveled over the ocean?"

Davenport and Neela shrugged. They had no better explanation.

"Can you tell me where he was when he posted it, Derek?"

"The best I could do would be a general location, and it would take time and external resources. When we got done, we wouldn't get anything more specific than saying he's in the Almaty area, and we already know that."

"Then all we can do is wait. We should be hearing something from Ostrakov any time now."

"Something I don't understand," Neela said. "What is the stuff about vermin?"

Chang frowned and said nothing. She walked to the window, pushed the draperies to the side, and silently stared out at the imposing Tian Shan Mountains to the south. Suddenly, she turned to face the other two.

"Fuck it! We're all in this together, and it won't change anything now."

Neela was confused. "What's going on?"

"It's another operation. It's need-to-know, but I just decided you need to know. You're isolated from Nousafarin now, so there's no risk of accidently saying something to her. There was another operation going on parallel to ours. It was designed as a diversion. We sent a Special Ops team to attack the Warlord. Or at least to engage his defensive perimeter."

"We know where his home base is?" Davenport asked.

"Not exactly. I'm not going to share the details, but we were given information that we might find him a hundred miles northeast of here an unpopulated part of the national park. The tactical assumption was that we could engage his men, although it would be some distance from his base. We still don't know where that is."

"But you're saying — Natalia is saying — that the people who were 'exterminated' were ours?"

"He's dissembling, Derek. I was advised that we sent in a small force a week ago — just three or four men. Our team engaged their forces and killed all of them. We had no casualties. At least no injuries that were life threatening. It's just the opposite of the Facebook post."

"That sounds like a real change," Davenport said. "He's always been arrogant, but none of his earlier posts were fabrications. Why would he suddenly change his style now?"

"I'll bet he doesn't know," Neela said. "Remember, I've met him. His men are scared of him. Maybe they were afraid to tell him his forces were wiped out."

"Could be," Davenport added. "And if that's the case, some discontent on their side would be to our benefit. If he's intentionally putting out false information to his followers, maybe it means that he's concerned he'll be attacked again.

"Yeah," Neela said. "And if somehow he has the wrong information about eliminating our team, maybe he'll be a little overconfident. Either way, it might make him a little less focused on what we're going to do here. A little less suspicious."

Chang held up her hand to signal an end to the exchange.

"Right now, it doesn't matter. All we can do is concentrate on our part of the operation and make sure we don't fuck it up."

• • • • •

Thirty minutes later, Chang's phone rang. She looked at the screen, and pushed a button.

"Are you encrypted, Andrea?"

Her already anxious expression intensified, and she hit another button on the phone.

"Go ahead."

Chang nodded several times and then asked several short questions. She motioned to Davenport and repeated the answers so he could make notes.

"The Ritz-Carlton … the LT Grill … okay, eight p.m."

Her words were followed by another period of silence in the room while she listened.

"All right, I'll see you in the lobby at seven forty-five. Be sure to remind her once again that she doesn't know us. She can't look in our direction. But she can't avoid looking in our direction, either. Shit, I don't know what I'm worried about. She's probably better at this than I am."

Chang ended the call.

"What's the deal?" Davenport asked.

"Ostrakov made contact with Canterbury. Actually, it was only a text exchange with someone he thinks is Canterbury. Allan is nice and comfy back in Langley. Anyway, Ostrakov is having dinner with Nousafarin tonight at the Ritz-Carlton. I'm meeting one of our local assets, a guy named Dariga Nabilov — that's his work name, at least — and we'll be having dinner there, too. Just to keep an eye on things."

"Won't you be a little obvious? Speaking English?"

Chang shook her head slowly. "Derek, please. I'm not a complete idiot."

"Sorry, Andrea. I didn't mean … I guess what I meant was that I didn't know you spoke Kazakh … or Russian."

"Enough to order a cup of coffee. But if that were all I could do, my dinner with Nabilov would be a bit obvious."

"Then how …?"

"I'm fucking with you, Derek. You wouldn't know it from his name, but Nabilov is ethnic Chinese. He studied for a while in China when he was younger, and he speaks remarkably good Mandarin. And as you might guess from my name, I have a Chinese background. There's a substantial Chinese presence in Almaty. The border is less than two hundred miles away, and people have been crossing back and forth for centuries."

At this point, Davenport began to roll his eyes. "Okay, Andrea. I've been properly chastised. I just never heard you speak anything other than English."

"No problem, Derek. I guess I'm a little edgy about tonight. And the next couple of days, too. We're not going to get any do-overs."

"Yeah. I know what you mean."

"What about you, Neela? You doing okay?"

"As well as can be expected. I haven't been this fucking nervous since my first day of boot camp."

* * *

The LT Grill, Almaty, January 22

At five minutes after eight, Nousafarin approached the entrance to the LT Grill. She spoke to the man at the reception desk in Kazakh.

"Good evening. I wish to join the table of Mr. Ostrakov."

"Certainly, Madame. He is expecting you. You are Ms. Rahmon, I assume?" He stammered, enchanted by the elegant and beautiful woman standing in front of him.

"That is correct." She smiled at him in a way that he found disorienting.

The headwaiter heard the exchange as he walked to the desk. "Please come this way, Madame."

He walked across the dining room, making sure that she was close behind him. As they passed one of the other tables, Nousafarin caught a glimpse of Andrea's profile. She was led to a table set for two that was occupied by a man of indeterminate age.

The man stood immediately, and when she extended her hand, he grasped it lightly. Then he leaned over and kissed it lightly in the European manner.

"Miss Rahmon. I am Gennady Ostrakov. I am delighted to meet you at last. I have heard many wonderful things about you."

As soon as she was seated, Ostrakov looked at the headwaiter. "You will please bring us the champagne now."

With a hint of anxiety, he turned quickly to Nousafarin. "That is acceptable, I hope. If you prefer, I will order something else. I chose it because it is the best on their list."

She smiled at him. The same smile that had captivated many other men.

"The champagne would be wonderful. Thank you."

It arrived in a silver ice bucket. After Ostrakov approved the selection, the waiter removed the cork and poured two glasses.

"A toast to the success of your business ventures, Miss Rahmon. With the assurance that I will do everything possible to assist you while you are in Almaty."

They clinked their glasses and sipped the champagne. They nodded their approval to the waiter, although Nousafarin did so only after she smiled at Ostrakov in the most sensual way possible.

"Tell me please, Miss Rahmon, exactly how I may be of assistance. I know you are seeking objets d'art for your business. As our mutual friend advised, I know many people in this city. I am familiar with many artists, and I know the owners of several galleries and the curators at museums. If you should need introductions, I can be at your service."

"That is very kind of you Mr. Ostrakov. It is exactly the kind of assistance I need."

"Very good, then. Do you have a business card?"

"Certainly." She reached into her purse and retrieved a small leather case from which she removed several cards. She took a pen from her purse and wrote a number on the back of one of the cards.

"You can reach me easily at this number while I am here in Kazakhstan. The other cards you may give to your colleagues."

His smile was genuine. "And I have a card for you as well, Miss Rahmon."

He handed her the card. She saw his name on the front, printed in both Roman and Cyrillic. He had also written something on the back. "The Royal Tulip." Below it was a time. "Tomorrow evening at nine." And a name. "Volkov."

She smiled earnestly. "Thank you so much. I am quite certain that my business ventures will work well on this trip."

While they drank their champagne, she told him about the kinds of artwork she was seeking. They spoke of her favorites and of his. Of the works she owned and those she bought and sold for her business.

"I would, of course, love to own works by the great masters. Even those we still call the modern artists of the 20th century. Can you imagine having a painting on the wall in your home by Chagall? Or Kandinsky?" She knew her choice of artists born in Russia would have a favorable effect on her dinner companion."

"My dear … if only I had such a thing in my possession, I would give it to you at once. Just to see that smile cross your lips again."

Their light conversation continued for several more minutes. When the waiter brought menus to the table, Nousafarin waved hers away, looking across the table at Ostrakov.

"Please. You know this city and its restaurants. I would be delighted if you would choose for me."

By the time their meal was finished, he was thoroughly enchanted with Nousafarin. Despite her protests, he insisted that he would pay for the dinner, and she yielded.

"This means, however, that I am in your debt, Gennady."

The progression to their given names had been achieved by the time their main courses had arrived.

"Perhaps I could begin to repay my debt this evening, Gennady. If you would accompany me back to my suite at the InterContinental, I could offer you a very fine brandy. I purchased it as a gift for an old friend, but my interaction with you is far more important."

She reached across the table and gently stroked the back of his hand. "Would that please you?"

He noticed the smile. The same smile, once again.

"Very much, Nousafarin. I would like that very much."

* * *

Holiday Inn, Almaty, January 23

Neela yawned and looked away from the TV as the final credits of the film scrolled across the screen.

"I'm beat, Derek. I thought we would have heard from Andrea by now. I've got to get some sleep."

"Me too. She didn't say she'd call tonight. Just that she'd tell us when she knew what the next steps were."

"That's not reassuring. Nousafarin was supposed to have called her after her dinner. It's way past midnight now."

"Things never go exactly like we plan them. It'll be okay."

"You really think so?"

"Who knows? I'm just as worried as you are, Neela, but there's nothing we can do about it. Go to bed. I'll fall asleep soon enough myself."

She stood up and turned back as she walked through the bedroom doorway.

"It's a king size bed. It won't bother me if you stay on the other side. It'll be more comfortable."

Ten minutes later, they were both asleep.

· · · · ·

The buzz of Davenport's phone woke them.

"Yes?"

"It's Andrea. Are you awake? It's past eight."

"Uh … yeah. I'm awake."

He listened for a few seconds. "Yeah, okay."

He put down the phone and looked over at Neela.

"You'd better get up. Andrea will be here any second."

They still looked half asleep when Chang arrived several minutes later. Her eyes paused briefly on the sofa bed, which looked as neat as it had a day earlier. She said nothing.

Davenport broke the silence. "You said there were some developments."

"Yes. I just spoke with Nousafarin. Everything is moving. Just about as well as we could have expected."

"I thought she was going to call last night. After her dinner."

"We had someone on her floor of InterContinental watching out, so we knew it was all okay. Something you'll learn with more experience is that an operative has to be given maximum flexibility and discretion."

The sharpness of her remark was emphasized by a brief glance in the direction of the bedroom.

"On the other hand, you're right about how we thought the night was going to proceed. She told me this morning that she wanted to make a very strong impression on Ostrakov so her introduction to the Warlord proceeds as smoothly as possible. Dariga Nabilov and I witnessed her performance at dinner last night, and she was incredible. Charming, witty, smart, seductive. Ostrakov was utterly enthralled. And I gather that his subsequent visit to Nousafarin's suite did nothing to detract from that frame of mind."

"So, I guess that's all good," Davenport said. "What are the next steps?"

"Ostrakov is meeting with the Warlord tonight, and he gave Nousafarin the details of the meeting. There is a reservation for two in the name of Nikita Volkov at 9 p.m. at the Royal Café, the main restaurant at The Royal Tulip. Probably the best hotel in the city."

"And Nousafarin?"

She looked at Davenport with a sly smile.

"Quite a coincidence. She has a reservation at the same restaurant for a late dinner at ten o'clock. Almost certainly, she and Ostrakov will notice each other. And it will go from there."

"And we'll have watchers?"

"Only briefly. We've got a team going in at eight. They'll finish their meal before nine thirty, but it will be enough to make a quick assessment of the guests of honor. Ghazi — under the pseudonym of Volkov — and Ostrakov."

"This team will know them?"

"Yes. One of the two is Dariga Nabilov. He was with me to observe Ostrakov last night, so he'll be able to learn what they put in place for security. And to convey any last-minute details to Nousafarin."

"What about Neela and me?"

"You have a reservation for nine thirty. You'll get a text if Nabilov sees or hears anything you need to know about."

Chang turned her attention to Neela.

"Your evaluation is essential. We're almost certain that this man Volkov is indeed Ghazi. But we don't have a positive identification. You're the only person on our team who has met him face-to-face. We need you to verify that Volkov is really the man we're after."

"I understand."

"Questions?"

Neela looked at each of her colleagues and then spoke hesitantly. "Yeah, I've got one. It's his name. Do you know what it means?"

"No idea. Derek?"

Davenport shrugged.

Neela continued. "I guess it's more of a comment than a question, actually. In the past, the names he's used have had a specific meaning. You've said it's like he's playing a game."

"So, you're talking about Nikita Volkov. Nikita, maybe? Like the Soviet leader, Nikita Khrushchev?"

"Not exactly Andrea. I guess I've spent more time speaking Russian than you two. The name Nikita has a meaning. It's got to do with being victorious in battle. It has a Greek origin and means *unconquered*. Or even more specifically, it can mean *unconquerable*.

"Then he's still fucking with us. Still trying to send us messages."

"I think so, Andrea. And there's more. The name *Volkov*."

"Like the German word Volk? Maybe meaning *the people*, like a Volkswagen, *the people's car*?

"It's different in Russian. Nothing even related to the German. In Russian, Volk means *wolf*."

"So it's an obvious play on the names he's been using for years," Chang replied. "Kaskyrbai is *fearless as a wolf*, and Ghazi, means *conqueror*."

"Exactly. Even if I couldn't point at him for you, you have your answer. It's him."

* * *

Royal Café, Almaty, January 23

Dariga Nabilov and his partner were experienced operatives. Soon after they began their dinners, they noticed the two men who had stationed themselves in the lobby outside the Royal Café. Nabilov and his partner paid no attention and gave no sign that it concerned them. But they understood it was Ghazi's security detail.

At ten minutes before nine, two more men entered the hotel lobby and walked up to the reception desk at the restaurant entrance. They were together, but they were not together. One of them, a well-dressed middle-aged man, asked to be seated, explaining that his guest would arrive shortly.

"If you would please follow me, Monsieur, I will show you to your table." Turning to the second man, he said "Just a brief moment, if you would be so kind as to wait."

The headwaiter walked past the American agents and stopped at a table that also had a view of the restaurant's entrance. He pulled back the chair that faced away from the door, but his customer only smiled at him.

"I think that the views of your restaurant would be much better from the other side of the table."

The headwaiter offered no argument, and moments later, the new arrival was comfortably seated. His gaze focused beyond the American agents as he waited for his guest to appear.

At almost exactly nine o'clock, Ostrakov approached at the reception station. He and Volkov could see each other, but neither made any sign of recognition. Moments later, the headwaiter brought Ostrakov to the Warlord's table.

"Ah, good evening," Volkov said as he stood to greet his visitor. "It is good to see you once again."

"And it is a delight for me. It has been too long since we have seen each other, my friend."

Soon the two men were sharing an aperitif, and their expressions had turned serious. Their conversation was conducted in low tones, and their waiter was waved away immediately after he placed menus on the table.

"Thank you. We will signal when we are ready."

Almost fifteen minutes had passed when the tone of the conversation suddenly lightened. The agents sitting nearby observed an exchange of smiles followed by a handshake. A major shipment of materiel, mostly small arms and ammunition, had been arranged. The arms would satisfy the needs of the Warlord, and the sales price would put a considerable amount of money in the pocket of the seller. Ostrakov, who was only an intermediary, would receive a substantial commission for his evening's work.

"I think the vehicle is the best part of our agreement, Nikita. It is the newest we could obtain of the Toyota SUVs. It has four-wheel drive, and it will go anywhere. Yet when you are in the city, it is a vehicle of elegance. People see you riding in this vehicle, and they will assume you are the richest of Russian oligarchs."

Ostrakov handed the Warlord a set of keys.

"At the time and place we have arranged, a vehicle will stop, and its driver will walk away. You will discover that these keys fit the vehicle, and its cargo area will contain every piece of merchandise you have requested."

They shook hands again.

"Thank you, Gennady. You are a friend to me. And to our cause."

Volkov signaled to the waiter, and soon they were waiting for their meals.

The choreography of the evening was remarkably complex, but everything was proceeding perfectly. At nine-twenty, the two American agents rose from their table and left the restaurant. They paid no attention to Volkov and his guest, nor to the third man who originally had arrived with Volkov. In turn, their exit went completely unnoticed by the Warlord and his security team.

As Nabilov reached far side of the main lobby of the Royal Tulip Hotel, he paused to send a text message.

• • • • •

Davenport and Neela had entered their taxicab at precisely nine fifteen. It was an ordinary Almaty cab that had been borrowed for the evening. The driver was another local asset. He reported to officials at the U.S. Consulate, although he knew nothing of the operation except that he was to pick up his passengers at the Holiday Inn and drive them to the Royal Tulip. Afterward, he would park on the street and remain until he was called for the return trip, turning down any other fares with the explanation that he was already engaged.

Davenport felt his phone vibrate as they drove along Dostyk Avenue. He entered a code to bring up the encrypted message and held the phone so he and Neela could read it at the same time.

> *Table for two near center of restaurant. Away from*
> *windows. Visible from entrance. Guest has back to*
> *entrance. Target facing entrance. Two watchers in*
> *hotel lobby. Third man eating alone in restaurant,*
> *back to entrance, watching target and guest.*

Quietly, he spoke to Neela. "That's good. We'll be able to scope him out immediately."

"I'm nervous as shit, Derek."

"I know. But we've got nothing to worry about. We'll be there together, and he won't be paying any attention to us. We're just looking, not confronting."

"It's not me, it's Nousa. If we do anything to screw this up, they'll kill her."

He put his right arm around her shoulder and squeezed her hand with his left hand. "Just take a deep breath. We're going to do fine."

When they looked up, they could see the golden façade of the Royal Tulip just ahead of them, and the driver pulled into the circle in front of the main entrance. Davenport made a point of handing several banknotes to the driver, who in turn acted quite pleased with the exchange.

"I will wait for you at the side of the hotel. Just call my number and I will come at once."

He handed Davenport a card with his telephone number, the same number that Davenport had previously stored in his phone.

After entering the hotel lobby and checking their coats, the couple walked toward the restaurant. They noticed two men standing idly in the lobby, but those men took no notice of the couple.

"Good evening," Davenport said. "We have a reservation for two at nine thirty."

When the headwaiter bent slightly to look at his reservations book, a new sightline was opened to them. Davenport looked toward the middle-aged man facing them and made his tentative identification. He also noticed a second man, sitting by himself at a table not far away, whose attention was focused on the same middle-aged diner. Davenport knew the second man was not to be ignored.

Neela had approached the restaurant with her arm linked to Davenport's, and once more her instructions came to mind. She and Derek were just two newlyweds on a vacation trip.

Suddenly her arm tightened, and she turned toward Davenport, clutching his other arm and pulling herself tight against him.

At the same moment, the headwaiter resumed his full height and smiled at them. "Yes, I see. Mr. and Mrs. Davenport, I assume? Your table is ready, if ..."

At that moment, he saw that something was wrong. "Is Madame ...? Is everything all right, Sir?"

Neela had spoken softly to Davenport at the same time. "It's him, Derek. No question about it. We can't go any farther or there's a real risk that he'll recognize me. We've got to go. Now!"

Davenport saw the man he thought was Ghazi glance up curiously toward the restaurant entrance. At that instant, the solitary diner who had been watching Ghazi turned his head toward them as well.

Davenport looked at the headwaiter and spoke quietly. "I'm afraid my wife has become ill. We are just married, you see ..."

"Certainly, Monsieur." He said it obsequiously, almost as though it were an everyday occurrence. "May I call a taxi for you?"

"You are most kind, but it is not necessary. We have a car waiting for us. Please forgive the inconvenience." He thrust several banknotes into the man's hand. A large but not extravagant tip.

The headwaiter responded with a serious, almost sad look. "It is unnecessary, Monsieur." But he did not return the bills.

"Perhaps you can return tomorrow. At whatever time you wish. You need only to call me. I will make sure you have a table."

"Yes. Thank you. That's very kind of you."

Neela had pressed against Davenport at the onset of her feigned illness. She shielded her face from view, but she was able to scan the dining room thoroughly.

As they turned to leave, Davenport put his arm around Neela, and her face remained hidden from those in the dining area. All they had been able to see of the minor commotion at the restaurant entrance was the quick departure of a young couple. The woman was young, and she was pretty, but nobody would have been able to recognize her if they saw her again.

As they walked through the hotel, Davenport took out his phone and made the call. A moment later, he put the phone to his ear. "Yes. We're ready ... right now ... thirty seconds at the most."

Forty-five seconds later their taxi was hurrying back toward the Holiday Inn.

· · · · ·

The dance at the Royal Café was not finished. About half an hour after the arrival and premature departure of the young married couple, a solitary woman approached the reception desk of the restaurant. This time, the two men stationed outside the entrance took notice. Not because she seemed dangerous, but because she was beautiful. One of the men had to nudge the other to get him to stop staring.

"Good evening, Madame. May I be of service?"

"Thank you. I have a reservation for ten p.m."

He looked down for a moment. "Ah, yes. Mademoiselle Rahmon. You will be dining alone?"

"Yes, thank you. Just a quiet table if you could. Perhaps across the room, near the windows."

"It would be most satisfactory, Mademoiselle. If you would follow me, please."

They walked almost directly past the table occupied by Ostrakov and Volkov, but the two men were just finishing their main course. Volkov had become so relaxed that he failed to notice the attractive woman who walked past their table.

Asim Ospanov noticed. But he saw nothing he might consider a threat. It was simply a woman of remarkable beauty. He smiled to himself when she passed by the others. It was quite unusual that such a woman would fail to attract the notice of the Warlord. Clearly the financial negotiations had gone well.

Nousafarin told her waiter that she only wished a light meal, and soon she was enjoying an appetizer and sipping a glass of wine. It seemed only to be pure coincidence when she glanced across the room and her eyes met those of Gennady Ostrakov. Broad smiles were exchanged.

"My friend, Nikita," Ostrakov said quickly. "Could you possibly excuse me for one moment? There is a lady across the room to whom I must say hello. She may be an important business contact for me."

Volkov turned, just in time to see Nousafarin avert her eyes. He paused for a moment and then smiled as he replied to Ostrakov.

"Certainly, Gennady. Our transactions are completed, so I suggest you might ask this lovely woman to join us. Possibly it would be good for your other business concerns. And under no circumstances will I allow you to leave me this evening without first making an introduction."

Ostrakov crossed the dining room to Nousafarin's table. From a distance, it appeared entirely polite and formal. And it would have seemed no different if others had been able to overhear.

"My dear Miss Rahmon. What a surprise. I did not expect to see you again so soon. I am still … how do you say …?"

He paused, almost as though embarrassed. "... still recovering from a wonderful evening."

Ostrakov made a small gesture toward his own table.

"My business colleague expressed interest when I saw you. When he saw you. Would it be acceptable for me to introduce you?"

"Certainly, Mr. Ostrakov. Perhaps after I finish my meal, I could join your table for a coffee. Or a brandy."

She reached into her purse. "Perhaps you could give him one of my cards in the meantime. I always welcome the opportunity to make new business contacts."

As Ostrakov walked back to his table, he realized that Volkov had been watching.

"Who is that gorgeous creature, Gennady? Tell me please, that she has agreed to meet me. Such a woman should never be permitted to remain by herself."

With considerable effort, Ostrakov restrained a laugh. He knew something of the Warlord's appetites.

"My good friend Nikita, you may relax. She will join us when she finishes her meal. She will come to our table for a coffee or a brandy."

Volkov took the business card from Ostrakov and smiled. "It is unfortunate, Gennady, that exactly when she comes to join us will be the time that you must depart."

Ostrakov nodded sagely. He had completed his obligations. Both to Nikita Volkov and to his old friend Ivan. He would be happy to leave this place and return to Russia, where he would feel safe.

• • • • •

It was nearly eleven p.m. when Nousafarin signaled her waiter. Volkov could not hear what she said, but he saw her extend a hand in his direction, and he saw the waiter nod in response.

Seconds later, the waiter who had served Volkov and Ostrakov appeared at their table.

"You would like me to set an extra chair for the lady?"

"Unfortunately, it will not be necessary," Volkov said. "My colleague has learned that he must depart, so you need only clear his place. The lady will make it two once more."

Ostrakov stood as Nousafarin was escorted across the room by her waiter. When the procession neared, Volkov stood as well.

"Miss Rahmon. I wish to introduce you to my colleague and good friend, Nikita Volkov. He is an important businessman here in Almaty, and I am certain that the two of you will get along famously."

He took a step, and Nousafarin seemed surprised. "But you are not staying?"

"Alas. Something has come up, and I cannot. But you will find yourself in good hands."

"Then good night, Mr. Ostrakov. I shall look forward to the next time we meet."

As Ostrakov walked away, Volkov took Nousafarin's hand and held it as she took her seat. Then he resumed his own place at the table.

"What may I offer you, Miss Rahmon? Tea, coffee, vodka, a brandy? Whatever you might wish."

"A brandy would be a lovely treat, Mr. Volkov. I would be delighted."

As the late evening continued, Nousafarin was surprised by the courtesy and sophistication Volkov displayed. She had expected someone considerably more boorish and vulgar, yet his conversation flowed effortlessly through a range of topics from political philosophy to the arts.

He told her the story of his life, of his university studies in Russia, and of his disaffection with the communist system. But it was not an accurate story, as it touched only on the topics he wanted her to know and skipped those subjects he wished to remain his secret. According to the words she heard, he had been a minor government functionary until the fall of communism when he leapt at the opportunity to employ his networks and skills and became a successful entrepreneur in international commerce.

She told him the story of her life — the story that had been fashioned and coached by Canterbury and Chang. She spoke of the things that were to be divulged and kept secret those things not intended to be shared. She related her childhood in Dushanbe and disclosed that her parents had been casualties of the civil war.

Nousafarin described her sojourn in Russia as a girl, a stage of her life that she portrayed as a long stay with relatives in Bytxa, a tiny village on the coast of the Black Sea near Sochi. In fact, Ivan had once taken her there for a brief visit, although neither the man nor the event was included in her narrative.

She also told Volkov how she left Russia to go to Paris — another event that was true, even if the underlying details she provided were not. She even spoke of studying at a small university after moving to the United States.

"My family and friends understood that I wished to study art, and they had friends who lived in a place called New Mexico. They sent me to study there at a school called Santa Fe College." Another half-truth, but it was accurate if one considered that Allan Canterbury — the man who was both family and friend to her by the name of Adrian Carter — had sponsored her registration in a course at the community college in Santa Fe one summer.

She told Volkov how she had returned to Paris after completing her education, at first working in a small gallery where she purchased a painting from someone she considered a rising star. Her judgement had been correct, she said, and she sold it five years later for a sum that allowed her to purchase the gallery from the elderly owner. Now, she earned enough that she could afford to travel throughout Europe to search for new artists she might exhibit.

The thread of truth was there. She knew the gallery — the place listed on her business card — and had been to it many times. Moreover, Andrea had assured her that any investigation of the gallery, or even its financial records, would show that Nousafarin had owned it for almost six years.

Over the course of several drinks and finally coffee, they had enchanted each other with their narratives. The only caveat was that Nousafarin alone knew they were nothing but fabrications.

The stories may have been a fiction, but the encounter was a success. Nousafarin had been successful in her seduction, and she was not in the least surprised. It was, after all, her greatest talent.

* * *

Holiday Inn, Almaty, January 24

It was a nearly 3:00 a.m. when Davenport walked into the bedroom to wake Neela.

"You need to wake up now. Andrea will be coming over. As soon as she finishes talking to Nousafarin. They're across the street at the InterContinental."

"Okay." She shook her head. "I really feel out of it."

"The nap probably did you some good. You want something to drink?"

"Just a Coke. Are there any left in the fridge?"

"Sure. Hold on a minute."

"Derek?"

"Yeah?"

"We did okay, didn't we? I didn't think the stress would hit me so hard."

"No problem. And we didn't screw up, Neela. You made the positive ID, and that was our assignment."

"It wasn't just him. You noticed the other man who was sitting by himself at a table closer to the door?"

"Yeah. One of his bodyguards, I guess."

"Not just a bodyguard, Derek. It was the man the Warlord calls Asim. He was in charge of security. That's why I knew we had to get out of there so quickly. When I saw him, I knew he'd recognize me even if Ghazi didn't."

"Then what you did was perfect. We never got into the restaurant area, so nobody had any reason to think anything was going on. They just saw someone who wasn't feeling well. The way you were leaning on me when we left, I bet those two watchers in the lobby thought you were about to barf all over me. Everyone there bought your act. The headwaiter was so concerned, he was ready to walk out with us to take care of you."

"It wasn't entirely an act, Derek. I honestly did feel like I was going to puke. It brought back when I first met him. It was Asim that told us what to do. How Samantha and I had to bathe and how to dress. All so the Warlord could fuck us. It all came back at once. It freaked me out."

"Doesn't matter now, and it couldn't have worked out more perfectly. Here, drink this. The caffeine will help."

• • • • •

Andrea Chang arrived twenty minutes later. Davenport had sent a text summarizing what had happened, and she knew Neela was upset.

"Feeling better now?"

"Yeah. I just got totally exhausted all of a sudden."

"Did they see your face? Could any of them have recognized you?"

"I've never seen either of the two in the lobby before. But I recognized both men inside the restaurant — Ghazi and the aide who was sitting by himself. Even with the change in my appearance, I think they would have known it was me. It was just something about how they were looking around. So I leaned into Derek before they had a chance to look at my face. They never got a clear look at me."

"Then we're okay. Things like this happen to agents in the field. The good ones get through it, just like you did."

"What happened with Nousafarin?" Davenport wanted to change the subject.

Chang's expression was hard to read. A hint of a smile, but also concern.

"Pretty much what we hoped for. I only had a short conversation with her, and I want her to sleep before we make any more plans. I'm encouraged, though. These last two nights have convinced me that she's everything we believed she could be."

"But she didn't invite him back to her hotel."

"No. She thought it would be a mistake to rush it. He has to think he's the one initiating the seduction."

"If she'd gotten him back to her hotel, we could have taken him. It would all be over."

"Not that simple, Derek. We've got a lot of leeway in this operation, but not enough to create a major international incident. It's clear that the Warlord doesn't go anywhere without an armed escort, and we can't have a firefight in the InterContinental."

"Then what's the plan?"

"It's up to the Warlord. And Nousafarin. We just have to wait and see. But Nousa was confident. She said he was acting like a teenager who was desperate to get laid for the first time. That he seemed so turned on, he was almost being careless. He'll contact her. Soon."

* * *

InterContinental Hotel, Almaty, January 24

Later that day, when Chang knocked on the door to her hotel room, Nousafarin let her in immediately.

"Please, have a chair."

"Thank you."

There was stiffness in their interaction that had not been present in previous meetings. Chang responded with a gentleness that was unusual.

"Are you okay, Nousafarin? Is everything all right?"

"I am okay. Perhaps I may be nervous a little. But it is okay. I feel better since I slept."

"Can you tell me about it?"

"Yes. Let me pour a drink of water. Then I will tell you."

She walked to a sink in the living area of the suite. "May I offer you something, Andrea? A brandy? A cold drink?"

"Just water for me also, Nousafarin."

They sat on opposite sides of a coffee table, and Nousafarin began to relate her story. "It was difficult for me last night. More so than I had expected. I think perhaps it was because of the things that have happened. Of what he did to Neela and Samantha."

She didn't know about Anja. Nobody had told her that part of the story.

"You don't have to do this, Nousafarin. You just say the word, and you'll be on a plane back home in the morning."

"You are wrong, Andrea. This is something I must do. It is a debt. A debt to Adrian Carter. You know that name? It is no matter. I can say it is a debt to Allan Canterbury. Without him. I would be nothing. I would be already an old woman begging for handouts in Russia. All used up and offering sex to pay for my next meal. He saved my life, Andrea, and I can never repay him."

"This could cost your life, Nousa. If you're not able to do it the way we planned, you'll be discovered. And the Warlord will kill you."

"You should understand that I must do it. There is no choice. It is a small thing on my part — something to help the man who saved me and the country that gave me a new life. Even if that life ends now, it is a price that is small for what I was given. My freedom."

They each took a drink of their water. Neither of them spoke for nearly a minute.

"He is a frightening man, Andrea. But last night I overcame my fear. I played the role I was asked to play, and he played the part we expected him to play. He is a man who listens only to his *khuy*. You know that word? It is Russian. It is a vulgarity. In English, you would say he is ruled by his dick."

"And that would not be a threat to you?"

"I think he is usually in control. This time he would not be so. But he will think he was in control, and that will make it easier for me so I can make him careless."

"Tell me about the contact, Nousafarin. Every detail. It may be important for our planning."

• • • • •

Everything happened almost exactly like we planned, Andrea. He suggested last night that I should accompany him to his hotel room. I think probably it is in the Royal Tulip, the same as the restaurant, but he never said so exactly. I pretended a little bit to be offended by his suggestion. I am not that kind of woman, I said to him. If you want to make love to me, you must first be nice to me.

He told me he only would be in Almaty for two more days. Then he would have to leave for important business reasons. I answered that he would need to move quickly if he wished to make good impression on me. I could see it did not make him too happy, but it was the point, no? As I told you last night ... I think probably it was early this morning, when I came back to my room. He promised he would call me.

So two hours ago, I received the call. Actually, it was the second call. The first came from the concierge of the hotel. To tell me that a delivery had come for me. They sent it up to me. Over there, on the table — the flowers. They are quite beautiful, don't you agree? I think they must have been quite expensive. And the chocolates are costly, as well.

As I said, the call came two hours ago. He did not say his name to me, but I knew it was him. He asks me, do you like the flowers? And the chocolates?

I answered that he was making a good impression on me. I said it was a good sign for him. It almost made me laugh, but I could tell he started to have a catch in his breath. I knew what he wanted to ask, but he wasn't sure. He was afraid if he moved too soon I would just say no.

So I told him the chocolates were also very good. I told to him that I especially liked the ones that were hard. That they felt so good when I put them in my mouth.

Finally, he couldn't stop himself. He said he must see me before he left on his business trip. He almost begged me. So finally, I say okay, I will see you before you go. Maybe you would like to take me to dinner, tonight?

He said it was what he wanted most of all. If it was okay, he said, he would tell the chef at the hotel to make something special. He told me it would only be the best. The finest caviar and champagne, second to nothing. He said the chef would prepare the top things from his kitchen just for us. Truthfully, Andrea, I think maybe he told the chef he would cut off his fingers if it was not good enough.

And then he asked the tricky question to me. He said, if it is okay, we will have this feast in his suite. He says to me it is the best suite in hotel. The Presidential Suite.

I ask him are you trying to seduce me?

He makes a sound like he almost is choking. No, he says. I want only to treat you like the beautiful lady you are.

I know then, Andrea. We have him. So I say to him, yes.

* * *

Holiday Inn, Almaty, January 25

Chang sat in the living area of the suite occupied by Davenport and Neela. She looked nervously at her watch. It was past midnight.

"Nousafarin said she would call me as soon as she got back to her room at the Intercontinental, but it probably won't be for another hour or two. Maybe not until the morning. I'll sleep here tonight. You're not using the sofa bed, anyway."

If it was meant as a dig, Neela ignored it. "Do you know where she is?"

"Only that she's with the Warlord. The Royal Tulip has a Presidential Suite, so I think we can be confident it's where she is."

"I wish she had a tracking device."

"Not this time, Derek. No point. This is still just to set things up. We saw the car that picked her up at the InterContinental. A black Mercedes S-class sedan. A car just like it pulled up a few minutes later at the Royal Tulip, although we couldn't get close enough to see her get out. Too much surveillance at this stage could screw up the entire operation."

• • • • •

Chang's phone rang at two-thirty in the morning, and she recognized the number. She was lying on the sofa bed, but she was only dozing. Davenport and Neela were both asleep in the next room.

"Yes, Nousa."

"I'm clear, so we can talk."

"Are you okay? That's the most important thing."

"I'm fine. Pretty good, actually. It's okay, Andrea. I still have my touch, if you know what I mean."

"I think I know. Tell me how it went this evening."

"Mostly like we expected. He had this big feast for just two of us. But it was clear he had more on his mind. He was just like a little kid. Or maybe a puppy. He had food and drink. Only the best, just like he promised to me. But he wanted something else. I made him wait for some time, but then I decided I would offer it to him."

"And he accepted the offer?"

Andrea heard a short laugh at the other end. "Sure thing, he did. He accepted right away. And he got what he wanted. I can say he's a tired guy right now."

"What about the next steps?"

"Even better than we hoped. I knew he would want more. It's why I say I still have my touch. I was afraid he would say I must wait until he comes back to Almaty. But no, he asks me to go with him."

"Where?" The question was preceded by a sharp intake of breath.

"Best of all the possibilities, Andrea. He says to his headquarters. He tells me it's real great. One time he calls it his country house. It's what we wanted. We go there, it's going to be isolated. It means you can hit him."

"When does he want to go, Nousa?"

"He says we leave at noon. He will send his car for me."

"Is your luggage packed? The special luggage we gave you?"

"It is by the door. Everything else I tell the hotel to store for me until I get back. One week he says. It is enough time."

"I hope so. Get some sleep. I'll call you later in the morning. For final arrangements."

Andrea put the phone down and looked up to see Davenport and Neela standing beside her.

"All systems are go. Nousafarin is on top of her game. It looks like that bastard Ghazi is on borrowed time."

* * *

28

Monitoring

Let your plans be dark and impenetrable as night,
and when you move, fall like a thunderbolt.

—*Sun Tzu, The Art of War, 6th Century B.C.* [*]

Almaty, Kazakhstan, January 25

Andrea Chang and her team were gathered in a suite at the Holiday Inn. Two computer technicians worked at a desk around which the others congregated. The desk was crowded with communications gear and monitors.

Neela looked at Chang curiously. "Do you think they searched her luggage?"

"Hard to say. We're fairly certain they did with Anja, which may have been how they caught her. Anja's tracking device was small, but they could have found it if they ripped the bag apart. If that's the case, we fucked up big time. But this time it's different. Nousafarin didn't go trolling for Ghazi. As far as he's concerned, he's the one who went after her. So there's a good possibility that he might tell his aides to leave her stuff alone."

"What if he doesn't?"

"We're going to find out soon enough," Davenport answered. "Not whether they look, but whether they find anything. I don't think they will. The devices we're using this time are a whole lot more sophisticated. I got to check them out before we left the States."

"Tell us about them," Chang said.

---

[*] "The Art of War," Sun Tsu (Sun Zi), 6th Century B.C., translated by Lionel Giles, 1910.

"So, first of all, this stuff is the latest generation of Blue Force Tracking technology. It was developed for combat units. It combines directional tracking with GPS, so we can pinpoint the exact location of something on a map."

Chang frowned. "But that sets up the same damn problem we had with Anja. It was the transmitter she was carrying that probably gave her away."

"What Nousafarin has is a new version of these tracking devices, Andrea. They're much smaller than the old ones, and Ghazi's people wouldn't realize what they were even if they found them. But they're functional. Take a look — the techs are optimizing the signal right now."

"Then we'll know where she is on a continual basis?"

"We should, Andrea. It's only been a few minutes since they picked her up. Our spotters on the ground say they haven't left the Royal Tulip yet. We'll know when they do."

"And we'll be tracking her?"

"Yeah. They'll only communicate her position. It's not a telephone. Ten years earlier, we would have needed a something the size of a pack of cigarettes, but these new devices are much smaller. In some research studies, they've been attached to individual insects — like a bumblebee or a butterfly. Nousafarin is using a basic airline carry-on, and the electronics are built into the molded plastic feet. Even if they suspected something, they'd have to break it apart to find anything. There's a backup device hidden the same way as part of her shoulder bag."

"What if they don't let her take those things with her?" Neela asked. "Remember how they made Anja leave her carrying case behind when they took her to Ghazi's room? They could tell Nousa to leave her luggage and handbag behind this time."

"Very unlikely," Chang said. "For several reasons. First, Ghazi is acting like he has a real hard-on for Nousafarin, so he wouldn't suddenly start treating her like crap. Second, there's no reason he'd suspect anything now, so he wouldn't be treating her like a prisoner. And third, he's trying to charm her."

"And she also has another backup," Davenport said. "The transmitters aren't as powerful, but she has some jewelry — a pair of earrings — that she could activate if necessary. They work the same way."

"What about the transmissions?" Neela asked. "If they scan for a bug, won't discover these devices right away?"

"That's what's so neat about it this new stuff. The technology doesn't broadcast electronic signals like a traditional bug, so they wouldn't detect anything, even if they had really sophisticated equipment."

"Then how does it work if it doesn't broadcast a signal?"

"It's called harmonic radar. And the devices don't even need batteries. All the power comes from our end. We have a drone waiting to follow Nousafarin's progress from several thousand feet, and it will periodically send down a directional radar pulse. The devices in Nousafarin's baggage will take the energy in the pulse and reflect back a radar signal at a different frequency. It's all completely passive."

"Can we trust it?"

"I sure as hell hope so, Andrea. It's been field tested. Like I said, they've even used them to track individual butterflies. The technology is starting to be deployed at some ski resorts. As a way to locate buried avalanche victims."

"So you think … when?"

"When they start moving out of the city. Probably another half hour."

• • • • •

Davenport's prediction was right on target. Twenty-five minutes later, at about 1:15 p.m., one of the techs raised a fist in the air.

"We got contact. The map's loading right now."

The others crowded around the small desk.

"Here it is. See that yellow dot? That's her suitcase. It has the larger transmitter, so it's easier to see. I'll double-check, but probably it's going to obscure the second signal most of the time. Hold on a sec. Yeah, here we go. Two signals. Everything is tracking fine. The signals are coming from about three blocks north of here."

"They're heading for Kapchagay," Davenport said.

"The reservoir?" Chang asked.

"No, the city at the west end of the reservoir. It's exactly like we thought. They're heading for the area north of the national park."

• • • • •

Progress seemed slow to those in the hotel room, but an hour later, members of the team could see a clear trail of dots on the computer screen. North from Almaty, past the city of Kapchagay, then turning eastward.

"They're following the A353 highway."

Another twenty minutes passed.

"They've been going northeast, following the highway after they passed Shengeldy. Now it looks like they've left the highway, and they're going slower. They must be using local roads. They turned southeast, toward the mountains."

Forty-five minutes later, a sudden exclamation brought everyone back to look at the tech's computer.

"They've reached their destination. Look at the pattern. These three dots are closer together, and now the last two are superimposed. They've stopped."

"Let's see some satellite views," Chang ordered.

* * *

Almaty, Kazakhstan, January 26

Members of the team had been able to get a few hours of sleep, and they reassembled early the next morning.

"Any change?" Davenport asked the tech who was sitting at the main computer screen.

"Nothing."

"Anything from home?" Chang asked.

"Green light just came through," Davenport answered. "For everything except the last step. I don't know why they let us go this far if they aren't going to finish it."

"You know they will, Derek. It's just the bureaucracy."

"I suppose. At least they've allocated additional satellite coverage, so we should have a better idea of the physical setup of the site later this morning. The embassy is still negotiating with the Kazakh government about air space, so our drone coverage isn't as good as we'd like."

"Assuming we get the final approval, how do we know when to make our move?" Neela asked.

Chang answered. "When Nousafarin tells us. That might not be until tomorrow. Maybe even the day after."

"I thought she didn't have anything but the passive communications,"

"It's more complicated. She can't send a message, but she can give us a signal. Her devices respond every time our drone sends down a radar pulse, almost like a mirror reflecting a beam of light. But there's a way she can permanently disable her transmitters. When she shuts down the secondary device, we'll know she's in place and wants to initiate the final step of the operation."

• • • • •

At noon, there had been no developments, and nobody wanted to speculate. It was beyond their control.

Shortly after two p.m., the techs said the satellite was about to make its next pass. Andrea and the others peered over their shoulders to view the computer screens.

"Looks like we've got something coming in now."

Everyone crowded closer, and the tech moved the cursor on the screen. He pointed to the location.

"The signal is coming from this building. It seems to be one of several buildings close together."

"Is that a wall surrounding them?" Chang asked.

"Looks like."

"How high?"

"Not sure," the tech answered. Then he pointed to a second computer screen. "This image was created at ten this morning. Let's see ... given our latitude and the length of the shadow ... I'd see it's five feet, maybe six."

"Hard for someone to climb over?"

"Depends on their size and how strong they are."

"I'm thinking of Nousafarin," Chang said.

"Then yeah, it would be hard for her."

"She's not an athlete," Neela added. "But she might be able to scramble over, if she had something to step up on. I hope she scouts it out before she hits the button."

"Here's another angle," said the tech. "More of a side view, and it confirms multiple buildings. I count four altogether. The signal is coming from the largest building in the compound. It seems to be a real house, but who knows what it might look like on the inside. The others don't appear to be much more than huts. Mudbrick, just like the wall around the compound."

Neela spoke again. "So to get out of there, she first has to get out of the house. Then cross the courtyard, or whatever you call it, and finally get over the wall. All of this without being seen. And aren't they going to notice that she's gone?"

She was looking at Chang, and the others did, also.

"There's a very specific timetable, Neela. Once she sends us her signal — when she disables her secondary device — it will be the start of a twenty-four hour countdown. We'll be expecting her to disable the primary device a day later. She'll be ready to move. And Nousafarin knows she has to have it all planned out."

• • • • •

The signal didn't come until late the following afternoon. The team members were wired with anticipation and bored from the inactivity. They were starting to snap at one another, and several times, Chang had to intervene to stop some petty bickering.

The signal came in as a beeping noise on the computer.

"What is that?" Chang asked, startled.

The tech turned to her with an excited smile.

"That's your signal. The one you've been waiting for. That's the alarm that says the secondary device is no longer responding. Five beeps followed by three more. Nousafarin says she's ready to move. Twenty-four hours. Give or take."

Chang forced a smile. "I'll tell Langley."

"What do we do if Langley calls it off?" Neela asked.

"Not a damn thing. That would be the whole point of calling it off."

"What does Nousa do, then?"

"She wouldn't know the operation was terminated. In twenty-four hours, she'd disable her primary transmitter and attempt to get away from the compound. We wouldn't be there to get her, and you can be damn sure the Warlord would notice her behavior. If Langley backs out now, they're signing her fucking death warrant."

* * *

Almaty, Kazakhstan, January 28

The tension was becoming unbearable. Chang knew she had to maintain control, but she was ready to bite the head off anyone who even asked her a question.

One of the techs turned to her. "We've got word that the drones are up, ma'am."

"Both of them?"

"Roger that. They're taking off from Bishkek, flying east. They'll stay in a holding pattern after about four hundred klicks. That will keep them over Kyrgyzstan territory. Just like you said before. We're not going to get permission to go into Kazakh airspace until the last minute."

"Andrea?"

"Yes, Neela."

"What happens if Nousafarin decides she can't do it? If she doesn't have a clear escape route?"

Chang frowned.

"She has two choices. Her safest option would be that she never disables her primary transmitter. We agreed on twenty-four hours after she disabled the secondary device, and she knows we won't wait more than thirty. At that point the operation is over. We all go home. Hopefully, she gets back to Almaty and goes home with us."

"What's the other choice?"

"She could push the 'go' button to deactivate the remaining harmonic radar device in her carry-on bag. She would know she couldn't get out, and she'd be telling us to proceed anyway."

· · · · ·

At three thirty, the tech monitoring the computer let out a whoop.

"The birds have been cleared. They're heading toward the target. Look at this! We're getting live video from the one that's unarmed."

The others remained behind him in frozen silence, staring at a screen that showed little more than a desolate landscape.

"They're turning video control over to us in thirty seconds. The flight paths will be a circle at five thousand feet above the target, and the drones will stay out of each other's way."

Another five minutes of silence passed before the tech spoke again.

"Okay, we're over the target. I'm zooming in. Damn, there's a whole lot more detail than we had with the satellite images. Nothing new, but it confirms what we thought. There's something back there by the wall. And it looks like she could stand on it to climb over."

"And I think that's another doorway at the back of the house," Davenport said.

"Come on!" Chang yelled. "Push the fucking button, Nousa!"

· · · · ·

Another hour passed. The hotel suite had been almost completely silent, except for a brief exchange in which the tech told Chang the specific sequence keystrokes she would need to use after entering her password.

Five beeps. Almost the same sound a large truck makes when it's backing up. It wasn't very loud, but everyone was startled by the sound. Andrea was standing next to Davenport, and her glass of water sloshed onto his shoulder.

The tech looked at her and spoke calmly.

"Those beeps mean that the primary device is no longer responding. Nousafarin has deactivated it, and she's making her move. Enter your password on the other computer, ma'am. Unless they've canceled the mission, you'll get the go screen. Then we've got a window of ten minutes for you to enter the codes."

Chang's face was completely drained of color. She entered the code sequence and waited for a response to appear on screen. Five seconds elapsed, then ten more. The others watched her with increasing tension.

Suddenly, Chang made a guttural sound that wasn't quite a word. Then she spoke in a near whisper. "We have our final authorization."

She turned to the tech. "You tell me when, and we hit our launch keystrokes at the same time."

"Where is she?" Davenport asked anxiously. "Where's Nousa?"

The tech shrugged his shoulders because there was no answer yet. No one else spoke.

Almost five minutes passed before motion was visible on the screen. The tech zoomed in as much as he could while keeping the entire compound visible on the screen.

"There!" he said. "It's a person. Moving across the courtyard. Right toward that box or whatever it is that we noticed."

They watched the progress of the figure, which appeared to be moving at an excruciatingly slow pace — as though it might be crawling rather than walking. The compound was in deep shadow, and it was difficult to make out any detail from the thermal image on the screen.

"It's got to be her!" Neela said through nearly clenched teeth. "It must be."

"We have to conclude that," Chang said.

The figure reached the wall, but it seemed to stop there. Several seconds went by. Suddenly, there was movement again.

"She's over. She's on the other side of the wall."

The tech turned to Chang.

"Alt-control-tab. Hit it ma'am!"

He and Chang tech pushed the same combination of keys at the same time.

Quietly, mostly to herself, Chang said, "holy fuck."

The computer screen showed a dotted circle, centered on the structure that had been Nousafarin's location for the past three days. The building they all believed was Ghazi's home.

Everyone in the room held their breath. There was no audio signal to accompany the display, and it was unnecessary in any event. Abruptly, the dark color that had characterized the Warlord's home disappeared from the center of the circle on the computer screen. It changed from dark to white. A small bright circle that grew in the course of a second until it covered the entire screen.

"Got you, motherfucker!" the tech yelled. Then he cringed, knowing he had spoken out of turn. Nobody cared.

There were no shouts of glee. Only a sense of awe at what they had seen take place.

"Where's Nousafarin?" Davenport shouted. "I don't see her."

"It'll take a few more seconds for the screen to recover. That was too much light for the camera to deal with all at once."

By the time the tech finished his sentence, the image of the compound had begun to reappear on the screen. But it was different. One of the rectangles, the one they had been calling the Warlord's house, was no longer there. The other structures were still visible, although there seemed to be some distortion, like cardboard boxes that had become wet and were beginning to sag under their own weight. On the other side of the wall, nothing was visible.

"There. Not where she went over but a little higher on the screen." Neela was yelling.

The tech spoke with confidence. "It's her. And she's moving. She made it."

A line of text scrolled across the base of the computer screen.

`Extraction team en route. ETA 4 minutes.`

The tech looked over at Chang. "Whatever bird they're flying, it's going pretty damn fast."

The team remained silent, their eyes glued to the screen. The tech had zoomed back out, to provide a wider view as the helicopter made its final approach. Even before it touched down, they could see two figures jump to the ground and run toward the wall.

Everyone continued watching intently and silently as those two figures were joined by a third as they returned to the aircraft. Finally, the team saw the helicopter leave the ground and move across the screen until it disappeared.

Chang was subdued. "I'll notify Langley."

* * *

29

Prayer Breakfast

*There is growing concern that IEDs might
eventually be used by other insurgents and terrorists
worldwide.*

—*Congressional Research Service, 2007*[*]

Washington, D.C., February 2

Will Desmond pushed the glass door open and stepped onto the K Street sidewalk. He had just finished a quick workout, and the bright morning sun was a welcome sight. With luck, he figured, they might get through the rest of the winter without another snowstorm. The last traces of snow from mid-January were gone, the temperature had already climbed to the mid-thirties, and it was only nine in the morning. He thought it would be a good day.

His new membership in the Mint Health Club showed every sign of being a good decision. It was a perfect location, situated on the ground floor of the Capital Hilton Hotel at the corner of 16th and K Streets. He could step off the bus, cross the street and walk right into the gym. Their equipment was great, and the people were even better.

The other members were the main reason he joined. On a typical morning, they were a mix of hotel guests and assorted professionals who worked nearby. He hoped the lawyers and bankers would help him expand his sphere of professional contacts, and it was a friendly crowd. It wasn't a place to meet women, although there were

---

[*] "Improvised Explosive Devices (IEDs) in Iraq and Afghanistan: Effects and Countermeasures," Clay Wilson, Congressional Research Service, August 28, 2007.

definitely some attractive women he saw frequently. It was a place to work out.

Conversations were casual, but he thought they might prove useful in the long run. Part of his responsibility at the Secret Service was vigilance, and the people he saw on the gym floor and in the locker room all had eyes and ears. If something strange was going on in the area, they would mention it. Not because they knew he worked for the Secret Service — most did not — but because it would be a topic of normal discussion.

Desmond crossed K Street and walked south on 16th, smiling to himself when he saw the top of the Washington Monument glinting in the sunlight. When he crossed the next street, the White House came into view beyond a truck in the southbound lane. He noticed the S2 bus approaching along I Street to his left.

The sequence began with a honk, but there really wasn't much noise. When Desmond turned around, it was basically over. The westbound bus had started its right turn onto 16th, but a utility van appeared to have cut it off. Desmond recalled seeing the van pulled over to the curb, so the driver must have pulled out in front of the bus. To avoid hitting the van, the bus swerved and crunched the rear fender of a car in the southbound lane.

There was little damage, and even as Desmond turned back with the thought of providing assistance, the bus driver was standing in front of his vehicle announcing that nobody was hurt. The driver of the utility van was standing beside his vehicle, shouting that he had to get his boss.

"He's right down the street. At McPherson Square. We're working on the boxes."

He pointed to the opposite corner of the intersection, where a greyish metal box about two feet square and four feet high was mounted on a concrete slab.

There was just enough chaos at the scene to keep anyone from noticing when the van driver crossed the street and ducked into the 15th Street entrance of the McPherson Square Metro Station. When people began looking for him a few minutes later, he had disappeared without a trace. Nor could anyone locate his supposed boss or any coworkers.

As Desmond surveyed the scene, he realized that the Secret Service agents stationed on the roof of the White House would have a clear view of whatever was happening. Vigilance. They were always alert when something out of the ordinary happened in close proximity to their post. And they were well-armed sharpshooters if any real threat developed.

A squad car from the Metropolitan Police Department rolled up with its flashers on, and Desmond realized there was nothing more he could do. He had not actually seen the accident, so he wasn't an eyewitness. And the police were better equipped to take statements and clear the scene.

A minute or two later, Desmond resumed his original path, crossed H Street, and began walking along the north side of Lafayette Square. He now had a full view of the White House, and there was a smile on his face. The smile broadened when he saw her.

It was the same women he had seen the previous fall. He was sure of it. He recalled how attractive she had looked in her short jacket and tight pants. He wished he had an excuse to meet her.

But there was no excuse, and the best he could do was walk along behind her. He recalled that when he had seen her previously, she went past the Old Executive Office Building, and he decided that she probably worked somewhere on 17th Street. He was surprised when she crossed back into Lafayette Square.

It struck him as odd, because she had been walking rather quickly. If she were in a hurry, why would she stop to look at the pigeons?

The answer to his question wasn't pigeons. Tracking her path forward, he saw someone on a park bench. It was the homeless man he had seen so many times before. It was a homeless man he had always considered a real nut case. He was always singing or shouting.

Then Desmond remembered that the other time he had seen her, she had stopped to give the man money. His curiosity was piqued, and he paused at the side of the square to observe. As she approached the homeless man, she reached into a pocket and handed something to him. But this time it wasn't money. It was a piece of white paper.

A note?

Desmond continued to watch.

The woman turned back toward her original path, but Desmond paid no attention. The homeless man had become more interesting.

The homeless man shuffled around for a minute or so, and he then began walking toward the northwest corner of Lafayette Square near Decatur House. Like many of Washington's homeless, he appeared to take all his belongings with him. He was pulling a cart behind him. Or maybe it was a collapsible luggage carrier. Desmond couldn't be sure. It held what looked like a backpack that seemed unusually heavy for its size.

The man continued walking west on H Street. Desmond followed, crossing to the north side of the street to be less obvious.

At the corner of 17th Street the man stopped and threw a scrap of paper into a trash can. Then he turned around and began walking back in the direction of the park.

He forgot his shopping cart. With his backpack.

The sirens interrupted Desmond's thoughts. They were coming from the north along 17th Street. Then the first motorcycle passed the intersection.

For a moment, Desmond couldn't make sense out of it.

Something's off. What's ...?

Then he remembered.

Thursday. The first Thursday of February. This morning was the National Prayer Breakfast. The President is just coming back to the White House now. The sirens are from the motorcade.

The homeless man began walking faster, almost running.

Desmond was still trying to fit the pieces together.

The bus crash was a diversion.

He turned toward the homeless man. He shouted.

"Hey you! Stop!"

The man broke into a full sprint.

"Secret Service! Stop or I'll shoot!"

But there were too many people in the vicinity. Shooting wasn't an option.

Desmond grabbed his cellphone as he started running back toward 17th street. The route of the Presidential motorcade. He scanned the area repeatedly, looking for one of his fellow agents.

They've got to be here! Where are they?

Finally, he saw them. Two of them, not far from the intersection. He had never trained for this specific situation, and he'd been caught off guard. He had drawn his service weapon, and the other agents had seen it. They were starting to react.

The words came out without thinking. He was screaming.

"Secret Service! I'm an agent! Don't shoot!"

Desmond aimed his pistol in a safe direction, but he didn't drop it. He had pulled his credentials from beneath his jacket using his left hand. They were already around his neck on a chain. A photo ID on one side, a gold badge on the other.

He continued yelling. "Stop the motorcade! Bomb! Stop the motorcade!"

Desmond saw a figure running up the street from the other end of the block, the Pennsylvania Avenue end, and he recognized the face.

"Jerry! Tell them I'm okay! Tell them to stop the motorcade! Call it in! Get the Roadrunner! Emergency! Clear this intersection!"

Jerry Kozinsky recognized Desmond and shouted to his team.

"Do what he says! He's one of us."

Desmond continued to yell.

"We're under attack! Keep Mogul out of here!"

He used the nickname that his fellow Secret Service agents would recognize. 'Roadrunner,' was an armored Chevy Suburban that served as the President's mobile communications center. 'Mogul,' denoted the President.

Moments later, one of the agents raised an arm and spoke to the other others nearby.

"Roadrunner confirms our request. They've diverted to Cloverleaf."

That meant the motorcade was headed to the Vice President's residence at the Naval Observatory on Massachusetts Avenue. The President was safe.

"We've still got a bomb here," Desmond said, pointing to the corner where the homeless man had left his cart and backpack.

"Bomb squad's on the way," the agent answered. "Roadrunner sent out the request. That's probably them coming now." He pointed to the flashing blue lights headed in their direction.

The bomb squad arrived in three vehicles, one of them a flatbed truck with a five-foot diameter metallic blue sphere mounted on it. The Secret Service agents pointed to the shopping cart on the sidewalk, and the new arrivals positioned an armored truck near it.

The leader of the bomb squad got out of his truck and motioned to the Secret Service team.

"You guys get the fuck out of here. If this thing goes off, we don't need any extra dead people. Stand back at least to the end of the block. And make sure nobody comes walking out of any of these buildings."

The bomb technicians, dressed in heavy protective gear, quickly threw a shield over the backpack. It wouldn't contain an explosion, but it would reduce the damage from shrapnel. They next used a robotic arm one of their vehicles to lift the backpack and place it inside the blue sphere on the flatbed truck. The sphere was an explosive containment vessel, capable of checking the major impact of a bomb.

A portable X-ray system was used to scan the backpack, and the chief technician reported that an electronic switch was mounted in one of the outside pockets of the backpack."

The head of the bomb squad walked over to Desmond.

"This thing looks like it could still go off. Did you see who put it here?"

"Last I saw him, he was running hard. Away from here. Toward Lafayette Square. I had to let him go so we could stop the motorcade."

"Okay. It was probably designed to be set off using a hand-held RF transmitter, and my guess is he moved out of range when he ran. Otherwise he would have set it off before now. Unless he's still waiting for the President to return. In any case, we're going to use robotics to kill the switch on the bomb. If this thing detonates, it could still cause a lot of damage. Even with the containment vessel."

"How much?" Desmond asked.

"You're asking if it would have taken out the President? Probably not. But there would have been injuries, even with all the armor on the limousine. We're all lucky you spotted this."

"Will you be able to analyze it?"

"If it doesn't go off on us first. So, let us do our job with that. You guys go find the asshole who put it here."

Desmond looked at Kozinsky. They were the two senior members of the Secret Service at the scene.

"Let's comb the square, Jerry. My guess is, he's long gone, but there might be something he left behind. And have someone get the contents of that trash can when the site is clear. I saw him throw a piece of paper in it."

There was nothing in Lafayette Square, and when they finally checked the trash can, all they found were a few receipts from a nearby Starbucks.

At Kozinsky's request, the team of sharpshooters who had been on the roof of the White House came down to talk with them.

"Yeah, I know the homeless guy you're talking about. He's in the square almost every day. Right over there. And he was here this morning for a while. He walked over toward Decatur House, and I lost sight of him."

"Did he return?" Desmond asked.

"No, he didn't. But maybe …"

"What?"

"After all the fuss started, I noticed a guy come from the direction of 17th Street. He was a big guy, and he had a beard. I couldn't see his face from my position. And at the time I never thought about it. He was wearing a sweater … maybe a hoodie … but not the long coat the homeless guy always has. I'm pretty sure he was wearing that coat earlier today."

"That's correct," Desmond said. "He was."

Kozinsky nodded to one of his agents and pointed to the Decatur House area. "Check for the coat."

"We already found it, sir. It's being bagged for evidence. It was just lying on the sidewalk around the corner."

"Did you see where the man went?" Desmond asked the sharpshooter.

"He walked right across the square and kept going. Like he was headed to Metro Center. That's only three blocks."

"Maybe we'll get some DNA," Kozinsky said. "From the backpack."

"Won't matter," Desmond answered. "He's gone. We'll never see him again."

* * *

30

Dead End

*Analysts often are susceptible to being unduly
influenced by a first impression, based on
incomplete data, an existing analytic line, or a
single explanation that seems to fit well enough.*

—*A Tradecraft Primer, CIA, 2009*[*]

Langley, Virginia, February 2

The team members drifted into the conference room ahead of their eight a.m. meeting. Everyone was apprehensive, a fitting reaction to the agenda for the meeting. The memo, which they all received by e-mail, had been under the subject line "Postmortem." Some of the younger members of the team had found it necessary to seek an explanation.

They were not familiar with a longstanding Agency tradition of carrying out a detailed examination of a concluded operation. What had gone right? What, if anything, had failed? And, why had the failures occurred? Ostensibly, the purpose of such an analysis was to ensure that things would go better the next time. But anyone who had ever participated in such a session was more likely to describe it as an inquisition. A search for blame.

The group was larger than it had been at prior meetings. The two technicians who had been in Almaty sat at a desk near the back of the room. They were at a workstation with two laptops and several

---

[*] "A Tradecraft Primer: Structured Analytic Techniques for Improving Intelligence Analysis," Central Intelligence Agency, March, 2009, p. 14.

additional computer screens. Their nametags identified them as Roberts and Weber.

The action team from Operation Gray Ghost was fully assembled by 7:55 at a conference table large enough to accommodate all of them. The leadership was gathered at the head of the table: Canterbury, Chang, and Hashan. Grouped toward the other end of the table were Davenport, Hartwell, and Pomeranz, along with Stephan, Martin, Neela, and Samantha. Only one member of the full operational team was missing. Anja.

Senior management was represented by Alford, but he was not alone. Accompanying him were two individuals that only a few of the others recognized. One was a senior attorney from the Office of the General Counsel, and the other was the head of the Directorate of Operations.

Stephan knew them by sight but had never met them. He knew they were heavyweights, and he didn't like the implications. As he surveyed the room, he counted thirteen people, not including the techs. A total of eighteen chairs had been placed around the table. He glanced back at Chang, who seemed unusually tense, as did Hashan. Alford looked ill.

The clock said 8:05, but there was no move to start the meeting. Moments later the reason became obvious. The door opened, and five men and women strode in together. They were a solemn group, exhibiting no trace of warmth and saying not a word. They marched to the table and occupied the remaining seats.

Stephan had only seen one of them previously, but he understood. They were all from the seventh floor. He looked at the more familiar faces, and noticed that Hashan and Canterbury had joined Alford in looking ill.

This wasn't a postmortem. It was a murder board. And they were out for blood.

The newcomers were the Deputy Director of the Agency, the heads of the Directorates for Analysis and for Science & Technology, the director of the Mission Center for Counterterrorism and the head of the performance audit staff for the Office of the Inspector General.

Alford cleared his throat.

"I think we should begin. Andrea, would you please recount the background for Operation Gray Ghost. Since we have a few people here who are relatively new to the operation, it would be good if you started with the events of last April in Rockbridge County."

Those who understood Alford's reference were careful not to look in Martin's direction.

As Chang related the early stages of planning, interruptions were frequent. Questions were cold, if not hostile.

When Chang first described how Samantha and Neela had been recruited immediately after the attack on the Sulley compound, the auditor from the Inspector General's office interrupted.

"Two years earlier, these same two individuals facilitated an attempted nuclear attack on our country," she stated, her tone aggressive. "Can you explain to us exactly how … and why … you decided they should be made part of a top-secret operation? An operation designed to bring down the same organization that sent them to the United States in the first place?"

A few minutes later, the lawyer from the General Counsel's office brought up a related issue.

"You're telling us that you 'encouraged' these two women to join the Army. Even if you weren't concerned that they might continue to work for their Kazakh handler, you haven't addressed the question of how you so conveniently arranged for them to be detailed to the CIA. You certainly were aware that it would have been illegal for the Agency to employ them as foreign nationals. But somehow you want us to believe that arranging for them to wear the uniform of our country's armed forces makes that all okay. This strikes me as an intentional effort to circumvent official policy, which could be considered a criminal act."

Subsequently, the head of the Analysis Directorate asked about Martin.

"I have a question about your recruitment of this young man. I'll grant that he's a U.S. citizen, but he was naturalized as a child. At the direction of his father. Now, I'll admit that his family was killed last year, apparently at the direction of the person who we believe was behind the original plot to detonate a nuclear device in Washington, D.C. But it was this same Martin Sulley who helped prepare a sample of uranium that was given to this madman you so amusingly named the Gray Ghost."

Andrea's eyes had narrowed, but she maintained her steely composure as the interrogation continued.

"So you ask him to play a central role in your efforts to hunt down this criminal. You give him a minimal amount of training and send him off to Asia with one of the two young women who had previously been foreign agents. And you provide virtually no oversight. On top of all this … I hate to bring it up, but someone will bring it up eventually. They're all Muslims. How do you expect those of us who run this Agency to answer questions like that if we're summoned to testify in front of a Congressional committee?"

Stephan was seething.

Where the fuck does he come off saying something like that?

The faces of his colleagues made him realize they felt the same way.

When Chang finally brought the narrative to the final stages of the team's hunt for Ghazi, she was interrupted by the Deputy Director.

"I'm bothered by how this story is unfolding. I've taken the time to review your original proposals for the mission. The proposals that were approved by senior officials of our government. We gave you authorization to capture this person you call the Warlord. Other options were available if that failed, but only if it failed. Our government does not conduct assassinations. It's not how we work. Did you understand that?"

"Yes, sir." She bit off the words in a flat tone.

"But nevertheless, you planned and carried out a mission that you permitted to slowly evolve from one that purportedly aimed for an arrest into an exercise that had had an assassination as its sole purpose. And in the process, you managed to lose one of our best agents. This entire sequence of events has been unacceptable."

When the Deputy Director finished, no one else in the room said a word.

Stephan glanced around warily. His fellow team members all seemed to be in shock. As far as they were concerned, they had worked hard, put their lives on the line, and accomplished their goal.

And now this?

He saw that the expression of shock and dismay extended to Canterbury and Hashan. And of course, to Chang. Even Alford's face was ashen. Stephan wanted to scream, but he remained silent.

The Deputy Director was in the chain when the operation was approved. We had approvals from higher up than that. Now he's just covering his ass. In case the media or someone in Congress comes after us. He's just getting ready to hang us out to dry.

• • • • •

It was shortly after ten o'clock when there was a knock on the door. Alford's assistant entered and handed him a note.

He scanned the message and frowned. Then he read it again. Finally, he looked up at the others.

"There's been an event. Downtown Washington. There was a bomb. Or at least a bombing attempt. The target was the President's motorcade. About a block from the White House."

The Deputy Director leaned to his left and whispered something to Alford, who in turn nodded.

"We're in recess for the next half hour."

The Deputy Director paused at the door and turned to speak.

"We'll continue when I return. I want you to remain here, and I don't want a bunch of chitchat while I'm gone. You're all still on the hot seat."

The executives departed as a group.

· · · · ·

The report of the attack on the President increased the stress levels of everyone in the room. But there was nothing they could do about it.

Roberts and Weber were the only two people in the room with Internet access, but their response to a question from Alford was straightforward.

"Nothing yet. The media haven't reported a thing."

Davenport quietly asked Weber if he could use the laptop for a few minutes. He sat in the corner working quietly.

The Deputy Director and other senior leaders returned in time to resume the meeting at 10:45. Alford called the meeting to order.

"We're going to resume with several more questions from the division chiefs. Andrea?"

Before she could answer, Davenport spoke.

"Excuse me."

Alford did not look pleased.

"What is it?"

"I was just checking something. On Facebook ..."

Nearly everyone in the room was surprised by the statement. The senior people were shocked.

The Deputy Director's face contorted as if he were suffering a stroke.

"What the hell do you think ...? he began to ask.

"Let him speak," Canterbury said evenly. His rank among the assembled officials was low, but they were aware of his history. They remained quiet.

"Listen to this post," Davenport said.

*We had exciting time in city today. It was day for
setting off big noise and big celebration. So now we
will return from our vacation."*

Some of the others understood immediately.

"When was it posted?" Canterbury asked.

"Just before noon today. Our time."

"Who posted it?"

"It was anonymous. But it was on Natalia's page."

"I don't understand," one of the division chiefs said.

"It's a message to the Warlord. He's Natalia on Facebook. This confirms his latest attack. We knew there would be another attempt to kill someone, but we thought it wouldn't be until later this month."

"What do we do?" asked another division chief.

"We don't do anything," Alford answered, emphasizing the first word of his statement. "But I'm going to give Carter Jennings a call. The FBI needs to know about this."

* * *

Langley, Virginia, February 2

The official postmortem meeting reconvened at 1:30 in the afternoon. Alford announced that they would hold formal presentations in abeyance for several minutes as they waited for an additional participant. Stephan noticed that one more chair had been brought to the table.

The last to arrive was only a contract employee, but everyone understood that she was essential.

There was a crisp knock on the door. Alford nodded, and his assistant ushered in a woman who walked tentatively to her place at the table. Several of the others reacted with shock, stifling gasps of astonishment.

Canterbury stood and held her chair for her. It was atypical behavior, not only for Canterbury but for all of them. They were accustomed to operating as professionals, and they did not normally hew to old-fashioned rules of etiquette. On the other hand, this situation was different. Canterbury had a highly unusual history with Nousafarin.

As she pulled her chair in closer to the table, Canterbury patted her gently on the shoulder before resuming his own place. Hashan waited several moments before speaking. He realized that Canterbury wasn't the only person at the table who needed a few seconds to regain composure. The others who had met Nousafarin were shaken not so much by her presence in the room as by her appearance. There had been rumors, but until that moment, most of them had been unaware of the gravity of her injuries.

In retrospect, they realized they should not have been surprised. True, she had made it to the other side of that mud-brick wall before the missile struck. But that only protected her from the trajectory of flying pieces of stone and metal. The blast wave obeyed no such restrictions.

• • • • •

She had been alive when they put her in the rescue helicopter, but it was little more than a technical definition. The medics on board were unsure if even that definition would hold for long. The mud-brick wall had sheltered her from the shrapnel produced by the blast, but her rescuers saw immediately that parts of the wall had collapsed on her. And she was bleeding from the nose and ears.

Arrangements had been made in advance for the possibility that the operation might result in injuries to Nousafarin or others. Because they were operating in restricted airspace in covert mode, local hospitals were not an option, and a medevac plane was waiting when the extraction team reached the airport. The C-17 Globemaster and its medical crew were airborne within five minutes. Seven hours later, they landed at Ramstein Air Force Base in Germany, and Nousafarin was quickly moved to Landstuhl Regional Medical Center.

The medical staff at Landstuhl quickly ascertained that she had suffered some level of traumatic brain injury, but they believed it was only a minor concussion. One of them remarked that the damage to her ears "didn't look that bad," and they concluded that the bleeding from her nose was the result of a minor injury when her face hit the ground.

Two days later, the chief of the medical staff spoke with Alford on a secure line.

"We think she's going to be okay. Even the partial hearing loss should be temporary. She's a lucky woman. They told us she was separated from the blast by a stone wall. If she'd been on the other side of that wall, she'd be in a box right now."

"When can she return to the States?"

"She's stable now. She could travel today, I suppose, but we'd like another day or two to monitor her condition. I understand you want to talk to her, so we'll release her as soon we're confident of a full recovery. How about we put her on a flight to Andrews on the second? It leaves here at four in the morning, and she'll be there in time to join you for breakfast."

"Send me the details, Colonel. And thank you."

• • • • •

Alford called the meeting to order.

"For the record, this is a resumption of the postmortem on Operation Gray Ghost. Some of you have been involved with this activity since its inception, and you are consequently familiar with its entire history. A few of you were focused on just one aspect of the effort, and some of you are learning details of the operation for the first time today."

He looked at Nousafarin.

"Ms. Rahmon. I want to express our sincere thanks for the actions you undertook. We owe you … your country owes you … a debt of gratitude. Your efforts led directly to the successful outcome of the mission. It could not have been done without you. You have returned to us with severe injuries, while the rest of us are seated at the table as though we'd never left the comfort of our living rooms."

Someone spoke at the other end of the table. *Sotto voce.* Alford couldn't tell who it was.

"Not Anja."

Alford colored. Then he made a choking sound that could have been mistaken for a cough.

"Forgive me. One of our own didn't make it back at all. Anja Dalbins. She made the ultimate sacrifice. Our country owes her a great debt as well."

He looked around the table, making eye contact with those who had known Anja. They all understood that nothing he had said was intended as dismissive. It was only an oversight in an emotional situation.

Alford continued his introduction.

"And there were other victims. Not directly involved in our operation but victims of the succession of attacks mounted by its target. The Governor of Michigan. Other citizens of our country, including the infants and elderly who died from food poisoning a year ago. And every member of Martin's family. They all died by the hand of this barbarian we call the Warlord. We just learned that were it not for the heroic actions of a member of the Secret Service this morning, the President of the United States might have become the latest addition to this list of casualties. All victims of one madman."

"They were loyal Americans, and he was nothing but a pathological murderer. But he's gone now. And he's gone because of the efforts made by all of you. Were it not for the tragedy of the events, we would be clapping our hands and drinking toasts at this moment. But it is all far too serious for such foolishness. The best step we can take now is review what happened and make plans to prevent anything like it from transpiring in the future."

He looked once again at Nousafarin. "Ms. Rahmon. If at any time you need to rest, please inform me. I will gladly put us in recess as needed."

She nodded to him. There was no smile.

Alford turned to Hashan. "David, would you be so kind as to moderate the discussion?"

• • • • •

It was only midafternoon, but the day had been an ordeal for everyone in the room. The field agents and case officers understood that their careers and futures were under attack, and even the Agency officials seeking political cover were worried about unexpected fallout from the operation.

Most of those in the room had been passive listeners. Some of the accounts they heard were horrific, conveyed with anguish and regret. But Nousafarin delivered the most compelling narrative of the day. It was a story that none of them had heard previously.

> *When I pushed the button — what you called the 'go button' on my overnight bag — I was ready to leave the home. Nikita was in the other room. I say Nikita because it was the name he continued to use with me. It required great effort sometimes for me to forget the other names we have for him. Just 'Nikita Volkov' I always had to remember that.*
>
> *When I sent you the signal, I knew to leave within five minutes, so I was prepared. Previously, I had walked into the courtyard to look. I knew the place where there was an old box, which I think was maybe a crate that once had contained packages of food. As a test the second day, I walked to the wall and sat on the crate. I was able to determine that it was strong enough to hold my weight. And I would be able to step on it to climb over the wall when the time came.*
>
> *Nobody said anything when I walked in the courtyard that first time. But I worried that Asim was suspicious. Asim — you all know him? He was the main bodyguard. From the beginning, I knew I could not trust him. He was a thug. Even Volkov could act like a decent man when he was not planning to murder innocent people. But not Asim. And I knew he suspected me after my walk in the courtyard. He did not know what he was looking for, but always he was watching me.*
>
> *I know he searched my luggage. I placed things in a certain way as I learned from Andrea Chang. And*

when I looked sometime later, things were not quite in the same way.

I realized he would always be watching, so when I sent the signal, I kept my eyes open for him. I walked quickly to the door at the rear of the house. I knew I had only four minutes remaining to be sure of my safety. As I reached to open the door, that is when I saw him. He was hiding in shadows beside the door.

I made no noise, and he said nothing. But he seized my arm. I had good fortune, because he took my left arm. And he pulled me toward him. I wanted to scream, but I understood it would only make things worse. When he pulled me toward him, it made everything less difficult. He used great force, and it aided me. The violence of my body moving toward him made it much easier for the knife to penetrate his clothing.

I must explain this to you. Nikita had a ceremonial knife — a Kazakh hunting knife that he prized greatly. The wooden handle was inlaid with silver. And it was very sharp. It was not a difficulty for me to take it as I prepared to leave the house.

Asim looked at me with great surprise. It seemed he did not understand what had happened. And still he said nothing. His mouth opened as if he would ask me a question, and that is when I lifted on the knife with all the energy in my being. It was as you trained me. I had no doubts that his insides were cut to ribbons. Some blood came from his mouth, and he loosened his grip on my arm. Then he fell away from me, and he fell to the floor. I am certain he was dead before I reached the wall.

As I climbed over the wall, I heard a noise in the sky. The sun was almost completely gone, so I could not see anything. But I heard. It is hard to describe the sound. I think I remember a sound that was a 'whoosh.' But then something happened. I do not remember any explosion. I only remember darkness. And silence.

*Even after I was taken to hospital, the silence
remained. Not until yesterday could I hear a voice
again. The day before I could surmise the doctor
was speaking. I saw his mouth move, and I heard
sounds. But it was only the kind of sound I have
heard before when I was swimming and my head
was beneath the water. It was a great relief I will
say, when I could hear words again yesterday. I
knew that it was really true that I was still alive.*

*It brings me joy that I am still alive and our enemies
are not.*

When Nousafarin finished her narrative, several people had
questions. Some she could answer. Others she could not.

The questioners were particularly interested in learning what
additional operations Ghazi might have been planning. Operations that
conceivably could still be carried out by surviving members of his
cadre. Did she learn anything about his financial networks? Did he
name any of his comrades? Were there other bases with warriors of
the KFB?

She was unable to provide much in the way of detailed answers.

"I did, however, hear him speaking once with Asim. He said it was
of great disappointment that most of their men had died for their cause.
That a new recruitment would be necessary if they would continue
working toward their goals. And he especially was disappointed that
Asim had provided incorrect information about Altyn Emel. I did not
understand what that meant."

"Was there nothing else?" Canterbury asked. There was hope she
had forgotten some small piece of information that could be of use to
them.

"One more thing I did not understand. I do not understand. He was
speaking to me as one does after ..."

She paused to assess how much detail was needed, but she quickly
realized that they all understood the nature of her assignment with the
Warlord.

"He was lying on the bed with his head on a pillow, speaking
almost as though it was a dream. At the same time, I think he was
trying to impress me. Show me he was a powerful man. A rich man.
He said he had great wealth. In gold. All right there in the house. Then
he changed what he said. Not in the house. Below the house."

"Below the house?" Canterbury asked.

"Not exactly those words. But it was clear he meant that."

"Do you remember his exact words?"

"I think yes. He said, 'It is underneath us. In the tunnel.' Those were his words."

"A tunnel?"

"Yes."

"Oh fuck!"

Chang wasn't running the meeting, but she had been responsible for the final operation against the Warlord. She looked at Weber, the technician who had been in charge of the computers in Almaty.

"Do you have the video here?"

"It's on the computer. I could put it up on the big monitor."

"Do it."

They all watched as the scene unfolded.

Weber explained that they had only viewed infrared images at the time of the action because the events had taken place in the late-afternoon shadows of the nearby foothills. However, the drone had also captured everything with its visible-light cameras, and subsequent processing had combined the two sets of images. The resolution was significantly improved from what they had seen at the time.

They saw the shadowy figure of Nousafarin emerge from the house. They watched her cross the courtyard to the wall, and they saw her climb over it to the other side.

"Here's the missile impact," Weber announced. "The explosion just makes the screen go white."

"Don't turn it off," Chang instructed.

They saw the helicopter land, and they watched the two figures emerge and run to Nousafarin. Then the figures merged into a single thermal image that moved back to the aircraft. The field of view widened to include the entire compound as the rescue mission neared its end. Nothing on the ground moved.

"Keep it going."

They all watched in silence. Some were almost afraid to breathe. The time signal at the bottom of the screen was at 10:57 when the helicopter lifted off. Weber had explained that the computer was set to Zulu time, and the local time in Almaty was 16:57, six hours later.

"Question. Pause it please."

Everyone looked at Hartwell.

"Why didn't they search the compound? Wasn't that the obvious thing to do? Make sure we got him?"

Chang answered. "Rules of engagement, Ash. The Kazakh government wouldn't agree to anything more than a rescue for our personnel. They had plausible deniability for the origin of the explosion, but they didn't want anybody going inside the compound. The helicopter was there only to evacuate an injured American civilian. Nothing more. Nothing less."

She turned back to the tech. "Resume the video, please."

At first, it seemed that Weber had not heard her instruction. The video screen remained frozen. But eyes were drawn to the bottom of the screen. The eye is always attracted to motion, and the only change that was taking place was the time stamp. It reached 10:58, then 10:59. The viewers were almost hypnotized as they watched the seconds changing. It went from 10:59:59 to 11:00:00. Twenty seconds later there was a cry from someone at the table.

"Look. There at the top."

What had been a motionless blob at the north end of the mud-brick wall began to change. It had been nothing recognizable by its shape, and it was unnoticed because its temperature was still much lower than burning debris created by the explosion.

The technician entered several keystrokes on the laptop, and the image changed.

"It's a person."

"Are you certain?" Hartwell asked.

"No way to be certain," Weber said.

They watched as the figure moved. Not far. But it was motion.

"Looks like he's crawling."

Then the motion stopped.

"It was him," Hartwell said.

"Maybe. Maybe not," Chang responded.

She turned to the tech.

"Could it have been an animal? Or even some residue from the blast that had a heat signature?"

"Anything's possible. But I already gave you my best interpretation."

Everyone continued to stare at the screen. At the now motionless blob.

"Even if he survived, we took out the rest of his people," Chang said. "He confessed that to Nousafarin. He's got nothing left. He's not a threat to us anymore."

"Whatever it is ... or was ... it's not moving anymore," Canterbury said optimistically. But his words could not hide the pessimism in his voice.

They continued to stare at the screen. It showed 11:00:15 ... 11:00:45 ... 11:01:15 ... 11:01:45 ... and finally, it reached 11:03:15. There had been no further motion.

The screen went blank.

"That's when the drones were recalled," Weber said. "There's nothing else."

* * *

References

Chapter 8

81 *Immigration and Nationality Act:* "Naturalization Through Military Service: Fact Sheet," Department of Homeland Security.

Chapter 9

86 *they use our highways and railroads:* "Kazakhstan to Permit Military Overflights to Afghanistan," Elisabeth Bumiller, *New York Times,* April 12, 2010.

"NATO's relations with Kazakhstan," North Atlantic Treaty Organization, 26 Oct., 2015.

Chapter 13

127 *from a scientific report:* "Impacts of Severe Space Weather on the Electric Grid," JSR-11-320, JASON, The MITRE Corporation, McLean, Virginia, November 2011.

Chapter 17

156 *caught on surveillance video:* "An Eye for an Eye: The Anatomy of Mossad's Dubai Operation," *Spiegel Online International,* January 17, 2011.

Chapter 28

289 *Blue Force Tracking:* "United States Special Operations Command: Blue Force Tracking Support for Special Operations Forces," Alaric J. Jorgensen, Air Command and Staff College, Air University, Maxwell Air Force Base, Alabama.

289 *like a bumblebee or a butterfly:* "Tracking Butterfly Movements with Harmonic Radar Reveals an Effect of Population Age on Movement Distance," Otso Ovaskainena, Alan D. Smith, Juliet L. Osborne, Don R. Reynolds, Norman L. Carreck, Andrew P. Martin, Kristjan Niitepõld, and Ilkka Hanski, *Proceedings of the National Academy of Sciences, USA,* volume 105 number 49, December 9, 2008.

290 *locate buried avalanche victims:* "Organized Avalanche Response: Team Member Field Reference Guide," Justice Institute of British Columbia, Emergency Management Division, 2012.

About the Authors

With the release of WARLORD, their fourth novel, Doug and Linda Raber cement their reputations as masters of the thriller genre. The Rabers made their debut as novelists with the 2012 release of FACE OF THE EARTH, which they followed with THE SAPPHIRE LEGACY in 2014 and EASTERN COLONIES in 2015. Their books bring the reader a unique mix of cutting-edge science, U.S. foreign and domestic policy, and current events.

Doug spent twenty years on the faculty at the University of South Florida before moving to Washington, D.C., to work on science policy at the National Academy of Sciences. He directed studies on topics ranging from chemistry R&D to forensic analysis of bombings and the use of technology to combat terrorism. He is a sought-after consultant in science policy arenas.

After stints on Capitol Hill and as a research chemist at the National Institutes of Health, Linda worked for more than twenty years as a reporter for Chemical & Engineering News.

The Rabers are longtime residents of the nation's capital. Their intimate familiarity with its physical and political landscape forms an integral part of their novels.

Forthcoming

THE BEST MAN

Secrets ... lies ... and more secrets. From his boyhood in Washington, D.C., through his Ivy League education and subsequent career, secrets and lies are always at the center of Timothy's life.

In THE BEST MAN, Timothy tells the story of his life as a series of betrayals. He savors his perfidy, becoming a connoisseur of deceit. His nuanced approach to secrets and lies provides the scaffolding on which he maintains a life of duplicity.

Timothy's work in international trade leads to his discreet service for the government, and the combination allows him to use his penchant for treachery as the basis of a successful career. Deception is his constant, but the reader must answer the underlying question. Who has been betrayed? And by whom?

ROCK CREEK, a Will Desmond Novel

A man is murdered at an embassy property in Washington, D.C. A dog is shot and wounded in Rock Creek Park. Secret Service Agent Will Desmond's home is attacked by gunmen, and a photograph leads him to Hamburg, Germany. He learns that the men who attacked his home are involved with trafficking young women from Eastern Europe. Desmond must uncover the links between a seemingly random series of violent events, and he must stop an international smuggling ring before he becomes the next statistic.